HIDING IN SUNSHINE

A NOVEL BY

JOHN STUART &
CAITLIN STUART

authorHOUSE®

AuthorHouse™
1663 Liberty Drive
Bloomington, IN 47403
www.authorhouse.com
Phone: 1-800-839-8640

Published by AuthorHouse 11/21/2012

ISBN: 978-1-4772-8331-8 (sc)
ISBN: 978-1-4772-8329-5 (hc)
ISBN: 978-1-4772-8330-1 (e)

Library of Congress Control Number: 2012919887

With love

John Stuart: to my wife and oldest daughter
Caitlin Stuart: to my mom and older sister

This was made possible only because of your encouragement and help.

FOREWORD

It was one thirty in the morning and the night seemed as if it would never end. Sleep, she knew, would not come. Her husband finally stopped tossing and turning and settled down into restless sleep. She listened to his breathing become even. She got up and went into the kitchen, with its depressing, yellowed linoleum floor. As she was pacing, she noticed the book in a gift bag on the floor. She sank wearily into an old armchair and read with a growing feeling of misery and failure.

CHAPTER ONE

Eyes Only
Department of Justice
Federal Bureau of Investigation
National Security Division
Washington, D.C.

MEMORANDUM: TOP SECRET

To: SPAC Marcus, Henley, SPAC D'Amato, Marissa, SPAC Martinez, Chaz, SPAC Moore Arthur, Field Offices
From: DDFBI Broomall, Thomas A.

Based on recently intercepted conversations and other activities, there is a reason to believe that **ZERIND ROKUS KAZAC** (REFERENCED HEREIN AS **ZRK**), reliably reported by informants and intelligence to be the head of a widespread global criminal organization, the **ENTERPRISE**, with suspected illegal and terroristic activities based in eastern Europe, including Russia, and reliably believed to be the master perpetrator behind recent cyber attacks on the United States, is intending to recruit selected top cyber security experts of the United States into his organization. It is further reliably reported by confidential informants and intelligence that the group has plans to kidnap or kill certain of those experts whom the Enterprise designates as non-cooperating.

A list of these top cyber security and other such experts in the United States, and their locations, will be issued in a subsequent memorandum. To the extent possible, this list will contain the names and ages of these individuals' immediate families, including spouses and children.

All bureaus and SPAC personnel: It is crucial to quietly monitor the well-being of such designated individuals and their families for reasons of personal and national security. This activity is to be kept strictly confidential with all field reports marked **TOP SECRET** to this office. Authority for such actions is contained in various statutes and Congressional Acts, and specifically as predicated on the Foreign Intelligence Surveillance Act (FISA) of 1978 (50 U.S.C. §§ 1801-11, 1821-29, 1841-46, 1861-62, 1871).

It is specifically directed that while designated subjects referenced in this memo and on the subsequent *List of Subject Individuals* are not suspected of criminal activity, and therefore should not be regarded as investigative targets, their crucial standing in the national security network, and their potential implication in international terrorist and other activities of the Enterprise criminal organization, allows for surreptitious surveillance under authority of the, FISA, Foreign Intelligence Surveillance Act.

CHAPTER TWO

Shortly after he turned thirty, Gavin Brinkley took stock of his life. He had graduated from the University of New Mexico with a double major in biology and computer science. Then it was on to Caltech, where his thesis focused on building advanced mathematical models of popular computer networks, and the risk-exposure to their security. It was a very theoretical body of work.

Then came a wife, Lisa, and in time a daughter, Becky, after a move to Pleasanton, California, an affluent, family-centered suburb in the eastern Bay Area. Pleasanton was a happy and bustling little town—take the name itself, Pleasanton. It even *sounds* like the kind of place academic sociologists conjure up when they publish studies of contemporary, affluent middle-class America. Pleasanton had a splendid suburban prosperity; burnished with the riches of Silicon Valley, it held the distinction of being the wealthiest midsized city in America by the time the Brinkleys arrived.

As the name suggests, the town was pleasant enough, if somewhat staid. It boasted the kind of excellent schools that well-funded suburban entities compete over. Weekday activities were characterized mainly by commuting to places like Silicon Valley, thirty miles south, or the Oakland International Airport, an easy twenty-minute train ride on the Bay Area Rapid Transit rail system. Weekends were dominated to a remarkable extent by youth sports and the juggling of family logistics to ensure attendance at as many of those events as possible, with perhaps a backyard barbeque afterward.

Yet, Pleasanton had a somewhat less complacent history. The settlement, then known as Alisal, lay along the main route from San

Francisco to the mountains where gold fields were swarming with fortune seekers after 1848. The farmers who had settled along the valley quickly realized that there was gold to be found not just in those hills, but on the road along the way. Known then as "The Most Desperate Town in the West," Alisal was known for selling provisions and whatever other services might be sought by the ragtag bands of fortune hunters headed to, and from, the gold fields. In those hills good luck could change abruptly to bad luck if a prospector had the misfortune of encountering a legendary local bandito, Joaquin Carrillo Murrieta.

Murrieta was a figure who would later be one of the inspirations for the Zorro tales, a dashing Robin Hood–like Mexican adventurer. Murrieta was famous for ambushing prospectors on their way back from the gold fields, and then seeking refuge in town, where he and his gang exercised the prudence of sharing their loot. Unfortunately, as the gold played out and the loot became more scarce, Murrieta himself became the prize. He was killed by locals who were motivated by the $5,000 bounty on his head. They evidently took that reward enticement literally when they chopped off Murrieta's head, which was on display in a pickle jar for those who paid admission at town hall.

Soon after, Alisal changed its name to Pleasanton. When the transcontinental railroad finally came through, Pleasanton enjoyed a less frenetic kind of prosperity as a center of agriculture and wine-making. The town evolved into the very prototype of an American turn-of-the-century small town—so much so that, in 1917, moviemakers chose it as the location for the setting of the movie adaptation of *Rebecca of Sunnybrook Farm*. In this classic children's novel, a spirited little girl, who is an excellent pupil, is forced into the challenges and adversities of a new life and emerges triumphantly as an accomplished independent woman.

In modern times, Pleasanton's boosters considered the conventional prosperousness to be of far more interest than the darker history of its founding. Gavin and Lisa too preferred to stress this aspect of their tranquil town's past, sometimes playfully referring to their lively, bright-eyed daughter, as "Rebecca of Sunnybrook Farm." Their second child, Jessica, born two years later, was an impressionable child who adored her older sister.

Like Rebecca in the movie, the Brinkley children were also to be presented with a new life at a young age, beginning happily enough with the family's relocation to New England when the oldest was just turning three. That year the Brinkleys took a July vacation to Nantucket, Massachusetts. They loved this summer colony for the affluent on a pristine island so much that they returned the following summer, when they also became enamored of Boston on a jaunt to relieve summer beach tedium. They took Jessica and Becky on the historic Freedom Trail, topped off by a Sunday afternoon baseball game at Fenway Park.

"Maybe they should grow up knowing the four seasons," Lisa told her husband that afternoon as they watched the little girls' faces beaming in the sun amid the merry tumult of the crowd in the field level of the third-base stands.

They often arrived independently at the same reflections, if not the same conclusions. "I take it you are not referring to the hotel chain," Gavin said.

She looked at him with a raised brow just as the stadium crowd erupted in a roar over a Red Sox hit that ricocheted with a metallic bang off the famous Green Monster, the 37-foot steel wall 310 feet down the left-field line. "Gavin, I mean it. Think about it!" she shouted above the noise.

"I am," he replied with a laugh, sliding his arm around her shoulder.

It wasn't just baseball and museums and a city with stature and bearing. It was also about intellectual culture, which they missed in the boosterism of Pleasanton. It was about great private schools, not just excellent public ones. And yes, it was about living in a place where the flowers bloomed only part of the year, hence with startling beauty rather than day-to-day insistence. The Brinkleys wanted Becky and Jessica to know those four seasons as children, even if one of them was New England winter.

They talked long into that night. That Saturday, on the ferry to the mainland, their bags packed and airline tickets in hand for the flight back home to California, they kissed with the sea wind on their faces. The idea of moving to New England had become a pact.

Gavin and Lisa were accustomed to following through fully on plans once an agreement was in place. With characteristic diligence, Lisa began researching suburban locations near Boston and soon had the prospects narrowed down to three. In October, the couple left the children in the care of a nanny and flew back to Boston for five days, staying, by mutual whimsy, at the luxurious Four Seasons hotel on Boylston Street in the Back Bay. Part of the trip was a second honeymoon, but most of it was built around that daunting American pursuit: house hunting.

In this venture, they were led as if on a forced march day after day by an indefatigable real estate agent, Sally. An apparently unflappable matron with a bouffant hairdo, Sally drove them from town to town in her expensive Mercedes-Benz E Class, which Gavin soon began calling "Sally's land-yacht." After a few days, the smiles all seemed frozen on their faces as they feigned interest, if not delight, with each successive property they saw and then eliminated. But it all came together on Friday morning when Sally announced: "Get in and hurry! We're going to Concord." With her Boston accent, it sounded like *CAN-kid*. "I just got the listing this morning for the house of your dreams, and I want you to see it before anyone else can."

Can-kid turned out to be perfect, and so was the house, a beautiful, modern Colonial mansion on eight secluded acres. The home had five bedrooms, including the sprawling master bedroom, and a total of nine bathrooms. Actually, the remarkable number of bathrooms was the only feature of the house that gave Gavin the slightest pause.

"Shouldn't the number of bedrooms and the number of bathrooms be roughly equal?" he said, as they stood admiring one of those bathrooms, which was so big that their voices echoed.

His wife gave him a look with a familiar smile that said, *please don't be stupid*. Sally watched with expectation and said brightly, "Wait till you see the barn and the horse stalls out past the pond. A lot of people in this area ride on the trails."

Gavin could tell that Lisa loved the house as much as he did. "How long did it take us to get here from Boston?" he said.

"Thirty-five minutes, with most traffic going the other way," Sally said. "It's maybe another ten minutes into the city in the morning. Would either of you be working in Boston?"

They would not, they replied. Sally already had plenty of background on them anyway, or she wouldn't have spent the better part of a week driving them around to view such expensive homes for sale. Bay Area money. Living in a home in Pleasanton that cost $2 million. He's a technology entrepreneur, self-employed, a high-tech inventor, evidently set for life. She used to be an international banker, but seems now to have become a stay-at-home mom. Big local philanthropists, mostly charities, nothing political, usually anonymous. These were people who stayed out of the spotlight. But the online background-profile service that Sally routinely and quietly consulted for information on clients in such multimillion-dollar deals linked to a local newspaper clip showing that the couple had given $1 million to Memorial Sloan-Kettering Cancer Center in honor of Gavin's mother, who had been treated there twenty-five years before when she was dying of cancer.

"So what do you think?" Sally said after they had thoroughly explored the house and the capacious grounds with the pond, a pool, and tall colonnades of stately oak trees and sycamores that ensured privacy.

Gavin and Lisa exchanged glances that merely confirmed their individual thoughts. Their unspoken answer was yes. "You need an answer today?" Gavin said tentatively.

"Not really, and you already know I wouldn't think of rushing you on a decision like this," Sally said. "But frankly, this one is special, and it will move fast. It's priced right, because the owners are being forced by circumstances to sell—"

Gavin felt Lisa's hand go to his arm, but not in time to stop him from saying what she knew he was going to say. "We'll make a cash offer. Contingent, of course, on all of the usual diligence including a home-inspector's report."

Sally nodded and said, "We'll see, but between you and me and that quaint gas-lit lamppost there by the end of the driveway, I believe that might do it. Do you want to come back to my office where we can draw up the paperwork, which will take about twenty minutes?"

Now Lisa took the lead. "Let's do that, Sally," she said.

The offer was accepted within a day. The Brinkleys put their own home on the market in Pleasanton and felt fortunate to receive an offer within ten days, and over the asking price at that, which sealed the deal quickly. As they put in increasingly exhausting days preparing for their long move across country, Lisa fretted about taking their daughter out of preschool.

"She has so many friends and she's doing so well. And the teachers adore her. Do you think she'll cope?" Lisa asked her husband.

"She's three," Gavin said reassuringly. "She'll cope. So will Jessica, who rolls with everything already."

*　　*　　*

Gavin had always marveled at the human capacity for change and adaptation. Certainly, a family uprooting itself and relocating its life across a continent would constitute major emotional upheaval. He was grateful, as always, for his wife, who with seeming ease managed the change from familiar to unfamiliar home.

Children, assuming they are secure in their young lives, were even more adaptable than adults. As they settled into the new house, Lisa made sure that Jessica shared a room with her sister, even though there were plenty of spare bedrooms, to ensure the youngster's feeling of security in an unfamiliar environment. The two girls were already close, and would soon grow into each other's best friends. Meanwhile, Becky's favorite possessions were among the most readily retrievable in the unfamiliar environment. Among those were jigsaw puzzles that, despite being a young child, she had an astonishing ability to complete—first carefully evaluating the scene to be assembled, and then putting the pieces into place with amazing speed.

In preparation for the move, and eager to ensure that her daughter would begin to feel comfortable with new scenes, Lisa had gone online and ordered several beautiful puzzles at what she thought was a high level for Becky to work toward as she became comfortable with her new environment. One was a two-hundred-piece puzzle depicting Fenway Park crowded with baseball fans and a beautiful streak of a rainbow in the sky. To her parents' amazement, the child curled up on a thick rug by the fireplace one afternoon and had that puzzle finished before lunch the next day. Then her mother brought out another new one, a three-hundred-fifty-piece puzzle of an intricately detailed map showing key events in the Revolutionary War that had occurred in Massachusetts—including Boston, Lexington, and their new hometown of Concord. With delight, the child fell to the task and had *that* puzzle finished by the weekend, then proudly moved the assembly board into place on the rug next to the Fenway Park scene.

"Where's the mountains one, Mom?" she asked, and Lisa unpacked old familiar puzzles, some with California scenes from one of the boxes that were still stacked in Becky's new bedroom. Within weeks, Becky had claimed a corner of the big family room for her completed puzzles, refusing to let anyone break any of them apart until she was satisfied with her collection. Then, she frowned as she reluctantly decided which one she would need to box away to make room for another.

There was another aspect to Becky's puzzle-solving skills that her parents found both amusing and remarkable, and that was her ability to find objects that seemed to have gone astray in the household. A set of keys lost on a counter, a remote control for a television, a wayward book on a shelf—she could spot them as soon as she was informed that they were missing.

"How does she do that?" Lisa asked one day when Becky had, in what seemed a matter of mere moments, come up triumphantly with a pair of Ray-Ban sunglasses that Gavin had spent forty-five minutes looking for.

"I have a theory," Gavin said. "Firstly, she seems to have a very sharp eye, a sense of how individual things fit together visually. . ."

"That would certainly account for her facility with jigsaw puzzles," Lisa said with a laugh. "Some of those would take me a week to finish."

Lisa nodded and replied, "Which means that when the time does come, we'll have to be very, very exact about which schools she goes to."

"Seriously," he agreed.

CHAPTER THREE

While Lisa worked with an interior decorator to apply her own good taste to the occasional startling displays of the previous owner's bad taste, she also researched the local schools. She especially liked the Hawthorne School, a venerable private establishment for kindergarten through eighth grade, on a thirty-acre campus whose facilities included two theaters, science and computer labs, an arts center, and a 6,000-square-foot gymnasium.

"Whoa!" Gavin had said when she showed him the brochure and the testimonials from far and wide. "How much?"

"It's one of the top private schools in the country. This way she'll be positioned for the best private high schools" Lisa assured him.

"How much?" he repeated playfully.

She slid onto his lap and said, "About sixteen thousand dollars for kindergarten, which they said Becky could enter despite being a year younger than the rest of the kids, based on the intellectual and social aptitude she showed during our visit."

Gavin did not interrupt to protest that the two had already made a clandestine visit, but let Lisa continue, "Eighteen thousand for lower grades and twenty-four thousand for grades six through eight."

"By my lightning-fast calculations, that's… let's see, that would appear to be one hundred seventy-nine thousand dollars."

"If you say so," she purred.

He looked at her teasingly. "U.S. dollars?"

"I believe that's the currency in use in Concord."

"I see," he said. "And this would include some books, and maybe a few pencils and some colored construction paper?"

"Doubtful. Those might be extra."

"I see. Incidentally, do you know how much my own kindergarten cost?"

"Not a clue. That was many, many years ago. But do tell me."

"Now, of course, I was quite young and living with my mother and father at the time; so my figures might be rough estimates, but—just ballparking it now—I would say... *zero! Free,* courtesy of the public school system."

"Inflation?" she said, kissing him. "Maybe you can go downstairs to your fabulous lab and invent something new?"

Becky was enrolled the next day.

*   *   *

Actually, there was no need to create any new inventions, or even to work anymore, at least in pursuit of a salary. Through his twenties, Gavin had become amazingly adept at keeping a low profile in the often high-profile world of high-tech. At the same time, he had managed to leapfrog profitably from one discipline of the industry to the next, inventing as he went. He was always careful to patent those inventions, and by this point he was the owner of seventeen such patents, some of which generated impressive royalties. His most important patent involved detecting a cancer protein using a blood test: a quick, painless, and reliable method that he had developed soon after graduate school.

Gavin loved coming up with new ways to solve old issues. The experimenting, tinkering, writing, registering, and watching a patent come to fruition, all were exhilarating. In total, the patent royalties generated about $7 million a year and required no day-to-day effort on his part. And the royalty stream would continue for another fourteen years. If he wished to work or even invent at any future point, it would be for personal satisfaction, and not financial gain.

So the usual stresses of going to a job while relocating and settling into a new home and town were lessened. Even still, Gavin preferred to be kept busy. Harvard and Massachusetts Institute of Technology were a short drive away, and he soon found stimulation attending academic technology and business conferences at those universities and their satellite extensions and affiliates in the region.

Concord was home to many professors who made the same twenty-five-minute commute to the colleges and universities of Boston and Cambridge. While being a small town (the population barely reached 17,000 when the Brinkleys moved there), Concord had a big and commanding footprint in American history, most notably as the scene in 1775 of the "shot heard 'round the world," the first battle of the American Revolution. It was also present in Paul Revere's mythic ride to rally countrymen against the British troops. Concord was so steeped in its history that at times Gavin thought it seemed to slumber in it. As his family set down its roots in this new place, one of those historical attitudes became apparent to the Brinkleys: anyone who had not lived in Concord for a few generations at least were regarded as newcomers.

Still, their new home was splendid in its setting. The driveway off winding Monument Street was a quarter mile long. The home could not be seen from the street, and a thick cover of trees separated them from their nearest neighbors, who stayed private. Weathered stone walls surrounded the whole eight acres, not—it seemed to Gavin—as a barrier against entry, for any agile deer or other determined intruder could easily vaunt their four-foot height, but more as a testament to one's place. The barrier for actual entry would have to be handled by one of the features that Gavin immediately approved of when the real estate agent first brought them to look at the property: an elaborate security system inside and out, including discretely placed video cameras outside, providing 360-degree coverage of the entire property.

There was a beautifully landscaped front yard with a serene Japanese garden in the back, and a six-car garage housed their four cars. The home had a tennis court and an outdoor saltwater swimming pool; it had an indoor pool as well. There was a movie theater that accommodated twelve people, along with a sauna and steam room, an exercise room, a recreational room, and a sunroom. Once they were settled, Gavin had an extensive technology lab built in the basement, the main feature of which was two banks of computers—eight wired to Internet and eight managed separately, one being a stand-alone unit. For security reasons, there was no wireless network in place.

The master bedroom suite that Gavin and Lisa shared was the biggest that either had ever seen—over eighteen hundred square feet, including sleeping and sitting areas, a dressing area with handcrafted cabinets, and a capacious master bath adorned with marble and granite imported from Italy. The shower had multiple heads, each fed by an unusual one-inch pipeline instead of the standard half-inch. Gavin loved the luxury of taking long showers with high-pressure water raining on him from all sides—it was often where he got his best ideas, and sometimes his showers could take upward of an hour if the ideas were really flowing.

There were two large-size closets—bigger than some small bedrooms. Lisa didn't realize how big her closet was until all her clothes barely took up one side of her closet.

"What am I going to do with a closet the size of a studio apartment in New York City?"

Gavin laughed and said, "Fill it up, of course."

This was the gaiety they shared, and they had every reason to believe that it would never end.

While the Brinkleys reveled in the opulence of their home, they also took joy in knowing that Concord was not just another serene and wealthy suburb with tended lawns, pretty parks, and a little downtown full with interesting shops. One of the greatest virtues of Concord, besides its beauty and its firm place in American history, was its equally firm place in intellectual and literary history. Among its past notable residents were Ralph Waldo Emerson and Henry David Thoreau. Gavin and Lisa liked having Emerson and Thoreau as spiritual neighbors, aware that the two men had been actual neighbors and spiritual comrades in the first half of the nineteenth century. And there were others as well, some of them drawn to Concord by the so-named transcendentalist philosophical movement established by Emerson. There was, for example, the novelist Nathaniel Hawthorne, who rented Emerson's home, called the Manse, with his wife in 1842. Thoreau created a vegetable garden there for them, a few years before Thoreau himself moved into a hut beside Walden Pond. It was there he wrote his most famous work, on land owned by his friend Emerson, two miles from town.

Gavin was familiar with Emerson, and especially so with these words of his: "*We live in succession, in division, in parts, in particles. Meantime within man is the soul of the whole; the wise silence; the universal beauty, to which every part and particle is equally related, the eternal one. And this deep power in which we exist and whose beatitude is all accessible to us, is not only self-sufficing and perfect in every hour, but the act of seeing and the thing seen,* the seer and the spectacle, the subject and the object, are one. We see the world piece by piece—as the sun, the moon, the animal, the tree; but the whole, of which these are shining parts, is the soul."

And Lisa, who had minored in literature and French while majoring in finance in college, loved Thoreau's *Walden*. The first weekend they had free from the chores of unpacking and settling in after moving to Concord, the Brinkleys took a picnic lunch to Walden Pond and watched their daughters play in the golden light of autumn.

"Did you know that Louisa May Alcott also lived in Concord at the same time?" Lisa asked her husband.

"They all knew one another?" Gavin asked with some surprise.

"Of course they did. It's a very small town. Louisa May Alcott used to visit Emerson in his library, and she went on picnics just like this with Thoreau. This is where she wrote her most famous work, *Little Women*. I don't suppose you ever read that because it was always considered a girls' novel."

"I once saw the old movie on television, I think," Gavin replied. "The second oldest of the girls..."

"...Jo March," Lisa prompted.

"...She's a tomboy who can outrace boys and climb trees. Full of pluck and spirit and energy, and at the end, I think, she overcomes adversity with sheer determination and becomes a strong and independent woman, right?"

"Louisa May Alcott herself was like that," Lisa said. "Smart and independent, and whoa, was she determined!"

They watched Becky toss a stone into the pond and saw her delight at the concentric circles rippling on the water in dappled sunlight, and then they watched Jessica try to do the same thing—always trying to keep up with her sister whom she adored so much. Gavin and Lisa held hands and sensed the presence of these long since departed writers and philosophers beside these wide-eyed children they had created.

As they gathered their things to leave, Lisa said to Gavin, "Emerson was the one who encouraged Thoreau to keep a journal. Did you know that?"

"Like me," Gavin said.

"You are just full of surprises, dear. You have a journal? How long have you had that?"

"A while," he said. "It started out as just scientific notes, basically annotated records. But in the last year or so I've been making observations."

"About what?"

"About us," he said, and they walked to the car through the dancing shadows of October.

*   *   *

As the fall season wore on, they occasionally found themselves missing California. Concord was certainly pleasant, and they loved to watch the changes in autumn, with the trees ablaze in color and the wind scattering brittle leaves across the soft ground outside the glassed-in patio off the kitchen where they shared morning coffee. But soon little patches of snow nestled in the flickering shade at the base of the trees, and before long the bold colors were abruptly erased by the wind as the sunlight started to dim with the insistent bite of cold in the air.

Gavin received an e-mail around Thanksgiving.

Hi Gavin: Guess what? I joined the Great Migration back East and am moving to (drumroll) Boston, where I'll be working at my firm's New England office, so no change in our relationship. Am looking forward to reacquainting myself with the pleasures of the Other Coast. They tell me that Boston is the antidote to Seattle, and vice versa, so here I am, certainly for at least a few years! I miss those dinners in Seattle. Hope you're settled in Concord, up with the veddy, veddy rich. Please give my regards to Lisa. How are the kids enjoying the new world?! Would love to catch up. I hope you are well. Regards, Cate.

He had met Cate four years ago through a patent attorney who told him that even though she was then just twenty-five years old, she had already established a reputation as one of the top private-wealth advisers on the West Coast. She was then, as now, working in a Seattle-based firm called Manhattan Advisory Group that specialized in providing advice to clients with a high net worth on matters such as estate planning and asset allocation, bonds, equity, hedge funds, private equity, trusts, and wills.

Cate was brilliant, in that intensely focused way of financial dynamos. She was also bubbly, pretty, trim, and always impeccably dressed in understated but clearly expensive fashion. All of her clients were wealthy families. More often than not, it was said, she knew more about clients finances than the clients themselves. Clients who worked with her soon discovered that she could relieve them of the quotidian chores of personal wealth management, which they readily ceded to her with their appreciation for her utter discretion. They relaxed in the knowledge that she had extensive relationships throughout the financial networks of the rich, including with banking executives and Wall Street tycoons. Her clients, like Gavin, invariably were referrals from trusted associates, friends, and colleagues.

Cate had double-majored in drama and English literature at NYU, and then graduated cum laude from Columbia Business School. During college, she also worked as a part-time model in New York City, which struck him as a fascinating twist on the usual financial world résumé. She had flown to the Bay Area on Alaska Airlines for their initial meeting in the lounge of a hotel near San Francisco International Airport.

When Gavin asked her to describe herself in a nutshell, Cate said:

"I'm basically a good, simple Catholic school girl who grew up in upstate New York where the snow starts falling before Thanksgiving and doesn't melt till Memorial Day. So I actually consider the Seattle weather a treat. "I have snow skills along with my financial skills," she said with feigned gravity. "I can get a car out of a snowdrift. I know how to hit black ice at fifty miles an hour and live to tell the tale, Gavin. I still carry a snow shovel in the trunk of my car because you just never know. Gavin, the nutshell is this: You can take the girl out of Skaneateles, New York, but you cannot take Skaneateles, New York, out of the girl. Now let's talk hedge funds and derivatives."

Opening his briefcase, he felt at ease with Cate immediately and liked her enormously. She spent her spare time with active sports, sailing on a snappy Bermuda rig sloop that she berthed on Puget Sound, engaged in mountain climbing and tennis—all of this showed in her trim and firm body and that tan that never seemed to lose its glow, even in drizzly Seattle. She was also an avid domestic and international traveler. Cate was smart but charmingly self-effacing. A model of discretion and poise, she brimmed with analytical information that she shared with as much delight as when she shared Wall Street gossip—those complex and sometimes quirky relationships and even the fiascos that make up real life in the supercharged realm of the very rich and their families.

Though he felt comfortable with her from the first day, Gavin was careful not to show undue enthusiasm. He exercised his customary caution before entering into any agreement about wealth management and asset allocation. He ordered the typical due diligence, including background checks done by a reputable investigative firm. But all of the reports came back flashing green lights: This was one of the most highly regarded people in the field. Gavin was delighted. In a few weeks, Cate returned to California, this time staying in Palo Alto, where Gavin drove to spend a day with her going over finances and establishing what would grow into a warm working relationship.

Subsequently, Gavin began visiting her in Seattle for the standard monthly updates. Gavin would fly in for a twenty-four-hour trip from California and spend all day with Cate at her office in Seattle, evaluating the performance of his investments in hedge funds, mutual funds, municipal bonds, private equity, and start-up companies. It is a common industry practice to entertain the client after a long day of meetings usually with dinner or a visit to a cultural attraction. After a couple of months, Cate started to make these events a bit more special. Their meetings usually ended around five o'clock and then Cate always had some fun adventure planned. She would go to her apartment, change into evening clothes, then pick Gavin up from his hotel in a car, whisking him away for elegant dinners or to see the Seattle Mariners at Safeco Field.

Although she initially chose a different restaurant for each of their excursions, they finally settled on a favorite, a quiet Italian bistro downtown where the lighting was low and the service was understated and elegant. Gavin looked forward to dishes like orecchiette con piselli—dreamily creamy pasta with peas, prosciutto, and parmigiano. By their third visit, the maître d', Mario, was referring to them as "mister and missus," which they found amusing. Over dinner, business was left behind at the office and the conversation was about life, travels, adventures, books, observations, and shared laughs.

Travel was an especially favorite subject, and the topic—as it often is with sophisticated travelers who never really leave business behind—was more often about the process of getting there and staying there with enough comfort and efficiency to get work done on the road.

"How many miles do you have?" she asked one night.

He shrugged. "I don't really keep count."

"You should," she said playfully.

"Okay. How many miles do you have?"

"Total, by airline? Elite qualifying versus basic miles?"

"What makes me think you have them all organized in lists and by accounts?"

"I do!" she said.

"I'm a million-miler on American. I have a card for that," he said.

Cate batted her long eyelashes and reached into her purse, opened her wallet, and flipped a shiny black card on the table.

"You have one of these?" she asked. On the card it read, American Airlines Concierge Key.

He studied it. "What is it?"

"I could tell you, but then I'd have to kill you," she said with a giggle. "No, really, what this is is the crème de la crème of elite status at American. They don't advertise it or anything. You can't even apply; it's by invitation. When you fly with this, you get treated like a head of state. Actually, I'm overstating it, but you do get treated extremely well, especially if anything goes wrong like a missed connection. You get very personal service to make things right."

"I'm impressed," he said.

"Trust me, I earn it with the amount of revenue they get from me. But you're also up there in status with them, so you should have one of these. And I know the guy…"

"The guy?"

"Right, the guy. I know the guy at American who makes the decisions on Concierge Keys."

"I can get one of those?"

"Consider it done," she said, sliding her hand into Gavin's hand on the pristine white tablecloth.

*   *   *

Cate was a die-hard fan of the Seattle Mariners. One summer she secured two seats right behind home plate and invited Gavin to join her.

Gavin asked, "These must be pretty expensive? You needn't spend this much money, Cate."

"Oh, don't worry about it, I enjoy the game—and your company, too."

She pouted her lips; her smile was so naturally adorable that it would get to any man's heart.

The game took place late in the season, and a playoff berth was on the line. Every time the Mariners scored or saved a run, Cate would get up from her seat and join all of the other fans in loud celebration. When the winning run was scored against the Tigers, in the heat of the moment she turned to Gavin and gave him a big hug while they were standing and cheering. Their embrace was lost to the rest of the crowd at Safeco Field, so jubilant were the hometown Mariners' fans.

At times Gavin would decline the invitation to join her after their meeting as he had something else to attend to—this would make her meticulously planned outing fall apart. She generally responded with, "No worries, Gavin, we will do it next time." Although Gavin could sense a tiny bit of disappointment in her voice.

During another visit, she mentioned to Gavin that her home computer had been hacked into, and that the IT guy at the office was having a difficult time trying to figure out the problem. Gavin knew that as a well-known financial adviser she could be a target of cyber thieves and volunteered to help her. "After our meeting, I can take a look," he said.

"Ohhh, but the machine is at my home. Would you mind if we stopped by my place for a few minutes before heading out for dinner?"

Gavin thought for a few seconds and then said, "Sure, I could stop by."

It was a beautiful apartment, tastefully decorated with various types of artwork and pieces collected from her travels around the world.

Cate showed him the computer while she went to change. It was taking Gavin some time to find the root cause of the problem, as the machine was infected with a nasty virus. While Gavin was still deeply engrossed in working on the machine, Cate took care of some odds and ends around the apartment. She then realized that they had lost their reservation slot at the restaurant and could not get a new one as it wasn't clear how long Gavin would take. She stood by his side while he worked on the computer and suggested that she cook something for the two of them at home.

"What are you in mood for?"

"Oh, I'm fine. We can go to McDonald's after I finish."

She pretended to be mortified and then playfully said, "OK, then I will decide!"

"I don't want to trouble you, anything simple is good."

Gavin finished fixing and rebooting her computer. Getting his help was like using a cannonball to kill a fly, but at least he took care of it in about an hour—something that would have taken someone else days to do. As Gavin looked up, Cate was busy in the kitchen. She was dressed in jeans and a T-shirt and had a white apron on. Her long hair was tied in the back. He had not seen her dressed casually before and could not help thinking how gorgeous she looked.

The dinner was served. Cate lit a couple of candles in exquisite candlestick holders and turned on some jazz. The apartment had an automated light system so with a flick of a switch the lights in the apartment turned soft.

Cate was an extraordinarily good cook. Gavin said with a smile, "Geez, you didn't have to do this—and how did you make something this good, that fast?"

Cate just smiled.

"Absolutely delicious!" Gavin murmured through his bites.

"I enjoy cooking," Cate said in her classic understated manner.

As they were finishing their dinner, Gavin's cell phone rang; it was Becky on the other line, and she wanted to talk to her dad.

"I miss you, Daddy. Too much! Come home now."

"Honey, I will be home tomorrow morning."

"But I want to play with you. What are you doing?"

"I am just finishing dinner."

"With whom?"

"A friend."

"But I want to eat with you, Daddy."

This conversation went on for a while and Gavin was completely oblivious that Cate had been waiting for more than thirty minutes. After the phone call, Cate and Gavin resumed their dinner and she brought out a hot fudge ice cream sundae—a favorite of Gavin's. They both started to share it when his cell phone rang once more. It was Becky again asking Dad to read her a story. Gavin tried to convince her to go to bed, but Becky would have none of it. Reluctantly Gavin started to tell her a made-up story, and Cate could hear a little girl giggling through the phone.

When Gavin finally hung up, a usually expressive Cate was still at the dining table expressionless with melted ice cream.

*   *   *

At these evening get-togethers, sometimes Cate asked about his family, and he spoke effusively of his wife and daughters.

"How is Lisa these days?" she asked during their most recent dinner.

"She's doing well. She's a great mother, as I think I probably told you."

"You certainly did, and I can tell from the way you beam when you talk about her and your daughters that you mean it," Cate said, her finger tracing the rim of her water glass. "What's Lisa really like, though? I'd love to meet her. Tell me how you got together."

Gavin told Cate about how he had met Lisa and delighted in her good humor and intelligence. They were at a party in California, where she had resettled after spending an exhilarating but ultimately exhausting and frustrating four years as an investment banker focused on Central America. They were married a year later. Like Gavin, Lisa was tall, but unlike him, she was blond. He was relatively introverted; she was relatively extroverted. Lisa had graduated from Berkeley, where her professors had been impressed with the versatility she displayed as a finance major who still managed to deftly carry those robust minors, American literature and French. She also knew computers well—long before she met a computer whiz like Gavin. She had learned Spanish with amazing speed right after graduation, when she spent a summer doing volunteer work in Haiti. Both her French and her Spanish were excellent to the point where native French and Spanish speakers remarked upon it.

"A good match for you?" Cate asked. "As we say in the investment-advice business…"

"Absolutely," Gavin said. "Long term."

"So you complement each other," she said. It was a statement more than a question.

"Well, I enjoy the world in abstraction, a bit on the edge, and she's as level-headed and deliberate as can be," he said.

"Opposites attract!"

"Is that always true?" he said with a small laugh.

She shrugged. "How about your kids?"

". . . Becky and Jessica."

"You have pictures, I presume?"

Gavin reached for his iPhone and chuckled to recall that it was not so long ago when a man used to respond to that kind of request by reaching instead for his wallet to slide out the family photos. He had a selection of happy pictures from the most recent family vacation in Nantucket. Their heads were close together as she studied the little screen.

"This is so cute!" she said in a tone that was almost girlish. "You guys have been married for five years? My parents got divorced when I was six. So I always wondered, how do you keep that spark?"

"Spark?" Gavin said, blurting out what he hoped she would regard as a joke.

Cate smiled.

At another dinner, when Gavin was describing one of his ideas, he said, "I ran it by Lisa. She gave me lots of good data points."

Her laugh made him blush. She said, "Data points!"

"I like to brainstorm with her, pick her brain," he said, and realized that he sounded defensive.

"Gavin, is she in the same space as you are?"

He wasn't sure how to reply to a personal question that almost sounded businesslike.

"No, not technically," he said. "She worked at a mutual fund for a short time, but she absolutely disliked the stress of stock-picking and the gyrations in markets, especially when logic did not seem to be the prevailing driver. So she switched to banking for a few years. But after Becky was born, she switched again to being a full-time mom." His finger flicked at his iPhone screen, trying to find one particular photo.

"At first, she fretted about giving up the world of finance for the domestic world of starting a family, but within a month after leaving the bank, the back-and-forth phone calls and e-mails ceased, and in the silence she realized how relieved she was to be free of it all. She came to enjoy the quiet time that being at home offered, especially because, like her husband, she was free to choose her intellectual and social pursuits without the encumbrances of a corporate job."

He found the photo he wanted and showed it to Cate. "See how relaxed she looks? This is what giving up the financial world will do for you!"

"Very pretty," Cate said appraisingly. "So this is my competition?"

They both laughed, although Gavin was the first to stop laughing.

After Gavin would return from one of his trips to Seattle, Lisa had to work to conceal being a bit put off by the obvious joy in his voice whenever he spoke of Cate. She grew anxious to meet this great personal friend, this financial Wonder Woman who had so captivated her husband's attention. She wasn't jealous per se, because she felt she knew Gavin so well, but she was very curious.

Gavin readily arranged for Cate to visit them at their home in Pleasanton, so that both he and Lisa could review their financials with her.

Lisa noticed, as she had anticipated, how her generally reserved husband lit up in Cate's presence. She had to concede that Cate was bright and personable and very attractive, though Lisa would have chosen the word "cute" if she had to choose one.

Now that Lisa had finished decorating their Concord home to suit their taste, and Cate had recently returned to the East Coast, they invited her for dinner. After dinner Lisa took Cate around the home, proudly showing her contributions to the house and its furnishings. It was such an impressive estate. The front door opened into a foyer with a massive chandelier. The living room and formal dining rooms were ornate, though the kitchen and sitting area were sensibly less formal, giving anyone who moved through the home a sense of having gone from refined to cozy. There was a library with a fireplace, as well as a fifteen hundred square foot home office with cherry paneled walls and cabinets, all with custom-built matching furniture and his and her desks.

Gavin was happy to hear the two women laughing together as they returned to the living room where he sat reading.

Over hot chocolate, Cate asked, "How did you guys meet?"

"It's a long story," Lisa said.

"And you've heard some of it," Gavin interjected.

"I like long stories," Cate said, hugging one of the throw pillows on the couch.

"Well, I was engaged to a guy named Jake Dolan," Lisa began. "I was young and naïve and it was love at first sight. I first met Gavin as Jake's new roommate."

"Do tell!" Cate said with real interest.

"I liked Gavin the first time we met, but that didn't mean much. I mean, obviously he and Jake were friends, and I liked Jake's friends as a rule. By the time Gavin and I met the second or third time and started having some more interaction, he grew on me. Jake was always such a Boy Scout..."

"And Gavin isn't a Boy Scout?" Cate pressed.

"Not really. It's hard to explain. He is a mental adventurist, if that makes any sense. I quickly decided that he was, for want of a better term, organically confident. Like, at ease, as if I had known him for years. Casual, comfortable in his own skin. Not looking for approval, you know?"

"My impression exactly."

Lisa sipped her hot chocolate and then said, "So not long after I met Gavin, Jake had an offer to do a semester at Oxford University in their cyber security lab, and suddenly, I was by myself."

"What about the engagement?"

Lisa made a quick nervous shrug. "Jake said the weirdest thing to me before he left. 'When I get back, we'll see about rebooting,' he said, almost like it was funny. I looked at him the way you'd look at a particularly annoying tech geek. Anyway, off he went, all full of himself and Oxford, leaving me confused. So I started seeing Gavin more, and pretty soon . . ."

"The love bug bit?" Cate prompted.

Lisa said, "Well, I was just smitten. But in all fairness, he did not make the slightest effort to woo me, even though my interest was, let's say, abundantly clear. I was still speaking with Jake over the phone every so often, but I knew in my heart that we were over. By the time Jake got back I had already decided Gavin was the one for me. "

"How'd he take that?"

"Like a jerk, a jerk with a new, phony English accent," Gavin added with a laugh.

Lisa shrugged again and went on, "When I told Jake that I wanted out of the engagement, he reacted as if I'd hit him with a shovel. He claimed he had no idea and certainly could not 'decipher this'—his words—from my tone of voice over the phone. You know how guys are tone-deaf."

"I know, I know!" said Cate.

"Jake was intensely hurt. The strange part was that he held Gavin accountable—but nothing could have been further from the truth. Once he even became physically agitated; when Gavin tried to help him with some boxes he was carrying out to his car, Jake pushed him against a wall. Gavin pushed back, cursing. Elbows got thrown. . ."

"His first," Gavin protested.

"Whatever. It got physical and ugly," Lisa said.

"Two men fighting over you. How was that?" Cate said.

"Terrifying," Lisa said. "Anyway, Jake stormed out, and I never really saw him again. A few months later he called me very drunk late one night and asked me to come back, kind of crying and whimpering."

"Eew!" Cate said.

"Actually, I did see him one more time, sort of. A year or two later, after we were married. I saw him in a car parked near our home. I was carrying some groceries into the house when I spotted him. He stared at me. A very hateful stare. Then he drove away. For a few weeks after that we got hang-up calls, no caller ID, usually in the middle of the night. And then, nothing."

"Sounds creepy to me," Cate said. "I once had a boyfriend like that, turned into a psycho after we broke up. I actually came home one night and found him in my living room, just sitting there silently. I changed the locks, of course, but eventually I still had to get a restraining order."

"Well, I never had to go that far with Jake, thank God. Although I did have the feeling for a while that he was hovering around somewhere."

"You mean stalking you?"

"Not physically. But in a weird way I knew he was still around. Like occasionally, I'd get e-mails that were forwarded links to travel destinations or weird news stories, really things with no apparent point, and I'd see that Jake had sent them to me and a long list of others. Very weird how he worked to keep me aware that he could reach me even tangentially. But that's all stopped now. Which is a relief!"

Lisa had assumed that this would be the end of that topic of discussion, but for some reason Cate persisted in her inquiries. "How long did you know Jake?" she asked, now turning her attention to Gavin, who had been mostly silent.

"Since we started grad school. He was a close friend, someone I worked with day and night analyzing computer security code and the attackers' code and comparing them."

"How exciting," Cate said with mock gravity.

"No really, it was. We would also examine and work through scenarios for various vulnerabilities to attacks by very smart hackers. We then used what we learned to devise new ways to secure the network. We were like two detectives."

"You collected attackers' data and studied them—but what if they changed the pattern?" Cate asked.

Both Gavin and Lisa were impressed by Cate's perceptiveness. Gavin explained, as if to a television interviewer, "Yes, that happens all the time. In fact, it's almost guaranteed to happen. The bad guys keep changing and enhancing ways to gain unauthorized entry."

"Then how do you know what they will bring on next?"

"We don't, so we develop our own attacks as if we were criminals."

This perked Lisa's interest. "And the government trusts you with that? What if someone goes rogue?"

Gavin turned to his wife with affection. "That is precisely the danger, but there is no alternative. Jake and I used to role-play all the time. Although I must admit that I was better than him."

"A man's pride and competitive spirit!" Cate said.

"Better how?" Lisa asked.

Gavin nodded. "I was better because I was more unpredictable. You're right about Jake being a Boy Scout. He had in fact been a Boy Scout when he was a kid, and he believed in the rules. Which at times constrained his thinking and narrowed his spectrum."

"Tell Cate about the contest," Lisa said, seeing that Cate was still following the discussion with obvious interest.

Gavin complied. "I participated in some of the most important cyber security conferences. I mean the kind that are exclusive, by invitation only, top-secret conferences, organized by government agencies. When you show up, you only give one word as your name, like a code name, and the deal is, that's all you use. You're divided into two groups—defenders and attackers. Each defender team is tested against each attacker, and if you lose as a defender, then you are out of the conference. I mean, literally out the door. But if you lose as an attacker, then you continue."

"Which side were you on?" Cate asked.

"I was generally a defender. At one such conference, my team was the last defender left; the attackers had all tried their best, but they couldn't even break through our first line of defense. That was the toughest conference I attended. They all had to leave—all but one."

"How many lines of defense were there?" Cate asked.

"Seven in all. The last guy left was named Rob. Cocky, intense, eerily focused, and with those weird eyes like you see in old alien-creature movies. Within a few minutes, Rob started to hack away at our defenses. By this time it was just me and my partners, this guy Rob, and the hotshots from the government agencies. Everyone was staring intensely at the screens as Rob grew steadily more focused and more confident. Bang, bang, bang, he kept breaking the doors down and progressively got closer and closer to the most secured data. Everyone was shocked, including me. The guy was unbelievably calm, no excitement or nervousness. One of my partners, Norm, even tried to say something totally out of context, trying to throw him off balance, but the guy was completely unperturbed.

"The rules allowed us to change code in real time, while the attack was going on. Me, I was sweating bullets, trying hard to calm my nerves while focusing on the defenses I could erect under the assault from this guy. Both of my partners were trying to create some last-minute blockade, but Rob kept coming through the doors. Then an idea flashed in my head and I conferred with my team.

"Finally, it worked! We spotted Rob's Achilles' heel. He knew, as he broke the sixth level, what the seventh one likely ought to be—but he got tripped-up because he kept thinking along the same lines as the previous six gates. I threw him off with something simple and even borderline silly, which he never even anticipated. After about two hours, for the first time, he grew annoyed. The more frustrated he got, the more he lost it. Everyone was just stunned at how close he came to the crown jewels, but in the end, he never got through."

Gavin went on, "We got the award. But then Rob created a scene, which was very bad form. In all fairness, we had a built-in advantage because, as defenders, we had to know the system, and as an attacker, he had to probe for holes. He was the absolute best any of us had ever seen. We told him so, too. But Rob still complained."

"Whined," Lisa corrected, having heard this story before.

"Right, Rob whined that he had broken through six of the seven defenses, and we could only protect the last one. So he should have been declared the winner. One of my partners laughed in his face."

"That would be Jake, our Boy Scout," Lisa explained to Cate.

"It was actually after that conference that we decided to become roommates so we could brainstorm all the time," Gavin said, remembering with a kind of wistfulness.

"A wonk buddy movie," Lisa said with a chortle.

Gavin paused for a moment, feeling the absence of Jake from his life. Then seeing that both women were still interested in his story, he continued.

"My other partner was Norm Porter, who had been my roommate during our first year at grad school before he moved on to MIT, where he finished his work in cyber security. Norm was a very likable guy; half Asian, half eastern European. His family once had money, but he actually grew up dirt-poor in the backwaters of Georgia. His Dad had died in federal prison—long story, but essentially the father, an immigrant from Serbia, had been framed by business rivals on some arcane securities-espionage charge in a prosecution bungled by the government.

"Anyway, Norm got a scholarship and majored in mathematics and linguistics down at Princeton. He was a natural scholar. He spoke fluent Mandarin and Russian, and spent a year at Tsinghua University in China—which is like the Chinese combination of Harvard and MIT—also on scholarship. He is one of the brightest guys I ever came across, just a free spirit. In a strange way, despite his elaborate university education, I would say Norm was really self-taught in many aspects. Maybe it was because of his rough background… Or maybe he was unaware of just how smart he was. He saw patterns when others couldn't even see a straight line. I remember that once he hacked into the school's computer and voilà!, changed the grades for everyone who got a C and below in one course to As."

Everyone laughed.

"What do you mean by 'self-taught' in that context?" Cate asked.

"Self-taught is a way of learning and conceptualizing that is very different than what is taught in classrooms or in textbooks. One learns in his or her own world in his or her own way. It's something that by definition cannot be taught. And here's the secret: Of all the people involved in network security, the self-taught ones are the most dangerous."

"Why?" Lisa asked.

"Because their approach to the problem, their modus operandi, is different. Which makes it extremely difficult to guess which path they might take, out of hundreds or thousands of choices available. It's like this: Those who learn from others tend to think similarly to those others; whereas those who learn mostly by themselves often wander along entirely different paths and, for better or worse, along combinations of those different paths. Sometimes it's actually a shorter and cleverer path that others just don't see, but the path also can have a lot more twists and turns and contortions. New patterns, entirely. The self-taught operate on very different wavelengths, making it nearly impossible to predict their behavior from empirical knowledge. Those who are self-taught and can connect the dots are an explosive combination."

No one said anything, and Gavin sensed that the evening was coming to a close. He worried that he might have bored Cate, but her eyes were still bright with interest. She was full of surprises and, come to think of it, unexpected nuances.

"Norm was a libertarian," Gavin said, as if further information was needed before the conversation could close.

"Well, that might figure for someone whose father was wrongly prosecuted by the government," Cate said lightly.

Gavin was impressed. "You really do pay attention, don't you?" he said.

"I do," Cate replied, as she slowly rose from the couch, and gave Gavin a warm smile that was just for him. "Well, this is all fascinating, but it's time for me to hit the road and head back to town. Early day tomorrow."

Gavin brought her coat and helped her with it. Becky and Jessica were sleeping peacefully upstairs.

Outside, the stars shone brightly in a moonless sky. The boughs of the trees swayed and rattled in the cold breeze. Lights of a neighboring house were barely discernible through the trees.

"How are your neighbors? Have you gotten to know them?" Cate asked as they came down the front path. The low-watt path lights had come on automatically.

"Not really, haven't even met them," Lisa said, her breath making a vapor trail in the chilled air. "The truth is, we've been so busy getting settled and getting Becky into school that we haven't made any real efforts.

And it's even more difficult with Mr. Reserved here." She tapped Gavin on the shoulder. "You know, even in California, we lived at that home for four years and only knew our neighbor across the street. We never really met the ones on either side or behind us."

"Well," Gavin said, "we were about a thousand feet away on either side with big trees in between. It's not like you just see them in their yard and go over to say hello."

"And here too you are a little ways away," Cate said, as she squinted at the dense foliage and towering trees, which formed a dense barrier even shorn of their leaves.

"I'm sure we will stop by to say hello as it gets a bit warmer," Lisa said.

They had arrived at her car at the end of the driveway, a shiny black BMW.

"Nice," Gavin said with a low whistle.

"Used," Cate said with a good-night laugh as she gave each of them a small good-bye hug and tapped the key fob in her hand, which made that familiar little beep.

The year had only a few weeks remaining in it. On New Year's Eve, Gavin and Lisa took the girls out to Boston for the famous Nutcracker ballet and to see the ice sculptures, returning home by 9:30 p.m. Upon their return, Lisa noticed that the digital clocks were all blinking 12:00 a.m. and realized that the power must have gone off.

"I don't get it," Gavin said. "We have a pretty powerful emergency generator for the whole house, and it is programmed to turn on within thirty seconds of an outage."

"It must not be working."

"Well, we'll have to get it checked in the spring when it's a bit warmer."

After that Gavin went down in the lab, restarted an experiment he was running, and then sat down at his desk. As he tried to access his machine, he realized that it was busy making backups. The backup mirror drive must have contained damaged data with the power outage. He went upstairs to use the machine in the home office.

CHAPTER FOUR

Right after the New Year holiday, Gavin got a phone call from Gary Cowan. Cowan was the executive vice president for information technology and their top man responsible for security at the First Bank of Northern Pacific, one of the biggest banks in the country. Gavin had never met Cowan, but he knew his name.

Cowan was all business after the brief introduction. "The reason I'm calling is that the top five banks in the country have formed a consortium to pull their resources together, trying to ensure foolproof system security. We have got to do a better job of combating online hacking attacks. As you know, it's critical that citizens and businesses keep faith in the highest level of the banking system, or our economic system will collapse."

"This I know," Gavin said, wondering why he was getting a lecture from a stranger who'd phoned him out of the blue.

Cowan went on, "So, to cut to the chase, the consortium is looking for someone with a strong network-security background, but with a low profile. You, specifically. We want to work on this quietly. I have seen some of your published work...."

"What can I do for you, Mr. Cowan?"

"Gary, please. Actually, I'm calling to see if you would speak with the group in New York. It would be a big help to the banks, and we will certainly make it worth your while in terms of compensation. Just, basically, take us through the current environment, as seen from your perspective."

For Gavin, compensation wasn't the issue, but serious attention to a subject that was near and dear to his heart certainly was. He already knew what he wanted to tell the group, in essence: That the current environment wasn't what worried him in terms of cyber security. It was the emerging environment. What was yet to come.

"Sure, I'll be glad to," Gavin said.

The meeting was set for the morning of January 14 at the law offices of Dana, Zingler, Matteson in midtown Manhattan.

Cowan told Gavin, "Someone from my office will call you with the specifics of the car that will pick you up at LaGuardia. I will also e-mail you a confidentiality agreement, if you don't mind. When you arrive at the offices, please do not go to the front desk. Write down this cell number, and call it a few minutes before your arrival—someone will meet you in the lobby. We want to keep as low a profile as possible, given the sensitive makeup of the group, as you undoubtedly understand."

"Low profile is always good," Gavin said.

"Wonderful. See you then," the banker said.

*   *   *

On January 14, Gavin took an early flight from Boston and arrived at LaGuardia around eight a.m. The car was waiting. He called the cell number a few minutes before it pulled up to the offices on 58th Street and was met in the lobby by a man who looked like a stereotypical high-priced attorney: Brooks Brothers suit, quality wing-tip shoes.

The stranger said only, "Good morning, Mr. Brinkley," and led Gavin into a private elevator off to the side of the elevator bank. They got off on the eighteenth floor and proceeded into an elegant, wood-paneled, windowless conference room.

Besides Cowan, there were four other executives seated at the table talking quietly among themselves. After the pleasantries, Gary asked all of the attendees around the table to provide a brief introduction of themselves, including their respective bank affiliation, title, and primary responsibility. Each person was the top executive in charge of technology security in his or her respective institution.

After Gavin shared his background in greater detail, Gary gave a PowerPoint presentation that highlighted some of the major recent hacking attacks on banks, the damage done, and what the various follow-up analyses had found about the respective vulnerabilities in the banks' existing systems. Here, for anyone who needed a reminder, was the reality of a profound threat to the global financial system that was almost universally unappreciated in the general population but was expanding with startling speed. Here come the barbarian hordes from all directions, boldly astride Trojan horses or stealthily burrowing through the walls with ever-proliferating cyber armament, bewildering even to the most vigilant: Malware, phishing, whaling, vishing, SMiShing, pharming... banks' payment systems pillaged, data hacked and exposed, there seemed to be no end to it.

"Of course, you can see that the fixes were made after the fact in every case," Cowan recited after the PowerPoint presentation. "So the question is, are we reacting adequately? Are we fighting the last war?"

"Exactly," the man from the fourth-largest bank said enthusiastically, nibbling on the tip of his pen.

Cowan said, "A really major incident could significantly shake the citizens' trust in our banks...."

"Well, to the extent that the public will still have trust after a really major incident—" Gavin interrupted, and several of the executives at the table looked confused. Mercifully, Cowan had come to the last slide in his PowerPoint.

Cowan smiled and said, "We all concur that a significant bank crisis could well be created by these hackers lurking all over the world. Which is why we asked you here, because we need all the help we can get. So Mr. Brinkley, would you mind sharing your views?"

Throats were cleared and chairs were scraped. Standing, Gavin surveyed the assembled faces, saw more skepticism than he had wished for, but hoped for the best. He had decided to begin with a light introduction: "Good morning. Let me start with a question that might sound odd, but please bear with me. You all have heard of the notorious old-time bank robber Willie Sutton. And why did Willie Sutton rob banks?" Gavin asked.

The men gathered around the table in the conference room shifted uneasily, and several made disdainful faces.

Then Cowan spoke up, playing along in his role as the host.

"Because that's where the money is, as Sutton supposedly said, of course," Cowan said, looking quizzically at Gavin. "So what's your point?"

"My point, Gary, is this, if I may," Gavin said, being careful to keep his tone amiable while trying not to sound as alarmed as he felt. "Willie Sutton is full of baloney, or he would be if he were alive and said such a thing today. Willie and his gang robbed banks in the 1930s, and 40s, armed with a Thompson machine gun that didn't even have live bullets. And yes, in his day, that's where the money was, and armed robbery was the best way to steal it.

"But consider the Willie Sutton style of bank robbery today. Guy goes into a bank with his accomplices, displays a gun, scares the tellers into dumping the dough from their drawers and maybe from the vault into bags—then they run out and make their getaway. But for what? Guess what the average haul is for a bank robbery in the United States today."

"Okay, I'll just take a guess: eighty thousand dollars," Barry Boltman said.

Shrugging, Gavin glanced down at the yellow legal pad at his place on the table. "These are data from the FBI uniform crime statistics. Last year, there were 1,081 bank robberies in the U.S., for a total haul, in cash, of… let's see, $7,502,097—and change. So the average haul per heist is…"

While many of the men around the table looked down and a few others shifted uncomfortably, Charles Kroger replied quickly, "Actually, it is $6,939—and 60.5 cents." He smiled brightly.

"Excellent!" Gavin said, "So the average haul for a bank robbery last year was less than seven thousand dollars. And remember that the haul almost always has to be split with at least one accomplice and often several. And that the cops make arrests in the vast majority of bank robberies."

"So you're suggesting that bank robbery is not a growth industry," Kroger said, and there were appreciative laughs all around.

Gavin waved a hand. "No, I'm not, actually. I'm telling you that bank robbery as practiced by some guys coming in the *front* door with a gun is a ridiculous waste of criminal energy. But as we all know, too well, that isn't how the bad guys rob banks these days. So let's talk very seriously about cyber security and the banking system. I know you guys are experts, but maybe we can let loose a little here and challenge some assumptions that are making the industry too secure, as it were, in its attitude toward security."

He was relieved to see an almost imperceptible straightening of chairs, a squaring off of legal pads in place. Heads were turned in his direction. He was relieved to have broken the ice with this tough group of masters of the IT universe. He now knew he could proceed to more serious business.

"I know you guys are the tops in your field, but let me play devil's advocate here for a bit," Gavin said. "Let me suggest that the resources that you are currently pouring into cyber security are probably woefully insufficient and misplaced."

Barry Boltman stiffened at this. "Come on guys, you know how I feel about this," he said. "No offense, Mr. Brinkley, but I believe that we are overly anxious and way too inclined to throw more and more money at a threat that we have under reasonable control."

Boltman went on, "There were always internal losses at banks. Spoilage is part of any organic process, including banking. Me, I am totally confident that my bank is secure. I have full faith in the system we have."

Charles Kroger said, "I agree with Barry in essence."

Erika Desker did not, however. "Barry and Charles, I seriously disagree with both of you. This is a major concern in my mind. I don't want to sound like an alarmist, but I think Mr. Brinkley is prodding us in a real vulnerability, and I don't think we can overstate the challenge. We just cannot play with our future, and the country's future, lightly."

Frank Lyman shook his head. "Oh, come on; isn't that a bit grandiose, Erika? Do you really believe that with a total IT budget approaching a billion dollars a year at your banks—and I think I'm in the ballpark with that average figure, right?—that we can be taken down easily by some punks in their parents' basement who were probably still using an AOL dial-up five years ago? I have faith in our software provider. MBI Associates is state of the art; they're miles *ahead* of state of the art. I think it's a gross overreaction to say that we're so vulnerable that we need to panic."

"I'm not saying panic—" Gavin put in, but Frank interrupted.

"Look. I did a major software upgrade three months ago. Since then, not a single attack has penetrated my system. Am I complacent? No. But am I comfortable that I'm protected? Yes, I am. How about you guys?" Lyman looked at Charles Kroger.

Kroger raised a palm dismissively. "My mind is on the Super Bowl. I just got two tickets. Upper suite, fifty yard line, by the way. So the main defense I'm worried about right now is the Patriots'."

35

"Where'd you score two tickets like that?" Lyman asked with agitated interest.

Kroger smiled. "Let's just say I know a guy."

"Some guy at MBI Associates?" Boltman put in.

Kroger smiled broadly. "Yeah, they have some good guys at MBI."

"I know," Boltman added quickly. "My wife and I will be there, too."

"I'm flying down on MBI's G4 Gulfstream," Lyman boasted.

Gavin waited for the chuckles to subside. Then he said, "Okay. Back to school. Let me pose another simple question, because I want to get you to focus just for a minute on the weakest link in security: passwords. Can anyone tell us what the most common passwords are?"

Barry Boltman actually raised his hand like an eager student. "123456," he said.

"Not bad," Gavin told him. "And yes, that is generally regarded as number one, closely followed by its dopey siblings '1234', '12345', and '12345678'. Any others?"

"Your pet's name?" Desker said with curiosity.

"Actually, that's not even in the top ten. But way up the list is 'QWERTY', which, of course, are the first six letters on the third row of a keyboard. Brilliant, huh? You'd be surprised that the smartest people often use the dumbest passwords. Also high on the list are the words 'football' and 'baseball.' Very popular, as well, are 'golf' and 'Jesus.' So hackers simply start off already knowing all the common passwords, which reduces the odds going in. Then the mix includes dictionaries of every language in the world and all the permutations. No problem, these go into the calculations."

"Hey, I didn't know he was going to give us a test today. I would have studied," Boltman said, looking around for laughs.

Gavin ignored him.

"Okay, moving along here, let's get serious. In the olden days there was one door to get in and out of the bank, as Willie Sutton knew. But nowadays, with multibillion-dollar computer and software systems, each bank has thousands of doors, mostly locked, some closed but unlocked, and one or two open. The *open* doors are known to you guys and to law enforcement. The doors we need to worry about are the ones that everyone *thinks* are closed, but unfortunately are unlocked.

"Software has gotten very complex, as you all are very aware, and it's not just the computing machines, but the networks we all connect to—"

"Wait a minute!" interrupted Barry Boltman. "We spent over $274 million last year to protect ourselves, and the hits we took were fairly benign. And quite frankly, Gavin, I don't believe that we have any door that is closed but unlocked."

"I agree," said Charles Kroger.

Cowan said firmly, "I urge you guys to take it far more seriously. This is not about the money you already spent on compliance, on reacting to known threats. Rather, the issue is whether our current security levels are adequate for future attacks, currently developing but unknown to us. I'm suggesting that we need to undertake a very aggressive program to find ways to fully secure our networks, and then overhaul each of our respective banks' infrastructures from the ground up."

Kroger snorted loudly. "Overhaul! Do you realize how much an *overhaul* costs? At my bank, we'd be looking at a cool billion for that sort of undertaking. I can just see myself going to my CEO, and him going to the *board* to explain the need for a billion-dollar *overhaul* and, oh, by the way, also explain why the current billion-dollar cyber-security system we have even *needs* overhauling! *No way, Jose!*"

"You better think again seriously about what Gavin is saying, guys. In order to save a billion you may be risking much, much more," Cowan said.

Kroger was the more vocal scoffer. "Look, this is all very basic. Can somebody who is unauthorized move money out of my bank account? Ultimately, that's what it comes down to, right? I'll bet money that no one can," he said, and looked for approval around the table, which he largely received.

Erika tried to steer the discussion firmly back to the purpose of the meeting. "Look, we've been at this for two hours. Why don't we let Gavin give his views without getting interrupted?"

Gavin thanked her. "Gentlemen, I hear what you are saying and I acknowledge your strong faith in your infrastructure," he said. "But are you certain that no one can take any money out of your bank without you knowing it?"

Kroger folded his arms across his chest. "Absolutely. I have gone through plenty of external testing and my system passed with flying colors."

"I assume you keep your money at your bank?" Gavin asked.

"The bank would fire me if I did not, and they should."

"Okay, will you be willing to give me permission to see if I can bang open some doors?"

"Sure, by all means, go ahead and I will bet ten thousand dollars, payable to the charity of your choice, that not a penny will be touched in my personal accounts. So be my guest."

"Let me test it. Do you have both checking and savings at the bank? "I do."

"Okay, please check your balances as of now and write them down on your pad."

He tapped at his notebook. A steward in a white jacket ducked his head in the door and made a signal to Cowan, who said, "Lunch is served in our adjoining conference room, guys."

"I'll join you soon," Gavin said as they all filed out.

*   *   *

About twenty minutes later, Gavin strolled into the adjoining room, where the bankers were still lingering over a sumptuous buffet as two white-jacketed stewards hovered.

"Sorry to interrupt lunch for a second, but Charles, can you do me a favor?" Gavin announced over the lunchtime chatter.

"What's that?" Kroger said a little sharply, looking up from the big deli turkey and Russian sandwich that he'd been demolishing.

The room turned quiet. "Would you mind dashing into the other room and checking your balances again?" Gavin said. Charles scowled darkly, but he rose and complied while everyone paused to watch.

In a few minutes Charles came back with his yellow pad in hand and an expression of disbelief.

Kroger said in a low voice, "I don't know what this guy just did, but a single penny has switched from my checking account to my savings account. One penny."

Amid murmurs, Charles took out his cell phone.

"Who are you calling?" Cowan asked.

"Tom Stapleton, the CEO at MBI Associates, is about to get a piece of my mind," Kroger said sharply.

"Charles, with due respect, would you mind holding off for the time being?" Gavin asked him. Charles frowned but snapped his phone closed.

The room was silent. "Okay, now would anyone else like me to bang open some more doors? No betting required," Gavin offered amiably.

No one took him up on it. Lunches left unfinished, everyone returned to the next room and sat down.

"When can you start?" Barry Boltman said gravely to Gavin, who could see the others nodding approval.

"I'm going on a family vacation for a week, so probably in the first week of February," Gavin replied.

Charles Kroger shook his head in disbelief. "What? Somebody can fiddle around that easily with a bank account? We're in grave danger, worse than any of us realized—and your priority is a family vacation?" he said with caustic disdain.

Gavin just smiled and replied, "I'm sorry, Charles. I'm not looking for a job. I came here out of a sense of responsibility. But I can only start on February 7."

The others quickly but reluctantly agreed that February 7 would be fine, if that was the best he could do.

Gavin gathered his things. "Till then I would ask—please—that no one does anything precipitant, like asking MBI Associates to come in and fix things. That would only advertise the problem we're seeing, and trust me, commotion will follow as they all try to cover their behinds. It's highly unlikely that anyone will find new ways into your systems within the next couple of weeks. And besides, why would anyone want to spoil those trips to the Super Bowl?"

Kroger stopped Gavin by the door and said with astonishment and approval, "Sir, you only took twenty minutes to switch money between my account balances. I do believe you have made a believer out of me."

Gavin shook Kroger's hand and headed for the elevator.

"Just trust me and enjoy the game, and I'll see you on the seventh," Gavin said. He didn't tell Charles that it actually had taken only five minutes—he'd built in the rest just for suspense, and to enjoy fifteen minutes of silence in the quiet of the empty room.

CHAPTER FIVE

When February 7 arrived, Gavin called the group back into session over a conference call. He urged them to move decisively on a concerted plan of defense that anticipated emerging threats based on intelligence, rather than just reacting to them based on experience.

Gavin addressed the whole group: "Public trust can turn into public panic if one of these cyber attacks gets too far out of control. So lady and gentlemen, do we agree that we have serious work to do?"

They agreed.

But just as a great ocean liner turns very slowly against the tide, so do big banks when they respond ponderously to new stimuli. The next meeting, scheduled for early April, was cancelled. Annual reports and annual shareholders meeting deadlines were invoked. May was the best anyone could do. Gavin worked to maintain a sense of urgency, but the crisis receded slowly.

While Gavin was trying to keep his spirits up about the banks' lack of responsiveness, good news came in the form of a phone call from New York. A major software company had made a significant offer to acquire his patent for an innovative method of detecting mal-intentioned software, whether they be viruses, Trojan horses, spyware, backdoors, worms, malicious adware, or the newly developed sub-classes like scareware, crimeware, and botware.

"Explain to me again the difference between botware and botnet?" Lisa said after he described the news to her.

Gavin sighed theatrically. "Forget about that stuff. Did I tell you they offered $17.2 million upfront to acquire the patent outright?"

"You did. Congratulations! Don't spend it all in the same place, as they used to say."

"Yeah, well, at least we know we can continue sending Becky to that insanely expensive school, and Jessica too, when she's ready for kindergarten. And after that Harvard or MIT, and the grad schools of their choice."

"Of *your* choice, is my guess," she said with a laugh and a nudge.

"Do you want a private jet?" he asked suddenly.

She looked startled. "You're kidding."

He laughed. "I'm kidding, I'm *kidding*," he assured her. "But you know those guys in that bank group I've been working with in New York? A lot of them went to the Super Bowl on private jets, can you believe it? Most went on their company plane, but a couple of them told me they had these jet-cards that basically buy you a certain amount of flying time—twenty-five hours, fifty hours, whatever—in a private jet, you, and your family. Wouldn't that be nice?"

Lisa shook her head. "We take the train to New York for an occasional dinner and Broadway show. We go to Nantucket for summer vacation, we drive to Hyannis and take the ferry, then we rent bikes on the island. I think a private jet would be seen there as slightly, oh, *louche*."

"This is one of the reasons why I love you: frugality," and he kissed her.

"Well, as to the frugality, within reason," Lisa said with a smile.

But it was actually true. Lisa was able to casually toss off the idea of wealth because so little of her character was invested in it. She was centered. Like Gavin, she enjoyed the good life, and when she spent, it was quality. She loved the security that money brought, the amazing ability of money to solve problems small and large, for yourself and for others. Problem-solving, that's really what money meant to her. She'd heard the saying that money doesn't buy happiness. Maybe not, but it does buy security and insulation. She and Gavin had been poor and they had been rich, and rich was infinitely better. Without the slightest doubt, many of the quotidian problems that confront any family, and can sometimes drive a family into misery, can be mitigated with a sufficient amount of money. Not all, of course, but *many*. That was the real value of money, not the acquisition of things and status. And she was proud that Gavin, who was able to generate money without submitting himself and his family to the travail and desperation that often accompanies its accumulation in a traditional corporate world, felt the same way.

"Let's you and me and the girls go out for dinner tonight, big spender," she suggested.

He nodded. "Pizza!" they both exclaimed.

In about an hour, they had the kids ready to go to their favorite Italian restaurant in downtown Concord. Jessica, by now two and a half years old, had become the family comedian, often prodded by her mother and her sister, Becky.

"Tell Daddy where we're going," Lisa prompted as she zipped Jessica into her coat.

"*CAN-kid!*" the child giggled with glee, while her older sister beamed approvingly.

After they strapped Becky and Jessica into their car seats for the drive into town, a drizzle began to fall, cold as snow. A low rumble of thunder could be heard along with the soft slap of the windshield wipers as Gavin pulled out of the driveway into the empty two-lane road. Moonlight filtered through the dark canopy of trees, making the street glisten wetly. Downtown, in the brightly lit pizza restaurant on Main Street, where the jukebox seemed to play nothing but Dean Martin songs, Lisa chatted with the girls after the waiter took their orders, but Gavin was distracted. Maybe it was the stubborn persistence of rain and cold in the early evening, when—at least in Pleasanton—the sun would still be shining and it would be warm, with flowers in bloom.

A few weeks later, on a Tuesday morning when the temperatures were slowly climbing into the 60s during the days, Gavin was driving into Boston when a blue BMW pulled into sight and then loomed bigger and bigger in his rear-view mirror. The BMW stayed almost right on his bumper on the Cambridge Turnpike and in the speeding traffic on I-93, all the way into the city, where the BMW finally made a sharp right just as Gavin turned onto Chestnut Street. The incident bothered him during a long morning meeting in the city, but by the time he was ready to drive back home, the annoyance was gone. Just another idiot with a fast car and a grudge, he figured. Who knows what sets people off? And Boston-area drivers were known as the most aggressive in the country.

But on his drive home a car drilled into place just behind his bumper, a black Mercedes SL500 tailgated him all the way to Monument Street.

Gavin tried slowing down, but the Mercedes slowed in tandem and stayed on his tail. He could see that someone wearing a Red Sox cap was driving, but not much more. Usually, a crazed tailgater will shake a fist or lean on a horn, but this one just stayed with him, menacing but silent.

In Boston, he realized that people often tailgated to avoid detection by law enforcement's radar; the police in the area were unrelenting when it came to speed enforcement. Yet try as he might to rationalize the two strange and aggressive tailgating incidents, he could not shake the idea that, somehow, this was personal and planned in advance. But why? And by whom?

Gavin didn't mention any of this to Lisa, but he appeared more and more impatient. Lisa attributed the entire family's crankiness to the seemingly endless chilly weather—it was their first delayed New England spring after all, at a time of year when Pleasanton would already be boasting the climate of paradise.

One Saturday afternoon after the landscape contractor came with his crew and their noisy machines to scoop up the endless sodden leaves and expose a few wan patches of new green, Lisa stood by a window and watched.

Gavin put down his printout and walked over to put his arm around her. "I think maybe we need a change of scenery and some sunlight, darling," he said. "Seasonal blues, that's what it is."

Gavin thought for a minute. "Easter weekend is almost here. I have an idea. Why don't we just have Becky play hooky on Thursday and Friday, and all of us get on an airplane and go to the Caribbean for four days?"

"Get out of my way!" she gasped theatrically, pushing past him with eyes wide.

"Why? Where are you going?"

"*Packing!*" she hollered, laughing. "Call the travel agent immediately!"

Gavin made the arrangements for a long weekend in resort accommodations at Caneel Bay on St. John, the lushly landscaped, exceedingly private gem of the Virgin Islands. But a day later, he suddenly had to cancel the trip, to the great disappointment of his wife and children. Frustrating business complications had arisen that required him to be on hand near home, and not on a beach. He had a call from the software company that had recently offered him the $17.2 million buyout. They had discovered a patent by someone else that might, arguably, contain several small elements potentially overlapping with his own patent. So instead of paying all the money upfront and running a risk of expensive litigation, the company's lawyers insisted that the payment be kept in escrow for eleven full years, and only then would it be paid in full.

Gavin didn't need the money or the aggravation of protracted litigation. The money could sit in escrow and accrue interest. Then, if they were to benefit from the patent without a legal hitch after eleven years, and that looked like a reasonable outcome, it was all his. But he needed to sign the papers and get the documents off by FedEx no later than Thursday night.

CHAPTER SIX

One night after dinner, when spring had finally sprung, Gavin was holed up in his lab running an experiment. While the test was underway, Gavin reviewed his security-system tapes as he did once every quarter. His was a good system with fixed-position wireless surveillance that showed the slightest intrusion or motion.

The archival logs visually documented a surprising number of critter intrusions, until Gavin realized this was his first spring at his new home. A wooded property in Concord turned out to have a lot more nocturnal critters meandering by in the dark than one would expect: deer, raccoons, wild turkeys, foxes, the occasional black bear and coyote. Gavin spent a few hours idling with fascination over the screen captures of those critters over recent months before he realized that it was getting late and he still needed to check the alerts early in the year. It was then he noticed that on New Year's Eve, the surveillance camera had inexplicably gone offline, gone blank, for about twelve minutes, at 7:14 p.m.

He mentioned the gap on the security tape to Lisa, and before he knew it he was telling her about being tailgated menacingly the previous month.

"Going to and coming from Boston," he said. "Different cars."

"*Both* ways? Gavin, what is going on? Do you have enemies I don't know about?"

He had no known enemies. Gavin could be slightly imperious at times in a business setting, but even when he was warning the bank IT security executive that they had better shape up, he did it with diplomacy and collegiality. Having been adept as an entrepreneur who stayed outside corporate bureaucracies for most of his career, he'd avoided even petty office clashes. He may not have had a wide network of close friends, but he definitely did not have any enemies, at least that he knew of.

"Should we call the police?" Lisa asked. "Maybe mention the tape?"

"And say what? That the power went off for a few minutes four months ago? That would sound a little nutty, especially since there is no physical evidence whatsoever that we were burglarized."

It was a Friday night, and as usual the family was heading out for dinner, this time in Bedford at All Natural Pizza, an informal place that served an excellent all-organic pizza. As they were halfway down the long driveway, Gavin felt that his Lexus SUV had gone heavy, as if the tires were low on air. It was dark. There were no driveway lights and no road lighting on Monument Street either, a nod to the town's insistence on preserving the historic nature of the area. He stopped, stepped out, and pressed a fist against the driver's side rear tire. It was flat. Then he examined the other side. To his alarm, that one was flat, too. As he was bent over the tire, he heard a police siren coming from Monument Street.

"We have a flat," he told Lisa and the children, who looked at him wide-eyed. He tried to remember the last time he had had a flat tire, and it struck him that neither of the girls had ever experienced that particular motor-vehicle phenomenon. One of the many great improvements in automobiles over the years since Gavin had been a teenager was the tires: Flats used to be common, now they were unusual.

He leaned into the open window. "No worries, we'll use one of the other cars. I'll pull this one to the side and I'll be back in a minute with the other car. You guys stay inside. It's cold out here... Still!"

He had barely finished the sentence when he saw a police car approaching the driveway. The Concord Police car stopped within inches of the SUV's front bumper. An officer jumped out. He appeared tense. Gavin stepped into the bright light.

"Sir, is this your car?" the officer asked, aiming a flashlight at the windshield. The bright flashlight beam and the pulsing lights from the cruiser's roof luridly illuminated the faces of Lisa and the girls.

"My car, my driveway, officer. As you can see, we have a flat."

"I see two flats, sir," the officer said, as if correcting inaccurate information supplied by Gavin.

"Two," Gavin agreed, "which is unusual."

A second police car, lights snapping through the dark, now bounced down the driveway and came to a stop behind the first.

"Mike, everything okay?" asked an officer who bounded out of the second cruiser.

"I'm looking," the first officer replied.

Lisa also stepped out of the car, which for some reason alarmed the officer named Mike.

"Ma'am, I'm going to need you to get back in your car," he said, aiming the flashlight at her. She complied.

Gavin then impatiently asked, "What is going on here?"

"Why were you out of your car in the middle of the driveway in this cold?" Mike asked Gavin.

"Well, as we see, I have a couple of flat tires and was just about to walk back to the garage and get the second car to go to eat in Bedford when you arrived, Officer. But why are you in my driveway?"

"Two flats," Mike said, as if stating something new.

One of the other officers was on his knees at the SUV's rear wheel well. He called out, "Hey, Mike, take a look at this!"

Lisa was now out of the car without any objection from the police. She and Gavin stood in the cold, bewildered.

A few minutes later Mike approached them and introduced the other two officers.

"Sir, I'm sorry about this, but I need to ask you. Are you armed? Do you have a firearm on your person?"

"Absolutely not," Gavin said, raising his arms the way an airline passenger is sometimes required to when passing through a TSA body imager at the airport.

"Okay, sir," Mike said, his tone now relaxed and cordial. "Please understand, we need to be cautious." He shone the flashlight toward the house. Gavin was impressed to see that its beam was intense enough to reach all the way. "Are you the new owners?" Mike asked.

"Yes," Gavin and Lisa responded simultaneously.

"When did you guys move in?"

"About a year ago," Gavin replied.

"What part of the country did you move from?" asked Mike.

Gavin was a bit surprised. How did a local cop they'd never met before know that they were outsiders? "From California," he said.

"Makes sense," Mike said, somewhat cryptically in Gavin's opinion. "Did you know the previous owners?"

"No," said Lisa.

Mike tucked his notebook away and said, "It's cold here. Would we be able to go inside the house and talk for a minute?"

Becky, who was listening at the open car window, called out impatiently. "But I really want pizza, Mommy. I don't want to go home."

Lisa shushed her and they all trooped back toward the house, with Gavin carrying Jessica. Out of earshot of the officer, Gavin said to Lisa, "Do we have any hot coffee?"

"Sure," she said. "The breakfast room. We'll get some coffee in them, and then we'll find out what this is all about."

But the other two officers did not enter the house. Instead, they began poking around the property with their flashlights.

As Lisa got the coffee ready, Mike asked them to send the children to another room. Then when they were settled around the table, he told Gavin and Lisa: "Look, Mr. and Mrs. Brinkley. Your tires didn't go flat on their own. They were shot out. We found one of the bullet casings nearby. "

"Oh my God," Lisa gasped.

"But how did you know to get here? Did someone report shots?"

"No," Mike said. "I'm afraid this gets worse. We had a call from another law enforcement agency that you may be a target of a kidnapping attempt, which is why we rushed here. So tell me what's going on. Has anybody been bothering you?"

Gavin said urgently and with great agitation, "Wait! What kidnapping? Are you kidding me? Who would want to kidnap us? We just moved here over a year ago. We barely know anyone, and we are very quiet, low-profile people. I don't understand a word you're saying." Gavin looked at his wife, whose face was contorted with fear.

"We have no idea what this is all about. You get crazy people making threats, overheard making threats. These days, there's crazy all around. But sometimes you need to take crazy seriously, you know? All I know is we were instructed to respond to this address, and to ascertain that you and your family were all right. Jeez, Mr. and Mrs. Brinkley, I know how this must sound, and I wish I could tell you more about what prompted this, but I do know we are supposed to take it seriously. Until we know more, we'll investigate and circle back. And we'll keep an eye on you, of course."

"Circle back? Meaning what, exactly?" Gavin said with exasperation.

"You haven't noticed anything suspicious lately?" Mike said, ignoring the question. "Say in the last few weeks. Have you hired anybody new for household or maintenance help? Anything going on at work that might be suspicious?"

"I'm self-employed," Gavin said.

Mike wrote that down. Then he asked, "Does anyone outside of the family come and go regularly in the house?"

Lisa answered. "Our cleaning lady, but she's very nice. On extremely rare occasions, the babysitter, a local girl who goes to Harvard, but we trust her implicitly of course or she wouldn't be the babysitter. The Orkin guy once a month, but I'm always here when he comes. The lawn and landscaping guys came by last week for a spring cleaning, but they're always outside."

"All local?" the officer asked.

"Right," Gavin said.

"Do you keep any large sums of cash in the house, Mr. Brinkley?" the officer asked.

"No, of course not."

"Do you travel much internationally, sir?"

The question made Gavin uncomfortable. "Not much. Why do you ask?"

"Which countries?"

"Here and there. Japan and China for ten days last year. I haven't been out of the country since. Again, why do you ask?"

"Just routine."

Lisa said, "Tell him about the tailgating."

Gavin felt a little silly complaining about tailgating, but the situation suddenly made those incidents more fraught with portent, so he explained them. The other two officers had come into the house, though Gavin noticed that one stood by each window, keeping watch on the outside. Mike was taking careful notes.

"Also, and this may be nothing, but I think someone might have tampered with our video surveillance system."

Mike looked at him with interest. "Tampered? How?"

"Well, as I said, it's probably nothing. But I noticed a twelve-minute gap on the home-surveillance tapes, although that seemed to occur during a short power outage. Nothing else. But look, that was more than four months ago. Nothing out of the ordinary since."

Mike scribbled more notes and then looked up. "That's it?" Mike said, sliding his business card toward Gavin.

"I think so," Gavin said.

"If anything comes to mind, Mr. Brinkley, I need you to call me immediately. I jotted my cell number on the back of my card. Any time, okay? And we'll be back in the morning to take a closer look around the home, and also examine the security system tapes, if that's okay with you. A couple of things, meanwhile. Make sure all the security alarms are turned on and working, okay? We'll be driving by the house all night, and we may also have a patrol car come down the driveway, with the lights on so you know who it is. But call immediately if you need us for any reason."

"Should we just leave and stay at a hotel tonight?" Lisa asked nervously.

"No, I believe you are safe here with us on patrol," the officer said.

After the police left, Lisa made some grilled cheese sandwiches and tomato soup for the kids. Neither she nor Gavin had an appetite. Gavin was very quiet, his usual attitude when he was mentally trying to connect the dots.

"What are you thinking?" Lisa asked softly.

"Nothing, just worried, plain worried. But don't you be. I'll figure this out."

"I am really sorry that I made fun of you about the tailgating," she said.

"And you think these things, the tailgating, the crazy kidnapping, are related?"

"I worry about that."

She was close to him. "Should we leave?"

"I think the police are right. We'll stay calm until we know more." he said.

Gavin was getting a little irritated. How was he supposed to know what to do, to protect his family as best he could? He had just shared everything he knew. He wanted to tell his wife there is no point now in talking for the sake of talk, because they had reviewed all of the known evidence and the only thing that remains now is speculation. And speculation feeds on itself as a night wears on. The dots were connected as far as they went. For now.

"You should get some sleep," he said tenderly.

"I'll try, but... will you?"

"No. I'm going to stay down here with a book, just to think things through. I'll check on you and the girls, but I'll be quiet."

She was crying when she kissed him good night.

He kept all the lights on inside and outside. He had programmed both of their cell phones with 9-1-1, so they only needed to press one button instead of four. There was a panic button in the security system base that immediately informed the monitoring station and the local police station of an emergency. He stared into space for a long time, feeling the night slowly edge by, sensing shadows adrift in the dark.

CHAPTER SEVEN

There is a concept called "wartime" that combat veterans know about. Both Lisa and Gavin had read about it but had never really experienced it... until now. Wartime is marked by a psychological tunnel vision, an intense shift from the broader perspective of life, with all of its quotidian stimuli as one simply proceeds through a day to a state of intense inner vigilance. It is a parallel and entirely distinct emotional universe. As a result of that one blustery and dark April night, the Brinkleys of bucolic Concord, Massachusetts, were suddenly thrown into a churning vortex of wartime.

Wartime started early. Around six in the morning, just as Gavin was finally dozing off from the tumultuous events of the night before, the home phone rang. The caller ID read: "U.S. GOVERNMENT." Gavin answered it on the third ring.

For a few seconds, he heard only office noise, with a phone ringing in the background, which seemed odd at this hour of the day. Then a deep male voice came on.

"Is this Mr. Gavin Brinkley?"

"Who's calling, please?" Gavin needed a few seconds to steady himself for whatever this conversation might bring.

"Mr. Brinkley, my name is Marcus Henley and I'm a special agent with the FBI. I'm sorry to bother you so early on a Saturday morning."

"That's okay. What can I do for you Mr. Henley?"

"Actually, it's what we need to do for you, sir. First, we owe you a few explanations. Then, we have very serious business to discuss. Do you have a few minutes?"

Well, of course I do, Gavin thought. Still, he remained unsettled by the police visit. He wanted to know for sure whom he was talking to. "Mr. Henley, I hope you don't mind, but would you give me your number so I can call you right back. I want to make sure I'm actually talking to the FBI."

This posed no problem. "Absolutely, it's a very good precaution," Henley said. "And please take a couple of minutes to double-check that the number I'm giving you is the Boston field office of the FBI. It's in the book. Or, it's online as we say now."

The phone number checked out. Gavin quickly googled "Marcus Henley FBI"—a list of routine mentions and news stories came up: *"according to Marcus G. Henley, a special agent with the FBI in Boston…"* He called back Henley, who answered on the first ring.

"Federal Bureau of Investigation, Special Agent Henley."

"It's Gavin Brinkley again."

"Great. Thanks for calling, Mr. Brinkley."

"Can you please tell me what is going on?"

"You spoke with the Concord police last night, correct? Is everything okay with you and your family?"

"Yes, but as you can imagine they're terribly worried… but about what, we don't know… Mr. Henley?"

"I'm here." The agent breathed heavily into the phone, then said, "Look, I don't want to go into a lot of detail on the phone. I need to come out there later this morning and talk to you. But I do need you to prepare yourself. The immediate threat is gone, and by immediate I mean imminent. But the danger is real. You'll need to be prepared."

"Prepared for what? Can we dispense with this cloak-and-dagger stuff?" Gavin said impatiently.

Henley was not amused. "Mr. Brinkley, you have no idea how serious of a situation we have here. First of all, you need to know that you are in the process of losing your identity. Do not use your computer or any digital device that's connected to the Internet. Understood?"

"Yes, but—"

"Your credit cards have been compromised. They are now all frozen."

"That's crazy!" Gavin shouted.

Marcus spoke calmly and deliberately. "Sit tight for now. I can be out there by seven thirty, okay? Stay off the phone and stay in the house."

"But—" Gavin protested.

The line went dead.

Lisa had wandered downstairs, dressed but disheveled, when she heard her husband on the phone.

"What's going on?" she asked fearfully.

"I'm sorry. I didn't mean to wake you. That was an FBI agent. He's coming here at seven thirty a.m."

She rubbed her eyes. "The FBI? Why? Did they give you any indication of what is happening to us?

"Not really." Gavin hesitated, unsure whether to tell Lisa more or remain silent. He chose the latter as he didn't really have anything concrete to share as of yet.

She had her arms around him. "Will we be all right?"

"The police and the FBI say so."

"This is crazy. Can we call someone?"

"Let me try Cate. The FBI guy said not to use the phone, but that seems a little extreme. She has connections all over. Maybe she can help us make sense of this."

Lisa did not object. As if in a trance, she went into the kitchen to start the coffee, and then padded upstairs to check on the girls.

Gavin held down the number 7 on his phone and three rings later Cate answered.

"Hey, Gavin, how are you? Are you calling to see if I'm working as early on a Saturday morning as you are?"

"Not really, Cate. I mean, I'm not okay. We have a serious problem that I have no idea how to sort out. Can you check on something for me? A supposed FBI agent named Marcus Henley just called and said that Lisa and the kids and I are in some kind of danger. Last night, the local police came by and said the same thing. We're on a kind of lockdown here, Cate. This makes no sense. Can you—"

"Gavin, slow down. Give me the details one by one."

He filled her in. It sounded insane, but she reacted with the logical mind he had come to trust in so many heady financial situations. He appreciated her attentive concern.

"Got it," she said. "My God, this is horrible."

"You don't think I'm nuts?"

"Gavin," she said, drawing his name out. "You're the sanest person

I know. Listen, the police and the FBI? You have to take them very seriously."

"I wonder if it's just a prank."

"I doubt that. You saw the cops and you verified the FBI agent. They're not in the business of pranking respectable citizens."

"Your firm has sources in law enforcement, correct? Can you make some inquiries on our behalf? I know this is asking a lot—"

"You stop that right now! Of course I'll check around. I know a guy in the U.S. Attorney's office, high up. He's on my speed dial, in fact. And he owes me. Let me sound him out. I'll get back to you as soon as I know anything. This is all very scary. I'd be very cautious right now. Who knows what's going on?"

Gavin saw the newspaper delivery van pull up in the driveway and heard the wet thump of the *Boston Globe* hitting the doorstep. He watched the van slowly turn the oval and head back out the driveway, and was glad to see its turn signal blinking red through the trees as she made a right on Monument Road. Was this what life would be like from now on? Afraid of the newspaper delivery woman?

Lisa was in the kitchen with the girls having breakfast. Still in her pajamas, Jessica ran up to Gavin and tugged at his sleeve.

"Daddy, come on!" she said, beckoning toward the bright glow of the kitchen. "Coffee!"

"Not right now, honey, I have some work to do. Go finish your breakfast."

Jessica made an unhappy face and said, "No work!" as if that was the greatest inconvenience she would face all day.

The phone rang again.

"Cate?"

"Gavin, stay calm."

"I am calm, I think. It's hard to be calm when you don't know what's happening!"

"Gavin, for some reason unknown to anyone, a very nasty element of the criminal world has got you guys in its sights. I don't know how to tell you this, Gavin. My guy at the U.S. Attorney's office practically jumped through the phone at me when I brought up your name. He was, like, stricken. 'How do you know this?' he demanded. 'Mr. Brinkley is a client and a close friend. He called me,' I said. 'Tell Mr. Brinkley to stay off the phone!' my guy said, very, very agitated."

"But what does this mean? What did I do?"

"Gavin, this is something—"

At that moment the doorbell rang, and Gavin saw a hulking man in a raincoat standing outside. He was by himself.

"I think the FBI guy is here," he said.

"Go!" Cate said. "And call me when you can. Be very careful, Gavin."

*   *   *

Marcus Henley was a trim, fit man, about six-three, with a conspicuous handlebar moustache. To Gavin he radiated how the movies portray FBI men: confident, businesslike, well-mannered, but with a steely gaze. Gavin felt more secure in his presence.

They exchanged very few pleasantries as the stress on each man was very clearly visible to the other. Suddenly Gavin realized that life was about to change drastically. With Lisa now hovering nearby, Gavin felt his head swimming as Marcus described the full extent of the threat. It felt like he was receiving body blows from an assailant.

The Brinkleys were in dire peril. "You're going to need to get out of here for a while," Marcus told them, carefully watching their reactions.

Lisa gasped. "What are you talking about?" she cried.

"You mean you can't protect us?" Gavin said angrily.

"Not adequately. Look, the compromising of your identity is just the beginning. We have intel—intelligence—that hacking into your personal data was just the prelude before… someone tried to kidnap you."

Lisa sat down shakily beside her husband. "Is it just us?" she asked. "Or have the children also lost *their* identities? Are they still our kids?"

Marcus seemed surprised. "No, it's only you and Gavin. Not the children."

For reasons not yet fully understood, a notorious Serbian criminal outfit called the Enterprise, whose boss was a figure known as ZRK, had not only infiltrated both Gavin's and Lisa's personal identities, but they had also targeted Gavin for personal "intervention," in an encrypted ZRK message secretly intercepted by the FBI.

"Intervention," Gavin pondered. "Do I want to know what that means?"

"They have a bull's-eye on you, and that's an absolute certainty," Marcus said.

"But why?" Lisa demanded, her face flushed. Gavin held back, listening carefully.

"We simply don't know. What we do know is that this gang can slip under the radar at will. They're deadly, and frankly we don't have a fix on them yet. We will, but we don't right now. Kidnapping is one of their more benign specialties.

"These people are very sophisticated criminals, highly trained ex-military out of the Serbian army, a very nasty breed, backed up by extremely smart computer expertise. Up until now their game has been money laundering, and we thought we had them pretty much under control, if not defeated. But they've begun moving in new directions. Politics. Terrorism. Score settling, and these guys have scores to settle that go back five hundred years.

"Once upon a time they confined their tribal battles to the ancient borders, but they have global scores to settle now, including with the United States for our attack on Serbia in 1999."

"You can't catch them is what I'm hearing."

"Not yet. This is a whole new world. There are no longer any borders."

"I knew that. Theoretically, mainly. This is the first time I've actually been a piece on the board, Marcus."

"Gavin—can I call you Gavin?—look, I know this is a terrible jolt to you and Mrs. Brinkley."

"Call me Lisa," she said hesitantly.

"And Lisa," he acknowledged. "Naturally, you're going to get some corrupt elements of the Russian intelligence into a mix like this. Opportunity beckons, plus they are still fuming over losing the Cold War and the dissolution of the Soviet Union. They have always had blackmail and violence in their bag of tricks, but now they also use some of the most brilliant minds in computing, which is why law enforcement has been caught flatfooted. Now we know they have even penetrated some of the biggest software companies in the world, and we know they're turning attention to the banks."

"The banks," Gavin said. It was not a question; he was beginning to connect the dots. Could it have been someone in the room with Cowan that day before the Super Bowl when Gavin made his impassioned Willie Sutton speech? Could it have been Cowan himself? If that were true, Gavin would have zero idea whom he could trust any more. Perhaps the room itself had been bugged, or other communications had been intercepted? After all, Gavin knew if it had been that easy for him to switch a penny from one of Charles Kroger's accounts to the other, it couldn't be that hard for someone even moderately skilled to intercept an email....

"Let me tell you about who we're dealing with," Marcus began. "The head of the Enterprise is an American-born, eccentric, UCLA-educated Serbian who graduated at the top of his class in both computer science and forensics. He went on to get a PhD in network security. That is ZRK, the mastermind—absolutely brilliant, both in cyber attacks and in criminal strategy. His deputy goes by the initials LSA and is even more brutal. If ZRK is the brains, LSA is the brawn, the muscle who enforces the writ. LSA used to be a contract killer but later joined forces with ZRK during the Bosnian War."

Marcus went on, "These characters don't think for a minute before killing anyone in their way, and local law enforcement is no match for them. They have hundreds of murders in their wake. These guys make the smartest of the Italian mob guys look like country bumpkins. Which brings us to where we are right now."

"Which is?"

"Which is the threat to you."

"But why us? Why would the Enterprise pick us?" asked Gavin. Gavin thought he had an inkling of the answer, perhaps they saw Gavin as a threat to their new operations in the highest tiers of banking security, but he wanted to know how much the FBI knew.

"Well, you have something they want, obviously. We can't be sure what. I've been following this outfit closely now for a couple of years, even before they emerged from the shadows to become a real threat in the United States. Some of their most recent actions led us to place you under surveillance—for your own safety—a few months ago. I'm the one who called the Concord Police last night, because we picked up some information that an operative was making plans to kidnap someone at this house."

"Last night?!" Gavin was still incredulous.

Marcus shrugged. "The timely intervention by the local cops undoubtedly scared them off."

"So what now?" Lisa asked.

Marcus took a deep breath and sighed. "Now you move."

Gavin blinked. "You're not serious."

"I am deadly serious," Marcus told them. "You need to be out of here for a while. We will move you to a secure, undisclosed location."

"For how long? Do we have any choice? This is an outrage!" Gavin was yelling now, letting the emotions of the past several hours rise to the surface. He couldn't stop them even if he wanted to, even though he knew his girls could hear him.

Marcus was implacable. He chose to answer only the latter of Gavin's two questions. "I'm afraid you have no choice. The safety of your family is gravely threatened, Mr. and Mrs. Brinkley."

The Brinkleys remained in a state of shock as they heard Marcus outline what needed to happen, absorbing perhaps 50% of what they were told. They would need to leave within twenty-four hours. They should pack only the bare necessities, such as clothing and toiletry items. They should not pack anything that could be connected to their current lives. No computers, no DVDs, no CDs, no cell phones, no iPods. Everything that could be traced had to remain behind until it was safe for them to return.

Marcus told them that he would phone with more details later in the day. Later that morning, Cate called back. Gavin, profoundly shaken, hesitated even to pick up the phone for her. When he did, he heard a tone of worry in her voice he had never heard before.

"Listen," she said, trying to mask her fear with a quiet, firm voice, "I checked high up in the Bureau with a very credible contact of our senior partner. You wouldn't believe the hoops I had to jump through to get to this person and to get him to say anything at all. The headline is this: Agent Henley may not even know the full extent of the danger. You're going to have to follow Henley's lead and go away for now, but they will try to get you back as soon as possible. My heart goes out to you, Gavin. You and Lisa and the children."

"This can't be happening, Cate."

"Get cash, Gavin. As much cash as you can without calling undue attention to yourself. And close your overseas accounts, which are far more vulnerable to criminals than your U.S.-based ones. Can you do that today?"

"I think so."

"Do it. Let me know what you get done, and if you'd like, I'd be happy to help any way I can."

"Would you be willing to take care of the finances in our absence?"

There was a long pause; Gavin suddenly realized that Cate would now be on the Enterprise's radar if she agreed to do it. "Are you OK? Would you be comfortable with that?"

"No, no, I am fine. I will do it."

Gavin could sense fear and trembling in her voice.

"Are you sure?"

"If I was in this kind of crisis, Gavin—wouldn't you be there for me?"

Lisa was crying. Gavin, on the other hand, began feeling oddly composed now that, at least, the vague outlines of a plan were coming into focus.

"I don't know how to thank you for this," Gavin said, and then hung up with Cate. He and Lisa made a frenetic series of trips to several banks, some of which closed at noon and some at one p.m., and managed to withdraw about $70,000 in cash.

Soon after they returned, Marcus arrived looking very grave.

"Just to go over a few critical things," he told them while the girls played upstairs. "One, do not contact anyone from your current life, and I mean *anyone*, under any circumstances until the federal marshals who will be working with you give you explicit approval. If you ignore to do so, it will be at your own and your children's risk."

Gavin and Lisa were too stunned to comment. They listened passively as Marcus recited to them a summary that sounded as if it had been memorized from a government text.

"You will be under the authority of the U.S. Witness Protection, Security and Benefit Act, also commonly known as the Witness Protection Program, in which the United States Attorney General authorizes the relocation and long-term protection of a witness or potential witness of the state or federal government in any proceeding concerning organized crime, or other serious offenses."

"A witness to what?" Gavin interrupted.

"That's just a technicality to get you into the program as a potential victim in a high-profile criminal investigation," Gavin explained.

He went on, "You will be transferred under the protection of United States marshals to an undisclosed location that you will learn about upon arrival. The federal marshals, whom you will become acquainted with very soon, are to be your primary contacts, and your only contacts unless explicitly advised otherwise. So long as you are located within the program and abiding by its various regulations and rules, the government will provide you with a living stipend to be described at your new location, but frankly it's not a whole lot, so you might at some point think about temporary employment. The marshals will explain everything in full to you. But a few things to really keep in mind: Absolutely no phone calls are to be made to anyone you currently know. You'll have a contact number for the marshals, and one for me to be used only in dire circumstances. No Internet usage. None whatsoever, because the Enterprise is known to have penetrated even search engines, and they can spot you via algorithms calculated on your previous usage, despite your new identities."

This hit Gavin like a blow to the head. Lisa stiffened suddenly beside him, her hand locked on his wrist.

"New *identities?*" Gavin said.

Marcus looked at him quizzically. "That's famously the key part of the program," he said.

After a long and stunned silence from the Brinkleys, Marcus opened a notebook and read aloud their new names and profile.

"You'll have a confidential copy of all of this, but ideally we'd like you to have it down right from the start," Marcus said, asking them to repeat the information to him: new names, new names for the kids, bogus but plausible birthdays. There were utterly false backgrounds to memorize: hometowns, educational résumés, work experience. A whole new fictional family portrait fell out of Marcus's notebook and was repeated dutifully back to him over a grueling hour's time.

Marcus gave Gavin and Lisa new identity cards, including driver's licenses, and asked them to surrender their current licenses. Gavin was now John Robertson. Lisa was Cindy Robertson. In an instant, Becky became Carrie, and little Jessica was now Erica. Everyone received new birth certificates as well; both children were now a few months older.

Finally, Marcus was finished. He firmly shook both of their hands. "You'll be hearing from me by phone once a month for a while," he told them solemnly. "Hopefully, we're going to get control over this situation before too long and you'll be back here in Concord as if nothing had happened except for a strange little family vacation. Most crucially, you'll all be safe. Any other questions?"

"What about our families?" asked Lisa.

"Please give me any contact information. We have methods for safely letting close family know that you're safe and being protected, but only close family. Parents, for example."

"My parents are dead," Lisa said.

"Mine, too," Gavin said. "We're both orphans, of a sort."

"So much the better," Marcus said. Then he saw on their faces that he had made a human error. "I didn't mean it that way; I'm sorry for your losses. What I meant was, for your safety, the fewer individuals trying to track you down, the better."

Gavin nodded. An insensitive slip of the tongue was the least of his worries. Marcus bid them farewell. Gavin and Lisa watched his car disappear up the long driveway.

Events happened quickly after that. The Brinkleys finished the last of their packing. They received a phone call advising them to be ready sometime after midnight. Finally, at three a.m., Marcus and another agent, Larry Oliver, arrived, both of them armed. They were packed into a black GM Suburban with their six suitcases and three boxes, and whisked away into the night. Gavin had observed Marcus's dictum and had brought along no personal effects, except one: his journals. He couldn't put his finger on why he needed to break this one rule, but he just had a feeling that they were going to be essential for maintaining his sanity.

Events occurred through dawn and the following morning with a staggering speed. Gavin and Lisa were careful to assure their girls that they were bound for an adventure, even as they began a new family game for vacation—calling each other by different names. Becky, who was now Carrie, enjoyed the game and jumped right in; Jessica, who was now Erica, didn't even seem to notice—she was so delighted with the attention she was receiving.

The FBI agents drove the family to Hanscom Field, a big general-aviation airport in Bedford. Two federal marshals transferred their belongings and escorted them onto a waiting government jet that took off as soon as they were in their seats.

One of the marshals remained with them as a flight attendant of sorts. He was taciturn but polite.

"Mr. and Mrs. Robertson, I'm Randy. Please let me know if there is anything you require." Randy took his seat just up the short aisle, as the plane climbed high above the clouds.

Gavin and Lisa had been deep in their troubled thoughts. They both looked up, startled at being called by their new names.

"Thank you, Randy," Gavin said. "There is one thing. Can you please tell us where we're headed?"

"They haven't told you?" Randy said.

"No."

"That's odd. We'll be arriving in Boise, Idaho, later this afternoon after a stopover near Detroit. It should be a comfortable flight, and there are snacks and sandwiches in the galley. Lunch will be available after Detroit. Would you like some coffee, or juice for the children?"

"Thank you, Randy," Lisa said.

"*Boise, Idaho?*" Gavin said in utter astonishment, looking deeply into his wife's eyes. Her shrug just said, "*Whatever.*" She was simply worn out and resigned. The boundary between reality and nightmare had evaporated. In a while, Lisa began muttering softly to herself. Gavin realized that she was repeating her new name and those of her kids.

After the short stop at a general-aviation airport near Detroit, Randy came down the aisle to serve lunch.

"How do you like the ride?" he asked Gavin sociably.

"The plane?"

"Yep. She's a Learjet 45XR, government fleet," Randy said proudly, and headed back to the galley.

Beside him, Lisa stirred from her slumber and mumbled something incoherent.

"Honey, what did you say?" he asked.

She cleared her throat and rasped. "Well, you finally got your private jet, John."

CHAPTER EIGHT

"Wolf season is open in Idaho," Gavin read aloud, rustling the newspaper as if to make a profound point.

"What?" Lisa said from behind the couch, where she was struggling with a television that was not hooked up to cable.

"It says here, right on the front page of the *Anton Weekly Sentinel*, that wolf season is open," he said. "I guess you can shoot a wolf here."

She looked up. "Why in the world would you want to shoot a wolf, Gavin? That's what I want to know."

"I don't want to shoot a wolf! I'm just reading you what's news in Anton, Idaho. You need a wolf license, of course. But if one shows up on your property, you don't need one, a license, I mean. You can just shoot it. Also sweetheart, we have to remember to use our new names even in private. Otherwise we could slip up."

"Okay, *John*," she said with a slightly anxious sigh. "Wolves! I have a feeling we're not in Concord anymore."

"*Can*-kid!" Erica (formerly known as Jessica) chimed in. Erica was sprawled out on a hooked rug by the fireplace, merrily helping her big sister, Carrie (formerly known as Becky), disassemble a jigsaw puzzle. The puzzle depicted a scene of jagged icy peaks of the Sawtooth mountain range reflected in a snow-rimmed lake.

"Can we see a wolf?" Carrie chimed in.

"There are no wolves! Your father is kidding. Help your sister put your puzzle back in the box," their mother suggested.

On a clear day, those actual mountains could be seen far to the north from the backyard of the family's new home, a modest three-bedroom cottage bordered by soggy, fallow cornfields. The Robertsons now lived in Anton, a small city that was boring but booming; with a population approaching 50,000, most of the employment was in farming and small retail, although there was an overlay of oil and gas industry jobs new to the area, which had brought relative prosperity.

John and Cindy Robertson, formerly Gavin and Lisa Brinkley, were at first appalled by Anton, which struck them initially as having none of the advantages of a town combined with none of the advantages of a city. Yet the wisdom of this choice made for them by the federal government as a sanctuary for their new lives presently became clear. Anton had, they quickly deduced, two factions within its city limits: a crusty old establishment of settler stock descended from long-gone mining and trading enterprises, these people kept mostly to themselves, except for keeping a wary eye out toward the second group: the oil and gas newcomers with their aboveground backyard pools and menacing SUVs plastered with aggressive religious and political bumper stickers.

So it was relatively easy for the newly named Robertsons to slip into such a setting and blend in largely unnoticed. Among the outsiders who had come to take part in the area's newfound wealth, there were folks from nearly every state. The town's population had grown tenfold within a span of less than ten years, due to sky-rocketing oil prices. Most people didn't know one another. There were many new homes, condominiums, and apartment buildings to accommodate the influx. And people generally kept to themselves.

"Why do you read that silly paper?" Cindy asked. "There's nothing in it but high school sports and school menus."

"Ah, but you're wrong, my dear. The police log alone is worth the price."

"There's no crime!"

"But I beg to differ. Listen to this week's report." He read from the column of police news:

*"**Tuesday**: Girls Charged—Two Vista girls aged 13 and 12 were arrested after they broke into a house and stole $10 worth of property. The girls admitted to entering a neighbor's house through an unlocked door. Once inside, one of the girls became hungry and prepared a serving of Top Ramen. When the homeowner returned, he noted that a sugar container, tweezers, and a doily were missing, and that the Top Ramen was gone."*

*"**Wednesday**: A Madison St. man complained that his neighbors 'go in*

and out all the time, talk in their apartment, and take the trash out at odd times.'"

"**Friday**: A twenty-seven-year-old Villas Road man reported 'out of control' by his father was only upset his girlfriend is moving to Seattle,' police said.

"**Saturday**: A Booker Road man said he received, but did not accept, a collect call from the 'Lottery Information Network.'"

"**Sunday**: A Renaldo Drive woman who was reported yelling 'Kill them' at her two young sons, it turned out, was 'watching a football game with them.'"

John and Cindy were laughing, a welcome respite of humor in what had been a dire series of events. Then John grew thoughtful.

"I confess, I am intrigued by the man who did not accept the call from the Lottery Information Network. Why did he choose to report it to the police? Are we missing something about the culture of this place? First, the man had common sense. But second, he decided to call the police to report something silly. Which means he's at least comfortable with the local cops, and they're at least familiar with his peculiarly fussy habits. All in all, a nice thing about a town, I think."

It was Cindy's turn to say something positive. "It is kind of pretty here, once you look out over the apartment complex and the abandoned factory with that awful smokestack, and see those magnificent mountains way out there. My God, they are beautiful!"

Despite trying to put the best face on matters, the move had been a serious jolt for both John and Cindy—the biggest they had ever experienced, in fact. Everything was different: their home, their neighbors, the weather, the roads, even their own names. It was as if they had moved to a different country. Truth be told, underneath the feeling of having been relocated to safety, they were traumatized and lived in a constant state of fear for themselves and their children. In a flash, everything they had worked so hard for seemed like it was gone forever.

Even a simple act such as arranging a pediatrician's appointment was fraught with anxiety. The threat was unseen but always felt, like humidity.

"What if we make a mistake in giving our names, or the kids' names, or their Social Security numbers?" Cindy fretted.

There were so many things that could go wrong, in both the big and the small picture. Agent Henley had warned them about the dangers of becoming complacent in their new lives. Marcus called them on the third day of every month to check on them, but the conversations were becoming increasingly perfunctory.

"Do not arouse suspicion. Do not stand out," Marcus told John, and there was no ambiguity in how he said it.

"Is it possible you're overreacting?"

Marcus grunted. "Look, John, you have to trust us here. The marshals have an eye on you guys, even if you don't see them…I know we have you living in the back of beyond. Rural Idaho, whoa. A state with an entire population about the size of Brooklyn, right? In the middle of nowhere, right? But this is a very small world, John.

"I'm going to give you an example, not to alarm you, but to illustrate just how small that world has become. Let me ask you a question: How far is the town of Twin Falls from where you are?"

"I don't know. I'm not all that familiar with the geography. South of here, that much I know. Down by the Nevada border?"

"It's due west, about two hundred miles. Did you know that, driven by a global refugee center run by the local community college since 1995, more than five thousand Bosnians and Herzegovinians have arrived to settle in the Twin Falls region?"

"You're kidding me!" John said.

"I am not. It's a good thing they've done, of course. These are good people. But I probably don't need to tell you that a growing ethnic population of Bosnians probably also draws attention from Serbians. Let's say it's on the radar."

"Why would you put us here then? Do you mean that Zerind Rokus Kazac has some connection in Idaho?"

"ZRK has connections everywhere, John. These are clannish people and they stay in touch across great distances. Which is my point. There is absolutely no reason for this criminal outfit to have any idea where you and your family are. But my point, John, is this: Keep your head down. Do not draw attention. They're clever and they're ruthless."

Without saying goodbye, Marcus hung up.

"Who was that?" Cindy said, coming into the room.

"Marcus."

"What is it this time?" she said in a worried tone.

"Nothing unusual. Turns out there's a Bosnian refugee settlement down in Twin Falls. So he warned us to be especially careful because you never know—"

"Gavin, does this ever end?"

"John."

"John, how long does this go on? I want to go home. I want our life back."

He grew a little impatient. "We want our lives period."

She said nothing, but he could tell she was holding back tears. Cindy was by nature a cheerful and optimistic person, but she didn't have anyone to talk to now except the children, who were oblivious and seemed to enjoy the different locale, thinking that they were still on vacation.

Their entire home, this wood frame cottage, was smaller than their bedroom suite in Concord. They sorely missed their old home: the hot tub, the swimming pool, the luxurious bath with two shower heads fed by that big pipeline that John had loved so much. The shower here was far too cramped for him to relax in to get one of his big ideas. There was no surround sound here; no flat-screen televisions. The kitchen was small, with an old stovetop. There was no workout room. The furniture was cheap and hastily assembled, like the kind they had had in college. The delicately tended Japanese garden in Concord? Here there was a scrubby patch out back with hard dirt where a previous occupant evidently had tried to grow beans, without much success.

Who knew there could be a place without Internet access? Marcus had warned them sternly against that, even as a dial-up option. Too easy to trace. Without it, they felt like they had landed on a different planet. There was no lab in the basement, either. In fact, there was no basement, just a dirt-hewn crawl space that the rental agent had optimistically referred to as a storm shelter.

John and Cindy, like hostages in a bad movie, resisted for a long time the idea that this was a new normal for them. They kept waiting for the phone call to tell them they were safe and they could go back to their lives in Concord. But slowly, summer faded to September, and Carrie needed to be enrolled into first grade. A new life gained traction under their feet, as reluctant as they were to feel it. John and Cindy realized they needed to at least make an effort to become a part of Anton, for Carrie's and Erica's sakes.

It is an astonishing fact of human nature, seen in war and civil unrest, in tragedy and relocation, that normalcy will try to impose itself, despite all odds. In December, working on paper and then on a cheap laptop he bought at the local Walmart and kept unconnected to the Internet, John completed a detailed project he had been involved in immediately prior to moving to Idaho. It was about high-frequency trading on Wall Street. He wrote the software and, using nothing more high-tech than a DBA filing at the town hall under a fictitious business name, a disposable phone, and a direct deposit account in a small community bank, he sold the module to a Wall Street firm. The front-end payment was $25,000, with royalties to come as a function of trading, about $5,000 per month initially, but that would hopefully go up over time. There was perhaps the slightest bit of danger in this—he didn't know how many innovative software programs were coming out of Idaho, and he felt sure that Marcus would not approve. But he strongly felt there was no way it could be traced, and the money was crucial toward leading a basic life of small comforts beyond the pittance the federal program provided.

They did adjust, but it was a bitter time. Back in Concord, John drove a Lexus LX470 and a Porsche Carrera; Cindy had her BMW X5 and a BMW Z5. Here they were assigned a 1993 Ford pickup truck. "She's a beauty; they don't make them any better than these F-150s—before or since. This baby has over 300,000 miles on her, same engine," the federal marshal who greeted them in Nevada had said with unbridled enthusiasm. "We even had her painted new for you. She fits right in with the landscape, of course."

The town had a library of sorts, which was little more than a room full of dusty books on the second floor of the firehouse, presided over by a fussy old woman who thought *Gone With the Wind* was the finest novel ever written and who insisted on asking new patrons if they had read it recently. The nearest proper library—one with present-day bestsellers and the tantalizing temptation of Internet connections on their computers, was forty miles away across dusty farm roads.

The Robertsons didn't know anyone except the UPS driver and a neighbor a half-mile away who waved suspiciously when he passed by. They followed the advice of Marcus and the marshals: Keep to yourself until you become firmly comfortable with your new identities. Don't worry about neighbors, such as they were. People took years to become acquainted in a place like this. Keep a low profile. And embrace the surreal.

The moon dipped below the horizon, but it didn't help her see the stars any more clearly. How long had she been reading, one hour, two hours? Each page seemed to bring up a fresh set of memories; she felt as if she were having an out-of-body experience. She couldn't even be sure that she was the one who was turning the pages. The one thing she was sure of was that this novel knew her more deeply than she could ever have thought possible.

CHAPTER NINE

The Robertsons hadn't heard from Marcus since well before Christmas, but didn't think too much of it. They had done the best they could to give their children a good holiday. With the extra money John had generated from the quiet sale of the trading software, the occasion was merry enough. Cindy had begun to take steps to express herself in the house, festooning it with natural wreaths of an exotic foliage which, truth be told, could not have been displayed in Concord.

They spent a quiet New Year's Eve watching television. Being in the mountain time zone did have its advantages; he and Cindy could let the kids watch the ball drop from that flatiron skyscraper in Times Square at ten o'clock local time, and still have them in bed by ten thirty!

It snowed on New Year's Day, one of those nasty, wind-slapped ice storms that reminds those alive today just how wretched life on these plains must have been during pioneer days. They stayed by the fire, cozy and warm. John had even become adept at splitting firewood, which he ordered by the full cord from a gnarly old farmer who advertised in the *Anton Sentinel Weekly*. The horrific storm conditions knocked the phone out for a day.

On January 2, the phone was back on and it rang at six a.m., which is never a time when pleasant news arrives.

"John, this is Larry Oliver. With the Bureau? I'm sorry to call you so early," the voice said.

It took a few seconds for John to place the name. Larry Oliver, the number two FBI man they had been working with under Marcus.

"Hello, Larry. Sorry I had to think for a minute. Marcus usually calls. Happy new year to you!"

"I'm afraid there's nothing happy about what I have to tell you, John," Larry said.

"Why? What's wrong?"

"Terrible news. I'm afraid Marcus is dead."

"Dead?"

"He drowned off that boat he loved so much. He was down in the Caribbean over the holidays. It isn't clear exactly what happened, but evidently a freak storm came up. He was alone at the time. When the Coast Guard boarded the boat, it was adrift, out of gas. No one on board."

There was what seemed like a long pause. John could sense that Larry was trying to hold himself back from sobbing.

Cindy sensed trouble. She was beside John at the phone, her eyes wide. He put his hand over the mouthpiece and said, "It's about Marcus Henley. He drowned in the Caribbean."

She gasped. "When?"

John asked Larry, who replied, "They found the boat yesterday. It may have been a day or two out there. It's impossible to say."

Cindy was slumped in a chair.

John asked Larry, "Could there have been foul play? The Enterprise?"

Larry replied with an edge in his voice. "We don't know for sure yet. There's no body found. But there were blood spots, broken pieces of glass. You know, signs of a struggle. You're not on a cell phone, are you, John?"

"No, no, this is a landline! Paid for by the government and untraceable—Marcus made very sure of that."

"Marcus was investigating connections between the Enterprise and Billy Dalton, a notorious local mob boss in Boston, and a very bad dude who disappeared a few years ago. Dalton was a cold-blooded killer but useful to us because he worked as an informant on the Italian mob based out of Providence. Dalton was playing both sides of the fence, which we figured was a possibility. What we didn't know was that Billy had a couple of agents in his pocket. We knew he had some local cops on his cuff, a couple of dirty assistant DAs—but *agents*?

"That was a stunner to us, and let's say it was a nuclear bomb to FBI headquarters in Washington. A huge embarrassment! The supervisor and others in the Boston Bureau were fired, and Marcus—with an impeccable reputation for integrity—was given the lousy task of cleaning up the mess. Meanwhile, Billy Dalton went on the lam, and one of the most astonishing things Marcus found out before he died was that Billy had established an entirely new criminal channel.

"The Enterprise. So we're looking into all the angles."

"Larry, I'm so sorry," John said. "I know that you guys were friends. And Marcus was a friend of ours. We owe him a lot. He was brave. And it looks like he died in the line of duty."

"Which is the finest and also the saddest thing anyone can say about an agent," Larry said. "Agent Henley was my hero. Everything I know, I learned from him. My fondest memories are of being out on his boat with him. He enjoyed everything that had to do with the water. Marcus was captain of his high school swimming team and singlehandedly led it to the statewide championship. He was very proud of it. So, between you and me, death by accidental drowning was not a likely outcome."

Larry came to himself, perhaps aware that he had said too much. "I have to go now, John. I'll be back in touch."

John wanted to stay on the line, as if to hold onto a thread of hope that he felt slipping through his fingers.

"What happens to us now?" John asked, convinced briefly that there was silence on the other end.

Then Larry cleared his throat huskily. "I will call you back in a few days with new instructions. In the meantime, John, and I cannot stress this enough, be extremely careful. Be alert to your surroundings. And whatever you do, do not do anything impetuous like try to reach out to your past. The danger may be at an all-time high right now."

After that fateful call, John and Cindy did their best to keep up appearances with the children, but it was difficult. Fear marked their every waking moment, and sleep was fitful. And worse, it was excruciating not to have any more information because Larry had told them not to phone him or anyone.

John had to fight off the urge to contact Cate. He missed her quick laugh and sharp mind. Most of all, Cate was a connection to the outside world and to their previous life. Making the call, he fantasized, might restore order; by reclaiming this friendship, perhaps the security and happiness of their previous life might return as well.

John never followed through on his plans to reach out to her or to anyone else. He just stared at the phone, willing for it to ring.

A few days later Larry did call again. John asked if there was anything he could do for Marcus's family. There was a pause.

"Marcus didn't have family to speak of," Larry said.

"Oh, I'm terribly sorry to hear that."

"Well, he has an ex-wife, Sarah. But there was a nasty divorce. I'm not sure of all the details because Marcus kept things close to the vest… divorce is a kind of occupational hazard for an agent as devoted to his job as Marcus was: The mob stuff is very, very scary and undercover work meant being away from home for weeks at a time. Tough on a relationship. They had a son named Timmy whom Marcus adored. There was a huge court custody battle, which Marcus lost bigtime."

"That must have broken his heart," John said.

"His heart and his bank account, too. After Marcus's memorial, they set up a fund for the kid."

"Where can I send a check?" John asked.

"John, I know your awful circumstance in this mess. You don't have dough to spare. Just you and Cindy remember him as a friend."

Still, John persisted and Larry gave him an address. John and Cindy sent $500 in cash to the fund and thought what an irony that was. They were used to writing much bigger checks for various charities—why, they had given away several million dollars in the last few years alone! And now they felt the financial pinch of sending money on behalf of a person to whom they owed their lives.

Months passed without any contact from Larry, and even the casual contacts they had had with the federal marshals based in far-away Boise had ceased. The Robertson family essentially drifted on their own, inexorably carving out a routine in a place that seemed less and less strange by the week.

And then one day there was another call from Larry.

"How well did you guys know a woman named Cate Whalen?" he asked casually after exchanging the usual pleasantries.

"Well, she was our financial adviser… and a good friend. And I hope she will be again when we get our lives back," John said. "Why do you ask?"

"John, I didn't realize you knew her, but then we were talking about her and someone here mentioned that you did. She died in June. I am so sorry."

John was speechless. His face turned ashen. As Cindy mouthed, "What happened?" flashes of Cate's smiling face, her youthful beauty and maturity beyond her years instantly flooded his memory.

"Noooooo..." John moaned. "Not Cate!"

Turning to his wife, he muttered, "Cate's dead."

Cindy was speechless.

"What happened?" John asked, feeling numb.

"I don't have many details. A sailing accident, three hours away from Nantucket on a windy day. Supposedly her boat was hit and demolished by a much larger ship—perhaps a freighter or a tanker—passing in the dark, early in the morning. But then, as you know if you knew her, Cate was captain of her sailing team at college, and so it seems unlikely that she wouldn't at least have had some warning—"

"Suspicious circumstances like Marcus?" John demanded. "Tell me it wasn't like Marcus!"

"I'm sorry, John. The indications we're getting is that the Enterprise could have been involved in this one, too. The Coast Guard noted that there was a Serbian-registered yacht in the waters of the immediate vicinity."

"Why am I just hearing about this now?" John demanded angrily. "Someone there should have realized that Cindy and I knew her well! What kind of police work is this?"

John wasn't sure if he was masking his grief with this outburst, or if he was afraid for his very life in a way that he had not been before. All he knew was that the emotions were coming fast and furiously.

"Well, I didn't know the connection as Marcus handled the case, and it's only during detailed review I realized it and thought that you ought to know. By any chance did you reach out to her in the past few months? That could have jeopardized her life as well."

"No, we did not," said John in a firm voice.

John was fulminating now. "What should we do? Both Cate and Marcus are clearly connected to me and Cindy and the girls! There has to be something! After all we cannot be sitting ducks here. It's just a matter of time before we are found out!"

Larry broke all rules of decorum and spoke directly to John as if he was speaking to a friend: "If I were you, John, I would get the hell out of Idaho. You need to find another location. Change your names and your appearances, close your bank accounts—and this time—*do not inform anyone* at the Bureau. Including me! I file my reports and they go to the organization; I have no idea where the leakage may be at this point, John. The Enterprise's reaches are deep and wide. At this point, any leakage can kill you or me—or both. I'm telling you this as a friend."

"You are not my friend!" John shouted.

"Look, I understand why you're furious," Larry said. "I'm not abandoning you. I'm just going deep into the background, for all of our sakes. When the risk diminishes I swear to you, I will track you down and follow up. I have ways to track you down. But do what I said. Leave, get new identities, change everything."

"And what brilliant ideas do you and your Bureau have about how to do this a second time?" John demanded fiercely.

But Larry had hung up.

Cindy was at John's side. What she hadn't heard from his end of the conversation she surmised. Her face was stoic.

What had happened to them? They were cut off from everything, including the hope that what was temporary would not become permanent. They were isolated, abandoned by the law enforcement, on their own, unable to reach out to anyone from their previous lives. They were like Robinson Crusoe, on an island, but surrounded by sinister forces unseen.

What would happen to their money, which had been in Cate's care? Did the Enterprise now have free rein with it, having killed Cate and perhaps dismantling the barricades she had erected to protect them? How difficult would that be for an international criminal enterprise, once they had eliminated a bulwark like Cate?

There was no one to trust. And now they needed to move again? But they had no ability to search for a new home. Internet access was beyond their reach. They needed to make decisions, but they were nearly paralyzed.

Saddest of all, they had lost two brave souls, Cate and Marcus; touchstones inside a life they had known so recently, were gone. If the Enterprise could eliminate a tough, seasoned FBI agent and a smart, savvy young woman like Cate, who had only an indirect connection to the entire episode, what chance did they have, being as exposed as they evidently were? Their lives were already in turmoil—but suddenly the roller coaster had ratcheted up once again, to the dizzying peak of still another very great height, and was suspended there, motionless for only a horrifying instant, nothing ahead of them except another terrifying plunge into a dark and twisting abyss.

CHAPTER TEN

Fear snaps on like a light at the moment the anxious wake up. Cindy was on full alert. Dawn had only begun to streak the sky.

"Where are you going?" she said to John, whose form she saw by the door against the dim light. He had pulled on a hooded sweatshirt.

"Out," he said. "I need to get online. We need information."

"Where?" she asked.

"There's a motel on the Baxter cloverleaf about ten miles up the Interstate that has an Internet kiosk in the lobby. I saw a picture of it in the paper."

"Is that safe?"

"As safe as we're going to get. It's one of those new units that are popping up in gas stations and convenience stores. Looks like an airport check-in kiosk with a keyboard. And it takes cash, not credit cards. You slide the bills in like a vending machine."

"Be careful, please," Cindy said. "Wear your dark glasses."

When John arrived at the motel, there were some truckers and an elderly couple in the lobby having breakfast at the rudimentary buffet for guests: wallet-size boxes of cereal, some tired bananas and apples in a white plastic bowl, along with dispensers for coffee, milk, and hot water. The male clerk watched John carefully when he came in, but then John realized that his only concern was that the strangers not try to get the free breakfast only available to guests. John smiled, waved, slipped off the hood, and strolled to the kiosk with a crisp five-dollar bill in his hand. He was relieved to see that no one else in the lobby had the slightest interest in him.

In a corner of the lobby, in a holder suspended from the dingy ceiling, a television blared the perpetually alarmed inanities of a morning network news program. John had to feed a second five into the machine, but he was pleased that the connection was good enough to enable brisk searching. He scribbled some notes, reflecting on how comfortable his family already was with a phenomenon that would have astonished them to consider just a year before: namely, how easy it is to disengage in America, once you decide to sever your links to the credit and banking systems and all government agencies besides a state motor vehicles department and the postal service.

John did some research about where to move, specifically where it would be easiest to assume new names without issuing any public notice such as advertising in a newspaper. A wealth of that kind of information, it turned out, is readily available online to the disaffiliated or would-be disaffiliated. He felt a bit more confident when he was through, and waved again toward the front desk when leaving the motel lobby. The clerk did not even look up, John was happy to observe.

*   *   *

"Montana," he said to Cindy as she poured him some steaming coffee at the kitchen table when he got back.

"Montana? We'd live in Montana? Does this ever end? John, *nobody* lives in Montana." She was very irritated, but she also knew that her pique was useless.

John sipped his coffee and took out his notebook.

"Actually, nearly one million people do, though mostly clustered in a few cities like Billings," he said, consulting those scrawled notes from the motel kiosk. "Shall I go on?"

He loved the fact that, even though she was afraid, she was still willing to play along.

"Please."

"Well, we wouldn't risk living in a city like Billings, which is too exposed. Somewhere in the western-central part of the state would be best. Rural, and almost isolated, but with, you know, *some* civilization. Plus, of course, clean air and mountains."

"We already have that here, but go on."

"Okay: Montana is the forty-fourth least dangerous state, according to FBI crime statistics—"

She waved a hand. "Don't mention the FBI to me"

"Sorry," he said. "The per-capita income, which was near the bottom among the fifty states, is changing because of the oil and gas extraction industry. In fact, the unemployment rate is pretty low, only about six percent, thanks to drilling."

"Isn't it, like, really, really cold?"

"Interesting you should ask. In fact, that is the case, although of course it gets pretty cold here in Idaho, not to mention, Concord, Massachusetts, in the wintertime, come to think of it. Maybe our basic mistake, sweetie, was leaving balmy California for the colder climes."

"Too late now," she said. "How cold? And I know you have the data."

"I do. The record low was set in 1954 at Rogers Pass at the relatively modest altitude of 5,400 feet. Seventy below zero. Fahrenheit. Though it never gets anywhere near that cold where we are headed: Wanton, Montana."

"Wanton?"

"Yep."

"Not Wampum?"

"Nope. Wanton."

"My God, that sounds terrible—"

"Population of eight thousand, but it goes up by another thirty-five percent in the spring and summer when seasonal vacationers visit. Also, regarding outdoor activities, one drawback that probably won't affect us. In Montana, to get a license to shoot a bear, you need to pass a bear identification test. Idaho has no such oppressive law. But there's an explanation for the discrepancy."

"Which is?"

"Montana has many more grizzly bears, which are highly protected. The bear identification test is to certify that you can tell the difference between a black bear and a grizzly bear."

"Which I could not," Cindy admitted.

"Me either, frankly. Not a clue."

"And this Wampum—"

"*Wanton*—

". . . This is our best choice, John?"

He closed his notebook. "Wanton is perfect for its isolation. I found a three-bedroom house just outside of town. Cheap."

She was crying. "When do we have to go?"

"Soon. I think it's best that we leave as soon as we can, without attracting any attention."

"How far?"

"About a ten-hour drive. And I'll rent a trailer so we can take as much as possible."

"Won't the kids ask questions?" Cindy asked with sad resignation.

"They will, and we'll have answers. We'll tell them that we're moving because we found a better school system—they're too young to really know the difference between bad and terrible in education anyway. Now if only we were back at, what was the name of that incredibly priced kindergarten? Hamilton?"

"Hawthorne School. Don't remind me. And what about our names, John? Do we have to go through all of that again?"

"We'll keep our first names the same but change our last name. How do you like, 'Stuart'? Should be ubiquitously American enough for Montana. And we'll change the girls' names as a precaution—we'll tell them it's so they'll fit in better at their new school. Kids will pretty much go along with what you tell them."

"Not our kids!" Cindy exclaimed. But it didn't matter. It was wartime again. Carrie (formerly Becky) was now Caitlin, an acknowledgment of their dear friend Cate who had likely given her life for their safety. Erica (formerly Jessica) would become Emma.

They made only one notification of their new relocation. The night before they left, John stopped at the Baxter motel to use the cash-operated Internet kiosk to notify the Wall Street firm that was paying him a royalty for his software about a new post-office-box address, which he had arranged for in a town about a hundred miles from Wanton.

This time there was no Learjet to whisk them privately, if tearfully, from one life to another. There was just the dented nine-year-old Ford F-150 pickup, with rust curled along its wheel wells, pulling a four-by-seven U-Haul utility trailer. The truck bed was piled and strapped with everything they owned that they could take to the new place. A digital television, a microwave, boxes of clothes and toys and books and household supplies, including food that wouldn't spoil. Cindy had also packed the only real luxury possessions, besides her jewelry, that she would not part with when they left Concord: two pieces of Louis Vuitton luggage, an expensive vintage steamer trunk, and a cowhide bag. John made sure to put those on the bottom of the pile of things stacked and secured in the truck bed. This way it would be out of sight from curious eyes that might question why a family that otherwise appeared to be just another stalwart unit of misfortune on the move would have among its meager possessions such fine designer luggage.

They stopped only for lunch, restroom breaks, and gas along Interstate 15 into Montana. When the kids fell asleep on what was to them just another fun adventure, John and Cindy discussed just how deep was the social dislocation of which they were now a part. Here and there, drifters and the desolate walked on the Interstate. They passed a family of four, including two teenage boys, hitchhiking, and were sad but also strangely relieved that there was not an inch of room remaining in the truck.

Great snowcapped peaks of ragged mountains loomed to the north. In a few hours, following a gas station road map, as they had forsaken any form of GPS, they turned off the Interstate onto a winding two-lane state highway. The road seemed good at first, but after a while it became bumpy, with accordion-like ripples in the asphalt. Every so often, a tire would hit a pothole with a sickening *whump*.

The volume of traffic on this highway, which included sections known in rural areas as a farm-to-market road, was odd. Whereas one might have expected to see only a few cars, there were many, traveling close together at high speeds over decrepit bridges and sharp turns. The worst traveling companions were the big trucks. One shiny tanker, horn blaring, passed them on a downhill and swerved back into the lane just ahead of them, splashing quantities of what looked like dirty water onto the roadbed.

"That's called drilling mud," John explained to his wife. "It's stuff they use for lubricating boreholes for oil and gas drilling. Nasty stuff, and slicks the highway, too. I can feel it in the traction right now. You get enough of this stuff spilling and it's like driving on black ice." For some reason, the term made him think of Cate, and then he recalled: *Snow skills.* Cate joked boastfully of her snow skills. Poor Cate!

Another big rig roared past, buffeting the pickup with wind.

"This road was not designed for this," Cindy said softly, trying not to wake the girls sleeping fitfully on the seat between her and John.

"Nor were we," John said woefully, turning on the windshield wiper spray.

Finally, they traveled down a long mountain pass and the first indications of the town of Wanton came into sight. A Walmart on the right, and just beyond that a highway intersection with a fast food restaurant, a coffee shop, an ice cream store, and a motel in each quadrant of the first major crossroads.

The town lay just ahead. On the left sprawled what appeared to be an industrial storage area behind fences, but the entrance told a different story: "Dixieland Oil Field Centre, Hospitality Services." On closer inspection, it appeared to be a sprawling trailer park covered with storage units rather than residential trailers. Row after row of industrial dorms resembled the kind of modular military barracks that contractors had built in Iraq for American troops. It occurred to John that this is exactly where these residential designs originated, in military contracts.

"This appears to be a man-camp," John said. "Though I was fooled at first by the affected spelling of the word 'Centre.'"

"A man-camp? What in the world is that?" Cindy asked, yawning.

"You always asked me why I devoured that awful weekly paper in Anton, and here's your answer. To learn about weird stuff occurring around us."

"What's it for?"

"Housing for new oil and gas field workers, all of them men. These places have hundreds of dorm rooms, in some cases thousands. Mess halls. And look at all those cars in the parking lots."

Cindy looked. The cars all seemed to have license plates from the states where the economy had been hardest hit. In search of work, unemployed men from these places had obviously come out West for the oil and gas boom. Just like in Anton, this would be the perfect place for the Robertsons, now Stuarts, to blend in.

Cindy pointed to a tattered Confederate flag that snapped in the wind from the broken antenna of a blue Dodge with Mississippi plates.

"Aren't these wild places?" she asked with some alarm, as this town did not appear to be big enough to provide insulation from this size of a man-camp.

"Actually no, except for the occasional shooting of someone on the outside—usually over pride, card games, or imagined slights. There is absolutely no alcohol allowed inside the barracks, and no women. A strict military style discipline is imposed on the men. The drilling companies pay the rent, but they don't put up with any trouble, so violators are evicted—and in a place like this, there aren't a lot of residential alternatives."

They waited at the last light before entering into the Town of Wanton. The girls stirred and awoke when they were frightened by a rap on the windshield. It had come from a skinny older man with greasy gray hair and a small bulldog by his feet. He held up a sign that said, "Vietnam Vet."

John gave the man a dollar and drove on through town. "Might as well start creating good karma," he shrugged.

The house was actually about five miles outside of town, which provided some comfort to John and Cindy. It lay on rugged, hilly terrain with scattered patches of muddy grass. The spacious forlorn three acres were enclosed, for a reason that was not apparent, by a sagging old chain-link fence. As they had expected, it wasn't much. But to Cindy's immense relief, it was clean and even reasonably furnished, with cheap but serviceable things. The curtains in the front room were plastic, and she was glad she had seen the Walmart on the way in.

The first night, after a visit to that store for some replacement bedding and groceries, they lay awake listening to strange new sounds in the dark. A clapping shutter. A moaning critter of unknown origin. Rustling branches. And from a farmhouse whose single light could be seen on a low rise about a half-mile to the west, a huskily barking dog.

Having made this kind of astonishing life adjustment once before, and rather recently too, the family now known as the Stuarts in time found traction beneath their feet. After roughly a week, John sold the red Ford pickup and bought a used Chevy SUV with lots of interior room and a powerful engine.

Wartime inexorably recedes. Uneasily, they enrolled the girls in school, little Emma (formerly Jessica and then Erica) was now in kindergarten and Caitlin (formerly Becky and then Carrie) was in second grade. Their parents were pleased to find that the children were routinely received as simply another manifestation of the social swirl that was transforming down-at-the-heels Old West towns like this one in a way that absolutely no one, not the local authorities nor the school district nor the tiny hospital, had foreseen. No one had seen this coming, that is, except maybe Walmart.

*   *   *

It was early November, with the Montana winter starting to push its way in and the big sky pressing down heavily. After the frenzy of moving had died down, John expected that the fear would diminish as well. It did not. He and Cindy were still frightened, often to the point of complete paranoia. Initially they wore bulletproof vests every time they stepped out of the house. That was something else you could find without any trouble at Walmart. Their biggest fear was what would happen to the children if something happened to their parents.

They had never felt so alone and exposed. The Stuarts took all manner of precautions. They looked out the window before they stepped outside. When they walked on the downtown street with the old broken neon cowboy figure swaggering in the wind from the long-closed hotel, they glanced furtively in shop windows to see if anyone was lurking. They always wore hats and caps, and insisted that the girls did, too.

They installed motion sensors outside the home that gave them a signal inside. They put up hidden video cameras outside, even though the clerk at the feed store had told them there was no need, that the town was safe and secure.

One of them always dropped the children at school; the girls were never left at a bus stop. Both Emma and Caitlin constantly pleaded and cried at times, wanting to join their classmates on the bus that crawled through their part of town, but their parents refused without explanation. There were three bedrooms in the home, but John and Cindy wanted the girls to stay together. They showed each of the children how to work a panic switch that John had installed under Caitlin's bed, in case they needed to raise the alarm.

In the parents' bedroom, and in a couple of other parts of home, they kept pepper spray in drawers and on the shelves. Again and again, they reminded the girls never to open the door without checking the twelve-inch security monitor.

The local Walmart had a big firearms and ammunition section, and

John decided that being armed was a good idea. To his amazement, Cindy, who had been horrified in her previous life at the idea of *anyone* owning a gun, let alone John and herself, agreed without protest. He bought a Mossberg 500 twelve-gauge shotgun at Walmart, where the clerk gave them the name of a gun dealer in town, who then sold Cindy a compact Glock 38 forty-five caliber handgun. The easy method by which they obtained licenses for the guns was, in fact, the same way they succeeded in obtaining the paperwork needed to get Montana driver's licenses in their new names. The gun dealer, upon learning that neither had owned firearms before, told them to take a three-day course in firearms safety and marksmanship training at a nearby shooting range. Cindy amazed John, the gun dealer, and the grizzled instructor as well, by quickly becoming a crack shot—not just with her new Glock but with John's twelve-gauge shotgun, too.

Oddly enough, acquiring guns firmed up their identities. The kids were also enrolled in martial arts. They kept money hidden under mattresses and in a few other places in case they needed quick cash, especially for an escape. In a town a hundred miles away, John had a single bank account to which the royalty money for his new patents and software was wired. They made all their household payments in cash; they had no checkbooks and no credit cards, knowing very well that a criminal operation like the Enterprise was able to scan trillions of credit-card transactions to find those needles in haystacks. They had no home telephone bill. For their cell phones, they used SIM cards they purchased from another town. They didn't even have a water bill because they had a well in their backyard. The only bill they had to pay was for electricity, which they paid by cash deposit a year in advance. On those rare occasions when he absolutely needed to use an e-mail function, John could always drive a distance and find an Internet kiosk. Each time, he needed to laboriously create a brand-new e-mail account ad hoc (including usernames and passwords, naturally) in whatever fictitious name and identity he dreamed up.

As winter crawled in, cattle huddled against one another in the fields. Ice formed on shallow ponds. The wind blew constantly, like a warning horn. With the weather gloomy and the holidays again looming, disconsolation mounted. They had no other family. Friends were, of course, out of the question. All they could afford to have were casual acquaintances, held at arm's length. At the children's school, they tended to be reserved and stuck to superficial chitchat with the other parents, just in case they got put on the spot about various personal details.

Still, a life had to be made. To his surprise, John found that he was not a bad handyman, and even a pretty good carpenter. The feed store a few miles on the east side of town had building supplies, and employees who were eager to explain things. Cindy, in turn, found that she had previously unknown plumbing skills, once someone told her how it was done. In the weeks after a Thanksgiving holiday they chose to ignore that year, she had both replaced an ugly, dirty old kitchen faucet with a shiny new one, and fixed a leaky pipe near the water heater. She was making plans to replace a rusty old toilet in the upstairs bathroom. She also began wondering whether she would be any good at tile work.

The family also spent some serious time in the woods camping, hiking, hunting, and enjoying nature. This was quality family time that also had the benefit of toughening the children. If an emergency suddenly arose and they needed to hide out for a few days or so, the girls had acquired the skills and stamina to do it, and to think of it as a lark in the bargain.

*　　*　　*

They had wondered about their nearest neighbor, a middle-aged man who drove a Ford F-150 pickup, but a new model, not like the rusty old one they had just sold. They had noticed the shotgun mounted in the truck's rear window one day when he passed them and waved. Not having a shotgun rack would, of course, have been far more unusual.

They met their neighbor a few weeks before Christmas, late in the afternoon. After a sharp rapping at the front door, John anxiously checked the monitor and saw the face of the man with the F-150.

"Howdy," the man said heartily but somewhat shyly when John slowly opened the door. Cindy and the children peered out from the kitchen.

"I hope you don't mind. I was passing back this way on foot to my house, doing some hunting. I thought it was probably time I came by and introduced myself. I'm Bruce Thomas. That's my place way out there on the hill." He extended his hand and John shook it and tentatively invited him in. John noticed how carefully Bruce stomped his boots and scraped them on the hemp doormat that Cindy had bought because of the mud.

John also noticed that Bruce had placed a shotgun against the boards on the porch. Back by the gate, a yellow hound dog paced, barking gruffly at his owner for leaving him behind.

"That there is Fred, my hunting dog," Bruce said as John closed the door. "He don't have the sense of an anvil, except when he's hunting, when he becomes nothing short of a machine."

Their suspicion eased in a fairly short time as it became clear that Bruce was a pleasant, and talkative, neighbor. He was merely seeking to reach out after an appropriate time, which in rural Montana evidently could be defined as a year or two.

Bruce was a shaggy man with an unmanaged beard. He was tall, well built, and had beefy arms covered with tattoos. Cindy had been cooking a roast and asked if he would like to stay for dinner.

"Thank you, ma'am, but me and Fred have to be getting home. Maloney gets home around six, and we like to have dinner waiting."

"Maloney?" Cindy asked.

"That's my old lady—sorry, I mean, my girlfriend. She works in town at the library."

The girls were clamoring to go out back, where John had strung a tire swing on the biggest branch of a sturdy oak. There was something about Bruce's cheery presence that made John and Cindy feel more secure. They let the girls go out back and after a while could hear their squeals of delight, along with the answering yelps from the hound dog, Fred.

Cindy served hot cider and molasses cookies she had made. Like most people in rural areas, Bruce talked freely but did not engage in much personal detail. They did learn, however, that he was originally from Arkansas, and that he had been a Marine in combat during the first Iraq war in the early 1990s. But they were most surprised to learn that Bruce had also been an Internet entrepreneur during the second half of that decade.

"That's where I met Maloney, in the Silicon Valley—after my divorce, that is," he said as they pulled a little more personal information from him.

John had to resist the strong impulse to engage over the Silicon Valley connection, as he did not want the favor of requests for personal information to be extended to him. Instead, he merely asked, "What did you do?"

"Made a lot of money, spent a lot more money. Decided that I did not want to work for the Man anymore. Even though, truth to tell, I was the Man myself. Couldn't stand me or anything about me. So I persuaded Maloney to run off to Montana with me."

"That's amazing!" Cindy said, brightening girlishly the way John used to see her brighten when she liked someone at a dinner party, in a life far away.

"So you were in Iraq," John prodded, eager to change the subject from his now unshakeable interest in hearing about all things Silicon Valley.

Bruce just nodded.

"And you're okay?"

"Well, like many things, I wish I hadn't been there. But sure, unlike some other people, I'm okay. Very okay, actually."

There was a silence, and finally Bruce asked, "Where you folks come from?"

John felt a slight panic but merely replied, "Back East, by way of Idaho. Long story."

Bruce nodded. There were lots of long stories in Montana that did not require telling. That was explanation enough. He got up and said good-bye to Cindy, thanking her for the hospitality. For some reason, John pulled on a coat and decided to walk him out front, where they stood on the porch in the gathering gloom and talked some more.

Without female company to wrap Western courtesy around, Bruce talked a bit more freely as they watched the hound dog scratch at a gopher pile, sniff a bit, and then decide to lay down and wait for something to develop before it got too dark.

"That's a nice gun you have," John said.

"Thank you. I'm a lifelong member of the American Rifle Association. She's a Weatherby 300 Magnum that will take down an elk and has, frequently. Not today, unfortunately."

"Beautiful wood grain," John said, confident at least in rudimentary protocols of gunmanship.

"Ain't it, though?" Bruce said pleasantly.

"So you're what, maybe three-quarter miles away?" John asked.

"That's about right. Rugged terrain once you get off the road, though. But like they say, the more rough the terrain, the more resources are generally available."

John had no idea what that meant but nodded affirmatively anyway.

Bruce cleaned his glasses while continuing to talk. "My cabin is a simple building, spacious enough, but without that obnoxious waste of space you see in those McMansions."

Bruce was watching to see if John caught the reference. There was an air of quiet appraisal about Bruce that John had only now begun to notice.

"You do see them all over," John said of McMansions.

Bruce went on. "We keep it real simple, once everything is in place. Kind of off the grid, if you know what I mean."

"How do you do that?" John asked, this time with real interest.

"Well, there is an initial phase of infrastructure development. My electricity is solar panels for which you got to have a good battery bank, four deep-cycle batteries. I bought my unit mail-order from Rolls Battery, which was founded in Salem, Massachusetts, but has since moved to Canada. I'll get you the address if you want."

John flinched a tiny bit at the mention of a town in such close proximity to his previous life. Bruce studied him in the dim light on the porch. And then he launched into a disquisition on batteries.

"Deep-cycle batteries are the major component in renewable energy systems that require electricity storage. A battery bank can give you a reliable source of power when the grid is down. Think of your battery like a big bathtub of pure energy. Same technology has been around for a century: Lead plates, sulfuric acid is what gives you the chemical reaction that makes the electricity."

John nodded again, this time in full comprehension. This was science, after all. And it was clear that, given an opportunity, Bruce would talk at great length about how things worked. John assumed that Bruce did not get many such opportunities. Despite his apprehensions about making any new connections, John was enjoying this visit.

"So they're always being charged," Bruce went on. "You tend to forget it this time of the year, but even in winter, there is a lot of sun in Montana. Even if it's shining on four feet of snow. Once the snow stops and the sky clears up, it doesn't take much solar power to supply an off-grid place like mine."

"So you're really 'off-grid?'" John asked, stumbling over the term he always thought was "off the grid."

"Well, not technically. There're some real off-gridders who would scoff at my lifestyle. I mean, I get bulk foods from Walmart; no getting around that if you like to eat. But the garden is easy to manage, and you'd be surprised how much you can grow for two people even in a place like this. We have chickens for eggs and some goats for milk. Plus with Old Benson here," Bruce added, slapping his rifle, "I've got the means to obtain wild turkeys, wild game... Elk cook up real good."

After a minute, Bruce went on. "So I'm not off-grid, but you could say I'm a kind of survivalist, and I would not argue with you on that account. There are a number of false assumptions about off-grid living, like you have to be some kind of crazy militia lunatic waiting for the apocalypse... Or some long-haired hippie with an old lady in a gingham dress and five rug rats hiding in a cabin, playing their Sheryl Crow CDs on a battery-powered MP3 player. Worrying about their carbon imprint every time they need to go to the bathroom. You talk off-grid to most people, and that's the image they have."

"I see."

"Some people, they always need to feel connections. Electronic connections, phones, peck peck pecking at keyboards. Beeps and whistles, never ending. And connected to what? Other beeps and whistles. Don't mean a thing. Ask them how to pitch a tent? They look at you like you asked them how to carve a canoe out of a tree.

"Here in Montana, you can easily find a different breed of man, one who not only isn't afraid to be disconnected, but who also will not ask you a lot of nonsense questions if it is obvious that a lot of fool questions serve no purpose except to make still another unnecessary connection. See?"

"I do," John said, intrigued about where this might be going.

"In light of our current chaotic economic situation, as well as the potential for social breakdown, for severe energy disruption, hyperinflation, freight and cargo and transportation disruption, and global war, the off-grid life is not just a hobby but a valuable form of insurance," Bruce continued as if he was reciting a creed, but John could see his passion had merely caught fire.

"There may come a day when, whether we like it or not, we will be forced to survive off-grid. Some will be prepared with the expertise required to make it work. Some will have at least a practical understanding of the methods and philosophies that drive decentralized and independent living. Many will not ever wake up to the social catastrophe looming in our country's future and the extraordinary significance inherent in off-grid knowledge."

"Others like this around here?" John ventured, now very curious.

"Well, the only connection we all have is this: We mostly belong to the Liberty Movement. You heard of that?"

"Nope."

"We are a group dedicated to peace and tranquility, and to the common goal of bringing a higher level of consciousness to this world, whose consciousness is being attacked by the lamestream media, bootlickers for the corporate oligarchy—and that includes the giant agriculture industry working to eliminate the organic food movement all over, while destroying our precious bodily fluids."

John had that moment where he began to worry about Bruce's sanity, but then he saw Bruce looking for a sign that John had gotten the joke.

John realized he was being cordially teased and that made him laugh. "Precious bodily fluids like the crazy air force general says in *Dr. Strangelove*, right before he unleashes the nuclear apocalypse?"

"And no, I am not going to press some pamphlets into your hands and ask you to come to a meeting. But I will suggest, you being out here basically in the wilds with your wife and kids, that you consider some survivalist preparation. Nothing drastic, just common sense."

He pulled something out of a pocket and showed John a cartoon he had cut out of a survivalist magazine, depicting a man sitting in the middle of stacks of canned food, smacking his head in dismay and wailing, *"I forgot the can opener!"*

"Don't forget the can opener, is all I'm saying. Several can openers."

"Okay. What else?"

"Well, for basic emergency preparedness you need to think beyond food."

"Okay."

"Water, of course."

"Of course."

"There are many ways to store water. Read up on it. And get you a good water filter."

"I will."

"Walmart has them."

"Of course," John agreed.

Bruce recited a small list: "Fire extinguisher, matches, flashlights, Sterno, extra blankets, battery-powered radio, or one of them hand-cranked ones. Extra gasoline. This isn't rocket science, though it actually could be, come to think of it, as rocket science ain't all that complicated. Basically, you put some gunpowder in a can and set it off. Anyway, you also have to think pet food. You got pets?"

"No."

"The girls might like a dog."

"Both Cindy and I are allergic."

"Sorry to hear. And remember prescription medications. Get a doctor who will write out anything you need. In emergency preparedness planning, the right accessories can make the difference between life or death, John."

"I'll remember that."

"Well, I gotta get going home," Bruce said, shaking John's hand and shouldering his rifle. He called out to the sleeping dog, who bounded toward them.

"That's a nice family you have, John. I should tell you, we mind our own business, Maloney and me, but if you ever have any need of anything, you or your wife or those two little girls out here, you fire off two shots in the air and here I come, no questions asked. Or you could call, if you're less dramatically inclined. I got a cell phone."

Bruce took out a pen and jotted down his cell phone number on a dog-eared card that said "LIBERTY.ORG" on the front and had his name listed as the president of the local Liberty Movement.

Bruce touched him fraternally on the arm. "If Maloney were here she'd yell at me that I don't get out enough except with that hound dog, so I can sound like a crazy man when I get to talking."

"I've enjoyed every minute of this, Bruce."

"Okay then. Don't forget the can opener."

Bruce rubbed his dog's ears and they trotted off. Light snow was falling. Over his shoulder, Bruce called, "Goethe said, 'None are more hopelessly enslaved than those who falsely believe they are free!'"

"That makes sense!" John replied in a shout.

Somehow, he was not the least bit surprised that Bruce had pronounced Goethe's name correctly.

CHAPTER ELEVEN

John was curious about whether the initial visit from Bruce would accelerate a relationship between the two homesteaders. John would have preferred to remain friendly but fairly distant, though he could tell that Cindy was being pulled more in the direction of establishing a real friendship. To his satisfaction, Bruce and his girlfriend still kept their distance, though Bruce did introduce them to Maloney through their car windows one morning when they passed each other near the elementary school. She was petite, dark-haired, and pretty, and it was clear she had Bruce wrapped around her finger.

This is not to say that the Stuarts shunned their neighbors on the hill once they'd made their acquaintance. In fact, they had them over for dinner on Easter and were delighted at how warm and sensible Maloney seemed to be. Who could figure out any couple? They just took Bruce and Maloney as a given, with only the most basic of social questions asked. Anything more would be pushy and nosy, and not the Old West way, which was fine with John and Cindy, who had quickly grown to like the Old West ways, truth to tell.

Sometimes John felt Bruce gazing at him and his family with interest that bordered on friendly concern. As much as John wanted to unburden himself to one other person—and Bruce seemed like the most reasonable candidate—all doors, physical and emotional, had to remain shut tight and locked. Just as a carelessly disclosed trivial piece of information, a birthdate, for example, could provide a tiny clue that ultimately could lead a hacker or a surveillance expert on to the trail, so a casually enhanced friendship held danger. Without anyone realizing it, a door would open somewhere.

Yet while John and Cindy maintained a vigilance bordering on clinical paranoia, they still wanted Emma and Caitlin to grow up as normally as possible. It wasn't their fault that sinister forces had created overcautious behavior in their parents. There was still every indication that Wanton would be the girls' home for a very long time in this bizarre new life they had been forced into.

It was always a tightrope walk between parents and children. The Brinkleys (then Robertsons, then Stuarts) had been fortunate to uproot the kids when they were, for all intents and purposes, too young to form key questions. Because of the developmental nature of the mind, coupled with enough false supplemental information supplied for their own good, those questions never did become conscious. Yet other events would occur, such as the children's birthdays, or invitations from school friends, and John and Cindy could see that the girls had figured out they were slightly different. They did not quite know why this was so, other than the fact that they had moved to this place from somewhere far away.

Bruce and Maloney sensed this and, without in any way intruding or overstepping bounds, they befriended Caitlin and Emma, each of whom they found delightful.

One hot summer's day, Bruce was watching Caitlin in the backyard throw a small rock that scored a direct hit on a tree stump seventy feet away. Caitlin looked at him with some uncertainty when she saw him watching.

"Caitlin, could you do that again, honey?" he asked with great curiosity.

Saying nothing, she picked up another rock and rubbed the dirt off it with her hands. Then she threw. *Swack!* Another direct hit on the tree stump.

"Caitlin, you got quite an arm on you, girl!" Bruce said with great enthusiasm.

"Again?" she asked.

"Again!"

Swack!

Now everyone applauded from their lawn chairs, where Cindy had served cider. Caitlin did not blush, but beamed instead like a lantern.

"That girl not only has a pitcher's arm, she has an eagle's eye, John," Bruce said after the children had scampered off to play fetch with the hound dog Fred, who never seemed to tire of the game. "She know how to shoot?"

Years ago, in another place, John would have been aghast at such a question asked of his well-mannered little girl, but that was a long time ago in another life. "I'm not good enough to teach her," he replied to Bruce.

Bruce said, "Well, I've seen that you already stress gun safety just by the attitude you and Cindy have toward firearms. Gun safety is the most important thing a child around any kind of firearm has to be taught. How to shoot the gun, that comes secondary. How to *not* shoot the gun unless you fully intend to, that's primary."

"I couldn't agree more," Cindy said.

"*I shot a man in Reno, jest to watch him die,*" Maloney sang lustily, imitating Johnny Cash's accent. She looked up quickly to make sure the girls hadn't heard. They were off with the dog. The adults laughed.

Bruce passed her a plate of crackers and cheese. "Sweetie, I'm glad you're enjoying yourself, but you didn't shoot no man in Reno," he said.

"Been to Reno, though," she protested.

"For a music-industry convention!" he said. "Fact is, you didn't even shoot *craps* in Reno."

She bit a flat cheese cracker. "Don't like guns, actually," she admitted with a giggle.

"Nor do you have to, darling," he assured her, and she kissed him lightly on the cheek.

John and Cindy were enjoying the couple's affectionate repartee. It occurred to Cindy that it had been a long time since she and her husband had felt relaxed and happy enough to flirt with each other like that.

Before the little afternoon get-together ended, though, Bruce did take John aside and offered to teach Caitlin how to shoot. He even offered to throw in some lessons for John as well.

To his amazement, John found himself considering the offer. He didn't realize that Caitlin had slipped up to join them until he heard her speak.

"Can we, Dad?" she implored her father.

"We'll see," he said. He caught himself in time, but he had almost called her Becky.

John and Cindy were sad when that day ended, as were the girls.

For a brief time, they felt more connected to a social system, even if that connection was just three-quarters of a mile away up the muddy hill.

The desire to be around people increased over time. Cindy began taking more trips with the girls to explore their surroundings; often they forgot to wear hats or otherwise shield themselves from company but just enjoyed whatever environment they found themselves in.

Cindy was sure to drive farther than necessary to fill their "people fix." One day in early fall, she took Emma shopping for back-to-school clothes in a mall that was a two-hour drive away. As Cindy was getting out of the car, Emma, always fascinated with her mother's key ring pulled the keys from her mother's hand while the door was closing. The door locked and Cindy panicked. She didn't know what to do, and especially did not want to call the police. She gestured frantically at the little girl, who merely waved back and laughed, as if they were playing a game. After a while, though, the child realized that something was wrong and began crying; her fingers were not strong enough to pry open the manual door lock. Three older women, passing by to take their shopping bags back to their own car, stopped to help, but their efforts were to no avail. Emma just screamed louder. Finally, one of the women called the police and a patrol car drove up.

A few minutes later, a beat-up sedan carrying a photographer from the local newspaper drove up to the scene. The two cops and the journalist greeted each other heartily.

"What do we have here, Billy?" the photographer asked one of the officers, who made a comic-face pose as he focused his lens.

"Late-breaking local news! Stop the presses!" the officer announced jokingly, while waving at the little girl in her car seat. Emma, witnessing of this scene assembling outside the car, stopped crying and watched with growing interest and a small smile. *How would this mess be fixed?* the child's face seemed to say.

First the officers introduced themselves politely and assured Cindy and the other women that all was under control.

One officer then said to the other, "Okay, let's get the door open, Billy. You got the slim jim in your bag of burglar's tools?"

"Wait!" the officer called Billy said excitedly. He signaled to the photographer to hold on while he scampered back to the patrol car, opened the truck, rummaged around the debris in it, and finally came up with a light-green tennis ball.

"You're gonna love this!" he said. "This is a front-page photo, with a service tip from Officer Billy Purdue on the new and improved way to open that locked car door. Burglars please do not watch."

Like a magician, Billy showed the tennis ball to all. It was a normal, used tennis ball, but with a small, oblong hole cut out.

"Observe," Billy commanded as the photographer snapped away. The officer took the tennis ball, put the cut-out hole firmly on the door's keyhole, and pumped it several times. Under the burst of pressure, the lock button popped up as if by magic.

Everyone cheered as Billy ceremoniously opened the door and Emma scampered out, smiling widely to see so many happy faces welcoming her. Billy bowed. The photographer took some more photos, and while Cindy was delighted to have Emma out of the locked car—to have the car door *open* again!—she was very worried about that busy, busy photographer.

"Thank you!" Cindy said to the officers.

"Where in the *world* did you get that silly trick for opening a car door?" one of the female shoppers asked.

"Ma'am, it works, doesn't it? Over Christmas, my mother down in Boise showed that one to me. She got it from somebody in her bridge club. I've been dying to try it in a real, honest-to-pete police situation, and this is the first chance I got," Billy said, grinning.

"Great story!" the photographer said with a big laugh, putting his camera into its bag. "Long as nobody falls into the river this afternoon, this should be on the front page as a human interest piece!"

Thanking them again, Cindy strapped Emma back into her car seat and bid them all good-bye, all the while feeling a sinking sense of anxiety.

The front page was the last place she wanted to ever be, even in a small-town newspaper in rural Montana. Early the next morning, Cindy made the two-hour drive again and picked up a copy of the local paper at a 7-11. Her heart sank. There, beside the photo of Billy triumphantly springing the lock with his tennis ball, were two photos of her and Emma, under the headline: "Match Point! Mother and Daughter Reunited Thanks to a Policeman's Tennis Bounce." Her heart sank.

She'd only told John she had some shopping to do and hadn't alerted him to the possibility of the newspaper story. When she got back early in the afternoon and showed the paper to John, he was furious.

"What in the world could I do, snatch his camera away?" she protested in tears. "As it was, I felt so bad having her stuck in the car. At that point, I was worried about a scene in the parking lot, where maybe, just maybe, somebody might come by and recognize us. Then these nice ladies came by and tried to help, and before you know it, the police and the photographer show up. This is how things work in small-town America, John! All I wanted to do was cover my face, take Emma, and run. But what could I do?"

"You could not go shopping at a mall!" he said peevishly.

"Really?" she demanded with an injured look. "You would take away from me that simple pleasure, which I have indulged in exactly twice since you dragged me to this place? Really, John."

He felt horrible. That afternoon, he himself took a drive without saying where he was going.

When he came back around dinnertime, he handed her a plastic card.

"John, we can't use credit cards," she protested.

"It isn't a credit card, Cindy."

"What is it?"

"A Montana AAA-Plus. It has numbers on the back for twenty-four-hour roadside emergency assistance. I'm sorry, I should have thought to make sure we had these."

When she placed the card in her wallet, as he had placed his, somewhere in the vast ether, the tiniest ping was heard as another small connection was made.

CHAPTER TWELVE

The Stuarts had always been a close family but now circumstances had brought them even closer. They realized how much they needed to cling to one another; life circumstances, for example, had ensured that the two sisters were each other's best friends despite their strikingly different personalities.

Emma was an adventurous child, brimming with energy and ideas that needed to be shared and required attention. Besides the tire swing that he had strung up the first summer, John had added a swing set and monkey bars in the yard. Once, when both girls were playing outside, Emma decided to get on the monkey bars in an attempt to emulate her older sister, but she did not have the strength to grab the next rung. Caitlin noticed and started calling for her mother, who came running and barely grabbed Emma before she fell. Emma just grinned. This sort of thing happened regularly.

Caitlin, on the other hand, was a happy child but quiet and observant; a child who seemed to enjoy watching the world more than being a participant in it. She had grown much taller over their last year in Montana and was now almost gangly in her preadolescence. Caitlin was an exceptionally bright child; John had bought for her a very sophisticated K'nex construction-assembly toy system, an intricate roller-coaster model that was designed for older children with precocious engineering skills. Caitlin pored over the complicated instructions, but mainly just followed the pictures and assembled the complex geometrical structures. She had the model finished in a few days—just as she excelled at putting together jigsaw puzzles that were designed for much older children. John looked on with astonishment as he realized that the task would have been too complicated even for him.

The family loved to play games, some real and some make-believe. Both children had unaccountably developed circus-like acrobatic skills and tumbled from couch to chair vying for their parents' attention. After they saw a sumo wrestling match on television, they enlisted their father in a session of that—outlining a circle in the living room with plush toys and whatever else they could find, struggling to see who could push whom out. The girls had become so well coordinated that John was able to keep only one of them out of the circle at any given time, but never both.

Initially, Emma had a difficult time reading, despite Cindy's tireless efforts. She bought a selection of educational books for developing early-reading abilities. These books were designed to teach reading logically, using letter sounds and repetition built around short stories. Day after day, mother and child sat down with a book, and soon Cindy realized that Emma was memorizing! If Cindy changed the page, Emma would give the wrong answer.

"What can I do?" she asked John.

"Don't sweat it," he advised her. "Memorizing takes a lot more brains than sounding out words. If she's memorizing, she'll eventually fill in the blanks and catch up on the reading itself." And to both his amazement and Cindy's, once Emma had memorized a book, she suddenly went back and deciphered the actual reading. That was simply an adaptation. Emma had devised her own learning technique, one that amused her as well.

In spite of the difficulties they had been through since they fled Concord, Cindy was determined to both impose and safeguard a healthy and emotionally secure mother-child relationship, and so spent most of her time with the children. They did paintings together, made beads together, planted flowers in the yard. Sometimes they created a huge commotion in the kitchen by cooking together.

John was the family storyteller. He made up tales involving animals, especially their favorite: monkeys. Even the word *monkey* caused the girls to giggle in delight. He devised stories that related to the real-life concerns and anxieties of children, usually with a hidden message. Every night, the children would not go to bed without hearing at least one story from their father, and usually forestalling the inevitable by clamoring for more.

John had stories with fantasies involving other planets and children who lived there. Inherent in these stories was a lesson based in astronomy and cosmology, because, after all, you had to get to those planets in the first place. The hardest time he had was when he told the girls stories of their lineage, which they sometimes demanded. What were their grandparents like? Were they both born in Idaho? Where did their mother and father grow up, and what were their friends like? These questions could be answered of course—and had to be—with a string of fictions, yet these fictional tales were the most difficult for John to produce. After telling the girls a story from their ancestry—usually based closely on the actual facts of a grandmother's canning hobby, for example—John would retreat to his room and make careful notes of the story he had just told. He did not want to be tripped up and caught by his own children, after all, for fear of the damage that such a discovery might do to them.

The children were always satisfied with the personal histories that John related; on those nights when the past was featured at bedtime, the girls seemed to go to bed the soonest and with the least fuss after John had finished. Conversely, those were the most difficult nights for John to go to sleep. One warm and humid July night, sleep came particularly fitfully.

"Don't go! Hang in there, Cate! Don't go! Help! Help! Will someone please help!" John screamed in the middle of the night. Cindy woke with a great start, snapped on a reading lamp and scrambled off the bed to lunge for her gun, which she kept in a holder beneath the mattress.

Eyes wide, she looked around. As usual, the windows were shut, though a small air-conditioner hummed in one of them. John lay supine, eyes closed, his words slurred as if he were a having a stroke. She heard him try to get words out. He sounded like someone begging for help. "Wake me up! Wake me up!"

Frightened, she shook him awake. He lay there with open eyes, barely breathing.

"What was wrong?" she said.

"Nightmare," he mumbled.

"And Cate?"

"I couldn't help her. I was powerless. I was terrified about her. She was drowning and kept calling me, but monstrous waves kept pulling her away."

"Tell me more," Cindy said.

"We were on a sailboat in the middle of the ocean. We were sitting on the edge near the mast and suddenly a big wave hit the boat from out of nowhere and Cate tumbled overboard. My heart stopped; she was screaming for help. I jumped in but could not figure out where she was. I kept hearing her voice, but every time I swam that way she wasn't there. Big waves kept rolling in on me, and I could hear her calling for me. Then I felt a hand trying to grab me, saying, "I love you, I love you, I love you," and then a wave came and we were apart; everything went silent. I kept calling for hours but no one responded, no one helped, no one was there; she was gone; I couldn't save her. She needed me and I was not man enough to save her. I left her to die. I'm responsible for her death."

"You didn't cause her death. And we can't change the fact of her death, John. You know this. You certainly did not cause her to die."

"Yes we did. She would still be around if she had not assumed our responsibility and tried to help us."

The *we* hit Cindy hard. She took a few seconds to compose herself.

John went on, "She was a good girl; sweet, with an air of electricity around her. She made me laugh." John's eyes wandered in the space as if he was looking for someone.

This intensity of feeling for Cate also caught Cindy by surprise. Looking directly into his eyes she asked, "Did you love her?"

"What?!" It was as if this was the first time the idea had ever occurred to John. "No! I enjoyed being around her, and she was fun to be with. She died for us, for our children."

"That's a little dramatic, if I may say so without sounding horrible. I understand your being upset still, but I am sensing something more here than just being grateful. At the very least, were you aware that she loved you?"

"I didn't know. How was I supposed to know?" John said, feeling innocent and intimidated at the same time. "I just didn't think about it. It didn't seem important."

"Not *important*? This woman was lovesick over you, and you think it was not important? What about our mutual commitment? What about trust?"

"It's not like I did anything, Cindy!" John said defensively. He then added, "You have to believe me, I didn't realize that I was leading her on, if I even was—she was great company and I enjoyed that," John said, protesting a subject that was not at that moment under discussion.

After a few minutes, John reached out and tried to hug her. She initially resisted but then relented. Through tears she said, "Did it ever occur to you that all I have is you? No one else. That I have loved no one but you, that I trust you, that you complete the only dream I ever had in life—that of a close, genuinely loving family? Please don't take that away!"

"I won't," he said. "I'm really sorry. Sometimes I'm lost in my own world, wandering through abstraction, at times unaware even of those who love me the most. I don't do this deliberately, but I can forget their needs, our collective needs. When I'm like this, those I assume will always be around me tend to get the short end of the bargain. These are my limitations and I am working on them."

"Please do," she implored him.

"I love you. But it's in my nature to sometimes withdraw from my surroundings, get disconnected in my own silos. That's how I can think outside the box. The conundrum is that with family, you have to be inside the box. I promise to do better; I had no bad intentions."

"I know," she said, but she was thinking: *What a frustrating man. There are times when I could strangle him!*

Instead, she returned to the subject of nightmares. "Look, this episode, or episodes, highlights something else I've been worried about—you haven't been to a doctor in years. John, we have to line up a family doctor and a pediatrician. And you need to tell a doctor about these nightmares to make sure there isn't some underlying problem."

"Some *other* underlying problem? Maybe you're right. We've put that off too long."

"And there is nothing we can do about Cate. She was a victim just as we are. You know that. It's horrible what happened to her, but we need to move on emotionally. Do you hear me?"

"You're right. And we'll figure out a way to handle the doctors discreetly."

"We will," she said, snapping off the light. "Now please go back to sleep."

Unfortunately, it wasn't always so easy. Every so often John had more nightmares, and the nightmares always involved Cate. He would wake up with sweat all over him. Cindy tried to talk to him about this obsession with Cate, but it seemed intractable. One day she suggested that he see a psychiatrist, to see if perhaps it was indicative of a deeper fear—fear that his own demise might be imminent, for example.

He exploded. "Are you kidding me? We can't go to a psychiatrist! They ask questions besides: 'How are you feeling?' and 'Does this hurt?' They want to know about your past. How you got to where you are. How you grew up and what you might be hiding. *Hiding,* Cindy! We don't have the option of talking honestly about ourselves anymore. That's one of the things that has been taken away from us. I am trying Cindy; I am trying, trust me. It's just the idea that she died because of me, because of us... it keeps eating away at me. I'm sorry. But a psychiatrist is totally out of the question."

Cindy bit her lip in frustration. These nightmares signified something deep and dark. Every time they happened, she hurt for days. Sometimes, and with great embarrassment, she had to suppress a feeling of satisfaction. Didn't Cate get what she deserved? After all, she had intruded into a marriage, into a family. On the other hand, Cindy knew Cate had been instrumental in saving their lives. Infatuation with an attractive and interesting man is normal, and John probably had to take some of the responsibility. Still, there were times when a little corner in her heart felt sharp needles.

CHAPTER THIRTEEN

The Stuarts got two newspapers, the weekly *Wanton Herald* and a morning paper out of the closest midsize city, two hundred fifty miles away. The *Wanton Herald* was useful only for strictly local news: school meetings, community events (such as they were in such a small place), and the crime blotter, which usually involved minor crimes although the nature of those crimes had escalated in recent years. With the influx of all those oil-industry workers from out of state, most living by themselves with lots of money in their pockets, robberies had become more common, and the occasional shootings and stabbings began to be reported as well.

The out-of-town daily paper had little actual news. Lots of feel-good stories, and a lot of advertising, but from the looks it of it, it was published cheaply, with few staff and even less concern for the rudiments of aggressive daily journalism. As such, it was fairly typical of newspapers in midsize cities all over the country.

John and Cindy referred to it as "The Daily Hopeless," but still, they read it. Bereft of the Internet, unable to find other options, it was all they had except for a few broadcast channel news stations on the television.

In early August, Cindy noticed a headline that seemed to convey actual news, however clumsy and annoyingly cloying the headline was. It read:

Withdrawal Symptoms: Hackers Target Hospital Deaths

Cindy read the AP story with interest.

Thieves, it seemed, had somehow hacked into several large hospital computer networks in the mountain states and installed very sophisticated monitoring software. The software scanned in real time for the individual patient codes a hospital entered when someone died while in treatment. It then immediately filtered out the names and profiles of those who had been single, and within seconds their bank accounts were automatically accessed and hacked—part of the money was then transferred to overseas accounts, according to a task force of insurance auditors in three neighboring states. The genius of the thefts was the knowledge that no family member would be around to check the deceased's account. In fact, that account may not even be looked at for several weeks.

The story was short, but it ended with the information that the National Association of Retired Persons had responded to the threat and planned to use its considerable influence on behalf of the victims. Still, it seemed to Cindy that a major news event was being given short shrift. She read the gist of it to John.

"How many accounts, does it say?" he said with alarm.

"It says here tens of thousands."

"Tens of thousands?"

"That's what it says. From one of the investigators."

"That's astounding and unconscionable," he said. "How could any thief stoop so low?"

"John, that sounds a little naïve coming from you. Of course some of these hackers would stoop that low. Lower, even. There's nothing some of these scum would not do, including murder."

"You're right about that, but still—"

"It says here they're estimating a hundred million dollars could have been stolen."

"A hundred million? I mean, don't newspapers do the simple arithmetic? A hundred million dollars siphoned from bank accounts of old people without spouses who die in hospitals? That would suggest that this scheme is wider than that newspaper story seems to indicate."

"Well, that's all they say, of course. You aren't expecting in-depth news in 'The Daily Hopeless', are you?"

"Silly me. I'll try to see if there's anything on the news later this afternoon," he said, suspecting that this also would be a fruitless venture.

"Why did they pick single elderly people specifically?" Cindy asked.

"Simple enough. Generally their children, assuming they have children, do not know exactly how much money a parent may have in his or her checking and savings accounts. Notifications to banks and other institutions take time. Probate court takes months to settle. So there is a very wide-open window, a lengthy period of time during which no one is really watching. This would allow hackers to move money out from various accounts with ease, once they know to push on an open door—or a closed door that isn't locked. And I know they have developed the skills to do this sort of thing. Their reach is astonishing. Look at us! They got to us easily enough."

"I know," she murmured.

"And then the two thousand or five thousand dollars, or even five *hundred* dollars, that they vacuumed out of an individual bank account, is sitting with the loot from all of those other bank accounts in some thief's account in eastern Europe, or somewhere else, in the blink of an eye. Then the money is going on a world tour," he said.

Cindy nodded and said, "I get that, certainly. I know from my banking days, once the money has gone through three or four national boundaries, it's nearly impossible to track it because of all of the overlapping and baffling banking laws, regulations, privacy rules, and uneven law enforcement across international boundaries. I remember a case when a couple of criminals in New York stole over a billion dollars from multiple banks, shuffled the money around the globe like card sharks, and were never caught. In fact, the theft hardly got any publicity at all," Cindy said.

She picked up the newspaper again and finished the story. "Investigative agencies are looking into it," she said with a trace of sarcasm.

John snorted derisively. "I doubt that will amount to much. The magnitude of the usage of computer networks has penetrated so deeply in our lives that these things are inevitable. It's shaping up to be a titanic a battle between good and evil. The truth is, law enforcement needs holes in the security so that they can keep an eye on the criminal activities. Unfortunately, the same holes can be found out by the best hackers in the world and abused. It's actually worse—law enforcement is only *aware* of the holes the software developers deliberately build in. Naturally, the best hackers not only find those holes, they discover other holes that law enforcement has no idea are there, right in the code. That's where the rub is."

"That's unbelievable! Why don't software companies tell law enforcement about all the holes?" Cindy asked.

"They don't know it themselves! Software without bugs is a myth. There is no such thing! These are extraordinarily complicated technologies, worked upon by thousands of engineers. Little mistakes are bound to happen. Besides, it's also possible that the big software companies have now been penetrated by highly sophisticated criminals."

"Like the Enterprise?" she asked anxiously.

He nodded. "You have no idea how much havoc a clever software engineer with bad intent can cause."

"Don't they test the code?" she persisted.

"No one ever reviews an entire code written by someone else, not line by line. You're talking about tens of millions of lines of code, Cindy. The testing, such as it is, is done at the black-box level, meaning externally trying every conceivable situation and testing for it. *Conceivable* being the key word here. If something is not conceived of by the test team, remember, it's simply not tested. The human mind has infinite capacity, and unfortunately in this case, that's a drawback because the testing is finite, by definition. And a top-tier software engineer can easily cover his tracks, with virtually zero risk. If it's found, then the test team shrugs and figures that it's just a bug, and they have the engineers fix it. And if it's *not* found—and this is definitely often the case these days—the secret door remains closed, but unlocked. *Voila*, the Enterprise or AJs of the world only need to push on that door, once they identify it, and walk right in."

"AJs?" she asked.

"That's a Russian criminal outfit that does high-level work in computer crime."

"Sounds like the Mafia."

"Yeah, but without the charm," he said sardonically.

"It's that simple? Just push on an unlocked door?" she asked skeptically.

"Trust me, I know a thing or two about cyber security," he said.

"But why does it have to be the Enterprise or the Russian outfit? Can it be foreign governments, too?"

"Possibly, but it's unlikely, at least in this case, as money is typically not the objective of foreign governments," John said. "They could have bigger fish to fry."

"Like what?"

He ticked off some things with his fingertips. "Espionage, civil or corporate. Terrorism on a scale that we can't yet even imagine. Diplomacy by disruption. Revenge."

"And this threat is growing?" she asked warily.

He replied, "As they say in the navy when the seas get rough: *Stand by for heavy rolls.*"

CHAPTER FOURTEEN

Cindy knew John was right, and that her going to see a psychiatrist was too risky. That didn't prevent her from researching local practitioners online at the local library, after swearing Maloney to secrecy. She found the man she thought she would connect with the best, Dr. Bennett, whose office was located in a midsize city about two hundred miles away. She stared at his picture on the computer screen. His kind eyes and sharp-looking horn-rimmed glasses, combined with his East Coast education, caused her to long for a conversation in which she could unburden herself.

Cindy at times found that what she persistently thought about during the day showed up in her dreams at night. But she was not prepared for her dream that evening in which she walked into the psychiatrist's office and began discussing the dilemma she faced regarding Cate with Dr. Bennett. In retrospect, this was how badly she needed to talk about it:

"And how well did your husband know her?" the psychiatrist asked her.

"Well, it's complicated. He was close to her."

"I see. Was it a friendship, a professional relationship, or was there more to it?"

"All of the above. They were close on a personal level."

"Just friends though?"

"Well, more than that. They liked each other; they enjoyed being together, laughed together, had fun evenings together—"

"Evenings together?"

"On his business trips. They got together for dinner and sporting events. She was a financial adviser he trusted implicitly."

"I see."

Cindy pointed out hastily, "I do trust my husband. At the same time, I just didn't know what to make of all that. And I still don't. Or maybe I do. I know what attracted me to him and that it still does. It's rare to see someone who is so innocently brilliant and self-assured, but not arrogant. But these same traits make him appear vulnerable, and therefore desirable. He grows on you fast. His obliviousness makes him unaware of the effect he has on others."

"You think he is responsible for their relationship?"

"No, I doubt that he realized what he was doing. I bet she, on the other hand, was smitten like anyone would be in her shoes, then you add money to the mix and…"

"Do you think she chased him for money?"

"No, I don't think so. My rational mind says that she wanted him badly and he was clueless to the effect he had on her. On the other hand, sometimes I wonder: Is it that simple? I don't know. I'm confused."

"That's natural."

"His mind thinks along both straight and curved lines at the same time. Which boundaries will he cross; which won't he cross? In my own mind, I can never be sure."

Cindy began describing her husband as a personality in contrasts—not bipolar, but someone who swings between the two ends of the spectrum with ease."He ranges between sheer brilliance and sheer stupidity, across the entire spectrum from violet to red, from being entirely predictable to quite unpredictable and everything in between. He is an utterly abstract adventurist, overjoyed in the unknown."

"Quite impressive," her interlocutor said. "But tell me, what does that all mean?"

"Well, he thinks outside the box. He's an inventor with lots of patents. His mind connects the dots where most people don't even see all the dots. On the other hand, he is largely oblivious to his surroundings; at times he can't see things that would be obvious to a four-year-old. I'm convinced that he himself does not know who he is."

"That must be frustrating. What about you?"

"I'm firmly footed in reality, well aware of my surroundings; I know who I am, largely. I enjoy doing things with my hands. I love painting, vibrant colors, fabric, nature. I love my children, watching them grow. I wish I could freeze time, always enjoy them the way they are, so sweet, so innocent, so curious…"

"No, I mean, do you have nightmares?"

"Yes, sometimes, but not as often as he does."

"What are they generally about?"

"Almost always about him going to the dark side."

"What does that mean, 'the dark side'?"

"Well, as I said, he's brilliant. He can use that brilliance for good, but there are other choices."

"There are many dark corners in life. Tell me about the ones you fear."

Her mouth felt dry. Was she going too far? She heard herself talking. "Well, he is a top-notch network security specialist. He knows more about network security and vulnerabilities than just about anyone."

"Computer security?"

"Sort of, but think much bigger. Networks, the lines that connect everything. Everything, you understand?"

"I understand. So go on."

"Well, let's just say you could combine this unusual expertise with his outside-the-box ideas; with incredibly creative, elegant yet simple answers to very complex phenomena, and you have an explosive combination."

"Are you worried that he is doing something illegal?"

She looked at him intently. "No, that isn't it precisely. It's far more complicated. He plays in the zone, or rather he's entirely capable of playing in the zones where virtues and vices are largely indistinguishable—and the only lighting guide is the intent. Which scares me.

"He has this uncanny ability to try on the proverbial criminal hat with ease and unbelievable depth, which is how a really good cyber security expert comes to understand the mindset of the bad guys. Once he is deep within that mindset and understands it, then he tries to figure out what would have been his scheme, the steps he would have taken, the distraction he would have created, and the counter measures he would have laid out. It's like playing mental chess, but both the players are you and only the hats change—white to black, back and forth.

"I feel like his thinking takes him to the precipitous edge of an abyss, and I always wonder whether he will be able to pull back. Oddly, he always does."

"Pull back from the brink of 'the dark side,' as you put it?" Bennett asked.

"Yes."

"And you say 'oddly.' Why oddly?"

"Because he goes so very deep into those depths, I think. But it's like he has this innate sense of where and when to stop. Yet each time it leaves me with this nagging fear. What if he misses the turnaround? What if he keeps going into the dark?"

Then Cindy woke up in a cold sweat.

John stirred beside her.

"You all right?" he mumbled.

"Yes. Go back to sleep."

"Were you dreaming?"

"It's nothing. I was just a little restless."

"You sounded like you were talking."

"Did I? Well, it was just a silly dream."

She held his hand, gave him a kiss on his cheek, and whispered, "I love you." After a minute, she could hear him breathing softly, back asleep.

Lying in bed in the depths of the night she kept thinking *Why am I always so worried? He is a good person, he truly loves me, he is great with the children. But then what really prevents him from being someone like ZRK, the odious master of the Enterprise? What if he does go to the dark side? He has the skills! He is fully capable!* Then suddenly a light bulb flashed in her head and she answered her own question, "I get it, this is the root cause of my fear: What if he crosses this boundary? What will happen to me, my children, our lives together? This is what scares me! He has never crossed it, but what if? What if he becomes ZRK? What if he is ZRK? Him? That's crazy. The man can't even tie his own shoelaces."

Then she smiled and felt relaxed enough to drift to sleep. She had finally gotten her therapy session after all.

CHAPTER FIFTEEN

It was a Wednesday in early September, the first day that both children had returned to school after a summer full of various activities, when John next took the long drive to the town of Baxter. He intended to use the familiar cash-operated Internet kiosk in the motel on the Interstate, but this time the clerk came around from behind the counter and stopped him.

"Excuse me," said the clerk, a short, skinny man with a protruding Adam's apple.

"Yes?" John said.

"That's only for guests, sir."

"But I've been using it for months," John protested.

"I know. Now we have to put restrictions on the use."

"Why? Nobody else is using it."

"Security, sir. This is not a public facility. Is there anything else I can assist you with today?" The clerk spoke in a high, whiny voice. Preposterously, he had walked over and placed himself between John and the kiosk, where he stood with arms folded firmly across his chest. His attitude seemed to convey the idea that he might have to physically restrain John, who was a good bit taller and far more fit. John didn't mean to laugh, but the man looked silly. He had no intention of trying to rush the machine.

Smiling, John walked toward the door, but as he left the lobby, he noticed a surveillance camera just above the front desk that seemed to be pointing directly at him.

On the long winding drive back home he fretted over losing access to the only Internet connection he had felt safe using.

"Why don't you see if Maloney can help?" Cindy said when he got back and expressed his frustrations.

"You mean at the town library?"

"Yes. She said they have Wi-Fi there. I'm sure it's fine as long as you're careful about covering your tracks."

"I don't know," he said. "I've been careful to not even turn on the Wi-Fi switch on the laptop I bought last year."

"Is there anything in it that could be hacked?"

"Some personal records. The journal I've been keeping," he said.

"What's in that journal of yours anyway?" she asked.

"Just notes and musings, nothing terribly important. But still, there are certainly clues in there for anyone who knows what to look for. I'd never risk using it to go online under any circumstances."

She put her hand on his and said, "Look, I know we're careful with money, but why don't you simply get another laptop? A cheap one. One that's totally clean. And use that for any time you absolutely have to go online for any reason."

"Where would I get that?" he asked, baffled but pleased at the suggestion.

"Walmart, silly. Where else?" she said.

*   *   *

Maloney was glad to see him when he strode into the Wanton town library a few days later with the low-end Compaq laptop he had bought for three hundred dollars on the last day of the annual Labor Day sale. The town library wasn't much to look at: Two crowded rooms on the second floor of the town firehouse, one crammed with books for adults and the other with children's books. Maloney sat at a battered steel desk wearing half-frame glasses. She looked like a comedy-movie version of a small-town librarian, cute and pert, with an expression that said, simply, "Shhhh."

"John, welcome!" she whispered, even though there was no one else in the room. "There's a desk over there that you can use. No password required."

"Thank you, Maloney," he whispered back, and retreated to the corner where he opened his laptop and quickly logged on.

This was basically a trial run. He had no pending business. All he wanted to do was feel the great joy of being connected without standing at a kiosk in some motel feeding bills into a machine like some slots addict at a casino. And it felt wonderful, having a high-speed connection! He surfed from pillar to post, and finally settled on the Web site of the *Wall Street Journal* to catch up on the news of the day and of recent days.

But all he could get was the headlines. The actual site was page blocked by a paywall. To access it, registration and a fee were required.

Impetuously, John threw caution to the wind, pulled out a prepaid debit card from his wallet, and typed in the information that would provide him with one month's entrée into the *Journal*'s site for about ten dollars.

He read luxuriously and leisurely, but then he noticed a medium-size headline on a story that would have been in the back of the front section of the print paper. The headline read:

Cyber Attackers Are Thought to Be Highly Sophisticated

The story reported that feds, while looking for clues in the most recent banking scandal, the one pertaining to hospitals, were finding, to their dismay, that this had not been limited to a handful of Mountain states. In fact, the crisis had spread throughout the entire West Coast. It was now suspected that the attacks were not done by run-of-the-mill hackers, but rather by a very sophisticated operation that could only be carried out by high-end groups. The federal investigative and regulatory agencies suspected the Enterprise, a Serbian criminal operation with a vast reach that was nevertheless unknown to most of the public. Also named as possibly suspect was an obscure and far more secretive Russian cyber-crimes group known as AJ—the initials of its leaders, brothers named Andrij and Josyp Marcovic. John felt nauseous to read that the Enterprise, AJ, and two other groups from the Ukraine were identified by the authorities as likely suspects.

What John read next caused him to sit bolt upright, scraping his wood chair against the linoleum. He saw Maloney look up, and he waved to assure her that everything was all right.

But things were not all right, not by a long shot. This meant that the FBI, the Treasury Department, and whatever other big guns law enforcement could deploy all were on the case. Certainly they all saw the implications. The Enterprise had become such a menace that questions were now being raised, tentatively for the time being but nevertheless pointedly, about the inherent security of the entire banking system. John realized, even if the downplayed story did not, that this was a huge bank heist. No Willie Sutton had barged in the door, but the money had gone out the door just the same.

Part of the reason the Enterprise was hard to track down was because it was both tightly knit and extraordinarily diffuse. Law-enforcement agencies knew very little about it. It was very carefully crafted, and the chain of command was highly confusing to not only an average law-enforcement officer, but even to the sharper eyes of the federal agencies. Instead of being vertically organized, as was just about every institution, including the Mafia, it appeared to be a matrix organization. Most of those who worked for it had no idea exactly whom they were working for. This made it difficult to penetrate the core shadowy figures whom, to the extent their identities were even recognized, had not been seen or heard from for nearly a decade. In fact, the last time ZRK appeared on national-security radar screens was more than eleven years earlier—and no one in law enforcement could say for sure they knew what this Zerind Rokus Kazac even looked like. The few surveillance photos that were supposedly of him were obviously the visages instead of a coterie of accomplice decoys, all of them masked or otherwise rendered unidentifiable. What's more, the Enterprise had developed sophisticated learning algorithms that allowed the organization to reconstruct anyone's voice simply after listening to their cell phone conversations for a few minutes. When a key member used a phone, the technology not only obscured the identity of the user and the phone itself, but also automatically transformed the voices in real time to the one the algorithms had just learned. This way, no one in or outside the organization knew who they were speaking with for sure—and any phone call tapped by law enforcement routinely pointed the finger at individuals who, under questioning, would turn out to be totally innocent. Attempts to track down the origins of the calls also led nowhere. Every time a lead was tracked in real time to a phone, it turned out to be false.

"Can I make a printout of something?" John called quietly to Maloney when he had finished with the story.

"Sure. The printer is over here. Just hit print and I'll get it for you."

He thanked Maloney profusely, then drove home to show it to Cindy, who read it quickly and with a worried expression.

"The Enterprise?" she asked gloomily.

"Yes, and they seem to be getting busier. This is a very nasty bunch of criminal geniuses."

"Tell me about it," she said sarcastically.

"It's very obvious that they're really starting to flex their muscles in the banking system."

"Maybe that means they're losing interest in us?" she asked hopefully.

"I don't think so, Cindy. Their interests are wide and vital. They're just expanding exponentially. Details never get overlooked in this kind of diabolical operation. So I'm afraid we're still on the to-do list."

She sighed heavily. "So will they be caught?" she asked. "I mean, ever?"

He shook his head sadly. "In the movies, the bad guys get caught. Even in the narratives that the newspapers covet, there's this sense that criminals are eventually discovered, at least, if not entirely brought to justice. But the older I get the more I realize that this is a myth designed to comfort the innocent. In fact, the guilty often operate with near-impunity."

"The thing I fail to understand is the lack of ability to track them in real time," Cindy insisted. "How difficult can that be? I always thought even local police has that ability."

John replied, "They do, theoretically. But this is much more complicated than people generally assume, even people who know something about criminal investigations. I believe that criminal elements have hacked into the phone companies' telephone switches. When you make a call to someone else, the calling number and the number being called are stored in a database as having been connected. Typically, law-enforcement agencies look into these switches via a management port, and then track them on the basis of the path taken. My hunch is that the management-port software has been hacked to the extent that access via the management port returns a *different phone* number than the one that's actually calling. To make it even more challenging to thwart, the number they swap the original with is likely one belonging to a large company that itself has hundreds of phone lines in its own system, making any one number virtually impossible to track. This undoubtedly flummoxes and, more critically, misleads the FBI, for example. The software behind these giant switches, which are called core routers, is extremely complicated and massive. This is some of the most complex equipment ever designed—far more complex and difficult to figure out than even a top-of-the-line super computer."

"That's terrifying."

"I know."

"Banks around the world already lose hundreds of millions of dollars *every year* to such thefts."

"Why don't we hear about that?"

"Well, we do, here and there, in bits and pieces. You have to add it all up to grasp the scope."

"And it's getting worse?"

"Far, far worse. And no one is sounding the alarm loudly enough. Banks already have these amazing losses, but they tend to sweep them under the rug as operating losses and various miscellaneous leakages, or whatever they want to call them: spoilage, shrinkage. That's what I was trying to warn those big bankers about back in New York when I was doing that consulting work."

"They listened, right?"

"For a brief time. But then they went back to complaining about the extra potential expense in getting all of those doors nailed shut. They insisted the losses were *manageable*, remember? And then, of course, events interrupted the process for us personally as a family."

"That seems like such a lifetime ago, Gavin," she said with great sorrow in her eyes.

"John."

"Yes, I know. John," she repeated with bitter resignation.

She blinked because something had just occurred to her. "John, you didn't leave any personal tracks online today, did you?"

He thought of the impulsive prepaid debit card payment he'd made at the library for the *Journal*'s Web site and dismissed the concern as too trivial to mention.

"Of course not," he said with a little more assurance than he actually felt.

CHAPTER SIXTEEN

November, and another winter was arriving. John had now come to fully understand and appreciate what Cate had meant by "snow skills."

The children were in midsemester now, and growing up nicely in a world that was familiar and reasonable to them, though still very alien to their parents. Cindy somehow held it all together for the family.

She was waiting at the front door when the bus dropped Caitlin off. Caitlin ran up the front steps excited, waving a sheet of paper.

"Guess what! Guess what?"

"What?"

"We have a new project. It's due next week. We have to make a poster. About me!"

Cindy blinked. "About you?"

"Yeah! I have to put a picture of myself from each year on it. From when I was age zero onward. Can we start right now? Please?"

"Zero," Cindy said, humoring her, while trying to absorb the challenge that this particular project would present. "Now, how in the world would we have your picture when you weren't even born?"

Caitlin said, "Whatever," and Cindy realized that her child was growing up quickly.

Cindy said, "That sounds like a great project. But first you need to wash your hands and have a snack… and then maybe we can start on it tonight. Or tomorrow."

Cindy was worried that this middle-school project would make the family's history available to outsiders, even if through a few innocent photographs seen by schoolchildren and a teacher in rural Montana. To make matters worse, she could not recall any pictures, or even computer images, that might be available from the earliest years of Caitlin's life. Hadn't they left behind all of her baby and toddler photos in Concord?

"Sweetie, I'm not sure we have anything from when you were younger. Remember, we told you about them being lost by the movers?" Cindy said, feeling guilty about the necessary lies they had laid down to give the children traction in a new life.

Morosely, Caitlin went into the living room with her milk and crackers on a plate and aimed the remote control at the television like a pistol.

Cindy was deeply saddened by her inability to provide Caitlin with a few simple photos that might prevent her from feeling like an outsider at school. Caitlin always handled these situations well in the end, but Cindy was always afraid that Caitlin's subconscious unrest would grow, and eventually... who knew?

Cindy was crying when John came in, and he asked what was wrong.

"This gets better over time," he told her, somewhat lamely.

"Does it? Does it, Gavin?"

"Please don't do that. Say 'John.' If you say Gavin, even in offhand moments, you might slip up. Like with the car door and the—"

She held her hand up and said through tears, "Just *stop!*"

He sighed. "I'm sorry."

Then he had an idea. "But wait a minute, about the photos. There was a box that I packed in Concord at the last minute, just threw stuff in, before the marshals arrived. There may have been some of the kids' photos in it from when they were smaller. I'm not sure, but I think there was a file envelope with some of those pictures you printed at Walgreens."

"Really? I remember those!"

John decided to look into it. The box was in the basement, in a room which appeared to be the old coal bin of the house and was always kept locked. He went down there after the children went to bed and opened it. Sure enough, the box contained an envelope that had a few pictures taken at the Concord home, some of Caitlin's baby pictures, and several more of her and Emma together as toddlers. He was both sad and happy looking at those photographs from a time before the horrors had happened. Tenderly, he brought them upstairs and scanned them into his computer, the one that was never connected to anything else. He added varied backgrounds to some of Caitlin's baby photos and cropped them to make them look like a lot of different pictures, rather than some variations of a precious few.

The next day, Caitlin was delighted to see so many pictures. She asked lots of questions that her parents still managed to deflect.

She brightened when Cindy showed her a baby photo of Emma. Cindy and John told her that they were visiting some place, but they couldn't remember exactly where the pictures had been taken.

Over the next few days, unable to resist vicariously revisiting their old life, John went into the basement and pored over what little memorabilia was contained in the box. A little bitterly, he recalled how sternly Marcus, the FBI agent, had warned them about "going down memory lane," that doing so might make it more difficult to adhere to their new identities. He decided that enough time had passed. Marcus was dead. Years had gone by. Life moves on.

"Well, it *does*, doesn't it?" John said aloud to himself, sitting on the floor with his thoughts and the family's meager remembrances of its past.

*   *   *

It became somewhat of a routine for him to go down late at night when the children were asleep, unlock the door to the room, and spread his old life out on the floor. Sometimes Cindy joined him, but she rarely stayed as long—or stared as hard—as he did.

"I'm going to bed. I have to be up early tomorrow. Poring over that life won't bring it back, you know," she said.

"It keeps it alive in my head," he replied.

She kissed him on the top of his head and tiptoed back up the stairs.

One night Emma woke up in the dark when the wind rattled a shutter on the girls' bedroom window.

She called out for her father. Both Cindy and John were in the basement, and John ran upstairs and tried to calm her. Failing to reassure her, he brought her down to the basement room, hurriedly put away the box and locked the door, then came upstairs with the child half-asleep in his arms.

The children knew that they were never allowed in that room, and of course it had become a source of mystery. But now that Emma had seen with her own eyes that it held no peril, just some battered old boxes stacked in the corner by a faded hooked rug, she prevailed upon her older sister to consider the possibility of exploration.

Emma teased Caitlin when she came back from school. "I was in the basement room and you weren't!"

"So, who cares? What's in there anyway?"

"Mom and Dad have secret stuff in boxes, I think."

The word "secret" intrigued Caitlin, a girl whose curiosity was becoming ever more an aspect of her personality.

Both Caitlin and Emma were growing into bright and highly creative girls. They had both already skipped a grade. They were very good with computers—though limited to using them only in school—and excelled at sports, especially basketball, softball, and ice skating, which their mother encouraged enthusiastically. Both girls acted more maturely than their ages and looked older too, allowing them to fit in well despite having skipped a grade.

Caitlin was especially good at working on computers. John took delight in occasionally showing her tricks about how to get deep into the computer systems in spite of normal security roadblocks and she absorbed his lessons rapidly. While her parents were proud of her abilities, John felt a certain twinge of anxiety as his older daughter became more deeply acquainted with technology, with connections he feared that he might not be able to limit or control at some point.

It was also ironic that Caitlin had far more Internet access at school than John could only dream of. He still felt it necessary to limit the trips to the Wanton town library's Wi-Fi–enabled computer to which he so looked forward. On one of his sojourns, he was preparing to take the family on a ten-day alpine backpacking trip—imagine that, a family from California by way of the Boston suburbs had acquired genuine wilderness skills—and he was surfing the Internet for wilderness protection. He came across the text of a congressional resolution marking an anniversary of the 1964 Federal Wilderness Act, which had mandated the setting aside of vast areas of federal land for the preservation of wilderness. Maloney printed it out for him, and he kept the copy in his backpack.

During their backpacking trip, the family camped and luxuriated in the mountains and valleys. In one particular meadow some elk grazed languidly on a hill not more than a quarter mile away. It was as if, to them, the humans were a part of the environment, as inherent as the animals and the stream that tumbled down over the rocks, still icy cold with snow-melt from the mountains.

After dinner that night around the campfire, with the last sunlight limning the jagged peaks, John took out the printout and cleared his throat portentously.

"Your attention please," he said to his wife and children, who smiled in anticipation of whatever he had in mind for after-dinner amusement at the campfire.

"I shall now read from a resolution marking the anniversary of the date of enactment of the Wilderness Act, which gave to the people of the United States the National Wilderness Preservation System, an enduring resource of our national heritage," he intoned.

"Here, here!" Cindy chimed in, striking her tin cup with a fork. The girls then did the same.

"The anniversary of said Act," John said, "happens to be this very day."

"Yay!" Caitlin yelled.

John cleared his throat and went on, "I quote from the Resolution: "*Whereas great writers of the United States, including Ralph Waldo Emerson, Henry David Thoreau, George Perkins Marsh, and John Muir, poets such as William Cullen Bryant, and painters such as Thomas Cole, Frederic Edwin Church, Frederic Remington, Albert Bierstadt, and Thomas Moran have defined the cultural value and unique concept of wilderness in the United* et cetera, et cetera, with many names evoked..." He turned the printed pages and skimmed over the verbiage. He continued, "*Whereas wilderness offers numerous values for an increasingly diverse populace, allowing youth and adults from urban and rural communities to experience nature and explore opportunities for healthy recreation...*" He frowned over the verbiage and found the conclusion, "*Whereas,* blah blah, *be it resolved then that the Senate of the United States of America is grateful for the wilderness!*"

"Here! Here!" Cindy and Caitlin cried together.

"Wilderness!" Emma hollered, pumping her little fist in the air.

John unfolded another printout, this one containing the text of the Wilderness Act itself.

"Definition of wilderness," he read. "A wilderness, in contrast with those areas where man and his own works dominate the landscape, is hereby recognized as an area where the earth and its community of life are untrammeled by man, where man himself is a visitor who does not remain. An area of wilderness is further defined to mean in this Act an area of undeveloped Federal land retaining its primeval character and influence, without permanent improvements or human habitation, which is protected and managed so as to preserve its natural conditions and which (1) generally appears to have been affected primarily by the forces of nature, with the imprint of man's work substantially unnoticeable; (2) has outstanding opportunities for solitude or a primitive and unconfined type of recreation; (3) has at least five thousand acres of land or is of sufficient size as to make practicable its preservation and use in an unimpaired condition; and (4) may also contain ecological, geological, or other features of scientific, educational, scenic, or historical value.'"

He looked at the attentive faces of his wife and children.

"Note the definition of wilderness as including the following: a place 'where man himself is a visitor who does not remain.' Tomorrow, my dears, we shall strike camp and head home, and leave the magnificent wilderness to itself."

"Boo!" Caitlin called out.

"And so to bed," her father instructed in a no-nonsense tone.

Later, when they thought the children were sound asleep in their sleeping bags, John had coffee and Cindy sipped tea as they watched the embers dying in the campfire.

"That was very funny, you reading the resolution," she told him. "The kids love that kind of thing. They think you're a real character."

"Well, and however we get it across to them, the girls are growing up with a profound sense of the value of wilderness," he said.

"It was interesting how, in what you read, the first names it mentioned were Emerson and Thoreau."

"Important inspirations, even in the suburbs of Boston," he said.

"It made me think of Concord," Cindy said with a small sigh.

They were silent. The fire crackled its last. And then they heard Emma pipe up from her sleeping bag, "*CAN-kid!*" she yelped.

The parents looked at each other with some concern.

"How did she come up with that after all this time?" John asked Cindy.

"Well, we used to laugh whenever she said it, and the child always liked a laugh," Cindy said, suppressing her own laugh.

*   *   *

They struck camp, leaving no trace of themselves behind, and drove home wearily the next morning. But late that night, back in Wanton, Emma started to throw up and when Cindy took her temperature, she was alarmed to see that it was 103.8 degrees. It was two a.m., and the nearest hospital was fifty miles away. John told Cindy to stay home with Caitlin while he drove the younger girl to the hospital.

At the hospital, a doctor ordered some tests and asked questions about Emma's medical history, particularly about her infancy. Had she been diagnosed with a heart murmur? Did she have any breathing issues? Were there any X-ray records for comparison?

John remembered that once a pediatrician in Concord had mentioned a minor heart-murmur issue, but had assured the parents that it would go away by the time the child was five or six. But they had no way to produce even minimal records, not to mention an X-ray.

"Which hospital?" the doctor had inquired.

Not thinking, John blurted out, "Emerson Hospital in Concord, Massachusetts."

"Well, we can call them first thing in the morning," the doctor said.

Having gone this far, John now realized that there would be no medical record under Emma's current name at Emerson Hospital in Concord.

John was deep in this quandary when he called an extremely worried Cindy to report from the hospital. He explained the dilemma over Emma's medical records from Concord.

Cindy replied with exasperation, "I don't care, John. We have to call Emerson Hospital for that information."

"Think this through. There may be better options," John said warily, knowing that reaching out to a hospital in Massachusetts would send a very loud signal to anyone monitoring all of the channels and waiting for a clue about where they were.

For the first time Cindy felt completely helpless. She turned quiet, but her anger started to build up.

Then she said abruptly, "I know how to get it! I remember her old Social Security number. I can call and ask them to fax the records."

"Fax? To where?"

"There's a Kinko's near that shopping mall where we got locked out of the car. I'll put Caitlin in the car and we'll make the drive."

John thought this through and said, "There is one hitch. What if they send the hard copy to our Concord address. I mean, we didn't leave a forwarding address naturally. As far as officialdom is concerned, that's still our permanent address."

Cindy said nothing.

John continued, "The doctor is also beginning to get a bit concerned why we don't want him to call where she was looked at earlier. The trouble is that, technically, Emma's birth certificate and other documents are in Idaho."

"What a mess. What do we do?" Cindy asked with grave concern.

"I don't know, I am so mad at myself for allowing this to happen."

She assured him, "It's not like it's your fault. What could you have done to avoid it?"

He breathed heavily into the phone. "This is so frustrating. We're stuck and can't even take care of our children. Goddamn bastards! If I could get hold of this ZRK person, I would break his filthy neck!"

"Just calm down," she told him.

"I am going to go ahead with the hospital in Concord, and if it blows our cover, so be it. I am fed up," John insisted.

"Don't do anything if you're angry," she advised him sternly.

"Don't tell me what to do!"

"John," she said, "take it easy."

"No, Cindy. I'm here in this godforsaken hospital in this rinky-dink place with our sick daughter, and—" He was almost screaming.

"She's all right, John. They just need to do some tests."

Then he suddenly calmed down a bit and said, "Okay. You're right. Why don't I just tell the doctor here to run all the scans again and create a new profile? I'll say her old pediatrician has retired and closed the office. Better yet, I'll say there was a billing scandal and he lost his license… and that we have no idea where her records are now."

"Just say he retired and closed the office. That will be good enough. They won't check. They're not the police, after all." Cindy advised him.

"Okay," he said. "I'll call you back as soon as we're finished here."

After she was given some medicine in the emergency room, Emma began to rally strongly. The fever was much lower by dawn. John called to share the good news with his wife, who had not slept and was waiting by the phone.

"Thank God," she said.

"Crisis averted," he said, forcing some gaiety into his voice.

She hung up and went to make dinner for Caitlin. "Crisis averted this time," she said to herself, feeling more lonely and afraid for the future than she had ever felt before.

CHAPTER SEVENTEEN

Eyes Only
Department of Justice
Federal Bureau of Investigation
National Security Division
Washington, D.C.

Re: Cointel Priority; DOD Operation Cyber Pearl Harbor, NSA RE 'ZRK,' MIT CA & task forces.
COPY POTUS TOP

MEMORANDUM: 567-34/A29

Top-secret meeting FBIHQ. Location: Situation room. Security: Top; highest, memorandum: eyes. Summary and transcript:

The four-person respond team and Deputy Director, DDFBI, **Thomas A. Broomall**. DDFBI: "Our country is under intense virtual attack with consequences far worse than a physical war. The enemy is virtually in, though physically removed. They have deeply penetrated our borders well into our systems and networks with severe potential consequences for our way of life, if we don't get it under control very soon and destroy those who are behind it."

(***Tone of DDFBI Broomall louder and more insistent***): "I have asked you to assemble briefly so that we can brainstorm. Brainstorm means just that: Anything goes, and nobody criticizes any observation and/or proposal. We are feeling intense heat from the political leadership from POTUS on down and rightfully so. There were four of the best network-security gurus who happened to have been all trained at the same time and kind of learned from each other. Three of them are accounted for, but the fourth one is missing. We need to find where he is and what his allegiances are. We don't know under what identity he is operating. His original name was **Gavin Brinkley.** His wife is **Lisa Brinkley**, and they have two minor children, **Becky Brinkley** and **Jessica Brinkley**. The profile of **Gavin Brinkley** is in your folders. The details behind his current whereabouts and possibly altered identity are unknown to FBI. There is not much material on the new identity. FBI Special Agent **Marcus Henley** was supervising the case and the **Enterprise/Billy Dalton** investigation, but **Henley** met an untimely death, presumably accidental but there are some indications that it might have been foul play. Apparently, Agent Henley filed minimal notes because he feared there was at least one ZRK and Billy Dalton mole within the Bureau. Need I remind you that he was sent to clear up the Boston office after that mess where so many agents and prosecutors were compromised. He had an urgent need not to be too forthcoming in his files. He was equally careful with other cases, too."

(***DDFBI Broomall addressing ASAC/Cyber Crime chief supervisor Arthur J. Moore***): "You are the top expert at the Bureau, assigned to lead this war on virtual terror. This is a command order. Spare no effort and report to me every week. Aside from the White House and the appropriate authorities at DOJ, who will be apprised as I see necessary and/or as they request, any information will stay strictly among this group only."

(**Agent Moore**): "Look, Tom, let's not kid ourselves here. We all know that Henley was murdered. People who work on the Enterprise case tend to have bad luck in terms of their actuarial tables." (***Some laughter***).

(**Agent Chaz Martinez**): "At least you're single." (***Some laughter***)

(**DDFBI Broomall**): "Okay, let's stay in focus here."

(**Agent Moore**): "You said brainstorm. So let's brainstorm without reprimands. How about you lay it all out for us, Tom?"

(**DDFBI Broomall**): "All right. Just remember, this is highest security level, and strictly background. This is what I know so far. **Gavin Brinkley** and his family were hustled into the witness protection program in a great big hurry some years ago by the bureau—but we don't have records on it. Nada! So is the Enterprise involved here? Who knows! So at this point the **Brinkleys** seem to have been lost in the shuffle. Yeah, I know. How do you lose an entire family in this modern age in America? Well, it happens. The alternative explanation, though, is that **Brinkley,** after entering into the program, went over to the dark side, as we say, and managed to engineer the complex identity changes and secret relocations that apparently were pulled off. The guy is smart enough to have done that, I think. Myself, that's the explanation I'm leaning toward. He fits a profile. He wouldn't be the first, but he might be the most dangerous: Super smart, white-collar tech scientists with fantasies of being world-class criminals dancing in their heads—fantasies accompanied by the knowledge that they're smart enough to pull it off and remain undetected. Clever, cunning people like these can move with ease between two extremes of right and wrong, with no pangs of conscience to hinder them."

(**SPAC Marissa S. D'Amato**): "But why would he want to deliberately switch his identity? What's in it for him, Tom?"

(**DDFBI Broomall**): "Then he can commit crimes under assumed names, and the trail will be left dead cold, Agent D'Amato."

(**SPAC D'Amato**): "But why does he need to change his physical identity and go through the enormous complications of dropping off the radar with his wife and kids to do that? If he's smart and cunning enough, why can't he just go over to the dark side and commit all the crimes he wants, just using virtual identities?"

(**DDFBI Broomall**): "Because in working exclusively virtual, you will inevitably leave a trace, the tiniest clue, by mistake. It's absolutely inevitable. So by severely altering the physical identities, and somehow managing to exploit the witness protection program to get that door open to a new undercover life, he now has two levels of insulation and protection, virtual and physical."

(**Casual chatter. The meeting ends.**)
END MEMORANDUM: 567-34/A29

*　　*　　*

In the long, startlingly polished hallway at FBI headquarters leading past the high-security station and to the elevator bank, Special Agent in Charge Rob Gillman caught up with Special Agent in Charge D'Amato, who was walking briskly and checking her iPhone.

"Marissa!" he said.

She stopped and looked at him, wordlessly tapping her high heel.

"Look, I didn't want to say anything in there because they were transcribing it."

"I noticed," she said curtly.

"All right," he said. "I'm sorry I tried to block your promotion last year. If I'd known you were going to end up as Broomall's protégé, on a track to becoming an associate director, I would have been a lot more careful." His high-pitched, nervous laugh annoyed her further.

She stared impatiently at her iPhone, as if it had an app for making him disappear. "What do you want, Rob?"

He unfolded a piece of paper that he fished out of his suit-coat pocket and showed it to her.

"And this is what?" she asked suspiciously.

"Well, it might be your ticket to ride, Marissa. Don't ask me where I got this, and do not involve me in this in any way, shape, or form, but an agent stationed in the West, who has since died of pancreatic cancer, passed this on to me. He and I went way back. We'd been in the Navy together. Here, write down these names."

She read the words and jotted them into a notebook.

"John and Cindy Robertson: Idaho/Montana. Case closed," she repeated, frowning. "Who in the world is that, and what 'case'?"

"I think this might be our Mr. and Mrs. Brinkley on the lam," he said.

"That's quite a leap just from two names and two states."

"I know. But as I said, my guy might have been in a position to know. He certainly acted that way, even though I couldn't get much out of him... he was extremely ill. In fact, he died the week after I went to see him in Denver."

"Denver. So who was he? You have a name?"

The agent used his fingers to make a sign as if he were sealing his lips with a padlock. "You got the names you need. That's all from me, Marissa. Good luck."

Without saying good-bye, Marissa D'Amato turned on her heels and hurried into the elevator, relieved to see the door close before Gillman could get there.

CHAPTER EIGHTEEN

Someone tapped on Cindy's shoulder as she stood in line at an ice cream shop, while John and Emma sat at a table outside, enjoying the sun.

"Hi, Lisa," the tall stranger said. Cindy didn't realize at first that she was being addressed because she was now so accustomed to being Cindy. When she was tapped again and heard the same voice, she turned around, startled.

The man was smiling at her. He had on a black suit and dark sunglasses, which alone made him stand out in the small group of customers making a routine afternoon stop at the Dairy King. Nobody wore suits in Wanton except the real estate people.

She was taken aback and tried to control herself and not say a word, but her body language was out of sync with her brain.

Thank God that John and Emma are not here, she thought, deliberately not looking toward the table farther away on the patio where her husband and younger daughter were sitting and waiting for her to bring the ice cream.

"I believe you are mistaken," Cindy told the man.

"I am not," he replied, smiling. He then added in an angry tone, "You dumped me, forgot me, took me out of your life, but I didn't know that you got me out of your brain, too."

"I don't know what you are talking about," she said with growing anxiety, but struggling to stay calm. "You must be confusing me with someone else." She turned away and studied the menu on the wall. The intruder persisted—to the point where several other bystanders shifted positions warily. He stared at her with steely eyes and said, "You know, I never forgave you. I never will. You can't escape me. I am like your shadow," he whispered menacingly, though through a supercilious smile. "Where is that no-good husband of yours?"

Cindy was now in a panic. "Why do you care?"

"I don't care, not really. Just wanted to see his pitiful condition, here in beautiful Montana. Quite a change from the old days, I see."

A second man in a dark suit approached and said to the first, "Let's go." They got in a silver sedan and drove off.

Cold sweat poured down Cindy's back. She wanted desperately to run to John and Emma, but her instincts told her not to go in that direction. She stayed to the side of the Dairy King for a few minutes and watched the silver sedan turn onto the highway and disappear. Then she quickly strode around the building and approached John and Emma.

"Did you get ice cream?" Emma asked with obvious disappointment, seeing that her mother had come back empty-handed.

"Not right now, Emma," Cindy said, feeling queasy.

"Mom, where is the ice cream?" Emma persisted.

"We have to leave now," she said, tugging at John's sleeve. He complied without a word. John dug out his car keys, and they jumped into the car and took off. Instead of the usual seating arrangement, in which Cindy sat in the front passenger seat with Emma strapped into her safety seat in the back, this time Cindy sat in the rear seat with her child, who seemed happy to have her mother beside her. John knew something was very wrong, but held his tongue while he focused on driving in random directions and constantly monitoring the rear-view mirror.

After a while, Cindy's heavy breathing calmed down. She was shaking her head fitfully, as if to expel an apparition.

"What happened?" he asked her finally.

"Give me a minute. Just keep driving," she said. Finally, she said in a thin voice, "It was Jake."

"*Jake?*" John repeated with astonishment.

She gulped and nodded assent.

John was quiet, still intensely focused on the rear-view mirror.

"Say something," she said.

"I don't know what to say. I'm still thinking, and I don't want to get distracted from driving." He was quiet for a minute, but then suddenly said, "If he knew where to find you, maybe he knows where to find Caitlin!"

Cindy replied abruptly, realizing that in the heat of the encounter and its aftermath she had not thought of her older daughter. "Caitlin! Yes! What are we going to do? Drive fast, John, we've got to get to her before they do!"

"Calm down, Cindy. We need to think. No emotions. This is the time to think. She's at play rehearsal at the school, right?" John said.

"I'll call!" Cindy said, brandishing her cell phone. She hit the button for the school.

"Hello, this is Mrs. Stuart. Is this Sharon?"

"Hi, Mrs. Stuart! It's Sharon! What's up?"

"Listen, Sharon, hi. I'm just calling to check on Caitlin. Have you seen her?"

"Of course, Mrs. S. I'm looking at her right now rehearsing with the other kids on stage. That girl is a natural on stage, did you know that? She could be a real actress, I'm telling you."

"Yes, Sharon. Thanks. Listen, would you make absolutely sure she doesn't leave till I get there to pick her up? I'm about fifteen minutes away."

"They should be wrapping up by then, Mrs. S., no prob. Is anything wrong?"

"No. Except please tell her that we're going to be there shortly and that she should take the medicine for her stomachache."

"'Medicine for her stomachache,'" Sharon repeated. "Okay, will do. Don't worry, she's just fine."

When Caitlin got the message, she quietly left the small school auditorium, went to the locker room, and then proceeded to the school cafeteria. Sharon discretely kept an eye on her.

In the car, as they drove toward the school, John said nervously, "I hope she remembers the action plan, remembers to follow the code," he said. He could see no sign that they were being followed. He drove to the front of the school, ignoring the red No Parking sign. Cindy rushed inside and, after a brief conversation with Sharon, came back out with Caitlin. They drove directly home.

Working to keep the girls from being alarmed, John and Cindy asked them to go watch television. At the kitchen table, they spoke in low, anxious tones.

"Does Jake work for ZRK?" John said.

"I have no idea. This is all baffling," Cindy replied.

"Has Jake maybe gone to the dark side by himself?"

She started, remembering her dream with the psychologist in which she had voiced some of the same distant concerns about John. How absurd that seemed now, even as the big picture was still not making any sense.

"Did he pretend to be surprised to see you?" he asked Cindy.

"No! Definitely not! I was the one who was surprised. He was standing there as if he had been watching me all along."

"Well, then that probably rules out any tiny chance that this could have been a very weird and unlikely encounter in Wanton, Montana."

"Yes, it does," she said shakily. "This was no coincidence."

"What was he doing here? In a dark suit that made him look like one of the Blues Brothers?"

She laughed despite her fears. "You know, he did look like one of the Blues Brothers. Which kind of stands out in a place like Wanton."

"And the other guy?"

"Same kind of suit. Same dark glasses. A little tubby, though."

"So why are the Blues Brothers stalking us?" he said, trying in vain to make her laugh again. But the humor was gone. In its place was a greater vulnerability than they had ever felt before.

CHAPTER NINETEEN

Now that she had made an informed guess at Idaho and Montana, Agent D'Amato's team started an extensive database search for those names and got a partial hit on a prepaid debit card charge at a small-town library in Wanton, Montana. It looked promising, as the cardholders' searches stood out from the typical ones in a town like that, especially in their repeated drilling into searches on cyber attacks and network-security threats.

"Bingo!" D'Amato said under her breath when she saw the hits.

Everything is connected. Everything, she thought. Needles still hid in haystacks, but those needles were immeasurably easier to find now. So it didn't take very long, just a couple of days, in fact, for the team to locate an interesting Internet kiosk in the general vicinity—a hundred miles being the "general vicinity" in a sparsely populated place like Montana. Interesting because whoever used *that* cash-operated kiosk anonymously every few weeks had been doing so for many months, running searches with the same tell-tale tags or keys as *the single session* of searches that turned up at the Wanton library in the single-month *Wall Street Journal* online subscription *that had been paid for* with a prepaid credit card *that on further analysis* connected to a driver's license number S45656458 *that corresponded* to the one registered to a John Stuart, previous background unknown before he had obtained a Montana gun permit and then that driver's license.

How hard this kind of thing must have been in the old days of paper records, before the Internet, D'Amato mused. *Now, it's so pitifully simple.*

She tapped away in the National Crime Information Center databanks. *Nothing.* But then the databank flipped her without explanation into

SIGINT, the staggeringly vast global databank that actually originated in the complex Echelon systems in East Germany, a system that was both infamous among intelligence experts for its astonishing reach into the everyday lives and activities of East Bloc citizens, and notorious for its futility. By the time the Berlin Wall was torn down and the Soviet Union collapsed, Echelon was virtually worthless. Almost nothing was categorized, prioritized, or even filed in a cogent manner. It was all just undifferentiated information, a universe of trivia.

But the computer revolution had changed that, and at least the collection, if not the evaluation protocols, of Echelon became useful in creating a truly global and indisputably useful surveillance system in which all of the connections could be sifted through—all of the dots could be connected—and all in the blink of an algorithm.

So it was that within a minute, Agent D'Amato was looking intently at grainy surveillance video from the small lobby of the independently owned Happy Daye motel along the Interstate in Baxter, Montana. A man with a baseball cap pulled low, his body crowding the Internet machine keyboard while the occasional motel guest wandered into the frame drinking a cup of coffee or spooning Cheerios out of a plastic bowl from the free breakfast buffet. The tracking origins on the video entry indicated that it had been routinely archived by the National Security Agency, via the Homeland Security Department, after a clerk at the motel called police to say that a man he thought was "suspicious" had been entering the lobby on occasion and using the Internet kiosk. The clerk had also helpfully followed the man into the motel parking lot and written down his license plate number.

In a whisper, D'Amato addressed the surveillance-camera image in front of her. "From this moment on, my elusive friend, you have a tentative A.K.A. in the files of the FBI," D'Amato said. *"John Stuart A.K.A. Gavin Brinkley."*

Later, as she worked on the file at her desk, D'Amato knew that Gavin Brinkley must have gone to great lengths to draw attention away from himself as he and his family faded into the shadows of off-the-books America. It fit a classic mold. So it figured: Something went wrong in Idaho, but what? Nothing had yet turned up on that. Then slipping further away into rural Montana. Building a new life in a sparsely populated spot where it's considered rude to ask too many questions. Where even a global criminal can prosper in obscurity, but is trapped in the delusion that he can also enjoy anonymity. And that is delusional because—

"—because everything is connected," she said, sitting back in triumph.

*   *   *

The task of confirming the existence of an entity now known in the files as *John Stuart* A.K.A. *Gavin Brinkley* fell to a perpetually dismayed man called H. Wallace Twilley, Special Agent in Charge of the FBI office in Butte, Montana. Twilley had been ensconced there for the last seven years with no hope of transfer, not even aware that a certain amount of derision was always directed his way because of FBI lore. In the old days, when an agent fell seriously out of favor with the legendarily autocratic former FBI director, J. Edgar Hoover, it was said—by Hoover himself, actually—that said agent (and in those days it was always a he) was going to end his career dispatched to the godforsaken Bureau office in Butte, Montana.

Agent Twilley had been sent to Butte, from Miami, long after Hoover died. In actuality, he enjoyed the assignment once he got used to it, and in fact planned to make his retirement as the Special Agent in Charge of the Butte Bureau, where supervisors and other snoops from Washington were seldom seen or heard. And where, as he told colleagues still chortling over the phone from Miami, "The fishing and other outdoors activities are wonderful."

Grumbling all the way, Twilley followed orders one morning to drive from Butte to Wanton, a trip of a mere two hundred miles that would nevertheless take eight hours because of the winding mountain roads, not to mention the infernal truck traffic from the oil industry.

Using police skills no more sophisticated than a GPS navigator and a pocket camera, Twilley did document that *John and Cindy Stuart* A.K.A. *Gavin and Lisa Brinkley*, previous addresses unknown, were living in a modest, old three-bedroom house in a rural part of tiny Wanton, Montana—nearest neighbors Bruce Thomas and Melanie Quinn, three quarters of a mile up the road. No known criminal records.

As instructed, he phoned headquarters in Washington and was put through to Agent D'Amato.

"You have this confirmed?" she asked.

"Confirmed."

"You talked to the neighbors?"

"I tried to. The man, Bruce Thomas, was very confrontational. I don't know what he knows, but he sure doesn't trust someone knocking on his door and pretending to be lost, that's for sure! So then I went to the feed store in town and made inquiries. Guy there told me that the neighbor lady, he said her name was Maloney, was the town librarian. So I visited this sorry excuse for a library and confirmed that. But a funny thing—"

"—What?"

"Turns out her name is actually *Melanie*. Melanie Quinn. Evidently people call her Maloney because she looks so Irish. Pretty girl, nice."

"Brilliant police work, Twilley," D'Amato said, trying unsuccessfully to conceal her sarcasm.

"You want me to go back?"

"You're not still there?"

"I'm in Butte," he said.

"Somehow that figures," she said, this time making no effort to hide the sarcasm.

"Well, what are we looking for here?" he asked, his pride wounded by yet another East Coast know-it-all. "It's not clear to me if they are working outside the law. I thought they were in the witness protection program, which is usually a place where we stash criminal informants."

"You're years out of date, Twilley."

"This guy is what, a hacker?" he asked D'Amato.

"Way more than that. He's a piece in a very complex jigsaw puzzle, and national security is at stake," she said.

"Wow, all the way up there in Wanton," he remarked.

"Twilley?"

"Yes?"

"I want you to go back there and snoop around a little. What's this guy like? Who does he know? What does he do all day? Who comes to visit?"

"Well, that part I already got. And the answer to that is, nobody except those two neighbors. The girls go to school and come home, very quiet. If there's an extracurricular activity, one of the parents is always waiting for them afterward. These people keep a very low profile. You don't want me to bring them in, do you?"

"I don't want you to confront them in any way! Is that clear?"

"Yup."

"Well, good luck, Twilley," she said with absolutely no conviction. "How about you head back up there for another day or two and see what you can learn. There's something going on or we wouldn't be so deeply into this guy. But please, Twilley, be discreet. Do not flash your badge unless you absolutely have to as a matter of self-protection, okay?"

"Got it!" he said. When the call ended, Twilley went to his computer and laboriously filed his mileage and meal expenses for the day.

*   *   *

Later that afternoon, D'Amato's supervisor Agent Moore came into her cubicle and sat down beside her desk.

"So you got a fix on this couple in Montana, the Stuarts?" he asked.

"Well, if this guy's who we think he is, if he's playing as big a part in this enterprise as we believe, he's going to lead us somewhere interesting. I'm sure of that."

"We're on it," she said, thinking with silent despair about Agent Twilley being on the case.

"My gut feeling?" Moore said.

"What?"

"—is that this guy is a first-rate criminal hunkered way down deep. Sometimes, D'Amato, criminals on the lam are extremely stupid. Like John Dillinger, the most wanted man in America in 1934. He hightails it off to Arizona with his gang, and do you know where we found him?"

D'Amato resisted the impulse to roll her eyes and said only, "Where?"

"In the hotel right across from the train station in Tucson! What a moron!"

"Didn't he escape?"

"He did later, from prison. Not our doing. But we got him again, and this time got him good, shot him dead outside a movie theater in Chicago. Bam! Bam!" He laughed in delight at the historical memory of an event that had occurred fifteen years before his birth.

D'Amato was beginning to wonder about her career choices, but she said only, "Before my time. And before your time, too, Art. Can we talk about this *'John Stuart* A.K.A. *Gavin Brinkley'*? I think we need a better plan than having Agent Twilley from the Butte Bureau keeping an eye on him and asking around."

Moore touched her sleeve. "Wait, we really have a Butte, Montana, Bureau?"

"Of course we do."

A big laugh convulsed him. "I always thought that was a joke! Butte, Montana!"

She smiled indulgently, trying to get him to focus. "Art, John Stuart is extremely smart. If we pick him up he'll get through interrogations easily because there are no digital trails tying him to crimes. I've validated that with our counterespionage digital team. Once we even approach him, he'll be tipped off, and that could be the end of the line for this investigation. So we have to keep him around under close surveillance and monitor his activities. If he is on the good side, by some chance, then let's keep him that way. If he's on the dark side, let's build the case with evidence."

Moore had turned quite serious. "And we've got the SPAC from the Butte office doing the on-site surveillance?"

She frowned. "It's all I could get approval for right now with the budget cuts."

He shook his head. "I want somebody from the task force here at headquarters out there," he said. "Approval for whatever you need hereby granted."

"Great," she said. "I have an idea to keep him on the straight and narrow, if he hasn't in fact gone over to the dark side." Just then, his cell phone whirred and he said, "The deputy director, gotta go! Fill me in tomorrow!" And off he bustled.

CHAPTER TWENTY

Naturally, the children's curiosity about the room in the basement kept increasing. Caitlin was much more interested than Emma in whatever lay behind that door, firstly because she had never been in there, and secondly, because she had been older when the family first moved out West. Periodically she would get flashbacks of a different landscape, a different kind of snow than the one she was confronted with six to seven months of the year, and occasionally a memory of playing at the beach. When she asked her parents about these gaps in her life story, they didn't seem to have any interest in discussing them—unlike her friends and *their* parents, who brimmed with information about their histories, with only the least bit of prompting. *Why are there so few stories about me?* Caitlin wondered.

One night she was up late finishing a homework assignment when she heard Cindy and John's voices from the basement. She decided to investigate and slipped quickly down the stairs, where she stood by unseen while watching her parents poring over the contents of boxes on the floor. Occasionally they would pass along a photo from one to the other. She heard her father say "that time in Paris" and her mother giggle about "that balloon trip over the Netherlands, when I was terrified of falling out." "How weird that the 2nd Avenue Deli is on First Avenue on the Upper East Side!" she heard her mother say with a bright laugh. "That dinner at Per Se," her father enthused. "I preferred Jean Georges," her mother said happily. "God, I miss New York." What were these places from memories that Caitlin did not know? She wished that she could visit New York. Somewhere dimly in her past, was there just a hint of a memory of New York—tall buildings, bustling crowds, that huge green statue in the harbor? Or did she just know these images from the movies?

Her parents also talked about things they had once done with the children, and here Caitlin's memories were more firm. A trip to Disney World in the winter, which she recalled now vividly as leaving a cold place of dingy hues of black and white—*where was that?*—and getting off an airplane in a visual landscape that magically manifested itself in Technicolor. It had been just like that scene in *The Wizard of Oz* where the black-and-white scenes of Kansas suddenly transform into the splendid, startling colors of Oz.

Why would they never discuss these things with her? She had a right to know! Why the secrets?

As she drifted off to sleep, Caitlin talked herself into becoming displeased enough with her parents to concoct a plot that would help her complete at least a portion of the puzzle. The following afternoon, after school, she pulled Emma aside and proposed a raid into the mystery room in the basement at a time when her parents were in the yard planting flowers.

"You don't have the key," Emma said, exercising her newfound, age-appropriate logic.

"Yes, I do. When I was vacuuming the other day, I found a key under the rug in the den, and I tried it in the basement lock. It worked. But I was too afraid to go in alone."

Emma looked at her conspiratorially and said, "I'll go with you!"

The next Saturday, when they saw their parents dirty up to their elbows in mulch, they stole the key to the basement and opened the door. Once they were in the room, they had little trouble locating the box, or the yellowing envelope within it. Caitlin's baby pictures were there, but also pictures of her parents in formal clothing, looking amazingly elegant at a party for a company with a name they didn't recognize. There was a couple of pictures of Cindy wearing high-fashion suits at what appeared to be a powerful job—*had their mother worked somewhere before that she never spoke about?* There were pictures of a beautiful, huge home, and a few pictures of children—*them!*—in the sun beside a swimming pool. There was a picture where Caitlin and Emma stood with Mickey Mouse and another one with Winnie the Pooh.

"Disney World?" Emma asked excitedly.

"Yes! You don't remember."

"No," Emma said dejectedly. "Does it count if I don't remember?"

Now both girls were more confused than ever. How could they be in two sets of lives, one not connected to the other?

"Who are all these people in the pictures? What do they have to do with Mom and Dad? Caitlin asked.

Emma thought for a minute and then chimed, "They're spies! Don't you remember the movie *Spy Kids*?"

"They're not spies! There are no spies in Montana, Emma!" Caitlin said with a sisterly laugh.

"I think they're spies," Emma said with the insistence of a child who has no narrative and is struggling to invent one.

Caitlin was in a more logical mode of thinking. She noticed that the name and store number of a Walgreen's pharmacy was written on one of the photo folders, and someone had scribbled "Brinkley" on it. She wrote the name down carefully on a piece of paper. Caitlin took out one of the photographs with the big home and slipped it into her pocket. Then the girls sprinted out of the room like bank robbers.

The next day, Caitlin and Emma decided to forego lunch in their cafeteria and met in the school library instead, which was permitted for students needing extra study time. They sat together at a computer. It took no time at all for Caitlin to find the location of the pharmacy with a simple search: Concord, Massachusetts. Then she used Zillow.com, the home-value and resale site, to browse through photos and other details of high-priced homes in town, of which there were many. But as luck would have it, within fifteen minutes she and Emma spotted a house that looked like the one in the photographs they had seen in the basement.

Most of the photographs had shown just a portion of the exterior of the house, but Caitlin assembled the fractured images in her mind like a jigsaw puzzle. The pieces fit together.

"This is the house," Caitlin told Emma, who moved in close to peer intently at the screen.

"Did we live there?" Emma asked.

"Maybe," Caitlin said.

"Why?" Emma asked.

"Because *maybe*, is all! You were too little to remember," Caitlin said with some exasperation.

"I mean, why don't we live there now?"

Caitlin had no answer for that, of course.

*   *   *

Caitlin was very distracted for the remainder of that day and the next. At her first opportunity, she sat again at the computer in the school library, anxious to fit more pieces into the puzzle. She googled "Concord, MA" and tried to absorb as much as she could. Some of the subjects stirred something in her: Monument Square, Walden Pond. Others she didn't quite understand. She was a young girl in Montana! What could these strange things, two-thirds of a continent away, have to do with her now? She read about Concord and was fascinated to see that there were two very famous private schools in town. She thought a lot about that.

At home the next day, while the whole family was having dinner, Caitlin suddenly announced her desire to go to a private boarding school.

Her mother sipped some water and tried to conceal both her surprise and her alarm. John moved some salad around his plate and watched silently.

"Private boarding school? Caitlin, why?" Cindy asked.

"It would be best for my education," Caitlin said dramatically.

Her parents were not inclined to disagree. Montana had its virtues, but it also had its limitations, most of them cultural. They had casually discussed the children's future educational options from time to time, but had steadfastly avoided discussing specifics, as if avoidance could postpone decisions that would inevitably have to be made.

"Where were you thinking of going?" John asked, attempting to appear nonchalant.

"Some of the best ones are on the East Coast, so it would make sense for me to go there," Caitlin said.

It was all her parents could do to not exchange worried looks. Wouldn't their child's leaving home cause a dangerous ripple in the pond of their anonymity?

"The East Coast is a very different place," Cindy said.

"I know!" Caitlin said with a burst of enthusiastic conviction that caught her parents by surprise.

"We'll think about it," Cindy said. "Who wants dessert?"

After the dishes were cleared and the girls were in their room, John and Cindy had a long and anxious discussion about Caitlin's future.

"This is too soon," John said.

"She's not a child anymore," Cindy advised him.

"We need to protect her!" he persisted.

"We can't keep her in hiding forever. Besides, she isn't on anybody's radar. Marcus said that from the very beginning. Her going off to school shouldn't cause any unwanted attention if we keep it low-profile."

"Private boarding school is expensive," John said. "In the old days that wouldn't have mattered. Now it matters."

"We'll cope," Cindy reassured him. "We are very good at coping."

The following night at dinner, it was evident to her parents that Caitlin had done even more research into her prospects.

"I know that private boarding school costs a lot, but there are scholarships," she said. John felt his heart sink. How in the world had he arrived at a state where his daughter had to try to reassure her father—him, Gavin Brinkley!—about money? His fury at the Enterprise, at the odious criminals who had caused him to put his family in such a place, was overwhelming, and even more intense because he could not show it.

"It's forty thousand dollars a year, the places I'm looking at—"

John swallowed.

She continued, "Don't worry, Dad. I looked into this. I'm applying for financial aid. So if I get it, can I go?"

"Where are these schools?" he asked.

"On the East Coast, like I said," she replied, carefully watching her parents' faces.

"We'll see," he said with morose resignation, feeling a cold chill, as if a door had suddenly been flung open to the winter winds.

* * *

Caitlin was very insistent in the coming days, and worked hard to persuade her mother at least to remain neutral. In turn, Cindy intervened with John, saying: "We need to be concerned with her future, instead of being solely focused on threats. And for all we know, the threats may be lessening. I saw online that the FBI is involved in an all-out campaign to take down global cyber-crime networks, and you and I know very well that the Enterprise is the biggest of them all. They've been arresting key players here and overseas."

John looked at her angrily. "Online? How many times have I told you, they have penetrated the entire Internet! Have you forgotten everything we've been through because of these people?"

Cindy felt unfairly attacked. *No,* she thought, *I have forgotten nothing. Not the fear and terror, not the sudden uprooting of my life and the lives of my children. Nothing has been forgotten.*

"So it's okay for you to do it?" she demanded. Her face turned red. "Maloney told me you've been surfing the Web in the library, too."

"I know what I'm doing. I know not to leave tracks," John said, almost shouting.

She gave him a spiteful look. "Oh, do you?" she said, and watched him back off in shame.

"Besides," she went on, "I did it the same way you do. I don't provide any personal information, nothing! There's no log-in. Who, besides Maloney, knows I'm even there? I use Google and the *New York Times* Web site—you get a certain number of free searches on the *New York Times* before they ask you to provide your information and pay for more. So it's totally anonymous! And I resent your implication that I would carelessly expose my family to more danger, John! I have *always* made my family's safety the top priority."

"I know," he said meekly. "I'm sorry."

"But how long does this go on, John? How long does the fear go on? Do we pass it on to our daughters? Because, mark my words, John: the girls are growing up. Do we want them to live with the fear that consumes us? *Do we?*"

"No," he said.

"So we will work with Caitlin on this, then. We will be part of her solution, and not part of her problem."

"You're right," he said.

And so it went. Caitlin enthusiastically began assembling the components of her application processes. John had allowed her to list five schools of her choice as her research went on. He and Cindy were impressed at how much time and energy Caitlin invested in the process.

Finally, she presented the list at dinner several weeks later. Looking at it, John had a sick feeling when he saw her first choice, highlighted in bright yellow.

"**Northpoint School: Concord, MA,**" it read in her bold, neat handwriting.

"Concord?" he asked weakly.

"*CAN-kid!*" Emma put in on cue.

"Shhh, Emma," her mother said.

"That's the one I like best," Caitlin said.

John and Cindy actively discouraged Caitlin to apply there, but her heart was set on it. In addition, Caitlin's best friend at her school in Wanton, a girl named Abby, had heard Caitlin talk about Northpoint School. The two girls, who regarded themselves as best friends forever, were soon conspiring to apply together.

They had memorized the course descriptions and the school welcome summary that they printed out from its Web site, which described a sylvan campus, a rigorous education in English, modern languages, the classics, science, writing, and critical thinking, along with an invitation to visit.

The welcome announcement read:

Northpoint School is a college preparatory, boarding and day school, Grades 9–12. It boasts a strenuous academic program in which students develop their voices and their intellects. Northpoint offers acclaimed co-curricular opportunities in sports, theatre, music, and other performing arts, environmental and community involvement, and public speaking.

Each school year, we look forward to welcoming approximately one hundred new students whom we believe will benefit from, as well as enhance, the unique ambiance of Northpoint School. Our students arrive with the highest accomplishments, and ultimately graduate with firm self-assurance and educational attainment that can be measured not solely in test scores, but also by the highest levels of intellectual and social attainment in life for which our graduates are renowned.

The two friends threw themselves into the preparation and application rigors required by Northpoint School, and before anyone realized how quickly the process had moved, the initial paperwork was finished and it became time for that personal visit to Northpoint School.

There was no way John and Cindy could accompany Caitlin on the school visit for obvious reasons, so they were happy when Abby's mother, a woman they knew only casually from school events, invited Caitlin to come along on a visit she was planning with her daughter.

Caitlin was disappointed and a little embarrassed that her parents would not accompany her on the trip to Massachusetts, believing that they had declined for financial reasons. However, her sense of anticipation for the venture took over, and Caitlin could barely contain her excitement when she left for the long drive to Butte with Abby and her mother. She thought it was the first time she had been on an airplane, but when the plane took off, the sensation felt vaguely familiar, as if she had done it before.

There was a hurried connection in Denver, and then a long flight east to Boston. Caitlin had her nose stuck to the window as the plane got closer and closer to the water. She couldn't wait to be in Boston for the drive to Concord in a rental car. The plane looked like it would land on Massachusetts Bay, but at the last moment, the runway appeared and they touched down with water on both sides. It was after nine p.m. when Caitlin and Abby excitedly led the way to baggage claim, and then outside to the car rental counter.

After getting the car and settling into an airport hotel for the night, the morning couldn't come fast enough. With breakfast from Dunkin' Donuts in hand and a surprisingly scenic drive once the gritty environs of the airport were left behind, the journey to Northpoint School was fascinating. Caitlin and Abby were excited and nervous. As the car arrived at Northpoint, they surveyed the green, pretty campus with awe. High school boys and girls strolled the campus with poise and determination that the girls had never witnessed in Montana. Faculty members headed to classes with coffee mugs in hand. Children and dogs chased each other on the athletic field, scattering piles of jewel-toned leaves as they scampered.

Abby's mother parked the car, and they all walked over to the admissions building, where a fresh-faced female Northpoint student introduced herself as Emily, their tour guide. As Emily led them out of the building, she began reciting statistics about every aspect of Northpoint

School. They marched through the academic buildings, the luxurious dining hall, and the athletic buildings and facilities. Caitlin was beyond awestruck. She had never seen a school like this! The campus was huge. Next, they saw a typical dorm and then the student center. They moved on to the chapel and the main green. Next came the library and the theater. A real theater, not an auditorium converted for a school play! Finally they ended up back where they began, and Emily suggested they make themselves comfortable till the interviews began.

The girls had been terrified about the interviews, but they were pleasantly surprised to find themselves put at ease from the start. Abby's mother was invited by one of the admissions counselors into an office for a separate interview, and the girls were happy to see her smiling broadly when she came out. After about two hours, they all left the campus. Abby had another tour and interview scheduled at a different prep school in the afternoon, and Caitlin was happy to tag along. But Caitlin already had her heart firmly set on Northpoint School.

Caitlin had been told to expect the admissions office to inform her of their decision sometime between March 31 and April 10. Each day, when she came home from school, she ran to the mailbox. On April 7, a fat envelope arrived with the magical return address: Northpoint School. Caitlin tore it open as she hurried back to the house.

"My Dear Miss Stuart," it read. "It is my distinct pleasure to inform you that your application to attend the Northpoint School as a boarding student in the coming Fall has been approved, and that we look forward greatly to your joining our unique community."

The letter went on to say that she would be receiving a full scholarship for all four years. When she showed the letter to her parents, Caitlin was crying with joy and pride.

CHAPTER TWENTY-ONE

#bankguard@XCV
Cybercrooks emptying inactive bank accounts, huge billions $ stolen, banks covering up but news to break soon Banking catastrophe looming?

Reply   Retweet   Favorite

That was the first notice about the Great Bank Collapse, a simple tweet on Twitter in early December, quickly picked up by the banking cognoscenti and retweeted across the digital universe. The author was unknown but was obviously well connected because, when the news broke a day later, it created headlines and "breaking news" bulletins all over the world.

Another massive fraud, the biggest ever, had hit the banks, and this time they couldn't sweep the problem under the rug. In a breathtaking assault, cyber thieves had mounted attacks on accounts that had been "inactive"—that is, accounts in the names of depositors who had not accessed them for a full year or more, either because the account holders had moved abroad, had become incapacitated in some way, had died and not listed these accounts in their wills, or because the balances were held in secondary accounts by affluent people who had simply forgotten they existed. There were hundreds of thousands, perhaps millions, of such inactive accounts in the United States. Under the law, it takes three years of inactivity before such dormant accounts are officially listed as "unclaimed." Well before this time, a government audit showed that billions of dollars had been silently diverted from banks all across the country by cyber criminals, clearly from a foreign crime organization, who had somehow cracked the elaborate codes banks used to flag the level of activity in any account.

At first, the banking industry attempted to downplay the revelations, abetted by the compliant news media and a federal government that was sufficiently alarmed but immobilized by the fear that admitting the extent of the assault would create mass panic. Finally, within two days, the government did admit the truth, in a tense news conference by the secretary of the treasury, and panic did, as feared, ensue. Within hours, long lines of angry people had formed outside bank branches, and the demands on online-banking sites were so intense that they became unavailable, one after the other, in a rolling system crash that piled up like a massive Interstate chain-collision from the East Coast to the West.

It became far worse. Huge sums of money, auditors discovered, were also missing from accounts that had been inactive not for a year or years, but for a mere few months. Then it was discovered that a massive breach of security had ripped through databanks containing Social Security numbers linked with names, account numbers, and dates of birth for millions of citizens. The devastating pileup of fraud and theft cascaded with terrifying speed.

Finally the president came on television to announce that law enforcement and national-security agencies were engaged in an all-out effort, which he called "the equivalent of war," to combat the fraud and bring the criminals to justice. The president also issued assurances that those who found their bank account looted could depend on the Federal Deposit Insurance Corporation and related agencies to cover their losses. In the meantime, word had gone out through intra-governmental channels with the greatest urgency. Further lack of progress was unacceptable. It was time to deliver. All over Washington, cell phones thrummed, whistled, rang, jangled, sang, and bellowed simultaneously.

*   *   *

In Montana, Cindy worried that their money—the Brinkleys' money—which they presumed was safe and untouched in various accounts in Massachusetts had now been looted.

"Since Cate died, no one is keeping an eye on them… and they have been inactive for a long time," she fretted to John, expecting that he would reassure her that the money, which they expected to be able to reclaim one day, was safe. She felt angry, frustrated, and helpless.

"I told those bankers in New York that the inadequacy of their security systems was going to leave us exposed to exactly this kind of disaster, and then we'd very quickly become aware of the other dirty secret, the inadequacy of the financial backing for the FDIC and the other safeguards."

"Please tell me some good news," she said miserably.

To her dismay, he didn't reply.

She said tearfully, "When will this stop?"

"I don't know," he said. "Everyone is connected and our lives are the better for it, yet that same global connectivity is a wonderful opportunity for criminals. It's worse in the case of the banks because ninety percent of the core banking-software market is dominated by only four companies. So all the Enterprise has to do is hack through four sets of software, and the vault doors spring open for thousands of banks."

"But how did they get hold of so many Social Security numbers and birthdays?" Cindy asked.

"Easy. In fact, just about everyone has allowed their personal information to float around cyberspace. When you go to a doctor's or dentist's office, they have it, right? When you go to a community hospital, they have it. When you apply for any kind of credit card, including a retailer's credit card, your Social Security number is online. Credit bureaus routinely provide this information to marketers who target individuals with all kinds of products unbeknownst to them. You have to proactively reach out to the credit bureaus and ask them not to share your information, as opposed to their default position to share without your permission. Schools and universities have all their students' Social Security numbers. Do you really believe that all these places have data-security systems that are adequate, especially in the face of a cunning criminal assault by an organization as powerful, ruthless, and far-reaching as the Enterprise?"

"What could anybody do with a college kid's data? Most of them don't have any money," Cindy said.

"Not yet. But remember, once they have it, schools keep this data post-graduation. Nobody ever relinquishes data, especially since paper storage is now obsolete and keeping vast amounts of digitalized data is utterly simple. A savvy criminal only has to hack into alumni lists and cross-check that data with easily stolen college data and, *voilà*, they have opened the lid to hundreds and hundreds of veritable treasure chests.

"All the years I spent in banking, no one ever talked about that."

"Why do you suppose that was?" John asked pointedly.

"No one knew?"

"Oh, some of them knew. They just did not want to tell others, because their careers came first and nobody likes a Cassandra."

"So, what's the solution?" asked Cindy.

"No idea. Every approach I've come up with so far breaks down when I try on the criminal hat to test it. Every single one. But I will tell you this, if I ever come up with one, it will be because of you."

"Why?" Cindy asked quizzically.

"Because you ask direct and logical questions—and that stimulates different parts of my brain. It creates dots in my head."

"Well, in that case, glad to be of help. Direct and logical, that's certainly me."

"Seriously, if I ever find a solution, I'll patent it and name it after you."

Her face clouded over. "Which name?" she said disconsolately.

He chucked her under the chin playfully.

"Okay," she said, recovering her equilibrium, "If I understand it right, the basic challenge is the centralized storage."

"Right."

"Well, that's as logical as I can get right now. I hope you figure it out fast. That's an awfully big responsibility you're taking on, for a guy stuck in the boonies of Montana without so much as a steady Wi-Fi connection."

John didn't seem to register that. Instead, he thought for a minute and said, excitedly, "Wait! Wait! So if we make every access transient, and do the same for storage, that could dramatically reduce risk." He kissed her and said, "Thanks, sweetie. I'm going up to take a shower."

At that moment Emma came in and said, "Can I take a bath?" while looking askance at her father.

Cindy smiled. "The shower is now tied up for an hour," she said.

CHAPTER TWENTY-TWO

Emma and Caitlin came home early the next day. Their principal, a Mrs. Conklin, had spotted a mouse in her supply closet and, shrieking, leapt in a single bound onto the top of her desk. Unfortunately, that mouse turned out to be the harbinger of an infestation of mice, rodents evidently fleeing the first icy blasts of winter for the cozy warmth of a school building. The school had to close around noon as every classroom now required emergency fumigation—a decidedly Montanan problem to have.

John and Cindy were not yet home. After the girls were dropped off by the school bus, Caitlin opened the front door with a key on her ring while Emma lingered outside looking at some red and orange impatiens that still stubbornly remained in bloom in her mother's flower bed despite the cold and the layers of ice that now formed on the puddles in the fields.

As Caitlin walked into the family room, she stopped with a jolt. There had been a home invasion. Everything was upended, including the couch. Papers were scattered all over the living and dining rooms. Drawers had been dumped on the floor. Caitlin wanted to scream, but stopped herself.

Moving noiselessly and warily, she traced her steps back to the mudroom, hurriedly unlocked a cabinet with another key, grabbed two hunting rifles, and ran out around the house to the front yard, screaming: "Emma! Come here now! Emma!"

When Emma came running, Caitlin handed her the smaller rifle.

"Go!" Caitlin ordered, and the two girls ran toward the road. "Run, Emma!"

Caitlin had gone on many hunting trips with her parents. The girls were not allowed to touch the guns on their own, except in cases of actual emergency, but they knew a lot about firearm use and especially gun safety, thanks to their patient and helpful neighbor, Bruce Thomas.

As they had also been trained, the girls hurried toward the home of Bruce and Maloney, three quarters of a mile up the steep narrow road. Caitlin kept looking around while covering Emma.

"Call Mom's cell!" Caitlin said when they were far enough from their house and saw no one in pursuit.

Emma complied using her own cell phone.

When Cindy answered from the car, Emma yelled, "Mom! Come home quick! Someone broke in the house!"

"Where are you?" Cindy said in a panic.

"On the road. We're going to Mr. Thomas's house!"

"Caitlin is with you?"

"Yes! Come home quick!"

"Let me talk to Caitlin!"

Caitlin, out of breath, assured her mother that they were all right, that they had seen no one in their house, but that they were terrified nevertheless.

"Caitlin, I love you, honey. Run directly to Bruce and Maloney's! Do you hear?"

"Yes, Mom!"

"I'll call him! Go!"

In a few minutes, before the neighbor's one-story cottage even came into sight on the crest of the hill, they saw Bruce Thomas's pickup truck coming toward them down the road.

"Get in!" he yelled through the open passenger's side window.

With Caitlin boosting Emma up, they climbed into the truck, pulling the guns in with them. He had his rifle in his lap, pointed away from them.

"You're okay!" he told the girls, who were shaking. "I spoke to your mom. You're okay. She'll be here in ten minutes." He flipped open his cell phone and called Cindy to tell her he had the girls and they were fine.

Cindy thanked him profusely, stopped in town to pick up John who had been waiting for her anxiously, and drove as fast as she prudently could on curving roads. A big tractor trailer laden with barrels pulled out from a side road and ground its way along at about ten miles an hour. They were on its bumper, unable to see enough to pass safely. Cindy flashed the headlights, lowered her window, and shouted toward the truck, asking to pass, but the driver did not budge. Unable to pass, frozen in fear and frustration, they wove along, looking for an opportunity to pull ahead that never came. The ten-minute drive to Bruce's place took a heart-stopping twenty-five minutes instead.

"Maybe we'd better go to the house first," Cindy said when they finally turned onto the road leading out of town where they lived.

"Good idea. I'll call Bruce and tell him we're checking out the house before we get the girls," John said.

They felt sick to see their belongings tossed around. The mess could be straightened up easily enough, but the feeling that they had now been discovered was a horrible one that would not be straightened out so readily. John went to the gun cabinet and was stricken to see it open, but then he realized that Caitlin had probably removed the two extra rifles. He took out his own shotgun and searched the house and the backyard.

After a little while, Bruce arrived with the girls, who ran to their mother. Bruce and John, both armed, searched the house and property again. No one was around.

"You want to call nine-one-one?" Bruce asked. For some reason, he had not expressed any curiosity about the Stuarts not having called the police.

"No," John said. "It's all right, really. Kids, probably." He felt a desperate inability to communicate. "Nothing valuable was taken, and calling the town cops would only cause them to be coming by all the time," he said, laughing weakly.

"Right. No good comes of that as a general principle," Bruce agreed. He saw Cindy put her own gun away, and he studied John with careful curiosity. He knew John and trusted him, and he did not probe. "Let me help you get this couch back on its feet," he said.

The intruders had not taken the television, the stereo, or any of Cindy's jewelry, which she kept in a small chest on her bureau. Yet every drawer and cabinet had been yanked open.

The basement was also a mess, but the box with photos and other memorabilia had only been moved, not dumped onto the floor.

"What were they after?" Cindy asked, clinging to his arm while the girls waited in sight on the basement stairs.

"Obviously something specific," John said. Suddenly, he realized what it had been.

"My laptops!" he said, referring to the one where he kept household records, as well as his personal journal, the one he always kept unconnected to the Internet; and the newer laptop, the cheap Compaq that he recently bought to be able to connect at the town library.

He kept them both under some shirts on a high closet shelf. They were gone.

But a broad smile came on his face as he pulled out a pen-drive from the pocket of his trousers. He showed it to Cindy.

"Scrubbed both of the hard drives last week," he said. "Everything is on this."

By early evening, the house had been put back together, as if no one had intruded into their lives.

They were planning to go to bed early and exhausted when they heard a car pull into their driveway from the lonely road. A chill went down Cindy's spine. She got her gun and passed the rifle to John, who peered out the window and saw a heavyset man in a suit holding what looked like a police badge. He opened the door while Cindy covered him.

The man seemed sweaty despite the cold. "Mr. and Mrs. Stuart, I'm Special Agent Twilley of the Federal Bureau of Investigation, Butte office."

Extremely warily, because he had no reason to trust the FBI, even if the man was legitimate, John inspected Twilley's badge and ID, which looked real enough. He noticed Cindy unobtrusively drift back toward the kitchen for better surveillance, and he could see that she still held her Glock handgun.

Agent Twilley did not stay long. He told them that the authorities were monitoring some criminal activity in Wanton, and had heard that a burglary had occurred at their house earlier in the day.

"Would you mind telling me why you didn't report this to the town police?" Twilley asked John.

John shrugged the question off. "It was nothing, really. You know how you have to worry about home-insurance rates. Just some kids, probably. All that was taken was a six-pack of beer from the refrigerator," he lied.

A tight smile crossed Twilley's face.

John asked him, "Tell me, how did you know there was a home invasion, considering we didn't report it?"

Twilley's eyebrows raised. "Oh, we got someone and he talked," he said. John's expression conveyed skepticism.

Twilley handed him a card and said to phone if anything came up.

When he left, Cindy asked John, "Now what was *that* all about?"

"Who knows?" John said. "We'll take the guns to the bedroom tonight."

CHAPTER TWENTY-THREE

"Come on, Mom, seriously, why can't you just be normal like the other moms?" Caitlin asked her mother for the third time. *If you only knew,* Cindy thought. Cindy had on a Dodgers cap and sunglasses, which had been the epitome of cool at one time. She told her daughter so.

"The Dodgers are very stylish," Cindy insisted.

"Where?" Caitlin asked, rolling her eyes.

"In California? Where I went to college?" Cindy said, unconsciously mimicking the inflections of a certain milieu in California.

"Mom, this is *Massachusetts.* Where the *Red Sox* are. And people don't wear baseball caps anymore anyway?" Caitlin teased, playfully tugging at the brim of her mother's cap.

Caitlin really didn't know where to channel her nervous energy. She decided she was being unfair to her mother, who had gone to great lengths to make the trip across the country pleasant for her daughter.

They drove up in a rental car to the historical Colony Inn hotel in the center of Concord, a sprawling clapboard building festooned with American flags and bunting draped over the roof and veranda. Caitlin noticed how deftly her mother navigated the way through town and seemed to know exactly where the inn was located, but she was too nervous to give it much thought. Cindy simply told her that she had memorized the directions from the map.

Caitlin was also too excited to sleep much in the deep plush bed, which had a canopy stretched above it. *What in the world was the point of a canopy,* she wondered. Though a sumptuous breakfast was available starting at six o'clock in the dining room, she could do no more than nibble on some toast and drink a glass of freshly squeezed orange juice.

She wished desperately that her mother would remove that cap and those pretentious sunglasses, which made her look, Caitlin thought with some horror, like a personal trainer at a West Hollywood gym.

All morning, mother and daughter trudged through the exhausting process of moving in to Northpoint: carrying boxes and luggage from the car into the dorm room, waving at strangers who also seemed to be trying to hide their anxiety. But by early afternoon, easing herself into the bustling flow as one would ease oneself into a swimming pond, Caitlin felt that first thrilling sense of belonging to something new and entirely exotic.

Luckily, Cindy did not engage in a long and elaborate good-bye ceremony, as many of the other parents did. Cindy was glad to know her daughter was secure enough to smile bravely through the separation. Right after she checked out of the Colony Inn, Cindy pulled her cap down low. But she could not resist walking a short distance to her favorite place downtown, an independent bookstore with excellent personal service that was a popular local gathering spot for book lovers whether they were children or senior citizens.

That night, as she flew back over the country, she thought about Caitlin intensely, and she took stock of her own deep and unsettled emotions at having come back to Concord, with her daughter no less, for the first time in nine years. Over the years she had slowly managed to mentally detach herself from her previous life, but seeing it all—the town, the houses—made her realize just how desperately she missed it.

*   *   *

Ten minutes after her mother left Caitlin realized that for the first time in her life, her mother would not be within physical reach. Her mind started doing jumping jacks. She had well-developed social skills—her parents had taught her which fork to use, and how to relate to adults with a firm handshake and a friendly look in the eye. At the same time she was frightened of the cultural and social judgments that she could already feel radiating from every corner of this new environment. She was a girl from Montana, a raw place with real mountains far to the west of this vast continent! Sometimes she even said "Howdy!" Could she remember never to say "howdy" again? And oh Lord, will she ever be able to remember not *ever* to say "Reckon"? Caitlin knew how to ride a horse and tie a clove-hitch knot and shoot a gun and make a campfire and read a compass and guess the snow that's coming by the light on the mountains. But she looked aghast at the fashionable clothes and accessories moving around her as new and returning students, mostly from the East, found their assigned places, and she realized with a sinking feeling in the pit of her stomach, "I know how to clean a rifle, *but I do not know how to shop!*"

In a commotion of color-coordinated suitcases and bags, she met a slightly older teenaged girl with perfectly made hair, a tan, and a polo shirt with a logo Caitlin knew did not come from the young adult fashion counter at Walmart.

"Hey! I'm Maddy," her new roommate said with confidence, holding out her hand.

Do not say 'howdy,' Caitlin sternly instructed herself. Instead, she managed to blurt out, "Hey! I'm Caitlin!" in reply, and the two girls shook hands. Caitlin felt the ground under her feet firm up a bit.

"Want some help unpacking? I already moved in," Caitlin said.

"Thanks, that would be great! Where are you from?"

"Montana."

"Oh, you're from the South!" Maddy said with interest.

"It's a lot more west than south...."

Maddy chattered on brightly, clearly not noticing her error. "We'll get to know each other," she said. "The one thing about me is, I talk a lot."

"Me, too," Caitlin said happily.

"I'm a repeat freshman," Maddy told her.

"What's that?"

"You come in after your freshman year somewhere else, but repeat it here. It gives you an edge on your application," Maddy explained. "Also, my brother graduated from Northpoint last year, so that also helps. Of course, it doesn't help on the tuition any."

Caitlin was afraid that her new roommate would ask about her acceptance, and would somehow learn that she was at Northpoint on a full scholarship. But Maddy chattered on about other things: the weather, the soccer team she planned to try out for, her home in Upper Saddle River, New Jersey, movies, skiing...

Thanks to her down-to-earth, outgoing personality, Caitlin made friends quickly. Especially useful, she found, was her strong memory, because she immediately remembered the names of everyone she met, from the girls in her dorm to the other students in her classes. At his welcome speech, the dean emphasized the need to follow the school's rules, and spoke of the implications and disciplinary actions that ensued if rules were broken. Memory for names and the like aside, Caitlin felt slightly overwhelmed. All of these rules and regulations! How could anyone remember them all, even though most of them were common sense. After the long speech, the girls returned to their room and asked endless questions of their proctor about what to expect from Northpoint School and its now-evident quirks. Before falling asleep, Caitlin managed to call her parents and mumble answers to their questions. She felt a twinge of homesickness, as if her mother's visit had never really happened.

"You're making new friends?" her mother asked.

"Yes, Mom. I'll call you tomorrow after classes with a full report," an exhausted Caitlin told her parents.

"We love you, honey," they both said before their images snapped off with a gurgle of electronic sound.

The next morning, Caitlin went to breakfast with Maddy, who turned out to be quite knowledgeable about the way things worked at Northpoint, obviously having had the full report from her older brother. The Victorian-style dining hall looked like a set from a Harry Potter movie. It was all done in dark wood, and banners and flags were draped from the rafters. Huge arched windows lined two walls, letting the early morning light pour in. There were long tables set up in a way that divided the room into four quarters. Underclassmen sat to the right of the buffet line, freshmen at the table closer to the food service, and sophomores across the aisle. Upperclassmen sat to the left of the buffet line and were mixed together, except for the senior stage, where only seniors sat.

After breakfast, Caitlin went to go meet her peer ambassador in front of the dining hall, a senior who looked like he might be twenty. Her group held about ten other freshmen as well. Caitlin was excited to meet more of her classmates. They seemed to be from all over the country, and some were from overseas—every fifteen minutes, or so it seemed, her world was enlarging. After an in-depth two-hour tour around campus, the group had lunch, and then the afternoon was spent getting their sports clothes and signing up for a fall sport. Caitlin chose field hockey even though she had never played before. She certainly was in shape for it, thanks to all of the hiking in Montana. After dinner they were all herded into the gym.

They sat on the bleachers nervously waiting for someone to tell them what to do, when suddenly about fifty seniors marched in costumed in decidedly wacky clothes: some had face paint on, others wore crazy hats and wigs, and all were festooned in neon. It was as if American Apparel and the circus had gone to the mall and rumbled in Sephora. By the end of the night Caitlin was exhausted, but she knew over half her class, and a good number of upperclassmen, as well.

The next morning Caitlin was able to sleep in. It would be her last chance to do so on a Saturday until Thanksgiving break. That was one thing Caitlin was *not* looking forward to—Saturday classes. She woke up around nine thirty, had brunch, and then hung out with her roommate and some other classmates. Around three in the afternoon she went to get ready for field hockey practice. After demonstrating to the girls the basics of a hockey stick, the coach had them break into groups and started practice with some warm-ups and agility drills. Afterward, the varsity girls taught the new girls how to run with the ball and pass. It was much harder than it looked, but Caitlin soon got the hang of it—to the point where making the varsity team seemed like an achievable goal. Two hours later, sweaty and exuberantly tired, Caitlin took the best shower of her life.

Sunday morning was Caitlin's first encounter with her academic adviser, Mrs. Grayson. As she walked into the library, excited to receive her schedule and buy her books, a tall woman in her mid-fifties greeted her with a warm smile. Mrs. Grayson taught history, while her husband taught English. They had both been at the school since their mid-twenties, making this their thirtieth year teaching at Northpoint. After five minutes, Caitlin was enthralled with Mrs. Grayson, who inquired politely about her family and home and how she liked Northpoint so far, and then asked what she might be anxious about.

"How do you know I'm anxious?" Caitlin asked.

Mrs. Grayson liked Caitlin's spunk and unbridled enthusiasm, but she sensed that this thirteen-year-old was perhaps a bit greener than some of the other girls. She said in a kindly voice, "Caitlin, all freshmen are anxious, honey. It comes with the territory. So just remember, I'm here for you. If you have any problems or questions, of if you just want to talk, you come and see me. Don't hesitate. No appointment necessary."

"I won't, Mrs. Grayson," Caitlin said gratefully.

That afternoon was the final part of orientation. All the new students got on buses that took them to downtown Concord in order to get acquainted with the place and its rich history. Their advisers organized the students into small groups and commenced a scavenger hunt that required discovering one place after another, while getting new clues at each place. Caitlin's team came in third, but she didn't mind because she got to experience the thrill of discovering a fascinating town and its role in American history, literature, and philosophy. At the end, everyone got ice cream at Simball's, a famous, local homemade ice-cream parlor.

Caitlin stared at the street corner opposite from the store with the odd feeling that she had been in this exact spot before. And not once, but many times.

"Whoa, this is the best ice cream I've ever had," Maddy told Caitlin enthusiastically. "What flavor did you get? Caitlin?"

Caitlin was broken from her reveries. "A thousand times better than Dairy King."

Maddy licked her chocolate-mint cone. "What's a Dairy King?"

Before Caitlin could figure out how to reply, one of the advisers blew a whistle and they all were off again—this time for a foray into BlueBrook. The leafy, sprawling Northpoint School campus was bordered by the pristine woods of this natural preserve where Harvard University scientists came to study ecology. In the woods, Caitlin finally felt completely comfortable. She watched the water sparkle in the sunlight as it tumbled down through a canopy of trees that were just now starting to transform themselves into autumn's golden hues. For reasons of safety, the Northpoint students were at present allowed only to go as far as the boardwalk by the pond, eventually they would be able to enjoy the full range of the preserve during an orienteering program. Caitlin awaited this experience with tangible anticipation; this was the kind of natural environment that she had been so familiar with at home. On the edge of the preserve, Caitlin closed her eyes and thought of her mother, father, and little sister. Just as the group was leaving she caught a glimpse of wooden beams in a tree. *A treehouse?* She was determined to come back sometime and climb into it.

*   *   *

As the school year took on a routine, Caitlin still could not shake her homesickness—but then again, even the girls from the East were homesick, especially the freshmen. It came with the territory, as Mrs. Grayson told her repeatedly. Caitlin radiated a cheerful nature and natural confidence, but she still was troubled with appearances. She didn't have the designer clothes, the shoes, and the jewelry—none of the trappings of the typical student at a prestigious New England prep school. Most of the parents were very rich; Caitlin was amazed to see that some of the students carried a lot of cash, hundreds of dollars in some cases, and most of them seemed to have credit cards—and not the run-of-the-mill cards, but the high-end ones that had words like *platinum* on the front. As if it were utterly routine, some of the girls chatted about shopping trips to New York City—and not to department stores, but to boutiques. They attended parties in New York, and not the birthday parties that Caitlin had grown up with. Elegant parties in clubs where one had to be approved before getting in the door! Caitlin was the youngest in her class. Her well-scrubbed Montana looks stood out, as did her athleticism and basic Old West friendliness that lacked a trace of attitudinal irony. Most of her classmates assumed she was a year or two older than she actually was.

Caitlin made one new friend in particular, Eva, with whom she felt a bond closer than any other student. Eva—a day student who commuted to Northpoint rather than a boarder like Caitlin—was outgoing and fun to be with, but also kind and compassionate. Eva openly admitted to enjoying kids' movies and childlike fun, in a milieu of girls who radiated studied sophistication. Eva said what she thought, a quality Caitlin found very appealing.

Eva was more concerned about Caitlin's homesickness than Mrs. Grayson. "Hey, do you want to come over for dinner on Saturday?" she asked after the two girls had gotten to know each other. "You might enjoy some old-fashioned family time away from campus, if you don't mind my crazy family."

"I would enjoy that very much. Are you sure your parents won't mind?"

"Are you kidding? They'll love you. But I have to warn you. My dad's an engineer and speaks in numbers, not words."

"We'll totally get along then," Caitlin said with enthusiasm.

"Sweet! I already told my parents you were coming, because I would have kidnapped you and dragged you home even if you said no," Eva said with a laugh and a hug.

"What should I bring?" Caitlin asked.

"Yourself and an appetite. Did I tell you that my mom is a great cook? She went to a culinary school for a year prior to switching to chemical engineering. She knows food chemistry better than anyone else."

"Wow."

"Yeah, which means we'll eat! *Bon appétit*! Then, luckily for you, you'll have the whole next week to work it off in field hockey, while I spend the week wallowing in sedentary guilt."

CHAPTER TWENTY-FOUR

U.S. Banking System Reels Under Cyber Attacks; White House Moves to Prevent Panic over Thefts as FBI Launches Global Criminal Investigation

The newspaper headlines screamed the story, and television news shifted into almost full-time coverage of new and breaking developments. John and Cindy now experienced a new level of *wartime*: the personal blossoming into the national, a shared alarm now in a terrifying assault on the banks that began with a sneak attack. When the talking head politicians bellowed allusions to Pearl Harbor, they were no less intense for the fact that much of the population now barely knew what Pearl Harbor had once represented to their grandparents and great-grandparents. Several of the basic elements held in common: It was a sneak attack, totally unanticipated. It generated fear. But unlike Pearl Harbor, the attack did not generate effective resolve.

This was a two-stage attack, not a single hideous assault—first a massive virus attack that pulverized the banks' Maginot Line–like security systems, and then, once the walls were breeched, a second firestorm assault that flooded into individual accounts and made off with a sum of money so large that no one initially had even an estimate of how much had been stolen. The thieves this time had not stopped at stolen Social Security numbers and birthdates; they had opened online accounts for existing bank accounts for hundreds of thousands of individuals who did not already bank online.

The thefts occurred over the holiday weekend but were not detected until Tuesday, because the banks were closed for Labor Day. Money was apparently moved on Friday night, because settlement in the U.S. happened at midnight. The trail was such that money moved to a bank in Mexico, where the settlement happens an hour later, and then to a Brazilian bank, which was another hour later. The money was then pulled out on Saturday, a working day in that country.

To head off panic, the government was assuring everyone that the situation was under control, an extensive investigation was underway at the highest levels of law enforcement, and that all of those whose bank accounts had been looted would be reimbursed through federal insurance.

"This isn't 'under control," John said woefully as he and Cindy absorbed the news.

"No," she replied, "it isn't."

"Do the insurance programs cover that much in losses?" he asked, acknowledging her extensive background in banking.

"Maybe, unless the figure is bigger than they're saying, which it may well be. At some point, somebody has to pay real money to cover losses, in any case. And even if they absorb one huge hit, what happens if there's another huge hit? Not to mention the damage to trust in the banking system."

"Without which there is no viable banking system?"

"Correct. Without an underlying foundation of trust, the banking system cannot function," she confirmed.

"And our friends the Serbians?" John asked.

"The news accounts kind of touch on the Enterprise, but way down in the stories in a kind of speculative way, which to me means that either the media or the government, or God forbid both, are not fully up to speed on what is driving this," she told him.

In the immediate aftermath of the attacks, the government froze each of the affected accounts and disconnected every affected bank from their network, until backup data could be validated and new protective walls could be built to repel any new attacks. Cindy was disturbed when she read about this phase of the reaction.

"Not a move I would have made," she said.

"Why?" John asked.

"They've shut everything down and created a vacuum, which only allows the Enterprise time and space to move money around outside of the United States. This is not good," she said.

And she was right. People who were out of cash because their bank accounts had been frozen were frightened, and that alarm spread through much of the unaffected population like a physical virus. In retail and grocery stores throughout the country, debit and credit card payments ran into brick walls, and purchases were rejected. People using subways, buses, and trains found themselves unaccountably stranded when debit and credit card transactions at ticket windows were declined. Many restaurants started posting "**Cash Only**" notices because of the growing number of bills that remained unpaid after credit cards failed. But cash also became difficult to acquire, not just for those whose accounts had been looted but, increasingly, for others who found that ATM machines had shut down and rather than giving cash, just gave infuriating messages like "**TEMPORARILY UNAVAILABLE**" on their screens.

The Stuarts were desperate for news, but were constrained by the meager news coverage of the local paper and their inability to go online for comprehensive news reporting, except for visits to the computer desk at the town library, which had to be kept to a minimum. Finally, John discovered that the national edition of the *New York Times* was available at a supermarket in Butte, and on several occasions, desperate for detailed news, he made the trip, over three hours each way, to buy a copy and bring it home.

Cindy was reading one of the stories when she looked up from the paper with a quizzical frown.

"John, didn't you know a man named Gary Cowan? The name is so familiar to me," she said.

"Gary Cowan? That's the chief IT guy from First Bank of Northern Pacific, the one who talked me into security consulting for that group of big bankers who met in New York, remember? Cowan was the organizer. Why? Is he quoted?"

She handed him the paper and said, "No, he's dead."

"Dead? How?" John asked, frantically scanning the report and finding the relevant paragraph, which read:

Meanwhile, a bank executive who had been coordinating industry efforts to improve banking computer-network security was found dead in his home in Sausalito, Calif., yesterday. Police identified him as Gary Cowan, 53, an executive vice president of First Bank of Northern Pacific, who died of gunshot wounds to the head. Police said they found no evidence of foul play, and a business associate of Mr. Cowan said he had undergone treatment recently for depression.

"I don't believe this was a suicide," John said, seeing the image of Cowan in his mind. "What makes you say that?"

"The patterns suggest that Gary was involved with the Enterprise. That's why he was pushing so hard and so openly for major spending on new IT security. One, he was laying down cover. Two, he knew—far better than I—that those other guys would never go out on a limb and commit their companies to spending that much for more effective security, not with the threat being so nebulous. So the whole idea simply died, and the status quo prevailed. And Gary Cowan thought he could play ball with the Enterprise, without knowing that he would become expendable."

"Really?"

"I'm betting that Gary, who had the highest security clearance level on the planet, was approached by the Enterprise and crossed over. Like all bank robberies, having an 'inside guy' is invaluable. So when the time was right, he surreptitiously opened a hidden gate in his own bank's software and told the Enterprise where to find it. Boom! Since banks are so interconnected, the virus was transmitted and spread like… well, like a virus. I warned these guys that their existing firewalls were totally inadequate…." John trailed off.

"What is it?" Cindy asked.

"Well, I had a very close look at Cowan's own security systems, and though they certainly needed a thorough upgrade in line with what I was advising, they were state of the art, such as it was at the time."

"Meaning what?"

"Meaning there is another dot needing connection. There has to have been at least one other top officer at Gary's bank involved for the initial entry by the Enterprise to have worked. The system was based on the kind of security that once protected our nuclear arsenal. Specifically, launching a thermonuclear ICBM required an agreement by two separate officers to turn two physically separate keys. As rudimentary as that system was, it arguably worked. We did not stumble into any unauthorized nuclear war with the Soviets. So, besides Gary Cowan, somebody else had to have turned a key. And that person is probably still there, undetected."

"So this could just be the start?" she said, following closely.

"That's what I fear. In all probability, assuming this theory is correct, the remaining insider is now actively plugging the forensics: the trail left behind in the form of IP packets that penetrated the network. From what I can see, those doors were left open a lot wider than was strictly necessary."

"Indicating that the barbarians are at the gate?" she said.

"No. Indicating that they're well inside the walls. And a lot more of them than the authorities believe," he said.

"ZRK is a top-tier criminal, brains like Einstein," John said after a minute.

"ZRK? You're talking as if you know this guy."

I sort of *do* know this guy…

"*Zerind Rokus Kazac.* Do you remember the top-secret conference I participated in where everybody used only their first names—and there was a contest, and a guy named Rob singlehandedly beat just about everyone? Remember how he beat just about everyone, except my team at that conference, which had been organized by government agencies. Then he made a spectacle of himself when he lost?"

"I remember," said Cindy.

"I did some research, there were eleven PhDs in network security awarded around that time frame at the advanced cyber-security center at UCLA, but I could account for only ten of them, all working for large companies or government or in academia. Except one, a Cincinnati born Zerind, whose middle initial incidentally was 'R'."

"I only vaguely follow you now," she said, as the subject went from banking to conspiracy.

John was animated by his own high-speed sleuthing. "Okay, so this is how it went down. By brilliantly and violently forcing me out of the picture, sending us all high-tailing into anonymous security in a secret location, he deftly sidelined a future nemesis. Then he had someone else assume my old identity. *Voilá*, he now has enhanced authority providing better access to the secret societies of those defending various public and private networks, not to mention law enforcement."

"That's some pretty freewheeling detective work, Sherlock," she said. "It's also terrifying, and we don't need any more terrorizing, John."

"All right, so let's find some good news," he said. "The good news is that the attacks don't affect us directly since we don't have bank accounts."

"Except for that out-of-town one where your royalty check goes."

"That's a small, obscure credit union that doesn't turn up on the radar for the Enterprise," he said.

"And of course our old bank accounts in Massachusetts. You know, back in our real lives?"

He had no reply to that except to shake his head solemnly.

"And money aside, we need to be even more careful, don't we?" she said in a low voice. "They seem to have a very wide reach. They killed Gary Cowan."

Again, he had no reply.

CHAPTER TWENTY-FIVE

Stocks Continue Free-Fall as Confidence Erodes in Banks; 401(k) Plans Plummeting With Mass Withdrawals of Funds

The news just kept getting worse. Within a week after news of the two-stage attacks, ZRK had become a familiar word in the headlines. But sources were also telling the media that the government and banks had installed the necessary backups and were comparing account balances and covering losses. Safeguards to thwart future brazen attacks were being rapidly put in place. But the news accounts were not coy, even if the authorities were desperate to avoid further panic. "Any subsequent major attack and run on the money could lead to the collapse of the entire financial system as we know it," one anonymous government source was quoted as saying—and it was obvious that the anonymous source was the secretary of the treasury.

As faith in the banking system wavered, many account holders rushed to withdraw money and hoard cash. The stock market had tumbled, with the Dow teetering at a dizzying 6,000 level, down more than half in a few months, and the vast majority of 401(k) plans, the bedrock of financial security for a huge segment of the working population, had nosedived into the red. With the economy in crisis, the Federal Reserve was scrambling to avoid a full-scale depression.

Like many other Americans, the Stuarts did their best to affect normalcy under extreme duress, but unlike so many others, they had long before become adept at it.

A few days later while jogging, John began brooding at the three-mile mark about their money in Massachusetts. His feet pounding with increasing fury into the hard earth, he thought: *Poor Cate has already been eliminated brutally by these vile bastards. And she was keeping an eye on the accounts. What's left? Anything?* It sickened him that, unlike in the old days when inquiries were answered promptly, when phone calls were returned, he was unable to reach out and ascertain the truth. He felt cold sweat soaking his back, a sudden illness in his stomach, and he mumbled "ZRK." He stopped running and stood frozen for a minute, feeling the wind tunneling down from the mountains. Sucking in deep breaths from frustration, not exhaustion, he turned and trudged back home.

*   *   *

Eyes Only
Department of Justice
Federal Bureau of Investigation
National Security Division
Washington, D.C.

Re: Cointel Priority; DOD Operation Cyber Pearl Harbor, NSA nb 'ZRK,' MIT CA & task forces.

MEMORANDUM: 658-09/A29a

Emergency meeting commenced at 0914EST (1414z), White House Situation Room. Attending: POTUS, VPOTUS, SECDEF, SECSTATE, SECDHS, SECDOJ, SECTREAS, JCS, DIRNSA, DIRCIA, DIRFBI, DDFBI

As a result of grave concerns in public at large around the safety of their money, the president called an emergency meeting on November 12. The consensus at this meeting, with no dissent, was that POTUS should address the nation on the grave crisis confronting the banking system.

Opening comments by the president of the United States:

"Our nation is suddenly at war, but no enemy soldier has set foot on our soil; no enemy has violated our physical space; not a single shot has been fired; no one has been injured or killed; there is no forward movement by any foreign armies. Yet our way of life is in imminent and grave danger as a result of brazen, cunning attacks on our national banking system being carried out via Internet viruses by shadowy criminal forces abroad."

"Their intentions can only be speculated upon until we know more. Who are they? Should we declare war against a criminal organization operating abroad with obvious impunity? Is this just a criminal assault that should be countered with an all-out law enforcement thrust? I submit to you that it is not; it is a war being waged upon our very way of life, and we must wage war, in return, against a new and insidious enemy. This enemy is waging a virtual war using WFD—weapons of financial destruction—and delivering substantial damage to the integrity of our financial system, which is the backbone of our global superpower status."

"No effort is being spared to isolate and identify the perpetrators of these heinous attacks, but there is no clear visibility. The suspects are two shadowy criminal organizations that have been widely identified as the Enterprise and AJ. We believe that, affiliated with them in nefarious, ever-shifting, and volatile alliances, are rogue elements of Russian intelligence agencies, including many with KGB backgrounds. We also believe that North Koreans cyber-crime operatives, as well as elements of Chinese intelligence, are working with these groups, though Director Toland [**DIRCIA JOHN C. TOLAND**] advises me that some of these are believed to be working in conjunction on an opportunistic basis, with no firm alliances. So I'll ask **Director Toland** to elaborate."

Comments by **JOHN C. TOLAND**, *director, Central Intelligence Agency:*

"Thank you, Mr. President. Besides the masterminds and their associates among Russian, Chinese, and North Korean cyber-criminal elements, we have ascertained that there are two other major criminal gangs involved, including one in the Ukraine whose role, apparently, is confined to violent enforcement to support the organization's on-ground activities, including the supplying of large amounts of military-grade weapons and other armaments, the purpose of which remains mostly unclear at this point. These guys are the muscle, and from what we know about them, they are very bad news. However, most of them aren't smart enough to log onto a Web site, let alone compromise a digital banking system, so we won't worry about them right now unless they start shooting people. Although if they do, we think the likelihood is they'll be shooting each other first because, as I always say, the first principal of geopolitical understanding is 'You Can't Fix Stupid.'"

(**NERVOUS LAUGHTER**)

SECSTATE ALICE H. TODD: "We do our best."

DIRCIA TOLAND CONTINUES: "Anyway, the motives are largely clear for the Enterprise, with some indications that they are backed up by Serbian nationalists who are still deeply aggrieved about our bombing and other military interventions in the Bosnian war. You know, when the Bosnian Serbs were slaughtering and raping innocent Bosnian civilians and thought it was none of our business? However, the motives behind the Russians seem deeper and more geopolitical. These breakaway characters seem to be motivated partly by an intense desire to avenge their unambiguous butt-whupping—oops, excuse me, Mr. President—*defeat* in the Cold War and the resulting division of the grand old Soviet Empire, oh *boo-hoo*."

POTUS: "Please, Johnny, just the facts."

DIRCIA TOLAND CONTINUES: "Yes, sir, Mr. President. So this time, instead of having the infrastructure support created by hundreds of billions of dollars' worth of what we have always known were second-rate weapons of mass destruction, they have decided that a new route has manifested itself. Their goal is to employ very sophisticated computer viruses and other hacking instruments to damage the nerve center of the enemy. Which would be us. Minuscule expense and the absence of potential exposure to actual armed combat make this very attractive. Their goal is to destroy us economically, and with the advent of networks and wireless devices with what we know to be extremely vulnerable security protections, they have been handed a golden opportunity while we are very exposed. Think of it as the same thing as having no security on our borders.

"Let me explain it in a bit more detail. The foundation of our economic system is the confidence in it by its citizens, businesses, and institutions. It's further buttressed by people around the world, their governments, and their own institutions. This is what separates us from the rest of the world. This is what makes us the sole superpower. If this reality becomes damaged or distorted, we can contemplate our future as a kind of glorified third-world country—but one saddled with a truly staggering first-world national debt. If people have diminished faith, the existing runs on our banks will become epidemic; people could really pull the plug by rushing to withdraw massive sums of money from the banks. Crashing down would come home loans, car loans, and that massive behemoth of credit card debt. Confronting significantly less capital, large and small businesses would be forced to shrink. Growth would be a memory. Consumer spending will plummet. Factories and retail businesses will shut down as current capacities and inventories become wildly excessive. Massive unemployment will ensue; folks will be stashing cash under mattresses; gun sales will go through the roof; crime will skyrocket, and tax evasion will grow to levels that we now see only in countries like Italy, Greece, and Russia. This will make the 1929 Depression look like a golden era. In effect, our system as we know it will collapse right in front of our eyes without a shot having been fired. And this could occur in such a short time—months, not decades. Rapid advances in technology have exponentially escalated risk and broadened the universe of unintended consequences."

POTUS: "Thank you, Johnny, for that rather horrifying summary of the fix we seem to be in. Why are we suddenly in this situation? For many years we have terribly managed our education with misplaced emphasis and consistently poor judgments about priorities. We had been acting as if we live in an insular world, and it's our God-given right to reign supreme. Well, it isn't. We forgot that our prosperity and our standing were earned the old-fashioned way, through hard work and persistence, and not handed down to us. The softer sciences yield us nothing in a virtual war. This is in sharp contrast to math, physics, or computer-science undergraduates or graduates, each one of who theoretically can become capable of delivering damage on a scale that formerly took a division's worth of soldiers in the wars of the past. Hence the discrepancy in our education systems. The enemy produces ten times more mathematics PhDs per capita than we do. Our top schools focus on churning out soldiers for Wall Street banks; the enemy is producing virtual soldiers to attack us on Main Street. So mark my words, this war is unlike anything else in history. It's a war of human capital, and to use a very old and subsequently discredited analogy, we have a missile-gap, ladies and gentlemen.

"So as a consequence, I am issuing a directive later tonight to make crash changes in the national educational system. We are at war, make no mistake about it, and we will act accordingly, and we will not need congressional approval to do so. I have also asked the secretary of education and the secretary of defense to come up with plans within seventy-two hours on how to train and equip 'cyber-army' divisions on very short notice, how to steer the existing pool and expand it quickly, and how to plan accordingly for the longer term. MIT, Stanford, Caltech, and Johns Hopkins have already been designated as point-universities for this unprecedented effort, and more will be selected.

"I should add that General Lee [**CHAIRJCS Gen. Joseph R. Lee, USMC**] has expressed concern that if we are determined to produce cyber warriors out of those schools, if we're really going to make them warriors, they ought to be as disciplined as United States Marines. These are free spirits, thinking outside the box. They don't march down the beaten path. It's gonna be a challenge, but we will succeed. We have to make them more like Marines."

VPOTUS: "Semper fi!"

POTUS: "I'm presuming that means that Vice President Snider would like for us to note that he once served as an officer in the United States Marine Corps."

SECDEF. SCOTT BROCK JR.: "As if we could ever be permitted to forget."

[**LAUGHTER**]

POTUS: "All right, then, maybe we won't send them to Parris Island for boot camp, but as we create this new cadre of cyber warriors, remember that our best hope is to somehow manage to come up with a force of outside-of-the-box thinkers and innovators who are nevertheless highly mission-focused and disciplined. Because these are really people we do not want going rogue on us. Okay, before we adjourn, I'm asking Dr. Guttberg [**SCIENTIFIC ADVISER TO POTUS DR. WILEM G. GUTTBERG**] to share some insights. As you know, Dr. Guttberg comes out of MIT by way of Stanford where he taught mathematics and developed that reputation as the nation's leading expert on encrypted coding and cyber security, Dr. Guttberg."

DR. GUTTBERG: "Thank you, Mr. President. I'll be brief. And all hail the outside-the-box thinkers, but keep your eye on them nevertheless—"

[**LAUGHTER**]

DR. GUTTBERG CONTINUES: "—With the advent and rapid dominance of these new technologies, each individual with their hundreds or thousands of unique attributes has been reduced to a commodity—numerized down to their Social Security numbers, dates of birth, credit card numbers, pin codes, and so on and so forth, ad infinitum. These specific identifiers, especially when collected in combinations, are profoundly stealable and fungible. In a cyber-universe, unique distinctions among humans have largely disappeared, as online transactions/communications/search online usage has skyrocketed. Bio markers certainly can help a bit in the short run, but they themselves can be hacked, and we may find ourselves in a situation that is even worse than what it is today. An example: A centralized depositary of fingerprints and optical scans, maintained by NSA and FBI, if hacked by those with ill intent, can then be used to beat just about any security measure in existence. The commoditization and anonymity facilitated by the Internet yields an explosive combination. This is exactly what the Enterprise and others have figured out—and their job is progressively getting easier by the day, as new technologies emerge. Look at it in part as a battle between convenience and connivance. And plan accordingly, because the threats are moving at warp speed. That's all I have to say."

POTUS: "Thank you, Professor Guttberg. Let's wrap this up because we all have to hit the ground running. These times demand urgent and an extremely careful approach to the grave danger we find ourselves in. And oh, I forgot, the FBI has one last thing to add. Director Freeman?"

DIRFBI CHRISTOPHER R. FREEMAN: "Ah, yes sir, Mr. President. The agency has designed a $25 million reward for information that leads to the capture of Zerind Rokus Kazac, whom we have designated as an international fugitive of direct interest to the United States of America. Thank you, sir."

VPOTUS: "A twenty-five mil bounty on this bird's head? Nothing high-tech about that!"

[LAUGHTER]

POTUS: "Okay, to work! Meeting adjourned and thank you all."

CHAPTER TWENTY-SIX

John was sitting quietly on the couch staring at a wall.

He thought, *the government certainly does not want me to be on the dark side with these criminals. So are they the ones who rummaged through the house, looking for evidence that I was working with the Enterprise? On the other hand, ZRK would definitely not want me working with the government while the Enterprise was attacking. So ZRK also has a motive.*

But why has ZRK not killed me? Thanks be to God and Marcus, it's possible that the Enterprise is not aware of my new identity and location. If the Enterprise is aware, which again is a possibility that finds some support in circumstantial evidence, then maybe ZRK would want me to join him—or at least stay neutral? One thing is for sure, if I do work with the government, I'm likely to be dead meat, the same as Marcus.

But why would ZRK want me now? I'll bet the Enterprise is feeling the full force of the government, intense international heat, probes galore. Maybe he needs another human dimension to keep him going at full-force. It's all so complicated! What did I do to deserve this? To see my wife and children deprived in this way?

He went into the kitchen, made a cup of coffee, and returned to his reverie on the couch. With a heavy sense of doubt, he thought: *I think the best way to stay alive is by not choosing sides. I hate this odious criminal ZRK. I would love to grab his neck and twist with my own hands—but on the other hand, how much do I trust the government? The Bureau has already abandoned me and Cindy once, left us high and dry to fend for ourselves. And whatever I might want to do myself, I always have to weigh the potential added risks for Caitlin and Emma.*

I am essentially caught between two forces. One is distinctly evil, and the other has a potential to abuse power that could result in it being evil. So staying neutral seems the only answer.

But on the other hand, is survival all that matters to me? Aren't there things bigger than survival?

The doors to the past are shut tight. The future appears to be as gloomy as a cold winter's day in Montana. I am stuck on a crossroad with nowhere to go, and the reward of staying in a holding pattern is staying alive.

With every minute going by, John got angrier and his resolve firmed up. *I cannot take it anymore; come hell or high water, I must get engaged, the nation is at war, and it is my responsibility, too. I cannot just sit idle. Besides this is the only ray of hope to get back to the past in the future.*

His thoughts were interrupted when Cindy and Emma walked in the front door after school. Seeing John so serious, she motioned him into their bedroom and shut the door.

"What is it? You look like you've been wrestling with a demon."

"I have been! I've been wrestling with ZRK. We cannot just stay on the sidelines while the country is under brutal attack."

"I wholeheartedly agree!"

"You realize there is a risk to all of our lives if I proceed?"

"John, as it is we are running around deathly afraid of this monster. Our lives have been reduced to nothing but day-to-day survival. The nation is at war, and if you don't do something about it, then there may be nothing left to go back to. You have beaten him before, and I am confident you can do it again."

"My only hesitation is the danger this would pose to your life and the kids' lives."

"We all have to die one day—that is the inevitable forecast for everyone. If I had your skill, I would have jumped already with two feet in."

"Okay, I am on it."

CHAPTER TWENTY-SEVEN

Eyes Only
Department of Justice
Federal Bureau of Investigation
National Security Division
Washington, D.C.

MEMORANDUM: TOP SECRET

To: DDFBI Broomall, Thomas A.
From: SPAC D'Amato, Marissa, Special Tactical Unit

Per order 267-76A2(DIR), Special Agent in Charge Marissa D'Amato has requested and received from Central Intelligence Agency Special Operations Unit (CIASOU) transcript of a surveillance recording NSA/CIA per DIRFBI/DIRCIA, subject **ZERIND ROKUS KAZAC** (REFERENCED HEREIN AS **ZRK**), reliably reported by informants and intelligence to be the head of a widespread global criminal organization, the **ENTERPRISE**, with suspected illegal and terroristic activities based in eastern Europe, including Russia, and reliably believed to be the master perpetrator behind recent massive cyber attacks on United States banking digital networks. *_CIA reports: As **ZRK** and associates are known to avoid standard and encrypted wireless communications, audio surveillance was conducted via networks of ISMI-catcher antennae installed (cyphering indication feature suppressed) at known suspect locations, cafes, and other frequented public and semi-public locations in and in the vicinity of Belgrade, Serbia._*

A summary of that recording has been made.

Intercept: Café Dtrazic, believed to be one of several headquarters locations used by ZRK in the Belgrade, Serbia, municipality of Barajevo, lower Sumadija.

Background: **ZRK** has been enormously ambitious in self-perceived goals, which he has described (MEMORANDUM 237A-67ZRK) as "the restoration of the respect of the Serbian nation for the sacrifices made over 100 years against Turk invasion to protect Europe and Christianity in 15th and 16th centuries and have the forces of evil that have dared to attack it be held accountable. [**The reference is believed to be to the United States of America**]"

Following is a summarized report on intercepted conversation between **ZRK** and a criminal associate identified as **LAADISLAO SYANISLAS ABADEZIEV** (REFERENCED HEREIN AS **LSA**), who had been described as **ZRK**'s top aide. **LSA** is a known enforcer for the operation.

It is noted that both **ZRK** and **LSA** speak English. **ZRK** speaks English like an American from the Midwest; **LSA**, however, speaks English with a Serbian accent. The reverse is true for when he speaks Serbian.

TRANSCRIPT FOLLOWS:

ZRK: Remember the guy I told you about?

LSA: What guy?

ZRK: The guy that got the first award at that top-security conference I was at years ago, where I cracked six of his team's seven gates? And the way I saw it, that meant he could only protect one?

LSA: I remember. You're still seething over that? His name was Gavin something?

ZRK: Gavin Brinkley. A first-rate guy, exceptionally bright. Did I ever tell you how he protected the seventh gate?

LSA: No. Tell me.

ZRK: Well, when I finished the sixth gate and proceeded to the seventh, he went in and made a change and somehow I stumbled. It defied logic. Unprecedented. I had never been stumped this way. So I asked a couple of the feds with the government agencies who were running this contest and how did I lose to this guy? They played cute. Told me nothing, zero, nada. Then that night I went to the lounge at the place where the conference was held and asked **JAKE,** who was Gavin's teammate, and he also refused to give anything up. Told me to go pound sand. Then the second teammate, **NORM** [*identity unknown*], comes by and he says, laughing, "Dude, you got royally stumped today!" The words felt like someone put a knife through me.

Norm says to me, "Look, you were incredible, very impressive feat. No one else even came close to what you did—and you did it single-handedly, no partner, no team. I was very worried when you knocked the fifth gate because there was no time to protect the sixth, and then the seventh would be relatively narrow to get to. Man, you were good." I told him, "Thanks, Norm."

And Norm says to me, "So did you figure it out?"

I tell him I did not. And Norm says, "Okay, I'll tell you, Rob. It's pretty funny. What happened was, Gavin changed the cyclic codes used in the security configuration so that 2 plus 3 was deliberately added and then coded as 4 instead of 5—so all the algorithms switched for you at the last minute." And Norm starts laughing and says, "Gavin is frigging brilliant, isn't he?"

I was shocked; I could not believe it! I couldn't *believe* that someone could do such a silly thing in this high-stakes game. But that is *exactly* what worked. It was like a kindergartener's move; it defied all logic, defied all that I had learned as a mathematician and blocked my ability to predict the next step. I am the best mathematician alive or who has ever lived! How do you explain this? Since then every so often I keep replaying it in my head: Could it come to haunt us if we do not learn from it?

LSA: Well—

ZRK: I keep analyzing what am I lacking and I finally realize, it's the human dimension.

LSA: Oh, man, don't let that human weakness come near you. It's forbidden for the very best. We need to protect each other against it. We must be resolute in our determination and maintain faith in our ability.

ZRK: I hear you, but listen: The human dimension is different than human weakness. The key to success is to learn even from your worst enemies, or at least the worthy ones. That's where you become formidable. We cannot allow our egos to blind us—*that's* the human weakness. I don't have that weakness, but the subjectivity introduced by the human dimension leads to uncertainty—and I loathe uncertainty.

Listen, Gavin is a nearly perfect mathematician, but his proximity to that human dimension gave him the edge in that instance. The good news is that, having the human dimension means he has the human weaknesses, too—and that prevents him from doing what we do.

Now, I would ask rhetorically: Could he provide a dangerous obstacle when he is not on our side? I answer my own question: Gavin on our side would be an insurance policy for our success. Now, I'm confident we will win; however, this is not a foolproof guarantee. *He* would make us complete, would round up that extremely high probability of success to a certainty. This would eliminate the risk of us getting stuck in a holding pattern, or taking longer to succeed than is advisable. I cannot and do not wish to delay our success a minute longer than necessary.

LSA: Why don't we just kill him?

ZRK: Absolutely not! We need him alive and willing!

LSA: So why don't I just grab him? Wouldn't that help?

ZKR: No! You cannot force someone into brilliance, no matter how much stress you put them under. One can always sub-perform at will.

LSA: Even if I had a gun on his child's head? In that case I'll bet he'd do exactly what you want him to do.

ZRK: But how do I *know* what I want him to do? If I knew that, I would have just done it myself. It's probing the unknown, anticipating the other side's defenses and coming up with a better attack. All these together are like playing a seven-dimensional chess game. There would always be that risk that he might deliberately leave a trace behind, which would be suicidal. No, we need him alive and willingly cooperating

LSA: But forgive me, aren't you being naïve, Zerind? Why would he do that?

ZRK: He hates concentrations of power and those forces who tell individuals what to do. So listen, if he feels that he is being squeezed by the big almighty government, he might join us. *There's* his human weakness, and he will likely succumb to it.

LSA: Oh. Okay, got it! So let me reach out and have him squeezed by the government then.

ZRK: Great. But by the way, first you've got to find him.

LSA: Not to brag, but when have I ever not found my hunt? What hole have I not pulled the rat out from?

[END OF TRANSCRIPT)

CHAPTER TWENTY-EIGHT

Cindy's phone rang around ten o'clock at night just as she had dozed off on the couch. She saw that it was John calling.

He sounded terrible. "I was in a bit of trouble, just wanted to let you know. I'm okay."

"What do you mean you're okay? What was even wrong?" she asked anxiously.

"Keep an eye out for Emma and yourself. Do not open the door for anyone. I'll call you back in a few minutes," he said, and the call ended.

Frantic, Cindy jumped off the couch, grabbed her pistol, turned on all the lights in the house, and walked into Emma's room. She was fast asleep.

Ten minutes later, John called back still sounding breathless. "You wouldn't believe what just happened. I had paid for my gas, and was heading back to the car... I was about to open the car door, when the headlights on another car about fifty feet away suddenly snapped on—high beams—I couldn't see a thing! Then the car started toward me. I tried to open my door as fast as I could. Two men jumped out of the other car, just as I was starting my engine; even as I started to take off, these guys were still trying to drag me out. I spun the car in a circle, which threw both of them on the ground. They fired a few shots but by then I was out of their reach."

"My God, John! Who were they? Did you get a look at their faces?" Cindy realized that in her self-protective panic, she had forgotten to ask the most important question: "Are you all right?"

"Yeah... I burned some rubber getting out of there, I'll tell you that.

The other car tried to chase me, but I was far enough ahead and knew the area well enough that I shook them."

"Are they still there?"

"I lost them I think. No idea who it was; they were wearing ski masks, bulky jackets—nothing identifying."

When he got home fifteen minutes later, Cindy was waiting with her gun in her hand. They hugged. Despite the cold weather, John was sweating.

Fear had returned in full fury.

CHAPTER TWENTY-NINE

Two thousand miles away, Caitlin had shaken some of her feelings of homesickness. In her first semester, she had received her adviser's permission to take elective classes in forensic science, in addition to the requisite full schedule of English, trigonometry, music, history, Latin, and chemistry. It was rare for a student to take seven classes, even as a junior or senior, but because of her obvious industriousness and demonstrated work ethic, she was cleared for the extra course. She had also made the varsity hockey team and was thriving as a forward. By the end of her first six weeks at Northpoint School, she could honestly say school life was both exciting and enjoyable.

One extracurricular activity that was required of all freshmen was to navigate through the BlueBrook nature preserve and come out on the other side with only the aid of a partner, a map, and a compass. No cell phones were allowed. Her partner was Jennifer, who hailed from a wealthy New York family. Jennifer always dressed in designer fashions and was not overly keen about classes. Anyone who met Jennifer soon learned that she had traveled with her parents all over the world. She had been on a safari in Africa. She had been to the Taj Mahal, to Machu Picchu, to the Duomo in Florence. Places like Disney World were beneath her perceived status, and only when pressed would she admit she had been there. "We stayed at the Grand Floridian," she would say, casually mentioning the most expensive five-star hotel at the Florida resort.

About a half hour into the woods, Caitlin and Jennifer had a disagreement about which path to take. Jennifer insisted that they had to go left, and a bit of an argument ensued, but Caitlin decided to follow Jennifer's lead so as not to offend the more fragile ego of her orienteering partner. The duo kept walking for another hour, until they realized that they had been in the woods for much longer than should have been required.

Jennifer panicked and started blaming Caitlin. Caitlin kept her cool and fell back on the navigational skills she had learned over the years with her parents in Montana, insisting that they walk in a specific direction based on the position of the sun. About an hour later they found a path, and soon they could see a home in the distance. They picked up the pace.

Tired and exhausted, they walked along an old farmers' stone wall. In the backyard was a big trampoline. There was a woman lounging on the portico reading a book, and on a path nearby was a young girl riding a bike. It was a very large home. The woman, who appeared to be in her early to mid-thirties, saw them, got up, and looked at them with patient understanding.

"Lost, girls?" she said, putting down her book.

"Yes ma'am," Caitlin replied.

"Northpoint School?"

"Yes, ma'am."

"How long have you been out there?"

"Like three hours," Jennifer said.

"Two hours and ten minutes," Caitlin corrected her.

The woman laughed and said, "Don't worry, you are not the first intrepid pair to get lost by a long stretch." She introduced herself as Lisa, and the girls introduced themselves in turn.

"Would you guys like to use the washroom or have some water?" the woman asked them. Both girls were very thirsty. Caitlin had tried to insist that they hike with bottles of water, as she had been carefully taught in Montana, but Jennifer sniffed at the idea.

At Lisa's invitation, they sat down for a few minutes. The interior of the house was the most beautiful Caitlin had ever seen. They saw another teenager walking around, and in the huge dining room, pushing a vacuum, was an older woman who appeared to be the housekeeper. There were a lot of family photographs on tables and shelves, but Caitlin noticed that many of them appeared to be in new frames.

"You have a very beautiful home," Caitlin told Lisa, who studied her for a moment and then thanked her politely.

"Why don't I drive you back to school?" Lisa suggested. "It's five miles away."

Jennifer seemed impressed that they had walked at least five miles. To Caitlin, the effect was the opposite. On a hunting trip with her father and their neighbors Bruce and Maloney, they had once walked eighteen miles and thought little of it.

They took Lisa up on her offer of a ride. Other than the lodge resort at Yellowstone National Park, Caitlin had never seen a home this big, inside or out. Jennifer, while curious, didn't seem quite as impressed. Lisa led them to the garage, where there were four cars parked. Jennifer admired the first one, a Porsche Turbo, and announced that her father had one just like it. Lisa led them to an SUV and the girls climbed in. They pulled out of the garage, drove down a side driveway, and then headed slowly toward a tree-lined two-lane road out front. Caitlin turned around, staring at the front of the vaguely familiar looking home from the long, winding driveway. Then Lisa turned right onto Monument Street.

A short distance away, Lisa pointed out a pretty, old-looking wood pedestrian bridge built on rock pilings that spanned the placid little Concord River.

"Do you guys know what that bridge is?"

Jennifer shrugged and made a face. Caitlin thought she knew, though she had never seen it.

"The Old North Bridge?" she said.

"Right! And what happened there, do you know?"

Jennifer wisecracked, "I didn't know we were going to have a test."

But Caitlin knew her history. "That's where the Battle of Concord began in 1775, on the first day of fighting in the Revolutionary War, right?"

"Right," Lisa said. "Actually, this bridge is a historical reconstruction, but that's the exact spot all right. It's a very popular tourist spot in the warm months. I'm surprised you two haven't seen it."

"We're still freshmen," Jennifer explained petulantly. "They don't let us out much except to go get lost in the woods without our cell phones."

Caitlin addressed Jennifer as they drove past the bridge. "We'll come back some day, now that we know the way."

"We do?"

"*I* do, Jennifer. This is worth seeing. This is where the Patriot militia and the British troops first engaged in battle. You know Ralph Waldo Emerson?"

"Of course I do," Jennifer said peevishly. "He was like, a writer, or something."

"Emerson was the one who wrote about that battle later on and called it the 'shot heard 'round the world'," Caitlin said.

"Oh," Jennifer replied without much interest. "How come you know so much about this when you just got here from Missouri?"

"Montana," Caitlin said. "I guess I'm just interested in history. Also, I'm always interested in my surroundings."

As they approached the playing fields of Northpoint School, the SUV dropped them off at their dorm beyond the hill. Caitlin noticed that Lisa was studying her with curiosity through the rear-view mirror.

It seemed that the dawn would never come. She both longed for the morning, and feared for the finality of events that it would bring. Would it be possible for time to somehow reverse its course and speed her backward to before the events described in the pages of her book? Both dreams and nightmares come to the same in the end—they vanish in the light of day. Her reality was certainly not a dream nor could it be described as a nightmare. In fact, it had all the makings of something far worse.

CHAPTER THIRTY

Hacker Attacks Cripple Social Networking Accounts Nationally; Grave Fears Spread Over Internet Privacy–Invasion Peril

At four o'clock in the morning Eastern Daylight Time on October 23, the profile pages of the largest social networking company, Friendsbook, abruptly went haywire in the northeastern United States. Those who were online at that dim hour of the morning—and their numbers were at least in the hundreds of thousands—were perplexed to find their computer, smartphone, and tablet screens displaying not their own individual profiles, but instead the profile of a total stranger, with a totally different and unknown collection of that stranger's photos and comments and friends.

After tapping away insistently at the problem, which of course was assumed by users to be isolated and probably immediately fixable, many people gave up and made phone calls or text messages to friends who they had reason to believe were also up and online at this hour of the morning.

My fb profile went insane! Acct unavail, but I get strangers stuff. Weird! U having problems? So went a typical text message being dispatched into the predawn ether.

And the reply came back: **At the keyboard but also nuts. C u ltr!**

A thousand times, and then a hundred thousand, and then tens of millions of times such messages beamed into the wireless spectrum and rippled westward across the country as the time zones came fully and successively online and requests for service hit into one another in sickening succession, the most catastrophic traffic pileup ever witnessed, or indeed contemplated, on the Internet superhighway. Shock waves radiated across the country as monstrous freight trains of words, caravans of urgent sentences, careened and jackknifed impotently into digital ditches. As word of the failures spread, people who normally would not even be online rushed to tap out text and e-mail messages that fell in the digital void like trees crashing in an empty forest, unseen and unheard. When one account failed to work, alternative e-mail accounts were utilized, adding exponentially to the pileups. Everything, of course, was connected. So the panic advanced through the Web like a vast tumbling tsunami, churning destructively over continents of digital terrain with terrifying impunity. Throughout the country, Internet service providers and wireless carriers crashed as the volume grew. Everyone with a Friendsbook account in the United States experienced a sudden and complete loss of the privacy they assumed they had—as foolish as that assumption might have been. The sickening realization infected every generation: from students to parents to grandparents, all linked together in social networks, all thoroughly stripped of their privacy.

And no one knew what force of terror had orchestrated this assault.

Vast Internet Blackout Stuns Nation; Anonymous Hacker Group Surfaces Denouncing Web Threats to Privacy

Company officials, horrified by the ease with which their supposedly impregnable security barricades had been overrun, emerged from an emergency meeting at the White House to announce that a herculean effort was underway to restore the situation to normal. This only resulted in an even more ferocious response from the anonymous hackers. A devilishly cryptic blog suddenly appeared on tens of millions of screens across the country warning, in text accompanied by a menacingly deep voice augmented with echo-chamber effects that the Friendsbook site would remain shut down for forty-eight hours.

"Any further arrogant and futile efforts to remedy this situation will

restart the clock for an additional forty-eight hours of darkness," the text and resonating voice said. *"We have done this to get your undivided attention, America. This is a protest against the concentration of so much information under one crypto-corporate roof. It is also a proclamation about the growing risks of an unprecedented, yet widespread invasion of the public's inherent right to privacy. We demand that serious initiatives begin immediately to desist the practice of sharing personal information to either the government or to private parties for unjustified financial gain, without due process, including legal warrant. We apologize for this deep civic inconvenience, but our goal is to galvanize public awareness of the risks inherent when so much personal information is carelessly shared on digital networks. If we do not hear of major changes to the policies of this company within forty-eight hours, access to its users will be restored, but each user's account will have randomly selected strangers appearing as 'friends.' In other words, you must be prepared to get to know your fellow Americans in intimate and detailed ways that you never thought possible previously. God bless America!"*

In Montana, the Stuarts, such avid online users back when they were the Brinkleys, were in the strange position of not being directly impacted in the attacks on Friendsbook. They found out not through accessing their own profiles, but through media channels such as the television and newspaper. Who, they wondered, was behind these attacks?

"Could this also be the Enterprise?" Cindy speculated. "The usual suspects, so to speak?"

John shook his head. "I highly doubt it. Consider, there's no money to be made by doing this, at least from what I can determine. So I have my doubts. Unless it's the world's most malicious prank by some tech grad students, it's from people who just want to make a very serious point, even at the great cost that this involves the country."

"They certainly knew how to make that point," she said.

"Precisely," he replied with no sense of irony.

Internet Attacks Laid to Loose Network of Serbian Hackers, U.S. Privacy Activists

Within days, the government said it suspected the attacks to be the handiwork of the Enterprise or AJ, possibly in conjunction with a shadowy group that called itself Citizens Anonymous. Several anonymous experts quoted in the news accounts, who had been monitoring the clandestine Web and other networking activities of Citizens Anonymous, suggested that the group consisted of some highly accomplished cyber experts and ad hoc hackers who were operating with the belief that they were protecting the public welfare, even if they did work under the radar.

"The government can point fingers wherever they want—I think it's just people, this Citizens Anonymous outfit, trying to make a point," John told his wife.

"And the point is?" she asked.

"That most people realize how thoroughly, profoundly, and *efficiently* our personal information is progressively getting concentrated in fewer and fewer hands. Most people don't realize that search engines, retailers, credit card companies, banks, and everyone else who collates this data, all collectively and cooperatively know more about the individual than anyone else does—including that individual's spouses, parents, children, close friends, and associates. The tragedy of the whole situation is that we're merrily cooperating right along with this! People are volunteering incredible amounts of easily connected personal data about themselves. Imagine how deliriously happy Stalin would have been if you had told him that one day—not all that far off from his time—an entire free society like that of the U.S. would end up willfully cooperating to compile personal data on an unprecedented scale into the hands of a few entities!"

Cindy sighed and sat down comfortably in a worn-in armchair, preparing herself for what she could tell would be a classic John rant.

"Take this for an example: Say someone is searching for a wedding ring online. What do they see? Instantly, boatloads of wedding related ads, even though they may not yet have selected a spouse! Search engines have the absolutely breathtaking ability to drill down right into your personal core, to slice and dice your preferences and quirks and experiences, your likes and dislikes, your opinions and attitudes and anxieties and health concerns and even your most intimate secrets—which can be so easily inferred and compiled logarithmically into a marketable narrative—and then boom! They sell that profile—that narrative of the real you—to anyone who chooses to pay for it. And not only is this narrative available for purchase to anyone, it also streams uninterrupted before the appraising eyes and rapacious archives of government agencies, of law enforcement, and of our burgeoning intelligence and surveillance apparatus.

"All of the Internet businesses and search engines raise their eyes to heaven and preach to you that they have safeguards, they have privacy standards, they have scruples—that the information they collect on you is protected. Well, as we're seeing now, protected against *whom*, exactly? Against the *amateurs*, basically. Because this data is easily pillaged by a cunning insider with criminal or other malicious intent; by rogue bureaucrats or corporate entities solely focused on profit at any cost. This is far worse than the old version of Big Brother watching you. Big Brother had to wait to see you do something, and you could distract him if you were smart and vigilant. But *Big Brother 2.0* is omniscient, fully capable of seeing into your most private concerns, utterly devoid of conscience or emotion, utterly confident that each citizen will submit to scrutiny at levels never before seen in human existence."

Cindy's eyes had grown wide listening to John, and she felt queasy. "You're talking as if you agree with all this nonsense," she said.

"I'm not saying I like that Friendsbook was hacked. But I do believe that the concentration of so much individual data, essentially in one vast and easily breached vault, is profoundly dangerous—dangerous to individuals, to their liberty, and if I might add, to their identities."

"Do people who surrender their private information so readily even deserve the right to privacy?" Cindy asked pointedly.

John replied, "Absolutely. The fact that usage of information beyond what was an originally a simple search or a transaction can evolve into something much more sinister isn't the individual's responsibility. The average Internet user can't necessarily be expected to see the larger picture. Reading the privacy policies of some of these websites practically requires a law school degree, not to mention patience with boilerplate and fine print. The truth is that once the information is in the hands of third parties, all bets are off about its protection. Freedom should be the *default*. Usage of the information should require explicit approval. Unfortunately, it's exactly the reverse right now."

"You sound upset," she decided, seeing how intense he had become.

"I'm beyond upset," John replied. "I'm deeply alarmed. Today, you can't drive through most major intersections in the country without being photographed and tracked by satellites. *Satellites*, for God's sake! You cannot buy anything in a convenience store or gas station without being photographed; where you are at any point is tracked by your cell phone. You can't even use a public restroom without it being noted and recorded! At home you can't type a simple keystroke without it being recorded and interpreted. You cannot send an e-mail over the Internet without it being scanned by the federal intelligence apparatus for key words. Read a newspaper and you're tagged as being part of a certain ideology. And forget about the kind of exposure you open yourself to when you're looking at your own financial data! Bottom line, you cannot read, write, move, shop, communicate, or have an opinion without being monitored and recorded."

"This is so depressing," Cindy said morosely. "So what do you suggest?"

He thought for a few seconds and replied, "Most importantly, people have to become aware of the pitfalls, to be vigilant against these omnipresent invisible chains of confinement that constitute a deep and fundamental threat to our privacy, and hence to our liberty."

"And that's possible?" she asked warily.

He shrugged the question off. "But we also have to be aware of the impending threat to our lifestyle. Most of the infrastructure these days, such as the chemical plants and nuclear plants, are automated and controlled by their respective software. Each is then connected, inextricably, by vast networks. So by infecting such equipment, they can be made to malfunction in ways not anticipated by their designers, protectors, and users, with consequences beyond imagination. Can you think what would happen if the systems in a big chemical plant suddenly malfunctioned? The equipment and the networks have to be extremely well designed and protected—but we're fighting the old war and are unprepared for the new one. This constitutes a vulnerability to our national economy, not to mention our national security, far worse than the one that existed in the old days of the Soviet Union. At least then it was only one enemy with not very sophisticated technology, even if they did have a lot of very big bombs and, like us, very efficient ways to deliver them. The Soviets needed a huge military infrastructure, and were struggling throughout the Cold War under the costs of maintaining that capability against ours. But today, a few exceptionally bright individuals, men and women in any corner of the world, can pose a threat to us of a magnitude greater than a nuclear attack, and they can do it cheaply, with technology available to anyone who knows how to employ it. That's the risk which is least understood by the public at large. They have no idea how quickly our lifestyle could be badly damaged, if not destroyed."

Emma padded in with a cell phone and dejected expression in tow. "Dad, I texted Caitlin two *entire* hours ago and she's not responding."

"I am sure your sister is at field hockey practice or chorus or something. Don't worry about it." John said half-heartedly.

"But she never talks to me anymore. Ever since she's gone to Northpoint, it's as though she replaced me with her other friends. It's not cool."

"Come on Emma, you know that's not true. I promise we will call her later this evening."

Emma pouted and sulked off.

John went on, "So we need to focus on the large picture. An extremely bright person acting alone today can cause more damage to a country than entire armies did even in World War II. A clever hacker can completely shut us down. Imagine how much misery they can cause in a single day! And then you have the matter of the concentration of data about every individual in the hands of very few, with such data open to immense abuse by the government and big corporations. I don't believe that there ever has been such a situation in the history of mankind."

Cindy had had enough of first imagining, and then fearing, the worst. She brought the subject back to the immediate present, the hacking attack that had caused much of the Internet to tumble along. "How can you be so certain that it's Citizens Anonymous? It could be someone else trying to malign that group's name?" she asked.

He said, "That wouldn't surprise me either. There are many organizations with these skills. Some are pure evil greed such as the Enterprise, and then there are ones in the gray area who move back-and-forth. The best ones are few and far between. Most are petty criminals.

"To make matters worse, individual agendas of each group can at times be hijacked by the others, sometimes to confuse law enforcement, sometimes only to discredit other groups. So to get back to your earlier question, yes, it's possible that the Enterprise did this, and deliberately left the virtual fingerprints of Citizens Anonymous behind to discredit Citizens and at the same time force the politicians and corporate oligarchy to respond to the public outrage by cracking down on them. But on the other hand, while it's entirely possible that Citizens did it to make it look like the Enterprise's handiwork—to force the government to crack down on the Enterprise—I believe the odds on that are low. The people who belong to the groups such as Citizens tend to be folks who are concerned about the public welfare of country. While they may break the law at the fringes, they're not really criminals at heart."

Cindy asked, "So what's your gut feeling?"

"I believe Citizens Anonymous is trying to deliver a huge blast of shock therapy. To wake up the society at large to these dangers."

Cindy was thinking about Caitlin, seemingly disconnected almost a continent away. "John," she said, "I think Caitlin has, or had, a Friendsbook profile that she started at school. She swore to me that she'd be discreet. All her school friends are on it, and she felt like the odd girl out."

John felt a jolt. "What are you talking about? Do you know how big a risk that is? I can't believe this.... Why didn't you tell me?"

"I didn't want to worry you."

"What did she have on it?" John demanded.

"Mostly school friends' pictures."

"*Mostly*?"

"Well she said she had some pictures of you and me, and also of Emma. Some general Montana stuff. I told her immediately to remove those pictures and that information, and she did without asking questions. I checked. But she was deeply confused and unhappy. She said, 'Mom, why can't we just be a normal family for once? What are we always afraid of? None of my other friends have any such restrictions. Why I am so different?' She was crying."

"What did you tell her?" he asked, unable to conceal his concern about a door that his daughter may have inadvertently opened wide in Massachusetts. *There are no borders on the Internet,* he thought with bitter frustration.

Cindy said, "I told her, 'Caitlin, honey, everyone has some wrinkles in their lives including your friends. It's just that ours are more unconventional than theirs. We are a loving family where everyone cares for each other so deeply and relies on each other.' She didn't fully understand, but you know Caitlin. She *comprehended*, in her own way. She's such a wonderful kid. And she deleted her profile page."

CHAPTER THIRTY-ONE

Halloween approached New England dressed in autumn's natural splendor of orange and gold. The ripe displays of foliage only added to the sense of anticipation Caitlin felt in the communal atmosphere of Northpoint School, where the holiday was a grand tradition. Students planned, designed, and executed elaborate costumes and spilled off campus into the surrounding areas for gleeful trick-or-treating starting around dinnertime. Unaccustomed to such frivolity, Caitlin eagerly sought details, and even made a few suggestions about which neighborhoods she and her friends should troop through that night. Caitlin consulted a town map and suggested a particularly ritzy neighborhood, assuring her friends that it was not that far away. In such an affluent neighborhood the bounty of candy was likely to be impressive for the effort involved.

"What are you going as?" Jennifer asked her, aware of how busy she had been in theater shop after class working on her costume.

"I'm a devil paparazzi!" Caitlin announced. "Actually, the correct form would be the singular paparazzo, but that sounds odd."

"You are so creative! What in the world is a devil paparazzi anyway?"

"A photographer who stalks famous people, but in this case it's a devil photographer, which some people would agree is appropriate. Wait till you see my costume with all the paraphernalia, like the big pockets I made for carrying accessories. And every time I click the camera shutter it triggers a spring that makes a *papier-mâché* devil's head pop out of the hat. That took me weeks to get right."

"This I have to see," Jennifer said, rolling her big brown eyes.

"This you will see," Caitlin assured her.

When Halloween finally arrived, Caitlin and three other costumed friends headed out to their chosen neighborhoods. Soon they were approaching the house that Caitlin so anxiously wanted to visit. As they neared the driveway, Caitlin felt her heart pounding. It was about five p.m. and there were a few early kids out trick-or-treating. There was some sunshine left as they walked down the long driveway and admired the beautifully manicured lawn and tasteful gardens. Some hazy image started to form in her head, elusive and perhaps a dream not recalled: the old stone wall, the pool, and the canopy of great tall trees.

When Caitlin pressed the bell, a woman wearing a tiara and a long frilly princess-style dress opened the door and, projecting delight, asked the girls in turn who or what they were dressed as. Caitlin had moved to the rear of the group and when her turn came to reply, she responded by snapping a photo of the woman. On cue, up popped the wickedly grinning *papier-mâché* devil's head, which Caitlin was relieved to see worked as designed. Everyone laughed in appreciation of her theatrical skill. As they were holding open their bags for the woman to drop candy in, a man arrived accompanying a preteen girl and greeted the group jovially. He had a beard and was wearing a Spiderman jacket with a web motif.

"Where do you go to school?" the man asked the girls. When they replied Northpoint, he and the woman stood smiling at the door and seemed impressed. Caitlin demonstrated her clever devil-paparazzi costume design again, snapping a quick picture of the man and his daughter. Caitlin suggested that the gentleman try the devil hat and take a picture of her and her friends. He agreed, and she gave him the demon's horned hat to try on.

"Be careful, I had to make the inside surface rough so it didn't slip off when the devil's head pops out," she warned him.

"Don't worry!" he laughed, pulling the hat onto his head, where it sat at an odd angle because of the tight fit. The man then took some photos of Caitlin and her friends, who trooped off happily with a growing haul of goodies from the bounteous neighborhood.

When Caitlin got back to her dorm room, she immediately looked at all the pictures of their Halloween jaunt, many dozens of pictures. She cropped and arranged the photos online, wrote a happy note and e-mailed the photo album to her parents labeled "Halloween Hijinks!"

John had judiciously acquired a nonbrand smartphone, which he was careful to use only for e-mail with SIM cards.

It was still early on Halloween night in Montana, two hours behind the East Coast. "Caitlin just sent some Halloween photos!" he happily told Cindy when he saw the e-mail.

Cindy bounded out of the kitchen to the living room. "Can we see them on a bigger screen?" she asked.

"Sure," he said. "I'll just transfer them to my laptop."

They bent over the laptop with delight, perusing each of the photos, zooming in on each in turn for a better look at the detail.

"Look how pretty and happy she is!" Cindy said of her daughter, who was growing up so fast.

"She's wonderful," John said with great pride.

"And such nice friends," Cindy added.

"You can tell, yes," John agreed. He looked at the dreamy gaze in Cindy's eyes and asked her, "Are you crying? Why?"

"She's so far away, John. Our little girl is growing up," she said through happy but poignant tears.

John sniffed a little himself, painfully aware that he had not been able to chance the trip to Massachusetts with his wife and daughter when she started school.

He clicked onto another photo.

They both froze.

There was their old home in Concord.

Cold fear descended on them, but mixed emotions also broke through. They had multiple and identical flashbacks seeing close-ups of their old lives in that home: the lawn and the gardens, the columns at the grand entrance, the farmers' stone walls.

Then the jingly sound of their own doorbell startled them back into real time in Montana.

Through a part in the curtain they could glimpse a group of children who had been driven into the rural part of town by a parent to do some trick-or-treating.

"I'll get it," Cindy said, hurrying off to answer the door. She expressed wonderment at the children's costumes, and dropped candy into their bags. She quietly shut the door as they chorused thank-yous and ran back to the idling car on the road.

Hearts pounding, they were at the laptop screen again examining Caitlin's photos.

The next picture showed a blond woman wearing a tiara. Her face was painted. The photograph was a bit dark because it was early evening and she was in a doorway between twilight outside and house light within. The next few frames provide more close-ups.

"She looks vaguely familiar for some reason," Cindy said.

John frowned, studied the photo more closely and then said in a low voice, "Not to me."

A few pictures later showed a bearded man with a little girl. This time Cindy thought she recognized him as someone they occasionally would see walking a dog in their old neighborhood.

"Looks like someone in the old neighborhood is living in our home," she said.

John remained quiet.

The doorbell rang again; Cindy didn't want to go open the door. Cindy hesitated, and Emma beat her to the door. "Mom, its Bruce and Maloney!" she called brightly to her parents.

"Emma, please. It's *Mr. Thomas* and *Ms. Quinn*." Emma frowned at this mouthful but remembered her manners and said, "Sorry!"

Bruce explained that they were driving by while headed into town to buy groceries, and saw the strange car parked out front. "Just thought I'd stop by and see if there's anything you needed at the Safeway," Bruce said.

"No thanks, buddy," John told him, while Cindy exchanged pleasantries with Maloney and Emma clamored for attention. After a few minutes their neighbors departed and John and Cindy returned to the laptop.

"Can I see? Can I see?" Emma repeated.

"Honey, you have to go read your book now. Daddy and I are doing something," Cindy told her.

"You have pictures from Caitlin," the child said. "Can I see?"

"Later, Emma," John told her. "Tomorrow, I promise. Now you have to finish your book and then get ready for bed."

Emma bounded off with her book, allowing the parents to return to the photo album on the laptop. Neither spoke a word as they drifted through their own thoughts. They even forgot to reply to Caitlin, who said she would be anxiously waiting for their reply to her e-mail and photos.

But Caitlin would not be so easily appeased. After ten o'clock, John got a short text from Caitlin that said, "Call me."

"It's after midnight in Massachusetts," John said to Cindy, who looked as worried as he was.

Cindy called and Caitlin asked anxiously, "Mom, did you and Dad... did you see my pictures? Did you like them? I texted you earlier, too. You guys really should remember to check your texts. This is the twenty-first century, Mom. Why can't we Skype instead?"

They both wanted to know why was she up so late, and then told her how much they liked the pictures, but gave her no hint that they had recognized their old home in them.

"I forgot to load the Skype, but I promise I will do it next week," John said, getting on the phone.

"But that was what you said a month ago," Caitlin complained.

John told her he loved her and passed the phone to Cindy, who talked for a while. Caitlin was somehow not surprised; she was accustomed to her father's distraction and the way he would tune things out when he had something else pressing on his mind. This was both a blessing and a curse. She knew that this trait was one of the marks of his brilliance, but it could also be exasperating. She wondered if her photos had anything to do with it.

CHAPTER THIRTY-TWO

Mrs. Grayson had her regular adviser meetings with Caitlin on Saturdays in the morning, but this week Caitlin arrived ten minutes late—an unusual occurrence, for the girl was invariably there early. More striking and unsettling to Cora Grayson, however, was the way the child looked, especially her exhausted, bloodshot eyes. After the customary hug, which Caitlin seemed to shrink away from, Mrs. Grayson fixed her with a stare.

"Caitlin, are you all right?"

"Yes, Mrs. Grayson, I'm fine."

"You don't look fine to me, Caitlin. Did you sleep last night?"

"Yes." The answer was not persuasive to the academic adviser, a woman who prided herself on having seen it all in dealing with troubled students.

"Caitlin?"

"Hmmm, a little, but I actually had a bad nightmare," Caitlin said with shy reluctance.

"What kind of a nightmare, Caitlin?"

"Please, I don't want to talk about it."

"Would you like some tea?"

"No, thank you."

"Water?"

"Yes, please."

Mrs. Grayson turned to a water cooler behind her desk and filled a clean glass with filtered, cold water, which Caitlin accepted gratefully.

"Tell me about this dream. I won't repeat it to anyone, but it will help you to say it aloud."

"Trust me," her adviser prompted further, as she could see that Caitlin wanted to talk about whatever it was that had her so dismayed.

Caitlin responded haltingly in a tentative voice. "I keep getting these dreams... I hate them!"

"About what, dear?"

Caitlin stifled a sob. "Dreams in which I'm holding Emma's hand, and we both are running away.... I'm yelling at her to run faster. Faster!"

"Emma is your little sister, as I recall."

"Yes, ma'am. She's eleven."

"And what happens in the dream?"

"Men are chasing us."

"Is it the same men in all the dreams?"

"Yes. With guns."

"And do you get away?"

Caitlin looked at her as if to say, *well, I'm* here *aren't I?*

"What happens, Caitlin?"

"I wake up. Like last night. I woke up and couldn't get back to sleep. I was so scared of losing her."

Mrs. Grayson passed her a box of tissues and asked, "Did anything like this happen before, when you were home?"

Caitlin hesitated and mumbled a small "No," while looking down at her fidgeting hands and avoiding Mrs. Grayson's gaze.

Mrs. Grayson was extremely worried about the mood that had come over this bright, spirited fourteen-year-old from out West. As an experienced and deeply empathetic mentor, she had been working with teenaged girls for over thirty years, and her reputation was that she could read their minds, at least the ones who were open and honest enough to trust an adult. She set aside the previous agenda she had prepared for Caitlin and rephrased the question.

"Caitlin, look at me. Did you have this kind of dream before you came here?"

"Once."

"When was that?"

"Last year."

"In Montana," said Mrs. Grayson, who knew when to back off a little. She recognized Caitlin's hardened countenance and channeled the conversation to her life before coming to Northpoint School. She asked about her middle school, her sister Emma, the kinds of guests they entertained at home. She asked about her parents: Where they worked, how they treated her. Did they attend college? Where? What was home life like in Montana? Why had she come so far to attend school?

To a degree that both surprised and relieved Mrs. Grayson, Caitlin answered the probing questions patiently and with no apparent protective disingenuousness, though also with no great amount of detail. Her parents had trained her well to be guarded about her background in all circumstances.

As she skillfully probed through the standard issues with the obvious questions, Mrs. Grayson felt relief tempered with a tiny bit of frustration. *What is this kid's story?* she wondered. She was filled with curiosity as much as concern. Recurrent nightmares fit no diagnosis she could apply to Caitlin Stuart. Then after twenty minutes of back and forth, Caitlin had to go to a Saturday morning class and left, seemingly happy again.

Although Caitlin had departed her office, the mystery surrounding her remained behind. She was a model student: hardworking, pleasant, brilliant academically, and gifted athletically. Yet there was something strange about this girl, and it wasn't just that she was from some exotic place like Montana. No, something else was unusual here. *The kid has a core of steel,* Cora Grayson thought. Not in any cold-hearted manner, because she was kind and self-effacing and open. She clearly came from a loving family, and there were no indicators for alarm there. But Caitlin could handle pain, dejection, or unpleasant news with remarkable aplomb for a girl the age of fourteen, when anxieties and self-doubt were often rife. Time and time again in their weekly meetings, Caitlin would indicate with clarity and purpose that her small school problems and routine adolescent social issues had no bearing on anyone other than herself, which in Mrs. Grayson's mind was an indication not only of impressive maturity but of basic *sanity* in any girl of the precarious age of fourteen!

Never before, in thirty years at her job, had Mrs. Grayson encountered a girl who presented such genuine mysteries as Caitlin did. When Mrs. Grayson searched for her family online, nothing showed up—not of her or her sister, which might of course be expected given their ages and rural upbringings—but not of her parents either. She kept trying different searches. Nothing. Local newspapers in Montana? No. Various name and word combinations? Not a single solitary thing. Having spent an hour and a half at this fruitless search, she was tired. She spoke of these matters at night with her husband, who was also puzzled—at the situation, and at the way his wife had brought this concern home, which was unusual. She couldn't get Caitlin out of her mind—and Cora Grayson was a woman who prided herself on her professional skill in maintaining emotional detachment, no matter how deeply she cared about a kid. She and her husband walked through this over and over again: There was no other way to do this job with teenagers. You guided them, you loved the ones you could, and you worried about some of them intensely—but *you were not their parent.* At a certain point, you needed to let go.

Cora Grayson could not let go.

Early the next week, Mrs. Grayson saw Caitlin in the hallway and gently took her aside.

"You sleeping okay?" she asked.

"I am! Why?" Caitlin said happily, her expression indicating that the question was strange.

"Caitlin?"

Her eyes still sparkled. But quietly, she told Mrs. Grayson, "I just pulled an all-nighter, so that will take care of any nightmare issues!"

"Caitlin! A bright student like you should not be 'pulling all-nighters,' as you call it."

"I know, Mrs. Grayson, but it was just this once. I can handle it."

"I know, I know. But you are not indestructible. Your brain needs a break! Get some rest. I know you have a math test later today, but I'll call your teacher and have it rescheduled."

"Thanks Mrs. Grayson, but really, I'm fine. I'll go to bed early tonight. My parents get unhappy if I avoid academic work, and 'tired' is an excuse they don't like hearing. Especially my Dad, who says you have to learn to be tough enough to push yourself through being 'tired,' all other things being equal. It was my choice to stay up all night, so I need to take the test!"

Caitlin finished this with conviction, but then failed to stifle a large yawn. Mrs. Grayson, who had not only seen it all but *heard* it all before in her thirty years dealing with adolescent girls, stood her ground like a granite monument to sensibility.

"No, no, no, dear. We shall reschedule this test. I'll write a note to your parents that it was at my insistence it was rescheduled, not yours."

This caught Caitlin off-guard because it conveyed the kind of logic her father would have acquiesced to readily.

"You are not taking this test today," Mrs. Grayson said in a tone that brooked no opposition.

Caitlin smiled at the triumph of common sense over blind determination, even though she had championed the latter.

"You know what, now that I think of it, that actually is the right answer," Caitlin said thoughtfully. "I'm too tired to do well. So I'll take a nap!"

CHAPTER THIRTY-THREE

By December, another depressing Montanan winter had begun crowding in, crowding out the days in which sunlight appeared with any strength. With one child away at school and the other growing well and securely into adolescence, Cindy grew increasingly desperate to re-engage with life and the world at large. Important national and international events seemed so far removed from this rural spot in the mountains! Even the Great Recession in the United States had occurred as if far removed from the quotidian routines of the Stuarts' life in hiding.

Yet the repercussions of the economic crisis still resonated for her. Cindy had once been an accomplished banker, and she was frustrated by her inability to immerse herself professionally in the intense machinations of the response to such an evolving crisis—besides her long talks with John into the wee hours of the morning. *Why didn't people see this for what it was, as a developing emergency, rather than something that had merely happened?* she thought to herself. Every indication was there that there would be another phase in the unfolding of this national disaster. *Why was this going to be such a surprise? Has society lost even the minimal ability to learn from even the most recent history?*

Her entrepreneurial mindset was working in overdrive.

Haiti, for example, was on her mind. In 2009, a major earthquake had devastated Haiti, with a resulting humanitarian and economic catastrophe: The currency tanked, inflation soared, and many small banks had runs on their money and were forced to close. Many more banks were still struggling, years later. But the great spotlight of world and national attention has swiveled elsewhere, leaving Haiti in the dark,

215

its struggles unseen now and unheeded beyond the island, except for the steady stream of world-disaster aid that continued to flow.

Cindy saw an opportunity in Haiti and, given her prior experience and contacts there, suggested to John that they buy a bank, Bank Port-au-Prince, which in dollar terms was relatively cheap, due to the severe currency deflation. John was initially surprised, but as Cindy explained the opportunity in terms of its potential upside, he became increasingly intrigued with the idea.

"But where are we going to find the money to buy this bank? We don't quite have two hundred thousand dollars," John said.

"Well, we still have some of the cash we withdrew when we left Concord, and I don't mind selling my diamond jewelry to make up for the rest."

"Are you sure you want to do that, honey? That will leave you with no safety net—we will be living on the edge."

"Trust me, I know what I am doing," said a Cindy with a mischievous smile.

*　　　*　　　*

Bank Port-au-Prince was a fifty-year-old full-service bank in the backwaters of Haiti. Once it had thrived, bearing a good reputation, but now it was a skeleton of its former self. It offered the usual services such as savings and checking accounts, bank CDs, deposit boxes, and money transfers between the U.S. and Haiti to serve the immigrant community. The number of employees had been cut back drastically; bank records were in disarray to an alarming degree; many manual records were missing. Some had been lost during the earthquake when the computerized data backups had been housed carelessly in a dusty and leaky warehouse. Yet Cindy also knew there was a large Haitian community living in the United States who sent money home when they could; many did so every month. For many families in Haiti, that largesse had become the principal means of survival. Most immigrants lived in the New York, Washington D.C., and Boston areas. Cindy saw it as an excellent opportunity to build a business by opening branches in these major metropolitan areas where the Haitian population was concentrated. Another motive was to benefit from the economic activity that was still arriving in Haiti for the many years of reconstruction that had followed the disaster.

John reluctantly agreed to maintain their secretive life in Montana while she went forth on regular trips, over the course of eight months, back and forth to Haiti—straightening out the mess at the bank, working day and night to restore and re-create records from damaged data. Cindy brought back some of the knowledgeable ex-employees and worked tirelessly to motivate the staff by instituting an employee stock-option plan.

Once she felt that she had established a degree of stability, she hired Dominique Jean-Francois as president of the bank and only stayed on as a member of the board of directors. Dominique was a native-born former banker who had worked in the United States for several years and was well versed in compliance laws. Although Cindy enjoyed the work and the potential of financial reward, the project was obviously creating huge demands on her time at home, and she constantly fretted about her family on those grueling trips which required a three-hour drive to Butte, Montana, and a thirty-hour airplane trip, with connections through Salt Lake City and New York, before she would arrive at the Mais Gate Airport in Port-au-Prince, Haiti—and then she'd repeat the arduous journey in reverse to come back home.

Under Cindy's direction, the bank hired twenty-seven employees who went through hundreds of boxes of printed data, some of it badly damaged, trying to match each record with either the deposit box or the bank account to which it belonged. At times Cindy felt overwhelmed. Was this just folly? When she was exhausted or frustrated, she would call John. She knew that record-keeping was typically shoddy at Haiti banks but she did not realize the sheer magnitude of the misfeasance and incompetence. She thought, *no wonder Haiti has the reputation as being a poor man's money laundromat.* No wonder it was such a haven for thieves to stash their loot, thanks to corruption, ridiculously lax banking regulations, and either indifferent or paid-off law enforcement.

After Dominique was firmly in control, Cindy quit the board but kept her significant ownership. She immediately hired an auditing firm to list all the ownerships of assets. Many account holders were American citizens, which was not unusual, as some had migrated and returned. This list with the names of the American citizens was submitted to the federal regulators as a routine part of compliance with new banking regulations enacted after it was discovered that thousands of Americans held secret accounts with a Swiss banking giant to avoid paying taxes. Since then the U.S. government had cracked down on banks and demanded that any American citizen holding an account overseas must report it. Banks were asked to provide such data on a monthly basis to enable cross-checking.

One of the names that stood out on the list was that of Billy Dalton, the notorious Boston gangster. Dalton's particulars turning up in Hispaniola, of all places, piqued the government regulators' interest. They demanded a deeper investigation into all activity that had been associated with that account. U.S. law enforcement arrived, collected whatever data they felt was necessary, and left. A few days later, they asked for all of the account and transaction details belonging to American citizens.

A world away in Massachusetts, Caitlin was having an advisory meeting with Cora Grayson. The topic had shifted again to family, and Caitlin's eyes became misty as she talked about Emma, the little sister she so desperately missed.

"We had wonderful times together, Mrs. Grayson," Caitlin told her adviser and confidante.

"Think about this, Caitlin. Maybe Emma could enroll in Northpoint next year, and then you two could be together."

"Oh, no. I don't think my parents would let that happen."

"Why not? From what you've been telling me, Emma is a terrific student like yourself. She could get full financial aid."

There was no way Catlin could tell her the true reason, that they had been gravely reluctant to see their first daughter leave the relatively secure nest they had created in Montana; it was highly unlikely they would let their other child do the same. The risks were—well, Caitlin could not really say herself what those risks were, but for most of her life she had been conditioned to know that the risks were grave, and she had seen enough evidence of this (the home invasion being the most recent) to know without demanding details that this was true.

She did not like avoiding the truth, but she had become expert at it, even with someone as perceptive as Cora Grayson.

"My parents probably don't want to be alone in Montana, with both of us so far away. Also, they can't afford to travel frequently to see us, either."

Mrs. Grayson was overwhelmed with empathy and said, "Caitlin, why don't I call your mother and talk this over? Would you mind?"

Caitlin tried to hide her fear. "Well, actually, you can't, because she's in Haiti."

Mrs. Grayson blinked uncomprehendingly and said, "Haiti?"

CHAPTER THIRTY-FOUR

In February, Caitlin tried to call her mother from school, but the connection to Haiti was out. Then she tried her father.

"Dad, I just got a very strange e-mail, and I think you need to know about it."

She heard silence on the other end of the phone. "Tell me," her father said.

Caitlin read: "I know who you are and who your mom and dad are. I know where they and your sister live."

John recoiled. *How had anyone been able to reach out to his daughter?* He hated the fact that she was now exposed, two thousand miles away.

"Caitlin, do you have any idea who sent that?" he asked in a shaky, barely controlled voice.

Caitlin could pick up on his cues and was becoming more deeply distressed by the minute. "No. There is no indication."

"Listen, could you try this for me. Get the drop-down menu on the e-mail and click on 'View Page Source.'"

"I did that, Dad. It was all encrypted, believe me. It was gibberish."

"Try 'Inspect Element,'" he suggested, masking his sense of urgency.

"I did! The same gibberish. It leads back and forth all over the universe, but there's nothing identifiable!"

"Caitlin, can you print those pages out along with the e-mail itself?"

"Yes, I can at the school library computer center," she said through tears.

"Would you do that, honey? And then fax them to me? You have the fax number, don't you?"

"Yes."

"Don't talk to anyone you don't know. Make sure you have your phone, with school security on the speed dial."

"It is," she said.

"You call them if you see anything suspicious."

"Okay."

John's worst fears were realized. He had always been opposed to sending Caitlin to Northpoint School but had acquiesced to please his wife and daughter. But now he was consumed with self-recrimination. In his head was the pounding refrain: *I should have never given in on this one; I should have never given in on this one!* On the phone, Caitlin could hear him muttering.

"Dad, are you still there?"

He snapped back into focus. "Look, it's probably some crazy person you encountered somewhere in Concord. I'll talk to your mom and we'll be on it. It could even be a prank message sent by one of the students."

Caitlin wasn't buying into that.

"What if it's not?"

"Don't worry, when I went to high school all kind of pranks would happen there. Far worse than this, believe me. Just be careful, okay?"

"Okay, Dad. I'll call you if I see or hear anything unusual."

"Yes, that's my girl. In the meantime, fax me that stuff and I'll try to figure this out."

When he got off the phone with his daughter, he immediately called Cindy in Haiti. He had to shout to have any kind of conversation with the atrocious phone connection, but at least he made her aware of the situation. Cindy was horrified and felt frustrated, being so far away in a place with such challenging telecommunication connections.

John was abrupt in the conversation they did manage to have. He wanted to think, while she needed assurance. This was generally the point at which they would have an argument—and they did, their rancor overcoming the inadequate phone service between the two places.

"What are we going to do, what are our plans?" she said through static that sounded like it had arrived from the distant past.

"If I knew I'd tell you, wouldn't I?" he snapped furiously. "I told you from day one that it was a bad idea to send her out by herself, smack in middle of the danger zone. I doubt that you still understand how dangerous these people actually are! This is not some movie; this is real life and she is in grave danger!"

After a few minutes, they calmed down.

"You will have to go and bring her home. I cannot go for obvious reasons," he said.

"She has exams right now and will be devastated if she were to leave in middle of the school year."

"The alternative is not acceptable," John insisted.

"Why don't I go there and stay with her for a few days and keep an eye on her?"

*   *   *

That night Caitlin was walking from the library and noticed a man in a Red Sox cap standing outside, staring at her, and smiling strangely. She wanted to scream for help but remembered all the training her parents had given her. She stared back at the man, maintained a confident posture, and walked back to her dorm. The man stayed back, and by the time she had walked two hundred yards, he was gone. It seemed impossible to call 911 with that kind of report. A man smiling strangely outside the library? She'd feel foolish, even though she knew he was grinning at her. She locked her dorm room behind her. Her roommate was off campus for a few days.

It turned out that similar threatening e-mails had been sent to two other students, and as the IT department searched the server, they realized that Caitlin was also a victim. The other two students had informed their advisers and the IT department, and of course the question was asked: Why hadn't Caitlin stepped forward? IT contacted Mrs. Grayson and shared the details. Under this circumstance, as a matter of policy, the IT department scanned all of her e-mails over the past few months. The only odd one they found had been sent to Emma. It read, "Halloween was fun, home—just like the pictures." The e-mail had been forwarded to Mrs. Grayson.

After a thorough investigation, the IT department concluded that it was a prank, likely done by one of the computer science students, and a routine watch was placed on those potential sources.

But Cora Grayson did not like the situation at all when she read the e-mails. Her face was tense. What worried her was that Caitlin had received the threat via e-mail but had not made the prudent decision—*and this was by all past evidence a prudent girl*—to alert security and especially to tell her, her closest adult confidante on campus. Mrs. Grayson e-mailed Caitlin to come and see her, but was careful not to sound alarmed. At the same time, she made ten extra walking rounds in the hallways of the building where most of Caitlin's classes were, hoping to encounter her, seemingly by chance, to assess her demeanor. But Caitlin, who had already shown that she was good at keeping her problems out of sight, somehow managed to keep herself out of sight that day as well—even though when Mrs. Grayson checked, Caitlin had not missed a class.

Mrs. Grayson did bump into Caitlin's best friend, Eva. Although Mrs. Grayson had never taught Eva and wasn't her adviser, the counselor made it her business to know every student in the school, and to at least have some idea of each of their interests. After inquiring about Eva's computer science project, she lightly asked about Caitlin.

Eva seemed nonchalant. "Oh, Caitlin just needs to get some serious sleep, Mrs. Grayson," she said, eliciting a deep frown from the adult. "Yesterday at dinner she told me she hadn't slept in thirty-six hours because she had an English paper due. But you know Caitlin; she's still so fun and bubbly even without sleeping that I can't even tell when she is tired except when she tells me! She's like a machine!"

"None of us are machines, Eva," Mrs. Grayson said gently, harping on one of her favorite topics. "All-nighters are a dangerous drain on someone's health. Please remember that."

"I will, Mrs. Grayson. Thanks. And I'll talk to Caitlin about it, I promise."

"And Eva, if Caitlin needs any help, she knows where I am, okay?"

Eva nodded gravely. "I know," she said. Then Eva spotted a group of friends and bounded off yelling, "Guess what?" with a whole new diversion in her attention span, something about a teacher who had inadvertently set his trousers on fire in chemistry lab and grabbed an extinguisher to douse the flames.

But Eva followed through on her promise, and spoke to Caitlin, who e-mailed Mrs. Grayson and said that she would come by at four in the afternoon.

When she did, Mrs. Grayson inquired in a calm manner about the e-mail. The question nevertheless made Caitlin uncomfortable. And then the girl began to cry.

Mrs. Grayson pulled her in and gave her a hug. "Don't worry, Cait," she said softly, using the name she had started calling her as a sign of affection.

When the girl settled down, Mrs. Grayson asked, "Are you afraid of this?"

"Yes."

"You are staying at my home for a few days," she announced.

"But Mrs. Grayson…" Caitlin tried to protest, but she was still comforted by the offer of a haven of this kind. Mrs. Grayson, more to the point, was implacable. And so Caitlin arrived at her adviser's house.

That evening over dinner, Mrs. Grayson gently inquired again about her parents, her relatives, family friends, hoping to understand the complicated girl. But except for the odd absence of relatives, Caitlin's answers seemed normal. Caitlin even described their eccentric neighbor Bruce Thomas and laughed fondly. Then she finished her homework and went to bed.

As Mrs. Grayson made herself a cup of tea in the kitchen later that night, she heard a small chime from the bookshelf near where Caitlin had done her homework. Realizing the sound was coming from Caitlin's cell phone, which Caitlin had not taken with her into the spare bedroom where she was sleeping, Mrs. Grayson shook her head. These endless texting alerts—*was anyone in this new world ever considered to be off-duty, out to lunch, gone fishing?* she thought with real amusement. She was glad that Caitlin was asleep.

As Mrs. Grayson picked up the phone to leave it on the table, she glanced at the screen and saw a text message marked "UNKNOWN." This raised a red flag. This was not likely a text from a friend who for some reason was not on Caitlin's personal contact list, as that would still come through with a normal phone number. *A text late at night from an unknown source, to a girl who had just received an anonymous threat?* Mrs. Grayson hesitated.

Yes, there was the issue of invading someone's privacy. Then again, there was the overriding issue of this girl's safety. While holding the phone, she debated, *What would I do if she were my daughter? I would read the text. There is no question about that! And in this case, I am, by school charter and indeed by law,* in loco parentis, *am I not?* She moved to touch the screen, but then held back again. She remembered what her husband had reiterated to her in the early years, when she became so involved with students' desperate problems that her heart was always breaking. *Maintain psychic distance. Although, does that fine and noble rule apply if a student's life could be in danger? When does concern about privacy policy end, and the responsibility to provide emergency assistance begin? What if I'm out of line, and invading a student's privacy becomes a school faculty discipline matter? On the other hand, how could there be any policy or higher priority than saving someone from potential harm?* She stood frozen for five minutes, and finally she put the phone down on the table, leaving the text unread and waiting for Caitlin.

Mrs. Grayson went to sleep that night deeply troubled. In the middle of the night she woke up abruptly, shaken into consciousness by Caitlin's ear piercing screams from the spare bedroom: "Run, Emma! Run, run, run faster! Run, Emma, run!"

Mrs. Grayson jumped out of bed and ran to the room where Caitlin was thrashing under the covers. She gently tried to shake her, softly saying, "It's okay, honey, it's okay. I'm here. Nobody is hurt… Emma is okay."

Caitlin's eyes were open and flashing with panic. "No! No! Emma is not okay! Where is she? Where! Did they get her?"

Mrs. Grayson finally got her to calm down and become aware of her surroundings. She gave her a glass of water and put her hand on her head. The girl drifted uneasily back to sleep. Mrs. Grayson stayed up listening for her, but the night passed without further incident.

Later the next day, Cora Grayson's husband, a famously deep sleeper who had been aware of nothing till she explained the situation at breakfast, tried to advise her not to obsess over Caitlin. He reiterated the advice about not becoming too deeply involved, about the danger to one's psyche that might entail. But she protested, "I do want her to affect my psyche. This kid needs me more than ever. Would you mind if she stayed here a few more days?"

He said that would be okay.

That day Mrs. Grayson called Caitlin's parents in Montana and explained the situation to John. John was in a dilemma, of course, because he was in no position to fully explain a situation so enormously complicated and fraught with peril. He was nearly paralyzed with remorse about the situation that had befallen his family, for which he blamed himself.

"I'll talk to her today, Mrs. Grayson. I'll work on reassuring her. I'm sure she's reacting to what's just a high school prank," he added, knowing that he did not believe this himself. "You know how kids get homesick."

CHAPTER THIRTY-FIVE

Stock Accounts at Two Big Wall Street Firms Rifled by Serbian Hacker Group, U.S. Says

The Enterprise was in the headlines again on February 28.

In what was their most devious and brazen attack yet, the Enterprise hacked into the accounts of two major financial-services companies, secretly "borrowed" stocks as short-sellers, meaning they made money when stock goes down. Then they pocketed the proceeds when those stocks were manipulated temporarily to lose a small percentage of their value. It was a complex and clever scheme, entirely dependent on the most sophisticated degree of hacking. Essentially, the Enterprise used the stock of unsuspecting investors to shake out quick profits, while at the same time the underlying account holders' risks were minimal unless the owner needed to sell the stock while it was secretly in the hands of the Internet criminals.

"Ordinarily the innocent account holder would not even be aware of it," Cindy explained to John when they tried to decipher the accounts of the latest major digital heist.

"But why did they raid accounts selectively, which is what I am seeing here?" she asked.

"Initially there was no apparent reason why money was stolen from some accounts and not others. But it appears that it was a two-prong attack, one on the registry where the electronic records of the stock ownership are kept, another on the corresponding individual accounts that were hacked into."

"Oh, and of course nobody keeps physical stock certificates in their possession anymore," she said.

"Well, except for some old-timers who might have a tin box to stash those certificates of shares of AT&T they inherited from their grandfather in 1954 and think will one day have spectacular value," he said with a laugh.

"Right. They're recorded at a centralized registry. That's where the 'stock' resides," she said.

"So the Enterprise went after those customer accounts that had enabled online-only account access and statements but had low frequency of access or click-through on the account statement."

"Like before, dormant or little-used accounts," she said.

"Precisely. It appears that the software that authorizes the short-selling on accounts was thoroughly compromised, and the electronic updates that occur when any transaction happens, including short selling, weren't noticed because the accounts were infrequently accessed."

"I'm seeing a pattern here, John."

"Yes, me, too. Let's hope we're not the only ones."

The industry responded to the latest attacks by assuming its defensive crouch. Immediately after the attacks were detected by federal banking authorities, the institutions hurried to underplay the extent of the problems. As usual, the mantra was "avoid panic." After all, the bankers' top lobbyists confided to their friends and patrons in Washington, there had been no real loss of equity. A stock that is lent comes back to the lender when the lending duration ends, even if the lender isn't aware of the activity. As one $2 million a year bank lobbyist told her favorite senator, the chairman of the Senate banking committee, "Isn't this a little like somebody who borrows a neighbor's rake while the neighbor is on vacation, and returns it in the exact same condition?" And the senator, who considered himself a legal titan by virtue of his law degree and the eternal fawning of lobbyists who invested generously for his unyielding legislative backing, sucked in his gut and replied with a wave of his fat pink hand, "Of course that's the correct analogy! Now, we want to be discouraging the borrowing of any and all property without prior permission, of course, but in this case, what is the tort? Where is the tort? Why cause unnecessary public panic and loss of trust, I say."

The scheme was detected only when Wall Street internal alarms rang, as the market tumbled after some of the account holders who did in fact try to sell stocks, but were locked out of selling and told that these stocks were already on loan. Only then did the government confirm the problem and announce that an intensive investigation was underway.

But it transpired that there was another twist to the story. All across the country, other small investors were encountering more than the usual instances of denial of access to their accounts, because passwords frequently would not work when they initially tried to log in. Typically, when this occurs, a user reasonably assumes that the password was merely mistyped, and tries a second time. A small annoyance, the glitch goes without comment. So it took a while for the anecdotal information, propagated mainly by social media comments, to elicit the attention of the banking and government authorities. They soon realized that systematic widespread hacking was occurring—driven by deliberate digital blocking of sign-in attempts. As sophisticated hacking software detected a sign-in attempt, it quickly determined if equity had been borrowed from that account. The sign-in attempt was then denied a couple of times, giving the hacking software the opportunity to "borrow" additional stock from somewhere else, making that specific account whole. This enabled the deception to pass the scrutiny of the relatively small number of chosen account holders who might be actually checking their accounts.

"It's clever, but obviously it can't keep working without detection," John told Cindy.

"The total losses they've been able to identify from this are over a billion and counting," Cindy read. "Nobody really has any way of knowing the full extent of the losses, but the biggest loss by far has been the trust that the general public held in the stock market as an unassailable system."

Even as the public accommodated itself to the assurances that the banks and the authorities had everything under control, there was another attack, the worst one yet.

But law-enforcement vigilance did yield some results. Somehow, the Enterprise made a few mistakes, and several of ZRK's top henchmen were arrested brandishing automatic weapons in a drunken brawl at a glitzy nightclub near Slavija Square in Belgrade. ZRK himself, and most of his organization remained intact, though ZRK's reputation for being strategically brilliant, cannily low–profile, and virtually untouchable took a bit of a hit when the gangsters in custody raised such a ruckus at police headquarters about their international "connections" that Interpol was notified.

The government was quick to declare a decisive victory in the battle against the Enterprise. The dreaded Enterprise was "on the ropes and now we're moving in for the knockout," one federal international task force official said.

"Is it?" John muttered, reading that hopeful and notably unsupported account.

"Is it what?" Cindy asked.

"Is the Enterprise finished?"

"I'm guessing that's awfully optimistic?" she said.

"Absolutely, although ZRK personally must be hurting."

"Why do you say that?"

John rubbed his chin. "I know the type. His ego is bruised now that he's been humiliated a bit. He'll be more tempted to prove himself, which means he'll probably move much closer to the edge. I believe he will use the very best mechanisms he has to carry on breaking networks and computer systems. It's a game of measured response—one does not use any more force than one has to in any single circumstance, allowing the extent and depth of the arsenal to remain secret."

"Not sure I agree," Cindy countered. "I see ZRK as being crippled; his organization is tattered. Besides, he is supposed to be this completely logical, emotionless, absolutely cold, and calculating individual. I don't believe emotions drive him in any way."

"Well, I disagree," John said. "He has pride. He's been compared to Einstein in his field, and for good reason. I've worked closely with his types. They're unique specimens, very rare indeed."

"Okay, but then how come you didn't become like them?" Cindy said with a teasing wink.

John didn't respond to the question. He was troubled about the extent of the fraud, and especially about the indications that Pandora's box had been opened.

"John. You have to jump in, there is no alternative."

"You know I am working on the design day and night; in fact I have never worked this hard in my life! But I need a couple more months before deploying it. The most difficult challenge is to find where the intrusive code is entering into the system and what it looks like, sort of like its signatures. With ZRK being the best in the business, it's like looking for a needle in the haystack except a hundred times worse. Every time there is an attack I get more forensics information to incrementally build my trap but, ironically, I need two or three more attacks to be able to identify it."

"There may not be anything left to protect after a few more attacks!" scoffed Cindy. "Have you considered reaching out to Norm? Maybe you two working together can do it faster?"

"Too dangerous."

"There must be a way, you got to do something and do it fast. You have beaten him before."

Then there was a silence, a silence of resignation. Then John suddenly blurted out.

"Wait a minute; you just gave me an idea, thanks Cindy!" John blew a kiss and ran upstairs to his work area.

Cindy smiled, she knew he had one of those brainstorms, and that meant he would be in there for a while.

John emerged from his office with nothing in his head, experiencing a kind of happy emptiness, as if he had just visited an enormous ocean shore.

"Guess what, I figured it out. I am much closer now! I am itching to test this…. When you mentioned Norm, I just remembered that he did tell ZRK (then Rob) at the conference why he lost. It was because in cyclic codes I had made 2 plus 3 equal 4 instead of 5. ZRK is a genius; he will not make the same mistake twice. So I analyzed the post-attack data from the U.S. branch of the Haitian bank and looked for the condition that avoids being fooled in that manner. Sure enough, I could detect that code! I found the signatures I have been so painstakingly looking for the past few months. My model is much better; I am nearly ready now. You know life is funny, sometimes what one knows becomes one's nemesis—and ZRK is in that boat!"

"This is brilliant! Exciting!" said an overjoyed Cindy. She then noticed that John had gone quiet and wore a blank stare as if lost in space.

"What's wrong?" she asked.

"It's everything," he said morosely, after a moment of reflection. The

FBI has dumped us. All these massive intrusions are becoming daily events. And the government seems to be unable to stem this tide. It reminds me a bit of Ayn Rand's book *Atlas Shrugged*."

Cindy shot back, "What are you talking about? The last nails on her coffin were hammered in by the 2008 financial collapse. Unabated greed of the few in the private sector, unconstrained by any moral compass, lacking integrity, did more damage than previously had been done in a hundred years. Millions lost their homes, and jobs through no fault of their own due to a philosophy propagated by Ayn Rand, who inspired free marketers who nevertheless had no qualms about using government as a back-stop. There ought to be a fair and common set of rules! A society that has one set of rules, or no rules, for the select privileged few and another for the rest is in deep trouble. Ayn Rand's philosophical poison tastes great but is fundamentally flawed—"

Like most people, Cindy was pronouncing the first name of the libertarian *laissez-faire* godmother as "Ann."

"It's Ayn, rhymes with 'mine,'" John said with a sardonic chuckle. "That's how she pronounced it, anyway. She made a big point of saying it rhymes with 'mine,' which kind of underlines the inherent selfishness of the woman."

"Well, that's an odd name in any case," Cindy said.

"Not her real name," John said. "Her real name was Alisa Rosenbaum. She changed it for effect. The 'Rand' she seems to have plucked out of thin air."

Cindy absorbed that with interest and amusement, and continued: "Well, no matter how she pronounced it, the woman has been a pernicious influence on two generations of zealots for an unfettered free market that can do whatever it chooses to do in the name of profits. Consider it just in the context of extensive corporate use of private information alone. The risk of abuse has never been greater. The risk to liberty and everything we stand for. The government may not even be a problem, or if it is then it's just one of few. It's any entity that has created a concentration of power or information about the populace at large, and decides to abuse it for its own benefit. They are nothing but two sides of the same coin. Both need be equally feared. The power is in the hands of a few and fewer, regardless of their affiliation."

"Do you do believe that government can actually play a role to rein in this abuse?" asked John.

"Oh absolutely, it is uniquely empowered to rein in the abuses. To the extent those with potential to abuse power are at loggerheads with one another, that is a good thing. Ayn Rand brings the best and the worst animal instinct out in humans. Well, excuse me, I aspire to be further evolved ethically than that. I really believe that Ayn Rand is the Marilyn Monroe of philosophy—all seduction, little substance."

CHAPTER THIRTY-SIX

A couple of months later, Caitlin was cast as one of the leads in the school play, a performance of the musical *Into the Woods*. It was a major event, and everyone's parents were coming except hers. When she landed the role, she happily called home and gave her family the performance dates, begging them to come. But both John and Cindy went very quiet. She sensed that her mother was becoming tearful, but there was no evident response whatsoever from her father. Nothing further was said. The quiet said it all. They would not be able to make it.

In their next meeting, Cora Grayson simply assumed that Caitlin's parents would be arriving for the spring show, which was one of the highlights of the school calendar.

"They're coming, right?" Mrs. Grayson asked, and the expression on the girl's face told her right away that she should not have inquired so directly.

"Mrs. Grayson, they have to travel on an urgent business trip, planned well in advance, so they won't be able to make it," Caitlin said, almost mechanically. She hated lying, and purposely played with her bracelet to avoid eye contact.

Mrs. Grayson tried to conceal a sad sigh. "I understand, honey. Sometimes schedules are just impossible. But don't worry, your friends will be there and I will be there."

"I know, and thanks," Caitlin said, putting on a brave face.

As the girl left her office Mrs. Grayson noticed that her shoulders were sagging, as if under a weight that never got lighter.

Deeply saddened, Cora Grayson thought once again, *What is this kid's story?*

Caitlin played Little Red Riding Hood, a musically challenging part in the work by Stephen Sondheim and James Lapine. The musical, very loosely based on the fairy tale *Little Red Riding Hood* was about the quest for family and security against the menace of the woods and the threat of the wolf.

Caitlin brought down the house in Act One with her performance of the musically complex song "Hello Little Girl," which showcased Little Red Riding Hood's first encounter with the Wolf as she traverses the dark, brooding woods with a fresh loaf of bread.

With haunting hesitation and fear in her voice, she sang:

> *Mother said,*
> *"Come what may,*
> *Follow the path*
> *And never stray."*

To which the Wolf counters:

> *Just so, little girl*
> *Any path.*
> *So many worth exploring.*
> *Just one would be so boring.*
> *And look what you're ignoring.*

Mrs. Grayson sat in the front row and clapped the longest at the end of the show, which left the audience cheering wildly. As soon as Caitlin came out, blinking shyly and freshly scrubbed of her makeup, Mrs. Grayson presented her with a big spray of roses, and they hugged in joy. Other audience members lingering for the cast members to come out from backstage were touched by this, and many assumed the two were mother and daughter. Many photos were taken, and later that night, Mrs. Grayson, careful to sound as unassuming as humanly possible, e-mailed a few of them to John and Cindy, whom she guessed to be in Montana and not on a business trip after all—though Mrs. Grayson was wise and thoughtful enough not to send any of herself and their beaming, happy child.

Meanwhile, as soon as she got back to her dorm room, Caitlin called her parents, who were eagerly anticipating hearing every detail. She gleefully gave them a minute-by-minute account, including the motherly kindnesses shown by Mrs. Grayson, and she did this at length even though she was deliriously exhausted.

Cindy was overcome with joy; she was both sad and happy in the same moment. At least there was someone who could give her daughter the support and the presence she so badly needed. She felt so limited by her own situation, but she could not do anything except bolster herself, as usual, against helplessness. She was very proud of her daughter, but at the same time momentarily felt a bit of jealousy toward Mrs. Grayson. For a moment, she wondered, *Am I losing my baby daughter to this woman?*

And then she was profoundly ashamed of herself. Her child had a life cosseted with parental love, but tonight she needed public acclaim, emotional support, and enthusiasm—and Cindy, who had no way of providing that on this occasion, was deeply grateful to a woman she had only met briefly during orientation, a woman who stepped in when a child needed someone.

CHAPTER THIRTY-SEVEN

MIT Student Found Slain
Was Cyber-Privacy Activist;
High-Tech Expert Charged

By now John should have been accustomed to being jolted by the news, but the account of Norm Porter's arrest on murder charges startled him out of his chair.

"Cindy!" he called.

"She's outside in the garden," Emma told him, ducking into the living room out of curiosity.

"Get her, honey," he told his daughter.

When Cindy came in brushing her hands on her jeans, John told her to sit down.

"What?" she said with understandable alarm.

"You're not going to believe this. Norm Porter was arrested for murder."

"*Murder?*"

"Listen to this."

He read:

"A leading expert in computer-security technology was arrested Tuesday in Cambridge, Mass., and charged in the murder of a graduate student who was a specialist in cyber attacks and an activist in the digital-security protest organization Citizens Anonymous, police said.

Karen Weinheart, 26, a doctoral candidate in computer science at Massachusetts Institute of Technology was found shot to death in a secluded area near the campus student center Monday night. Ms. Weinheart was described as a brilliant researcher who specialized in so-called Big Data and cyber-attack technology. On her personal website, she also described her activities with the activist group Citizens Anonymous, which works to counter what it says is the growing threat to individual liberties posed by digital invasions of privacy.

On Tuesday morning, acting partly on an anonymous tip and partly on blurry images from a security surveillance camera near the murder site, Cambridge police, including a SWAT team, conducted a raid on Mr. Porter's home in Cambridge and arrested him. Blood stains on the dead woman's clothing had been sent for forensic testing as well as a sample of Porter's DNA, confidential sources reported. A gun was also found at his home and forensic tests confirmed that the gun was the murder weapon.

A neighbor who declined to be identified said that she believed Mr. Porter and Ms. Weinheart were romantically involved, but her family and friends declined to discuss the matter. On campus, students who specialize in the nascent field of cyber security said they were stunned by the killing.

A police investigator speaking under condition of anonymity said that text messages between Ms. Weinheart and Mr. Porter were recovered from both his and her cell phones. "This guy was getting angrier and angrier at her as the texts flew back and forth, apparently because Ms. Weinheart wanted to call off their relationship," the officer said.

When he was arrested, according to police accounts, Mr. Porter had scratches and abrasions on his body, indicating that there had been a struggle between him and the woman before she was shot. The video surveillance evidence shows two people scuffling in a darkly lighted area, without clearly showing the alleged assailant as he fled, police said.

"Norm Porter was the most respected person in the field, universally accepted as a genius," said Rashaan Ombuto a doctoral student, who knew both the slain woman and the accused killer. "Karen was also one of the most promising and outspoken researchers I know. She was a very sweet person, extremely involved in her work."

After being charged with first-degree murder and assault, Mr. Porter was taken to Massachusetts General Hospital for psychiatric evaluation, and then transferred to Middlesex County Jail awaiting arraignment, which is expected to be on Thursday.

John folded the newspaper and put it down.

"I can't believe it," he said, shaking his head.

"I don't know what to say," said Cindy, deeply disturbed. She had never before known even a criminal, let alone an accused murderer.

John was flabbergasted. "Norm? *Norm?* Norm can't be a murderer! I mean, he's a *vegetarian!*"

Cindy looked at him quizzically. "John, *Hitler* was a vegetarian. Diet has nothing to do with this. Besides, wasn't Norm the one whose father was arrested for espionage? And didn't he study for a time in China or Russia? Maybe there's more here than meets the eye?"

John was obviously worried. He said, taking account: "Now Norm is behind bars. Jake has gone to the dark side, and I am living in anonymity, totally out of the picture. Norm, Jake, and I were the three team members who beat ZRK, remember?"

"So what are you saying?" she asked.

"I don't know. I'm trying to understand. Maybe we're lucky that we got whisked away into the witness protection program and then found our way to a new life under new identities here in Montana."

"*Lucky?*" she exploded. "Are you out of your mind?"

"We're alive!" He tapped his fingers with agitation on the folded newspaper and said, "That could have been me instead of Norm!"

"But Norm committed murder!" Cindy shot back with profound exasperation.

John was silent for a moment, and then he said, speaking each word as if it were a separate sentence: "I. Am. Not. So. Sure."

She stared at him in exasperation for a minute, but then her attitude softened. *John can be clumsy and infuriatingly obtuse,* she thought, *but at least he sees the whole picture.* So she just retreated into silence, thinking as usual about her children and whether this meant more potential trouble for them.

He stunned her back into focus.

"It may be a trap, and if it is, we'll be next," he said darkly.

CHAPTER THIRTY-EIGHT

Cindy was at her wit's end. She was dreading the stubborn interminability of the longest season between winter and spring in places like Montana—mud season—when the cold defines the advances of the sun, and the melting snow leaves behind a landscape of mud. Desperate for fresh perspective, she made the long drive to Butte and came back home with a bagful of AAA maps and guidebooks.

"We have to take a vacation," she told John. "A drive along the California coast. My eyes have got to see something other than these dark mountains, muddy fields, and potholed roads."

"We can't do that! What about Caitlin?"

"Caitlin is fine now. And if we have to, it's a lot easier to get to Boston from California than it is from here in the back of beyond."

John realized he owed at least this to his wife, so he agreed. Emma's spring break was coming up after the weekend, and they set off in the car, feeling more free than they had in years.

Driving along Highway 101 in California, Cindy's phone rang. It was Caitlin, with a routine account of life at school.

"I wish I could be with you guys," Caitlin said. School was fun and exciting, and Caitlin was prospering in every way in the atmosphere of Northpoint School.

"Ugh, I have tests tomorrow in history and English, so that means six or eight hours of studying," she told her mother, who looked at her watch and saw that it was five in the afternoon.

"Caitlin, it's eight o'clock there already. No all-nighters, okay?"

"Don't worry, Mom."

"Don't 'Don't worry, Mom,' me! I want to hear, 'No, Mom, I will not pull an all-nighter.'"

Caitlin sighed theatrically. "No, Mother, I shall not pull an all-nighter," she said.

John interrupted and said to Cindy, "Problem?"

Cindy told her daughter, "Hang on, honey. Your father is trying to take part in a conversation he can only hear one side of. Hold on while I try to bring him up to speed."

Speaking to John, Cindy said: "Caitlin says she has two tests tomorrow, history and English. And it'll take six to eight hours of studying. And I said, 'Do not pull an all-nighter.'"

John glanced at the dashboard clock. "Do the math," he said with a laugh.

Cindy suggested that Caitlin get off the phone and get cracking on her books, but Caitlin was in high spirits and chattered on. A few days earlier, it seemed, a couple of students had decided to sit on the still-frozen pond, using a fully upholstered but ratty couch they'd discovered in a dorm basement storage room. They dragged the old pink couch across campus and situated it on the pond not far from the edge of the land. Soon the ice cracked and shattered, and the couch began sinking end-first into the murky, cold pond. But instead of merely observing this remarkable sight, the two students decided to go down with the ship, as it were. Laughing hysterically, unheeding the icy water, they perched on the sinking coach, aware that it could not sink all that far, as the water was only a few feet deep at this spot. What they failed to calculate, however, was that, as the couch became waterlogged, it sank further into the mud, becoming so heavy and entrenched that they couldn't hoist it back to land and drag it back to the basement from which they had liberated it. Finally, everyone decided to just sneak back to their dorms and say nothing, with plans to rescue the couch sometime later in the spring when the ice was fully melted. This plan, however, failed to account for the energies of campus security, which spotted the ruined hulk within hours and made sufficient inquiries to determine who the perpetrators were, with punishments duly forthcoming.

"They got a tow truck to drag it out," Caitlin said, unable to contain her mirth. "Or so I was told. I, of course, knew nothing about this prank."

"Of course," her mother said dubiously, though she was amused by the way her daughter portrayed the hijinks.

"Can I say hi to Emma?" Caitlin asked.

"Just for a minute, Caitlin. Look at the time. You have to get off the phone and study, honey."

Emma took the phone with great delight. "Hello, Caitlin! We're in California! I love you!"

Caitlin replied, "I love you and miss you so much, Emma!" She was quiet for a minute, and then said, "Oh, guess what just happened here, Emma? We just lost power! It's totally dark now!"

"Like when we had snowstorms at home and would sit next to the fireplace for hours?"

"Kind of like that. But dark! I can't wait to see what pranks the junior boys are going to play! I'll let you know tomorrow."

"Don't forget to tell me!" Emma said. "Bye! And good luck with your tests!"

Cindy took the phone and asked, "Your lights are out?"

"I'm looking across campus. Everything is out! All you can see is the campus lit by the moon."

"Is there bad weather?" Cindy asked.

"Nope, it's fine. It's probably just another squirrel that got stuck in the system. But it better come back because I really need to study!"

"Well, you have a field-grade flashlight from Montana," Cindy laughed. "Besides, if the lights don't come back on I'm sure they'll postpone your tests."

Suddenly John slammed on the breaks hard. The car in front of him had stopped abruptly. They were just south of Santa Rosa, and ahead of them stretched a long line at the traffic light. Cindy told John to pay attention and told Caitlin to conserve her phone battery. Mother and daughter made their good-byes.

They waited at the light for a very long time. Then the light itself went blank. In the mounting confusion, some suddenly aggressive drivers started to edge around the snarled line for space to get ahead, but the road was too narrow. Tempers flared.

Cindy had a theory. "Since the budget crisis, California hasn't paid enough attention to highway and infrastructure maintenance. And now the chickens are coming home to roost," she declared.

Agonizingly slowly, the cars crawled ahead. A half mile away, John followed other cars turning onto an exit, and stopped at a service station to top off his tank. But the pump he'd pulled up beside seemed broken. Nothing was showing on the display screen. At the next pump ahead, the same problem presented itself.

Cindy went inside to inquire.

"Power's out," the teenaged clerk at the counter said, as if that weren't perfectly obvious.

"When will it be back?" Cindy said, and realized how absurd the question was.

"Soon," the youth replied laconically and with no apparent authority whatsoever, since he had never before seen the power go out before and didn't have the slightest idea why it had.

They decided to continue driving on two-lane roads northeast toward the spa hotel they had reserved in Calistoga, and stopped at the next gas station they saw about eight miles onward. The power was out there, too. John decided to buy a few cans of dry gas just in case, as well as an extra supply of batteries and, almost as an afterthought, a few gallons of water. But when he brought those purchases to the counter, the clerk told him she could not ring him up.

"Power's out," she said.

"But can't you just add it up on paper?"

"Can't do that," she said.

He thought for a minute. It was getting dark outside and soon the sunlight would leave the store. "Okay," he said, slipping three twenty-dollar bills out of his wallet. "This would certainly cover it."

She looked at the bills suspiciously, as if this were the kind of con the police on television were always warning against. But then she decided that sixty dollars would be better in her pocket than in his—after all, the cash register did not open without electricity. She palmed the bills and said to him, "Okay, mister. We're even."

We are by no means even; you are significantly ahead in this transaction, John felt like saying, but he didn't. Instead he merely thanked her and hurried back to the car.

In the car he found Cindy in a deep gloom.

"Should we call Caitlin and find out if she got her power back?" Cindy said.

"We're getting a weak signal here," he said. "I was trying to get news on the iPhone, but nothing."

John tried to find some news on the car radio, but all he got was canned music that probably emanated from a satellite, and talk-show hosts, origin unknown.

Cindy tried calling but her phone was returning a "circuit busy" tone. Then she tried to text Caitlin. *"Did your power come back on?"* They were relieved when the text box at least showed that the message had been sent.

"We'll wait a few minutes and see if she responds. It's pretty late, but we know she's up studying. Or will be, if she has power. Maybe they'll cancel the tests if the poor kids can't study...." The phone then chirped the alert that a text had been received, but Cindy's heart sank when she saw a canned message saying the text could not be delivered.

"Do the wireless networks all go down when the electrical power does?" she asked.

John looked at the phone as if he wanted to shake it. "This is weird. They're supposed to have backups. Let me bang out a few more messages and see if anything gets through." He did that, and within minutes five of the six bounced back like dead tennis balls. But one evidently did get through.

They were still in the parking lot of the convenience store with the windows open to the cool northern California spring air. Emma was sleeping in the backseat.

After ten minutes, Cindy's phone chirped feebly. *"It's all good,"* the text from Caitlin said. *"Power still out. You guys having fun?"*

And that was the last message they were able to see or send.

*   *   *

After about an hour of driving on dark roads, they arrived at the hotel in Calistoga, but all of the lights were out there, too. John spotted the hotel's roadside sign only when his car headlights swept over its surface. The clerk, working under a yellow battery-operated earthquake emergency lamp, was unable to confirm their reservation.

"The backup is only good for thirty minutes, and that went dead hours ago," the man said, and then turned back to the two other people ahead in line, whose reservations he was trying to process manually from the paper printouts they had in hand.

The reservations could be accepted only as long as someone presented them with confirmation on a piece of paper, or even as an image on a smartphone. Two hotel employees, vying for the limited light, were writing down credit card numbers in a process that seemed to take about thirty minutes per guest. Then, unable to consult the reservations system, they were merely assigning rooms to arriving guests based on educated guessed about which rooms were available.

"Please knock first. If somebody's already in there, come on back down and we'll try another," one of the clerks said apologetically.

Cindy and Emma waited with their bags on a sofa in the lobby, whose only light came from another emergency lantern, when John approached them looking triumphant in the darkened gloom. He waved the room key.

"Eureka!" he said merrily. "Which, incidentally, is a town a ways up the coast from here."

And at that moment, the power came back up with a roar from idled machines, as if they were loudly proclaiming their return. People applauded, pumped their fists in the air, and cheered. The Stuarts, now bathed in full soft-glow light, proceeded to their room, where the first thing John did was turn on the television.

Fiddling with the confounding remote device, he finally found CNN, where the announcer was describing a dire situation.

"To repeat: There have been major power outages across the country, for unknown reasons. Reports arriving in our CNN newsroom show that about half of the country—half of the country—is currently without electrical power. This is a developing story, and I need to warn you that our reports are still sketchy. Some regions, we are told, have erratic power and others are not affected at all. In a few minutes, we will have as complete a rundown as we can of where the power is out. Obviously, the effects of this massive power outage, the greatest in the history of the United States, reach deeply into everyday life. Traffic is snarled on city streets and on Interstate highways. There are reports of street disturbances and unconfirmed reports of looting in several cities, and we'll have more on that shortly. Across the United States, wireless networks are down because of massive demands from data, voice, and text messages...."

John felt Cindy at his shoulder looking at the screen. Emma, exhausted, had already crawled into the spare bed and was fast asleep.

"This looks horrible," she said.

John nodded without replying. His face bore a stricken look.

The broadcaster continued on with Cindy transfixed to the screen. John anxiously dug his emergency radio out of his bag and slammed it into its charger, worried about how long the power would stay on and hoping there would be sufficient time to do the same for the cell phones. He then asked Cindy to run down to get at least a dozen bottles of water from the vending machine.

"A dozen? Didn't you come out of the store back down the road with two gallons? Aren't you overreacting a little? I mean, it's not like power hasn't gone out before."

"Not on this scale it hasn't," he said flatly. "Trust me. I'm on this."

Cindy went to the shop in the lobby and bought microwave dinners, tins of Alaska salmon, and cereal. She was surprised to see that the milk was all sold out, but then she noticed that the shop was crowded with people stocking up on provisions. Feeling a little guilty, she bought the last two twelve-packs of AA batteries on the shelf.

In their room, they used the microwave to make dinner, having abandoned previous plans to eat at an excellent restaurant in town. Emma awoke and joined them watching the television.

John was flipping channels so quickly and furiously that Cindy became irritated. "Will you stop doing that? It's totally annoying," she said peevishly. "It's the same news, just different people reading it."

"Not at the same time," he said without any emotion. "I absorb it quickly and move on and then come back."

She was about to comment more, but he waved her off and turned his full attention to the television. He had heard the words "deliberate attack."

"We're now being told that an emergency meeting is underway at the White House, where the subject is whether this at has been a deliberate attack on the United States, rather than just a failure of the power grids. One Homeland Security official has just used the words 'terrorist attack,' but we need to continue to stress, this is all speculative at this point...."

"A deliberate attack?" Cindy repeated in a tone of disbelief.

And then with a sinking whoosh, the power went off again.

Now the only news available came from official government bulletins that were being read in a toneless voice on the emergency radio frequencies, as part of the Homeland Security disaster and attack-response plan. John and Cindy listened into the night, and when dawn arrived, nothing had changed. They had coffee, made breakfast for Emma, and listened some more, registering the horrific details as if in a trance.

Massive traffic jams had occurred across a large swath of the country as signal lights had ceased functioning. Cars were abandoned on roads and highways where they had run out of gas—causing deadly pileups. Route 101 was a clogged river of cars. Some cars had been abandoned when people just walked away seeking food and water, but hotels and bars were turning them away, and restaurants and fast-food outlets had run out of stock and locked their doors. Wireless phone service collapsed under unprecedented demand. The data network for Internet access also collapsed under the strain; John knew this was the dirty little secret of the telecom industry: such networks were built for a small percentage of users at any given time—when a critical mass of users attempted access at the same time, the networks suddenly and spectacularly fried from the overload.

One radio announcer said that the wireless cell service and remote Internet access would be restored within forty-eight hours, but that the companies had told the government that they hoped to be back in operation before then.

"How can they be sure when they don't even know the root cause?" John said in angry exasperation.

"John, you're yelling at the radio. It can't hear you," Cindy told him in a confidential tone, and for the first time since the night before they both laughed. Twenty-four hours without power had now gone by. The emergency radio droned on.

The mayhem was unprecedented. Most stores and supermarkets and grocery stores were closed. People were walking aimlessly in some parts of the country, hungry and thirsty. Police said they could not provide adequate assistance because roads were blocked. Helicopters could operate and were circling cities and residential areas making overhead announcements, asking the indisposed to proceed to Red Cross, Federal Emergency Management Agency shelters, and churches where beds, food, and water were available. Children were at school, where they remained.

Office workers were stuck at their businesses with food running out. Airports had closed under federal emergency order—but hundreds of thousands of travelers were stranded in terminals, and the backups reached into Europe and Asia as planes failed to arrive from or take off for the United States.

The situation kept worsening. Looting spread in cities and towns, partly as a result of people searching for food. Most municipal water-pumping stations had emergency power backup only for forty-eight hours, and after that they would require large deliveries of diesel fuel to run generators, and the fuel trucks could not deliver if the roads all were blocked. Sewage pumps stopped working in office buildings and dorms and apartment buildings, where toilets backed up, adding to the growing misery of citizens.

Even overcrowded shelters were running low on supplies and provisions because deliveries could not get through. The relative few who had emergency generators at home, and had stockpiled enough fuel to keep them going, were extremely relieved that they had made those preparations, even if others had scoffed when they did.

John thought of their neighbor Bruce Thomas, and his exhortations on emergency preparedness, on being prepared for a life off the grid.

"Remember the can opener," John pronounced aloud with new appreciation.

John turned to Cindy and they both thought of the same thing. Their Concord home also had backup generator capability, a precaution against New England snow storms, that could keep the house up and running for days.

The drumbeat of civil disruption beat on. The children and teachers who were stranded at schools where cafeterias were out of food. Emergency teams were delivering food by helicopters. Food was rotting at supermarkets due to the lack of refrigeration, but supermarket doors were locked and guarded. Food distribution centers reported lines of desperate people that stretched for many hours. There were reported cases of people helping other people, but desperation was also common.

The emergency radio droned on with the litany of abject misery. The government now suspected that a massive network-virus attack had infected control systems of power plants, causing them to go haywire. Worse still, this had caused severe damage to some of the physical plants, to the turbines and coolers and other systems. The virus was capable of self-destructing, hence difficult to track or even identify. Its properties included the ability to keep coming back randomly to take over the besieged control systems anew.

More clarity emerged from the bulletins, which John was paying rapt attention to. The nascent cyber-war force had managed to track down the virus, which left deliberate traces of its name, *"TENXUTS."* Apparently it traveled over power lines to avoid detection by standard firewalls—but then through machines that had interface to this power line; it extracted data and then subsequently made entry into the network. *"TENXUTS"* was the most disastrous virus and most damaging attack ever mounted. And it was devilishly smart, with the ability to erase its own footprint in a manner that made the power come up and then go down, as if designed to toy with everyone's hopes, to play with lives.

In Washington, the president met with the newly formed cyber-war council, but the enemy was not readily identifiable in a virtual war fought with virtual weapons that nevertheless caused real damage on an astonishing scale. The generals were just not used to it, as 99 percent of the defense budget was still being channeled into preparations for conventional wars. The Army and Navy had become lame ducks.

CHAPTER THIRTY-NINE

On the president's direction, the deputy chief of the FBI formed a series of "cyber army" units at MIT, Stanford, Caltech, and Johns Hopkins, where many faculty members and their top researchers were already working on their respective secret networks designated to experiment with and hopefully prevent cyber war. The problem was that many of these individuals simply could not be reached once the actual cyber disaster occurred. In Washington, Marine Corps General Joseph R. Lee, the chairman of the joint chiefs of staff, grumbled sourly at that prospect, which he saw as a basic failure of military planning.

General Lee exploded to his adjunct, a high-strung army colonel: "What kind of a sad-sack army is this, where we can't even deploy the troops to the front lines? Strategic military planning since the time of Alexander the Great has started with the fundamental requirement of getting your troops to where you need them. And when did that occur? When did Alexander the Great first confirm that strategy, colonel?"

"A very long time ago, sir," the adjunct said nervously.

"You're damn right it was a very long time ago, colonel!" the general hollered in a fury. "It was 335 B.C. when Alexander needed to secure his northern flank in the Balkan Campaign. And what did he need, colonel?"

"He needed troops there, sir," the colonel said, wishing the general would stop yelling at him.

"He needed troops! That is *correct*, colonel. *Boots on the ground.* And tell me, colonel: Where are my boots right now?"

"At colleges, sir," the colonel stammered.

"At *colleges*! And why can we not speedily deploy these so-called cyber boots at a joint command in D.C.?"

"Roads are blocked, sir."

"The *roads* are *blocked*," the general repeated with such scorn and agitation that the colonel rushed to bring him a glass of water from the nearly empty officer cooler.

While the military did its best to round up the new brigades of cyber warriors, a consortium of intelligence and military agencies under the direction of the FBI assembled the best experts they could get their hands on. As a consequence of this crucial need for intellectual firepower, the federal government had the state of Massachusetts grant bail and safe passage to one Norm Porter, explicitly so that he could take part in the high-level response to the cyber onslaught.

When the group was assembled at FBI headquarters, the deputy director of the Bureau, Thomas A. Broomall, outlined the extent of the problem.

First Broomall briefed the group, all of whom had been expeditiously cleared for the highest level of security, on the state of the Enterprise as it was currently known.

"A week ago, there was an assassination attempt on one of our top people, Special Agent Arthur J. Moore, the agent in charge of our cyber-crime operations. Many of you know Art Moore, and you'll be happy to know that he's going to live, though he was severely wounded in the car-bomb explosion. But the unconscionable attack on him shows just how dangerous the Enterprise is. Let me play you an excerpt from a surveillance audio recording of the Enterprise's top leaders in Belgrade, which we received through the CIA. The conversation, made shortly before these cyber attacks began, is between the Enterprise's number one mastermind, the boss, Zerind Rokus Kazac, also known as ZRK, and his top aide, Laadislao Syanislas Abadeziev, also known as LSA."

Broomall cued the recording in Serbian, accompanied by English subtitles on a large monitor.

"What happened, Laadislao? This FBI guy Moore is in the hospital, not in the morgue! He was supposed to be dead!"

"We hit him hard, but he got lucky, Zerind."

"Luck? Luck is what the weak rely on. What I see on our end is

incompetence, a failure to execute the critical mission. You might be losing your edge, Laadislao."

"My edge is razor-sharp, Zerind."

"I am beginning to wonder..."

"My sources in the FBI told me Moore was the agent in charge of Gavin's case, and that they had located him. I needed Moore alive and talking so we could learn where Gavin is. And only then we could dispose of Moore!" said Laadislao.

"Do you realize how bad this is now? Have you ever seen a wounded cobra in a fight? A snake should be killed—or left alone untouched. Never wounded. And now we're in a fight with a wounded cobra!"

"I hear you, Zerind."

"He will be definitely difficult to get to now! We will be attacked with far more vengeance—remember the Cobra nature of the human!"

That was the extent of the recorded conversation and Director Broomall let his eyes sweep over the group when it ended. "So this is who and what we're dealing with, ladies and gentlemen. Nothing abstract there. These are vicious killers engaged in a cause. And no, we don't know exactly what that last statement by ZRK means. So if you can help us out with any ideas there, please sound off."

No one said anything, so Broomall continued his briefing.

"Desperation is the operative word," Broomall told the group. "Our top cyber-security and technology people have been working to the point of physical exhaustion to clear the viruses from any and all suspected host machines. The challenge is that half of the grid is presently working for some unknown reasons, and we do not want the virus to infect the working networks, so we have been methodically untangling the two halves at every connection point—the power-line point and the actual network connection—to ensure their isolation. The biggest problem, I'm sorry to say, has been the simple lack of electricians to execute the basic tasks because most are stranded elsewhere and are unable to assemble. The military has now taken over the task, but it will take time to understand such a vast network. And if even one mistake is made, among hundreds of touch points, we will have an even greater disaster—a full-blown disaster instead of a half-blown disaster, if you will."

He continued, "Our worry is that the second half may succumb to the first half. That's because the desperate zeal to bring back normalcy can burn us completely. On the other hand, the public and, obviously, the political pressures are building up intensely. To make matters worse, the incredibly sluggish public data-com network will be going down very soon, and regular landline phone calls will also disappear. So whatever semblance of civil order remains will likely dissipate. At that point, only the military with its backup parallel networks will be operational—but that will be of precious little value to the civilian population.

"The enemy is operating silently and stealthily from deep shadows. We can't see and can't shoot. All our military hardware, worth trillions of dollars, capable of destroying the earth thirteen times over, is laughably useless at this time. This is worse than a nuclear strike, which, God forbid, would be horrible, but at least locality-centric. Some areas are nearing the end of drinking-water supply; others are only running at half the capacity to preserve fuel. Fortunately some of the pumping stations were in forward-thinking jurisdictions that employed solar power and wind power locally, so these are able to continue to work. That is one lucky stroke. But overall, it's the centralization of everything that is causing the unprecedented magnitude of damage. I wish that many more people, many more institutions, even supermarkets, were self-sufficient. Unfortunately, that's still in the future. What do we do now?"

"What's the current situation, Director Broomall?" one of the experts asked.

"Communications are poor but not totally dead. Many radio stations continue to operate with backup power, and the good news there is that radio stations and reception require a lot less power than television stations and reception. As most of you know, Homeland Security has been utilizing the emergency broadcast system for a running stream of news as we process it. Nothing fancy, but it's reliable news, and thank God a lot of radio stations are still close to their local markets and to the idea that they provide public service, unlike a lot of TV stations. So radio has been a real blessing.

"Air travel is back as of this morning, when Homeland Security lifted the emergency order that had grounded all flights for fear of a physical security attack. Now the planes can fly, but of course the roads are often impassable, the airports are still jammed with people who have no way to get home, and passengers and airlines employees are not working because the networks are dead. So except for government and military flights, there is very little traffic in the air."

"Trains?" someone asked.

"Similar situation. The rail system's electrical network is separate, but there's the same basic problem. People can't get to train stations, including crews, and the ones still there are totally exhausted. The stock markets are closed as no one can place a sell or buy order, and this has affected the world markets which went down by nearly twenty percent in two days, and a further plunge is likely. All over the country, ATM machines are off-line. Banks are closed, so it's hard to get money, and we're seeing signs of a barter economy developing already. Except for radio, communications are basically dead. Newspapers can't print, let alone deliver. With the networks down or almost down, there's no Internet Explorer, no Google. Oddly enough, only AOL, which still supports slow landline connectivity through dial-up modems, is still largely operational!"

There was some stilted laughter about that from the assembled computer and technology experts, who had long ago dismissed AOL with disdain, a service as obsolete as a telephone party line. As the proverbial cockroach with the best chance to survive a nuclear attack, amongst the telecom industry it looked like AOL was going to have the last laugh.

*   *   *

At Northpoint School, meanwhile, 380 students were basically idled. Teams and other students on indoor basketball and squash courts, and on the campus ice-skating rink, found themselves suddenly frozen in pitch blackness. Several students were injured on the rink, trying to grope their way back off the ice in the dark.

After a day with no power, hunger became a factor, though cereal and salads still were available. To consolidate resources and for better safety and security, students in the older dorms were moved into the newer dorms. An almost hysterical situation arose as students and parents were unable to contact each other by phone or e-mail. On a more basic human level, the sewage system had failed and all the toilets were backed-up. Water was rationed strategically. Luckily, there was some communication in place with the occasional text message here and there sent by the few who had conserved battery power.

Caitlin was equipped with a manual hand-cranked charger that Bruce and Maloney had given her as a going-off-to-school present. With that and her landline telephone, she did her best to accommodate desperate fellow students who crowded into the room she now shared with three other girls, all of who were attempting to contact home—sometimes with success if there was also a landline at their parents' end of the connection. Even the dean of students had claimed space in Caitlin's room and was making as many phone calls as she could to parents and guardians. Caitlin was seen as a savior, and was repeatedly complimented for her prudence and disaster preparedness.

Darkness arrived early in New England at this time of the year, and the cold was creeping in. With darkness, fear intensified. For most students, the novelty of an extended blackout had long worn off. Now they were just tired and frightened and confused. Then, with morning, the school ordered all students transferred from the dorms to the theater.

As Caitlin had feared, a group of junior-class boys exploited the opportunity for anarchy. As she and Eva walked across campus toward the theater, she felt ice trickling down her back. Before she even turned around, Caitlin saw a slushy snowball made from not-yet melted mounds of snow hit Eva in the back of her head. Caitlin and Eva soon found themselves, along with most of the school, on the main green flinging slushy balls of snow at everyone. For the first time in what seemed a long time, the students felt a kind of joy in the merry melee. It took twenty minutes for things to calm down, and by then all the students were cold and wet. As the student body sat absentmindedly listening to their instructions about procedures and emergencies for the duration of the crisis, their chill and damp clothing, and the awareness that there was nothing they could do but live with it, was an abrupt return to reality.

And then, forty-six hours after the blackout had struck, it was over as power rumbled on in a great surging wave from the East Coast to the west. Apparently cyber boots had finally succeeded in stopping the inexorable march of the Enterprise and AJs. There was a calm jubilance among the technology minds that had stemmed the tide of the crisis. The government, however, was still tense—they remained tight-lipped as the perpetrators were still on the loose and no one knew what they would do next. In addition, there was a negative judgment in the court of public opinion to deal with; the whole affair had revealed the government's visible lack of preparedness.

The deputy director of the FBI called Norm that evening.

"Congratulations, Norm, this is Tom Broomall. The bureau cannot thank you enough for what you did. Mr. President called and thanked Director Freeman and the entire Bureau team—and wanted to pass this gratitude along to you, for your help in getting us out of the most severe crisis we have ever faced in the history of our nation."

"No worries, Tom. That's my job; the country was under attack, and we all are on the same side. Besides it was not me alone, I had my band of brothers and sisters here at MIT helping me."

"Well, you guys were just plain amazing, absolutely brilliant; sometimes the boundary between outlaws and not-so-outlaws is so thin it's nearly invisible... at this time and age it's difficult to sort out one from another."

"All depends on how you define the law," a smiling Norm mildly retorted.

"Speaking of which, don't worry about your Friendsbook troubles anymore," the deputy director said. "I have taken care of that, with the assistance of Jake Dolan. You know him, I gather? But please stay out of trouble, while you are free on bail awaiting your trial in the Weinheart case. And go get some sleep! I think you guys must have been up for forty-eight hours straight."

CHAPTER FORTY

John had already decided that he was not going to take these attacks lying down, but rather he would try his level best to both fight for his country and get revenge on a personal level with the criminal, ZRK. He was angry but made efforts to calm himself down—otherwise, in this world of cyber warfare, he might lose his edge. He carefully analyzed the signatures of the previous attacks. He had access to all of the data he might require, as the U.S. branches of Cindy's Haitian bank had also been attacked. He then devised a plan.

One day he called Caitlin and asked her, somewhat out of the blue:

"I assume you know how to get deep into your school's computer system?"

"Yes, Dad, you showed me," said Caitlin with a tone that said, "I am not stupid."

"I need your help; can you help me test something?"

"May I ask why?"

"No."

"Okay, tell me what to do and I will take care of it."

"You get in the system and ping the IP address I will text you right after this call. Half an hour later, ping the IP address again, and that's it."

"Dad, I have the biggest dance of the year tonight, everyone's gonna be there. Can I do it tomorrow evening?"

"It will take no more than thirty minutes of your time."

"Dad, I already picked out my outfit, and I'm about to get ready."

"Just do it, it's important. Even better if you did it during the time everyone is at the dance."

"Fine. But only if you promise it'll take half an hour!" Caitlin said.

Caitlin successfully managed to sneak out of the dance twice and still have a blast with her friends. The code tested successfully. There had been no risk to the school's system, it was only a test but John did not have access to a safe site except for that hosted by Northpoint School.

*   *   *

In response to the fierce and repeated attacks on the country, citizen soldiers at their own initiative started to join the cyber war to defend the nation. It was just like the 1700s, except the soldiers' weaponry was comprised of computers and connectivity, as opposed to cannons and muskets. General Lee's ragtag brigades of cyber warriors were also on duty and, as he put it, "just itching for a fight." With a ferocious, if virtual, roar, the defenders were advancing on the attackers.

One such cyber warrior was a brave blogger with a Web site named Newtidbits.com. It was a popular blog that had recently gained some notoriety by publishing provocative theories about white-collar criminals. By now, it had a track record for accuracy and reliability among those who followed the minutiae of white-collar crime, a growing field. The blogger was a shadowy figure who stayed anonymous. Occasional threats were left on his blog by the aggrieved, but that only helped enhance the blog's popularity. John approached the blogger and bought his blog for $25,000, taking his place as an anonymous blogger with the same name.

A few days later, a Newtidbits.com entry on ZRK created a stir in these circles when it appeared with the provocative headline, **"ZRK: Just What Serbia Needs: Another Blowhard."**

The anonymous blogger claimed to have interviewed many people who grew up with ZRK—in the decidedly non-exotic environs of Cincinnati. It was clear to the discerning that the blogger had in fact spoken with people who knew him from elementary through high school, including teachers and also some of his friends and relatives who were still in the area.

The story was highly insulting to Zerind Rokus Kazac, suggesting that many of his so-called accomplishments were exaggerated in the manner of folklore. He was bright, but not as outstanding as the media and their minders in politics had made him out to be.

"He was a crybaby," one old anonymous schoolmate recalled. "He bawled like a three-year-old when a teacher we had gave him a 98 instead of a 100." His relatives did not speak kindly of him, either—though none would risk being quoted by name. "He was an arrogant egomaniac who never cared for anyone and was never loyal to anyone but himself," one of them said. "If you crossed him in any way, like making a trivial joke at his expense, he'd go after you like a junkyard dog," another recalled. "I simply avoided the guy after we grew up."

The long blog entry concluded by saying that the infamous Zerind Rokus Kazac "is nothing but a cheap criminal and a loudmouth." Furthermore, it asserted that the original and actual ZRK had died years earlier, and that the show was now being run by "this ludicrous impostor."

The blog was widely read and linked to on the Internet. Even the major newspapers made note of it.

Within two days, a threatening comment appeared on the blog, ostensibly from the Enterprise, with a death threat to blow up the blogger. It read, "We know who you are, where you are; we know every click you make; we know when you type. So enjoy yourself, Cowardly Typist, because you have only seventy-two hours to live."

The blogger responded boldly, taunting ZRK to disclose his true identity to the world. The blogger went even further and ridiculed the Enterprise. He boasted how well secured his blog was "unlike those national banks that were so easily hacked by pathetic amateurs from a ridiculous country like Serbia." Virtually bellowing with contempt, he challenged ZRK to attack his blog.

A day later a fierce attack occurred but the site survived. The emboldened blogger wrote: "Is this the best you got, ZRK? I would think a real man could do better. Or maybe you're just a fake genius?"

In the pantheon of things, the merely good hackers typically hack into a site, collect the information they require, and bring it back to their machines. The very best ones *never* do that, as there is a risk that the information brought back may itself be tainted, with a concurrent risk of detection. That is why the Enterprise never brought back data. So when the blogger challenged ZRK's manhood, personally attacked him, his childhood, his family, taunting him to bring the site down, at first ZRK could not succeed in bringing the site down. But apparently, ZRK lost his cool and included a tracer in his attack. A tracer is a cleverly designed packet that works like a sponge; like a sponge collecting fluid around it, it absorbs all. The tracer traveled back, and gave ZRK sufficient information about the blogger's computer systems and the path it traveled. However, there was a *return* tracer the blogger had included in the original tracer itself that ZRK did not recognize.

Oddly enough, John noticed that there was another sophisticated tracer active in his machine that he remembered from his grad school days. The only two people who could have done that were Norm and Jake. John created a return tracer and that brought the information confirming it was the FBI. To John's utter surprise, it turned out that Jake was working for the FBI. *Why then had Jake confronted Cindy at the ice cream parlor? Had he done this as a kind of warning?* John profusely thanked God that Jake had not gone to the dark side as John had originally suspected. Had he done so, ZRK would have been impossible to bring down. John was happy to realize that the government by now had gotten their act together and was trying every which way to gain access to ZRK and nab him. John added a message in the tracer to the FBI: "LOL, it's us again." He got a message back through the same channel: "Not so fast, just doing my job."

John just laughed.

John proceeded to disable Jake's tracer as he was worried that ZRK may detect it and then his own plan would be compromised. Then, just as he suspected, a massive attack occurred late that night that truly blew his defenses away, reminiscent of the time when he was competing with "Rob"—who had destroyed his six gates in no time.

Far away, somewhere in Serbia, ZRK enjoyed some satisfaction as this had been a tough nut to crack, even for him.

But there was another twist. The tracer John had created for the Enterprise brought back every piece of the data he needed to identify ZRK's location. He extracted the data and immediately forwarded it to Jake through the back channel they had established.

Coupled with Serbian intelligence, the feds moved in and ZRK was arrested within thirty minutes.

Later that day the notorious ZRK was on every television channel and newspaper front page in the world. There he was, handcuffed and being hustled into an unmarked plane at some unknown location, bound for some other location unknown. It was unfathomable that this diminutive individual had brought the entire nation to the brink of an unmitigated disaster worse than World War II—without firing a single shot.

Wild jubilation ensued at the FBI headquarters. A beaming president came on the television and addressed the nation. Bankers everywhere took a deep breath of relief. The U.S. stock markets shot up over 20 percent in a day and the same held true for the global markets. Citizens everywhere were celebrating, as were the cyber warriors at MIT, Cal Tech, Stanford, and Johns Hopkins. The president personally called Jake Dolan, congratulating him on a brilliant job, for the heroic and smart effort that he had put into this difficult war. The director of the FBI, Chris Freeman, also came by and patted Jake on the back and then told him that never in the history of the Bureau had someone done so much to save the country and bring it back from the brink of disaster. He would recommend a Presidential Medal of Honor for Jake. Of course, Jake would have to go to the White House to pick that up.

Back in Montana, Cindy broke out in shouts and hugged John when they saw the news on the television. She had tears trickling down her cheek, her cheeks were twitching and she was speechless. Her happiness wanted to burst out and scream at the world, *we got him!, we are free at last!,* but she remained silent and sobbed happily. Emma came by, confused as to what was going on; John explained in some basic terms and Emma was able to join in the celebration. Cindy quickly texted Caitlin, "We won, got him."

John felt himself relax as years of a massive burden had finally lifted from his shoulders. He heated some water in the microwave, made some green tea for himself, and sat down on his favorite couch, putting his feet up on the ottoman. An immense internal joy was reflected outwardly as a sense of calmness took over him—it was as if John had just come out of a deep meditation. He stared at the ceiling or at the walls with purposeful blankness as his mission was finished. He was back to being a small boat in an ocean, something he occasionally enjoyed. Only Cindy understood his mental state. They held hands tightly for a few minutes. Cindy leaned her head against his and left him alone in his own abstract world. They stayed together on the couch and dozed off that way; night came and for the first time since they left Concord they even forgot to turn the alarm on.

*   *   *

Back in Washington, Jake was happy as hell when he finally came back home to go to bed. The events of the past months had been a constant source of nearly overwhelming anxiety and now they were gone—replaced only by a nagging feeling, as if something was still not quite right. It was as if someone in his head kept saying, *the real hero remains quiet, unsung and unknown while you are getting all the accolades. Is that fair, is that right?* Jake could not sleep. He just lay in bed restless as the voice inside got louder and louder. The Boy Scout in him kept telling him to do the right thing. He got out of his bed and started typing an e-mail.

> *Gavin,*
>
> *Many thanks for what you did! You are the true patriot, who responded to the call of duty while taking immeasurable risks to your own life and that of your wife and children. You are the real hero not me. I wish the world would know that. I truly enjoyed working with you; in fact, it was an honor. I feel downright ashamed for the pain I caused, known or unknown to you. My most sincere apologies to you all. When you took the bastard down in your own quiet and unassuming way, then and there I realized why Lisa fell for you. She made the right choice. Hope our paths will cross again. Say hi to her for me."*
>
> *Warmly,*
>
> *Jake*

Since Newtidbits.com was gone, Jake's only access to Gavin was through Caitlin as he was the one who had sent that threatening e-mail to her earlier, as part of his not entirely holy plan to scare Gavin into helping the United States against the Enterprise. He encrypted the contents above and sent a note to Caitlin requesting she forward it to her dad, which she did right away.

As John read the e-mail, a big smile spread across his face. He murmured, "Thank you, Jake."

The next day, as John and Cindy tried to settle down from the big news of the day earlier, John said in his own understated way: "I am so glad that they got ZRK." His tone of voice radiated a happy satisfaction.

"Does this mean our troubles are over?" Cindy asked, hating to think that there might be reason for her elation to fade.

There was.

"No, I don't believe that for a minute," John said. "Criminal enterprises always find a new CEO, and there is a continuous supply of applicants. Look how long it took to bring down the Mafia, after generations of bosses went to prison. I am sure that Russian and Chinese intelligence using Serbians as proxy have someone ready to take over. The market rules!"

Meanwhile, a few days later the *Boston Globe* had a story headlined, "Feds Closing in on Billy Dalton." The story recounted how authorities had found huge sums of money belonging to Dalton in an overseas bank, along with lists of names of federal agents and state police he had paid off, and the corresponding amounts. Unfortunately, the FBI concluded, the lists largely matched other lists of people already known to have been compromised. The article said that the investigation was ongoing.

CHAPTER FORTY-ONE

One of the things that kept John returning to the computer at the town library in Wanton was the ability to access academic and technical publications. This was a service that Maloney had insisted the library provide free to the public, although at the total cost of several thousand dollars a year to her own small operating budget. She considered it important that scientific research be readily available and from many sources. John was grateful for that access that otherwise would have been out of reach. Without having to risk the purchase of a session each time by credit card, he had full access to a wide range of scholarly archives. Among his many fruitful searches, however, he was disappointed to find one resource that was not in the archives: the *Journal of Innovation*, an old, obscure niche quarterly that published scholarly articles and examined issues and controversies related to patents. It had once been his favorite scientific magazine. The *Journal of Innovation* had inspired him in his college days when it was a fat print publication. He himself had once published an article in the journal.

He mentioned the *Journal of Innovation* to Cindy and his longing to gain access to it again.

"I remember you mentioning it a few times when we were dropping off old copies to the high school library in California before moving to Concord. Whatever happened to it?"

"It fell on hard times, unfortunately, and closed down a while ago."

"Is it not available online?"

"No it was prior to that time," said John.

"Hey, I have a thought, why don't we go to California, scan all the copies and put them online. It's been a while since we went out there, and it will give us a change of surroundings, too." said Cindy.

Cindy and John registered its name, the rights to which had been abandoned by its former publishers. They drove to California and visited the high school housing the old journals for a few days and were able to laboriously scan every page of each issue. The journal had closed its doors abruptly eighteen years ago, with one Winter issue being the last—but, confoundingly, that issue was the only one missing from the ones he had carefully saved and presented to the high school library. Maybe, he thought, it had been lost due to a change of address. He searched the Internet, but was disappointed that only few references were available for the journal. Unfortunately, not a single reference existed for the final Winter issue. He searched for the editor, but he had died years ago. There were a couple of other names listed on the masthead of the old journal, but he could not trace them either. John went onto a community board for inventors and enquired if anyone had that particular Winter issue. To his delight and astonishment (he would never get over his wonder at the speed and the reach of the Internet), a man responded almost immediately and explained that only a few copies of the last issue had been printed because cash was running low, and so subscribers' copies of that issue were likely not mailed out. The man reported that he had no idea where a copy might be found.

Owning the *Journal of Innovation*'s name was a matter of pride to John, who wanted to revive and continue its legacy.

At dinner with Cindy that evening, they discussed how patents had been so central to their lives.

John said, "I am happy about putting this journal online. That was a great idea, Cindy!"

"A great idea in many ways," Cindy responded.

With some nostalgia and a little bitterness, they discussed John's agreement with the software company while he was still living in Concord; the long-delayed payment of $17.2 million plus interest would be due within just a few months.

"It would be nice," Cindy said longingly.

"Well, let's hope the criminals spend it wisely once they get their mitts on it," John said.

CHAPTER FORTY-TWO

Norm Porter was innocent, just as John had believed.

After a few days in jail, followed by two months on bail awaiting trial on murder charges, Norm was abruptly released by a judge acting at the behest of the federal government. Freed of all other charges, Norm agreed to pay a token fine on a technical charge for keeping an illegal clone of his SIM card—the very card that turned out to have been his salvation.

According to the news accounts, which quoted law-enforcement officials, the case was strange—and stranger still was its outcome. Norm had anticipated an entrapment of some kind and had begun to carry two cell phones that were clones of each other. One morning when he was jogging along the Charles River, he collided with a man on roller skates, and both of them tumbled into some hedges. Norm took a particularly nasty fall into a rose bush, sustaining bruises, scratches, and a cut on his arm that bled profusely. The skater, who had been the cause of the collision, apologized profusely and gave Norm some Band-Aids and a gauze pad that he had in a small personal first aid kit he carried in his backpack. Another pedestrian stopped by and helped. When Norm got home he turned on his cell phone, which he routinely turned off while jogging. That's when he found strange text messages that led him to believe that someone with malicious intent had gained access to his phone while it was switched off and had replaced his text messages with others. Seeing that, Norm quickly opened up his second cell phone and immediately flipped the battery out and tossed it away, hoping to prevent an intruder from accessing that one remotely.

The next morning, Norm was rudely awakened by a police SWAT team pounding into his bedroom, barking orders with weapons pointed at his head. During the arrest, the police seized both of his phones. During the preliminary investigation that led him to be charged with the young woman's murder, the police and prosecutors neglected to compare the two cloned phones, which anyone who knew anything about the technologies involved would have realized that both phones should have contained exact copies of the supposedly incriminating text messages. If Norm had sent those texts, they would have been on both phones.

They were not.

During the interrogation, before his lawyer arrived and told him not to talk, Norm had tried to explain that he believed he had been framed, that the mysterious roller skater who had seemed merely to be providing assistance had probably managed to obtain a sample of his blood, and if the skater had had anything to do with the woman's murder, that would certainly explain how traces of Norm's blood were found on her clothing. And stealing his gun and using it in the crime would not have been a problem. Detectives did not want to hear this theory, however. In fact, they shook their heads wisely and laughed.

Only later, after federal authorities expressed their need for Norm to be let out of custody to assist in the cyber-war response, did a detective follow up on his hunch that maybe Norm's story made sense.

When Norm's defense was established, investigators kept asking him about what possible motive anyone would have for framing him. They had known about his credentials, but by now they were aware of exactly how prominent Norm was in network security, given that the federal government obviously thought enough of him to reach out to have him released from custody even before the murder charges were dropped.

Cindy read the news account and ran to John to show him. "You were right. He was entrapped. But how did you know?"

John read the story with intense interest and said, "I believe the Enterprise was behind it."

"They killed that girl?"

"Absolutely. She and Norm were both involved in Citizens Anonymous. She was just a pawn in this play by ZRK. Norm couldn't be purchased—all that nonsense about him being corruptible because his father had once been falsely accused of being an agent of a foreign country aside. Norm was a thorn in ZRK's side. This took care of them both, supposedly."

She was trembling. "So why has he not gone after you?"

He looked at her sharply. She rephrased the question, "Why has he not got you?"

He replied, "Because we are hiding in sunshine."

CHAPTER FORTY-THREE

Redwood Biotech had been reliably wiring royalties from the cancer-detection patent to Gavin's bank account in Massachusetts every quarter.

Redwood had a policy, standard in the industry, of scanning the Internet annually for the patents they worked with, or had exclusive licenses for, to guard against misappropriation and piracy. During one of these routine searches, Redwood analysts encountered a keyword-string that retrieved an old scientific paper that was quickly deemed relevant. The paper was archived on a Web site called JournalofInnovation.com, which was an online resurrection of a long-defunct scientific trade journal for patents. It was listed as having been written by a Jonathan Demarcolus, who had not published previously—but that was not uncommon since the journal routinely published papers from authors who were not mainstream academicians with fancy titles. In fact, that had been part of its appeal to inventors, who tended to be independent-minded people who worked outside the box.

The paper briefly described Demarcolus's work. The patent attorney at Redwood Biotech searched for the author, but found no further references, nor could he be located through other search measures. The attorney conveyed his findings to a supervisor as part of an overall report. When the supervisor, who had been around for a while, reviewed the results, and checked cross-references made to the patents of interest, he became very curious. Demarcolus's paper appeared to describe a subject similar to the patent that Redwood did not own, but had exclusively licensed from a highly respected inventor named Gavin Brinkley, last known address in Concord, Massachusetts. The company had been paying huge royalties, several millions of dollars a year on the patent that now seemed to have been invented by Demarcolus. Not able to comprehend this conundrum, the supervisor checked the dates on the patents—all of Brinkley's patents had much later dates than the date of the publication of Demarcolus's work. *Should the patent itself never have been granted and the royalties never paid?* He immediately informed the chief general counsel, who sprang into action.

Redwood Biotech sent notice to Gavin Brinkley at the Concord address, explaining that what was called "prior art" had been discovered on his patent. Prior art is the legal term for any earlier knowledge that directly relates to a specific patent or an invention, including previous patents. The letter was not friendly. It stated that Gavin's patent should not have been granted, and that litigation was pending to challenge it. Redwood Biotech was demanding the immediate return of all of the many millions paid out in royalties over the years, with interest.

At the house in Concord, that alarming notice was signed for and read by an impostor Gavin Brinkley, who had assumed that identity. The impostor Gavin was initially surprised, but he shrugged it off. He was accustomed to opening letters from all over the world, always trying to do something with his patents. He and his wife, the impostor Lisa Brinkley, were getting ready to attend the debutante ball of a good friend, and the impostor Lisa did not like to be delayed.

When Lisa came down the stairs, she looked gorgeous. There was a limo waiting in the driveway to take them to the Ritz-Carlton in downtown Boston for the ball. The lifestyle of the very rich was extremely pleasing to them. They handled the necessary appearances with the requisite aplomb and flair, flaunting their exquisite tastes in everything from the wine they served to the destinations they traveled to, from the cars they drove to the clothes they wore with such confident style. The impostor Lisa loved diamonds, nothing vulgar, of course; Tiffany knew how to do a breathtaking necklace or earrings with precisely the right unmistakably starry-night sparkle. The impostor Gavin enjoyed sailing and racing cars on the track. Lisa loved to shop in Manhattan, Bergdorf Goodman was her favorite store after Tiffany, and she knew where all the designer houses were. The couple had two nannies at home, one for each child, along with household help to do the cleaning, the errands, and the driving. The couple had retained a personal chef as well. They flew commercial only when absolutely necessary, and always first class. But private jets were their usual mode of transportation, and the impostor Gavin loved to kibitz about fractional shares and jet cards at the country club—where both he and Lisa were known for somehow always working mention of their seventy-five-foot yacht into any conversation.

They each had their own personal trainer who came to the house six days a week. Lisa hated wrinkles or even the anticipation of wrinkles, and consequently had "some work done," as she would put it when she chose to grace a confidante with the insight. She'd had a nose job and a cheekbone enhancement, in fact, and was considering a neck lift, *nothing drastic but, well, you know…* . The impostor Gavin kept a beard, but he had wrinkles on the forehead removed along with some work on his eyelids, especially a scar he had from an old sports injury.

The couple enjoyed riding, kept two expensive warm-blood geldings at a nearby stable, and often trotted out into the woods. They owned a mansion in Nantucket, and spent summers there, feeling at home among the entitled who often inherited their privilege as well as among the nouveau rich who were building their own rival mansions. The impostors Gavin and Lisa were hence seen, among most of their social peers, as a model couple, jolly and friendly to all who enjoyed similar standing, and it was frequently remarked upon how very good they seemed for each other, as well as how fabulous they looked.

Ten days after the earlier stern communication from Redwood Biotech, a FedEx envelope arrived with a similar, but definitely more forceful, letter from that company. Mightily annoyed but at least feeling that he had been put on notice, the impostor Gavin called a prominent patent law firm in Boston to review the situation. When he reported back, the patent attorney advised Gavin that Redwood seemed to have a strong case. The best option was to contest it. It would be expensive, but there was no choice—the lawyer held out the hope that a judge might settle somewhere in middle.

A month later, his attorney informed Gavin that a deposition had been requested and two choices of the dates were provided. Gavin's face turned pale.

"What happens there?" he asked with some trepidation.

"Don't worry; this is all up your alley. Just tell the truth," the lawyer said.

The impostor Gavin became uncustomarily jittery as the chosen date approached.

When he arrived at the law firm for the deposition on the appointed day, Gavin was asked to take an oath, state his name, educational background, dates of graduation, area of expertise, and to attest that he was the owner of the patents.

Then the opposing lawyer took over, inquiring how he had come upon the idea, what he was aware of at the time of invention, and what he knew of other work in the same area.

Under polite but firm questioning, the impostor Gavin began to struggle. He had excelled in high school, but biology was never of particular interest. The rapid-fire questions were unnerving him.

Grasping, he pleaded some ignorance since many years had passed since he came upon those ideas.

"It's only been fifteen years," the Redwood Biotech lawyer reminded him. "Besides, some of what we're talking about here is basic biology. Considering your impressive educational credentials, these should not be difficult questions to answer directly."

Gavin's lawyer then intervened, protesting that his client was on antidepressant medications and had not been sleeping well. He asked for a postponement until his client was feeling better.

Over the objection of the Redwood attorney, that was granted.

Afterward, Gavin felt shaky. He told his lawyer as they walked to the parking garage, "Listen, I need you to keep these jackals at bay for a while."

"For how long?" the lawyer said skeptically.

"Get me a few months. I'm in no shape to handle this stuff right now."

"A few months might be a problem," the lawyer said.

"Get me a few months," Gavin instructed.

Gavin set about learning more biology, but his lawyer was unable to get him more than four weeks. The deposition resumed, and while his scientific answers were somewhat better, he contradicted himself under the pressure. Sensing Gavin's discomfort, his lawyer took him aside a couple of times and asked if he was okay. At the end of the deposition, his lawyer did not look confident.

"Get ready for a protracted, unpleasant, and very expensive court battle," the lawyer warned.

Gavin went home despondent. The lawyer had told him, as a way of assessing the extent of his future ability to pay large legal fees beyond the already huge retainer in hand, that the monthly royalty checks from Redwood had, of course, ceased.

"If I lose, how much will this cost?" Gavin asked.

"Ballpark, $120 million. Excluding attorneys' fees."

"They willing to settle?" Gavin asked weakly.

"They are not. They believe they have an ironclad case."

"Do they?"

"We'll see, we'll see."

A team of contract lawyers was assembled to prepare for the case and the impostor Brinkleys were paying $450,000 a month out of their money market accounts. There was another squad of patent attorneys on the case, while the Brinkleys hired another firm for a second opinion, looking for better coverage and determined to leave no stone unturned. With so much at stake, Lisa became actively engaged in the case, and worked side by side with Gavin.

The case went to court in three months and the preliminary hearings alone lasted for ten days. Gavin and Lisa were always in the courtroom, projecting mutual affection and invincible confidence. The trial lasted two weeks.

The jury did not at all buy the Brinkleys protestations that they were being persecuted by a rapacious biotech company. It took six hours for the jury to come back with the judgment.

The Brinkleys were ordered to pay $120 million, plus interest, to Redwood Biotech.

That prospect marked a turning point in the fabulous life of the impostor Brinkleys of Concord, Massachusetts. Now bankruptcy of the rudest kind loomed, as their assets, considerable as they might be, were not worth $120 million plus interest. The stock market had tumbled badly during the banking and blackout disasters, and their net worth had been cut by nearly a third. The lead counsel told them that while they had the right to appeal, the odds were stacked heavily against them, especially since the case against Gavin was so clear.

"So while you might have some money left after a bankruptcy to take care of your future, an appeal may not leave anything in your hands at all." In addition, he said, "The law firm would require additional payment in advance of three million dollars."

When Gavin and Lisa came out of the lavish law offices, they didn't say a word to each other. They just got into the limo and headed home. The driver was used to frequent chitchat, but Lisa just told him to be quiet. Bankruptcy loomed with ferocious menace. Glancing surreptitiously in the rear-view mirror, the driver noticed that the Brinkleys' smiles had faded. All at once, they both looked ten years older.

Redwood Biotech moved with ruthless speed against the Brinkleys and sought immediate court enforcement of the judgment after thirty days. Far sooner than they had expected, the Brinkleys were forced into bankruptcy.

Word spread fast in their chattering social circle, and at the country club hands that had once been offered in greeting became backs that were turned in disdain. Friends even avoided their calls, or at least any conversations beyond stiff pleasantries during a chance encounter in town. They were all afraid they would be asked for money.

Gavin and Lisa were stricken. Their possessions, the houses, the jewelry, the cars, the seventy-five-foot yacht, all would soon be gone. So would the fine vacations and private jets. *Would they have to fly coach?* The ghastly question was as unthinkable as it was unmentionable!

For the impostor Brinkleys, wartime had commenced. Forty-five days later the home went up for auction, along with all of its possessions with the exception of some personal items.

At the end of the auction, which was not attended by the impostor Brinkleys, the new buyer quietly approached the auctioneer and said that he and his wife would like to meet with the now-dispossessed owners within the week to inspect the home and to collect warranty papers and maintenance-schedule information. They were also asking that the home be vacated within two weeks.

The auctioneer called the impostor Gavin and informed him that an out-of-town family had bought the house. He explained the new owners' request that they be given a walk-through and a briefing on the various maintenance contracts for landscaping, snow plowing, swimming pool upkeep, security and audio and video system, electricians, and plumbers who were familiar with the home. Gavin protested that he needed time, but the auctioneer was adamant that the Stuarts were heading back home in a week, and reminded him that his options for delay were limited, as they no longer owned the house.

The impostor Gavin reluctantly relented, and said the meeting could be arranged after the weekend.

In the interim, the dejected impostor Brinkleys decided to flee Concord and snatch a few days' vacation in the sun before the inevitable occurred. The house did not feel like theirs anymore; in reality it wasn't—it now belonged to the new owner. Terrified that this would be their last trip in the style to which they had become so accustomed, they ordered the private jet—and were vastly relieved that they still were in good standing, that the bankruptcy referee had not yet sold off their one-eighth fractional share in the shiny $12 million Learjet 45XR.

Putting brave faces on, they took off for four days in St. Bart's, charging the five-star hotel on a credit card that had not yet been revoked. But when the impostor Gavin called to confirm the Learjet for the trip home to Massachusetts, he was told that their account was closed, and their share had been confiscated by the bankruptcy court.

They flew home in coach.

CHAPTER FORTY-FOUR

The time was set for ten o'clock in the morning on a pleasant spring day in New England when a Lexus SUV pulled in the driveway and a middle-aged man wearing a cowboy hat and boots emerged, and then out came his wife, a pretty blond in her late thirties. She was wearing a hat, too, and then emerged two teenagers. They looked like a nice family but looked a bit out-of-state in the quintessentially chic and fashion-conscious New England town of Concord.

They lingered by the stone wall for a moment, and then proceeded along a flagstone path to the portico. The man rang the doorbell.

"Hi, I am John Stuart, this is my wife, Cindy, and these are our daughters Caitlin and Emma," he said.

In a weary voice that conveyed no interest, the impostor Gavin responded, "Good to meet you."

"Good to see you again," John said casually.

Gavin stared at John and mumbled, "Have we met before?"

John laughed, delighted to see that the years, the change in character, and the very subtle plastic surgery work he and Cindy had had done when they first arrived in Idaho had been successful. *A new identity is not all that hard to create,* he reflected. Watching what appeared to be Gavin's genuinely bewildered face, John chuckled and said. "I'm a New Age guy and a fiction writer. I believe in reincarnation. All of us have met at some point in our previous lives."

With hooded eyes, Gavin gave him a look that said, "Whatever, you and the wife and the kids just get this over with." Still, there was a nagging reflection. *Had he come across this guy before somewhere?*

As he waved them in, Gavin asked John, "Where are you moving from?"

Cindy responded cheerfully. "From Montana. But our daughter goes to Northpoint School. We liked the area and, well, here we are. I guess we liked it a lot!"

As she was speaking, an attractive blond woman approached from another room and introduced herself as Lisa. Lisa then introduced her two teenaged daughters, who seemed to be about the same ages as Caitlin and Emma. Their names were Becky and Jessica.

John and Gavin sat down and went over the various details about maintenance and service employees. John made careful notes. While Lisa took Cindy on a tour of the big house, the four girls went off into a bedroom and chatted amicably. Cindy marveled at the irony of the situation: Eleven years ago, it would have been her giving a tour of the house, pointing out the special architectural details and clever turns in the decorating. Now it was her house again, a joy to be sure, but the painful memories of all of the intervening years threaten to overwhelm her. Memories of her previous life here with her husband and two little girls came rushing back as she struggled to regain her composure. To steady herself, she complimented Lisa on her taste. As Lisa was showing a big walk-in closet, really a cloakroom off the high-ceilinged foyer, Cindy noticed a mink coat with "Lisa" embossed in gold letters on the label. A cloud of memories engulfed her. Her husband had given that to her on their fifth anniversary.

"I just love this coat! Where's it from?" Cindy asked innocently.

Lisa didn't seem to hear, and moved along on gleaming hardwood floors to the library, where there were hundreds of books, many of which Cindy recognized with fondness.

"You must love reading," Cindy said.

"I do. I especially love fiction. I planned to be a writer when I got out of college, but you know, things took a very different turn." Lisa forced a smile.

"Life sure has more unexpected turns than we realize, until they happen," said Cindy. "Don't you think that life is truly more of a collection of random events, not a series of sequences in a fixed narrative, as everyone tries to make it out to be? I wonder what it might actually seem like at the end."

Lisa just shrugged.

Cindy went on, "My husband, in fact, is an aspiring novelist. He's very good."

"Really? What name does he write under?"

"Well, he's just about to be published. This will be his first novel!"

Lisa's attention had waned, though. Without much further comment, she led her through the rest of the house.

Lisa did notice that the girls all seemed to be in good spirits and even seemed to like one another, which somehow made her actually feel better. The girls chattered on about the schools they go to and the grades they were in. Both sets of girls were in similar grades but Becky, the one who was Caitlin's peer, went to a different local private school, BlueBrook School.

Caitlin asked about their summer plans and both Jessica and Becky responded that they were not sure.

"How about you?" asked Jessica.

"We are actually heading to Switzerland for skiing. My mom was born there."

Emma chimed in, "Yeah, and she has both Swiss and U.S. passports. She came here when she was a baby."

"That's very cool," responded Becky.

Caitlin inquired, "Where were you guys born?"

Becky responded, "Actually we both were adopted. From Canada."

Once the home tour was over, Cindy, Lisa, and the children reassembled in the foyer. Jessica said, "Guess what, Mom? Emma and Caitlin are going to Switzerland for skiing. I'd love to go there! Did you know that their mom was born in Switzerland?"

"How nice," Lisa said pleasantly but without much interest.

John asked if he could come by early the next morning to collect the keys, and Gavin assented. They had already packed their personal possessions and were moving the next morning, as soon as they handed off the keys, to a small two-bedroom apartment in Methuen, an old mill town a few miles from, and several social strata lower than, Concord.

John, Cindy, and the children then proceeded to the Colony Inn right next to the Monument Square. But this time Cindy did not wear her Dodgers cap, nor did she feel the need to wear her dark sunglasses!

The next morning John, Cindy, and the children arrived a little after seven o'clock. John and Cindy had brought a gift bag with them containing an advance copy of the novel John and Caitlin had coauthored, *Hiding in Sunshine*, which was going to be released in two days' time.

"This is our first work of fiction, written by a father-daughter team. I hope you enjoy it," John said modestly.

Both Gavin and Lisa murmured their thanks. Then they quietly left the home with heads down and misty eyes and walked to their SUV, which was crammed with moving boxes. The children were holding their parents' hands and seemed very subdued.

The Stuarts settled in, though the truck with their possessions from Montana was not scheduled to arrive till the afternoon. As Cindy and John enjoyed their home, murmuring to each other about how surreal everything was, Caitlin and Emma came by wearing mischievous smiles.

They announced in a semiserious tone of voice: "We are finally your children, Mom and Dad. Technically we were Brinkleys until now. Remember, you two lost your identities, but we did not!" Then they both laughed and ran away.

At ten o'clock, the front doorbell rang. Emma opened it and saw the FedEx man, and by habit she asked him to wait outside and closed the door.

She called her father, who pulled on a cap and opened the door halfway. The FedEx man appeared somewhat bored but was friendly enough. He handed John two packages, one addressed to Gavin and the other addressed to John—as the delivery man studied the landscaping in front of the house, he didn't notice that John took both packages, moved away a bit from the door into an adjoining room, and quickly scribbled two different signatures that were difficult to decipher. Then, thanking the FedEx man, John closed the door. He quickly opened the first package addressed to Gavin and smiled; it was a big check from the software company, as exactly eleven years had gone by. The second package, the one addressed to John Stuart, was from an address he did not recognize. He leisurely opened it and his jaw dropped. It was from the Department of Justice notifying him to collect the $25 million bounty on ZRK's head with a handwritten note from Jake that only said in big block letters "THANK YOU." John could not believe his eyes. Jake had apparently sacrificed his claim on the money. As he was about to walk over to Cindy, she came down into the foyer; when John let her know of Jake's actions, his eyes became misty. Cindy was stunned by this entirely unexpected gesture of apology on behalf of a man she had once known so well. She and John hugged tightly and for so long that Emma objected and said, "Come on, guys! You are *so* embarrassing."

CHAPTER FORTY-FIVE

In their depressing new rental apartment, they wondered if they could get back to their old lives. But the prospect was immediately clouded by their arguing.

Cate could not constrain herself, and shouted, "It's all because of your stupidity at the deposition."

Marcus heard that in a fury and lashed back, "If it wasn't for your greed we would have been just fine! I would have been a senior agent at FBI headquarters by now."

Cate retorted, "What about the good life you craved?"

He replied, "I rue the day I first met you at the high school. I wish I had gone to a different school!"

"Oh, stop this nonsense!" shouted Cate. "If I hadn't married you, you would still be struggling with your ex-wife, living in a dump, working 24/7. I did all the work and you just enjoyed the fruits of my labor!"

"Oh, really?" retorted Marcus. "Your heart was set on Gavin. You tried your best to entice him romantically, and when that effort failed, you roped me in. I was just a spare tire."

Cate was sobbing. "Not only are our lives ruined, but so are the kids," she stammered.

"Don't blame that on me. I was never for adopting kids, but you insisted so as to avoid any risk. You were the one who drove to Canada and brought them back!"

"We didn't adopt them to *avoid risk*," she said, spitting the words out bitterly. "We adopted them because they filled our lives. I can't believe you can be so cruel! Once you got what you wanted, you abandoned me. You were two-timing me!"

"What are you talking about?" Marcus demanded.

"You certainly know what I am talking about! I didn't send you that Valentine's Day gift with a big heart carved on the card; someone else did! You never admitted it, but the truth remains you were not faithful to me. I should have never trusted you."

He slammed his hand on the table. "Oh, stop badgering me with that! How many times have I told you that I never had a relationship with anyone else?"

She screamed back, "You lie and cheat. You are scum!"

After a few minutes when things were calmer between them, she said in a low voice, "I didn't try to trick Gavin. I had genuine feelings for him. But then I had you in my heart, too. There were days and weeks when I longed for you, and then there were days when all I did was daydream about Gavin. I was torn; I wanted you both—which was impossible. You were two banks of the river, and I had to pick my side... except I kept vacillating and couldn't get either of you out of my mind. I wanted it all! Why can't I have it all? Life is so unfair!"

Marcus wasn't buying that. "Oh, come on, this is all rationalization in the rear-view mirror. If that was the case, why did you cook up this whole scheme?" he said in a tone of sarcasm.

"I wanted him *badly*. I was just infatuated. Some days he would be all attentive, charming, and so desirable, but then there were times when he just was not that much into me. Friendly, but more businesslike. I couldn't understand that. First I rationalized that, after all, he *is* a brilliant mind, a wealthy man with a lot on his mind, and so I thought that he must be merely distracted. I certainly had his heart but could not get into his head. Without him, I felt incomplete. But then as time went by, I could not get him to take that last step. I grew angry, yes, jealous at times, and wondered aloud if he was too tied to the anchor he had. I still to this day don't quite understand what was holding him back—so close, and yet so far."

"Maybe it was Lisa. Did you consider that?" said Marcus in a more conciliatory manner.

"I don't know. Actually, I didn't dislike Lisa. To the contrary, I thought she was a good person, a good mother. She had everything I ever wanted. I admired her. She fell in love with Gavin, broke off her engagement with his roommate, and went after what she desired—and succeeded at getting it. As opposed to me. I have failed miserably at everything!"

"So, I was just a pawn in this game of revenge?" Marcus asked.

"No! Not at all! Once I decided to move on, Gavin was mostly out of my mind. Then I ran into you at the airport and suddenly felt as if years had shrunk into days. Then and there I chose my bank of the river: you. Everything else became secondary, even the grudge. I know it sounds strange now. But as you know we all have our internal conflicts; a little bit of the devil is in each one of us. We can hold contrasting positions at the same time. Once you and I started seeing each other again, I began gaining more insight into your life, and every day was exciting. The tricks of the trade, the fuzzy boundary between law enforcement and criminals along with the occasional trespassing on either side, it all germinated some devilish thoughts. I was still doing business with Gavin, and every time I saw him, I saw the devil become a bit bigger. Every nice, affectionate comment he made, every wink of the eye, even the honest, hearty laughs—all felt like someone was stabbing me with a sharp knife. I felt like someone had to stop this monster on the dark side. I had to be the enforcer and do something about it. That is how it all started and then it had a life of its own. When Gavin was about to go into the witness protection program and asked me to take care of his finances, momentarily I was frozen. I did not realize he trusted me so much. My mind for a moment got cloudy and hesitation crept in. I started to reconsider the direction on this last crossroad as there would be no turning back. I struggled to regain my composure and finally, in a trembling voice, responded yes. Gavin thought that I was afraid of the Enterprise. As always he was clueless how I was feeling. From then on I was at a point of no return. I found solace in you; confirmation that we would get away with what we were doing. You must know after all! You're in the FBI! Or you were. . ."

He said nothing.

She said, softly: "I don't even know who I am any more. But then, maybe I *never* knew? Maybe no one ever knows? Cindy is right. We are more defined by the random events in our lives and how we respond to them—that, eventually, is who we become as opposed to any plans we might have ahead of the life experience which changes us."

283

Marcus said in a halfhearted, yet conciliatory way, "Well, there's no going back now."

*   *   *

During this crisis, Cate did a deep online search of herself, and discovered that the IRS had a lien against her for past taxes from the money deposited in an overseas account. There were copies of 1099s for a couple of years. *How had that happened?* She wondered. Her status as a missing person was suspect. She realized that while she had planned everything to become a missing person, she had forgotten to figure out who would ensure that she went from a missing person to a dead person. She had listed Lisa as the beneficiary of a $5 million life-insurance policy and collected on it. Now that would make it impossible to set the clock back. Furthermore, her Lisa incarnation had recently received notices from the IRS about the bank accounts she possessed in Switzerland and had never declared. She was now guilty of multiple frauds, in her identities both as Cate and as Lisa. Both versions of the person were caught now, and there was no way out.

Marcus had done the same kind of online search. It didn't take much sleuthing. He already knew that a locker bearing his name had been discovered at an overseas bank in Haiti and was found to contain a stash of cash. It was a story for several days in the media and a subsequent investigation by the Department of Justice found irrefutable evidence of his involvement. Worse, there were also some transfers from Billy Dalton to his overseas bank account—according to the media, Marcus was a prime suspect in the eyes of the government as someone who had deliberately thwarted the investigation against Dalton. Those crimes alone carried a punishment of up to fourteen years in jail.

But I never took money from Billy Dalton! How did this happen? He demanded angrily. The time behind bars would be further increased for faking his own death, not to mention whatever federal and state laws he had broken by falsely forcing someone into the witness protection program, without any authorization. As the impostor Gavin, Marcus had squirmed when he saw his name in the paper. Clearly, Billy Dalton had played a dirty trick with him years ago, back when the untainted Marcus was aggressively leading the investigation and was closing in on the gangster. But then things changed and that Marcus was no more. It was clearly Billy who had him set up in case he were caught, and used this as a trap, a bargaining chip for future use.

"It all makes sense, Cate," he said. "The only problem is that if Dalton set me up, why are you in trouble with IRS? We weren't married then. Dalton couldn't have known you when I was aggressively investigating him."

Cate blinked. "I am confused," she said.

Marcus suddenly was jolted with a realization. "Goddamn it, it's my ex-wife's husband, Kent!" he said in a fury.

"No! How would he know about us?"

Marcus thought for a moment. "About three years ago I called Sarah. I hadn't seen Timmy for years and I was missing him badly, so against my better judgment I called her."

"You did not! Please tell me you did not!" Cate pleaded desperately.

Marcus had a pained expression on his face.

Cate understood that he loved his child, but he had also broken a solemn commitment to her, and this hurt her deeply.

"I just couldn't control it anymore," Marcus said miserably. "I told Sarah that I had gotten married and moved to another country. I asked about Timmy. She got agitated and told me to stay wherever I was, and that I'd better not come back. Then she hung up. I know she's vindictive. And I knew that the new husband works for the IRS. How could I be so stupid?"

"What?" said Cate, as if she had not just heard what he told her about Sarah's husband, Kent.

"The IRS," Marcus repeated darkly.

She felt her heart pounding. "Well, that certainly explains the delinquency notices I got from them. I cannot believe what I am hearing! After all the commitments you made—'I am a man of honor; it's my sacred duty; I will never divulge,' Blah blah blah! Whatever happened to all that?"

Marcus looked down morosely. "I let you down, I did. Timmy is my son, my own child; I love him more than anything in the world. I miss his little arms he used to put around me, his baby smile; I just miss everything about him...." Tears started rolling down from Marcus's eyes.

"You should have thought of that before we went down this path,"

Cate said unsympathetically. There was a long silence while Marcus struggled to regain composure.

"Regardless," he said. "It's suicidal to go back to who we were, and prison time awaits us if we stay as who we are. So who should we be, Cate?"

She had no ready answers. "We are in a perfect trap if we proceed as either person. The present is unpalatable, and a future reverting back to the past is already poisoned."

He slumped on the sofa. Neither he nor Cate spoke in the gathering gloom of despair and resignation.

Lying in bed that night, Marcus fought to understand what had happened to him. His thoughts were tortured. *Cate's right; we only find out who we are after the fact, not before. To think otherwise is an illusion. I am now completely alone, afraid of the past, the present, and what will come. I have never felt so alone before, not even among the most dangerous criminals while on undercover work.* He reviewed his life with bitter remorse. *I was a swim-team captain in high school, got a full scholarship for college, loved ROTC. After college the only thing I wanted to do was join the Marines. I was so proud of myself! Honor! Courage! Commitment! It's all gone. I betrayed it. I went from being a decorated Marine to being a third-rate criminal. How could this be? I joined the FBI to serve my country, to uphold the Constitution, and what did I do? I betrayed that, too. But maybe it's not my fault alone? After all, the FBI didn't pay enough—but then everybody at the Bureau was in the same boat, weren't they? And they are still serving honorably.*

Marcus tossed and turned in his guilt and misery. *It all started with Sarah, who brought me to this self-destruction. I was busy with my work, chasing criminals, undercover for months at a time. I loved my job! It was Sarah; she didn't like it a bit! She was alone, needed company. Once we had Timmy, I thought that would change her outlook on life. But life only got worse. What happened? She filed for divorce! And I couldn't afford the alimony and child support. Had I been fair to Sarah? A good father to Timmy? No, not really. I never found that balance. All those demands on my life were turning out to be incompatible with my commitments, and my moral compass went bad. Money was tight; I was late on payments. I didn't even have the time to get to know Timmy; work engrossed me completely.*

I needed a way out, out of the emotional wreck I had become, guilty of not helping raise my child! Always short on money, doing long hours. Cate was an old flame, and when I ran into her at the airport I didn't even recognize her. Dressed like a million dollars, she was. So sophisticated! So successful! But she had that same pert smile I fell in love with when we were in high school; the same bubbly personality. I fell for her again. So sue me! She's really the one who brought me into this mess! I wish I'd never run into her again. She is the devil incarnate! But then, why did I agree? It's all so messed up. I am nothing now. Nobody. No honor, no courage, no commitment. No respect. I am just a frightened man with no options left. Semper Fi, Marcus!

He sighed heavily. *When I single-handedly battled Billy Dalton, I wasn't afraid! I went after the mob, la Cosa Nostra, like gangbusters. Got threatened practically every day. But that didn't stop me! And when there were no takers at the Bureau for the thankless and very dangerous assignment to go undercover and infiltrate the Enterprise. Who stepped up and volunteered? I did! Who didn't think twice before jumping two hundred feet off the deck of an aircraft carrier in the middle of the night to save a fellow Marine? I did not!*

That proud memory, that churning cold sea with the pulsating sweep of the on-deck searchlights and the desperately anxious faces of the sailors and Marines who were lowered in the boat to retrieve him, and the man he had saved wrenched him into thinking about the sad but effective excuse he had contrived to explain his own supposed death, a boating accident.

For the first time, he regretted not actually dying in the boating accident that he had merely concocted.

The more Marcus thought, the more time and space opened up and blurred between what he aspired to be, what he used to be, and what he had become, what he faced. Physical identities had undergone a concrete swap, but mental identities were less compliant. They were very fluid and interactive, forward and backward in time. With troubled thoughts seeping through his mind like wet fog, he eventually dozed off to sleep.

CHAPTER FORTY-SIX

The night seemed endless. Marcus finally stopped tossing and turning and settled down into restless sleep. Cate could hear his breathing. But sleep eluded her. She got up and went into the galley-size kitchen with its depressing yellowed linoleum floor. As she was pacing, she noticed the book John gave her in the gift bag. She sank wearily into an old armchair and started to read. The first paragraph of the very first chapter brought flashbacks, and as she read on, she could not stop. Cate was always a fast reader, but she raced even more quickly than usual into this one, devouring the words. She was shocked; the book was replaying her own life. The boundary had collapsed between reality and the fiction she had been living. At the end of the penultimate chapter, she felt dizzy. Her head was spinning. How could this book be occurring in real time? She was living the book at that very second, reading this very chapter! Someone was certainly playing mind games with her, the smoke and mirrors in it were real and telling a true story.

She was terrified to start the next chapter. All the events had mirrored her life so far. Marcus's, too. Did she really want to know what came next? The question Marcus and she had been asking was still unanswered. How did it all tie together? How would her future unfold? It was her story, and she was unable to alter it, shape it, or steer it; it was already committed to ink and paper, immutable through time. Just a few months ago, she was in control of her life, now she was utterly helpless, a mere subject at the mercy of time, fate, and a narrative created by someone she didn't even know.

The past cast deep shadows on her future.

Should she stop reading? Then maybe there would be no more?

The book was driving her crazy. It was as if she was reading her own mind, but it kept leaping one step ahead of her the whole time.

Dawn was streaking the sky. Out in the apartment complex's parking lot a car door slammed and an engine turned over. Cate took a deep shaky breath and turned the page.

The last chapter was titled "Dispersed Dots, Curved Lines."

CHAPTER FORTY-SEVEN

Dispersed Dots, Curved Lines

A circle of life had been completed. John and Cindy sat down in their backyard sipping iced tea at their new home, which was also their old home. The sun was setting.

Cindy said, "You know we've had very tough times, but then, we've been very lucky, too. We barely made it, though. Moved in the same day when the big check from the software company was to arrive. Had we been delayed even by a day, these bastards would have gotten it and we would have had to fight in court tooth and nail. It's nice to have some money, lots of it, at our new start."

"The chief virtue of money is its unique ability to solve a whole lot of problems," John allowed with a sigh. This was something that he had once known, then learned how to live without, and now could enjoy again—although it felt different the second time.

"And the kids are well. They came through this like troopers," Cindy observed.

John agreed. "I cannot believe how bright and mature Caitlin is for her age. If it was not for her efforts, we wouldn't be here. Curiosity saved the day! If she hadn't taken such a keen interest in the photographs, we'd still be in hiding in isolation in Wanton, Montana."

"But we had a good life there," Cindy interjected. "Montana was good for us."

Again, he agreed. But his heart swelled with pride over his resilient daughters and their invincible grit. "To top it off, Caitlin took her own initiative to apply to Northpoint School, and got in with full financial aid! But there's another part to that story, of course, because it was really little Emma who truly started it, and Emma gets lots of attention but little credit."

The facts were, Caitlin had Jennifer deliberately lead her the wrong way out of the BlueBrook nature preserve that day. She had previously already navigated her way to the mansion on her own, in definite violation of school rules. Then when she and Jennifer were invited into the house that day, she stared at the beautiful family photographs in the sitting area and foyer and carefully memorized the images. Her idea of being a devilish photographer at Halloween was one ploy, but she also collected a hair sample of Marcus's when she asked him to put the tight-fitting hat on and take pictures as the devil's head popped out to create such merry diversion from her true goal.

"After Caitlin e-mailed them to me, I enhanced the pictures of Marcus and Cate—they matched Cate's original picture. I knew it was Cate right away as soon as I saw the pictures in spite of the nose job and other changes made along the way. I instantly knew that we had been manipulated and cruelly tricked," John said.

Cindy said, "Yeah, but I'm still mad at you. Why didn't you let me in on the secret right away?"

"I was startled! Flabbergasted! I kept saying it couldn't be, it couldn't be, it's impossible!" he told her.

"Actually, I knew something was up. You retreated into one of those silent modes of yours."

"Well, when you get a jolt like that, it takes time to get back on your feet. I felt like someone had pushed me into a deep well with no possible means of escape. What a sense of helplessness! Anger, betrayal, too many thoughts all occurring at the same time! Quiet was the best shelter."

"Especially when it was coming from an old flame?" said Cindy with mild amusement in her voice.

John did not reply. He continued, "As the storm in my head settled, all I wanted to do was to connect all the dots. That was my sole focus. I didn't want to think anything else. I kept thinking, *How this did happen? There has to be a method to this madness!* That night you went to bed, and I stayed up and kept replaying the past several years until finally the dots started to connect. First a shadow of a picture emerged, but the more I stared at it, the clearer it became. I soon realized that there indeed was a theft of an external drive from my computer when we were still living in Concord. That was my backup drive. The thieves then must have added a new drive as backup. That is why the machine was busy when I tried to use it, as all the data on primary needed to be mirrored in the backup. This was the start of the conspiracy to get access to my answers to the security questions for our various investment accounts. Questions such as what town I was born in, my mother's maiden name, the name of my first pet, and so on. Without this, Cate could not have gotten access to our money. The whole job on the hard drive was done extremely fast, precisely, and in less than six minutes, because she knew where the drive was and where the security system DVR was. Do you remember when you took her around to show her the home in detail?

"The tail-gating was an attempt to get my nerves rattled and be ready for the preposterous situation we were going to be placed in. Obviously, the two flat tires and subsequent call to the police by Marcus was staged by Cate and Marcus together, a plot to put us under further severe psychological strain and fear. When you are in an irrational state of mind and a source you naturally trust, like the FBI, shows up, well then you are predisposed to readily believe—and we agreed to move out on extremely short notice and to get into the witness protection program under new identities. The FBI call was further validated and reinforced by Cate, someone I completely trusted. It was a sinister, very ingenious plot using shrewd mind games.

"But then later on Halloween night I kept wondering: How did Cate and Marcus connect? I could not recall Cate ever mentioning any friend at the FBI. The name never came up in the many events and anecdotes she casually shared when we were together. A thought struck my mind. I knew where Cate had gone to high school, so the next morning I went to the library and logged onto Classmates.com and looked up Marcus. Sure enough, there he was: captain of the high school swim team. And sure enough, there were some photographs of him with his high school sweetheart, none other than Cate! That was the day after Halloween— the day the masks came off!

"That's when I realized that the Enterprise was used as a proxy by Marcus and Cate to execute their nasty plot. ZRK had a lot of vices—but stupidity was not one of them. He was a tremendously analytical thinker and planner and would have never made the mistake of using a potentially compromised agent's services to assume someone's identity. Simply put, a compromised federal agent is most useful inside the Bureau, not outside."

"That makes a lot of sense," Cindy said, refilling their glasses with iced tea.

John went on, "By the next morning, my head was clear and I woke you up. Remember, how shocked you were when I told you? I had never seen you that angry. Ever. Your eyes were spitting fire. Oddly, you went silent for what seemed like a long time. I didn't interrupt you; I knew exactly that you were in the thick of a mental storm."

"I don't remember that," she said.

"I am not surprised."

"The good news is that it all worked out," she said quietly.

He said, "I still cannot believe that you thought I was living out on the edge—but guess who actually crossed all the boundaries," he said playfully. "You! The levelheaded one, the straight arrow. No one, no one who knew you would ever believe that you came up with the plan to buy a bank, in Haiti, of all places! Then you conveniently had the bank president put money in the deposit box, as the accounts were not properly kept or were partially lost, even the entries that were made between Billy Dalton and Marcus—entirely unknown to them. You are one clever and conniving woman! Knowing what I know now, I would never dare to tangle with you," John said, laughing.

Cindy said, "Well, Billy Dalton was bad news, a very dangerous criminal. So some cash and a previously published list of people he had bribed and the corresponding amounts was helping law enforcement anyway. That was part of my rationale."

"Sure, and Marcus's name mysteriously got added in the list, considering that the rest of the names were known to law enforcement anyway," John said with admiration. "But I'm curious: Why did you list $65,000 against his name?"

"Because Marcus's deposit box contained the exact same amount: $65,000—and it also had his hair sample that Caitlin had gotten on Halloween."

"You are unbelievable! I love it, just love it! I also loved the way you managed to get the IRS onto those guys as well. How did you get 1099s on their names?"

"I actually had an old California driving license, prior to the one I got in Massachusetts when we moved here—the one we were forced to surrender when we moved to Idaho. So I went to a motor vehicle registry's office in California and got that license renewed. Then I opened a bank account using that license, and that account received money from the Haitian bank."

"Received?"

"Well, you know what I mean, someone was generous enough. There was interest earned on those accounts and a 1099 was issued; a copy was sent to the IRS as required by law and the copy that was supposed to come here must have been lost in the mail."

"Really? Two years in a row?"

"Happens sometimes," Cindy said with a faux innocent smile.

"You have a criminal mind," John teased.

"It was all in self-defense," she said.

"Cate got stuck in a jam two ways. How did you pull off the second one with those Swiss bank accounts?"

"Well, seemingly the damaged bank records showed Lisa having an account in the Haitian bank for eight years with about three million dollars, and apparently there were records of wire requests made to transfer funds to a couple of coded accounts in Switzerland. You know, life is interesting, unforeseen. Random. This bank had some ultra-rich Haitian customers who routinely wired real money to coded Swiss accounts, so naturally the wire requests were made to those accounts."

"Wire requests, not necessarily wire transfers. Clever!"

"As you know, I was adopted in the U.S. when I was five, from Switzerland. There was a small old account there on my name at the UBS bank. It turns out that Cate was not aware of it when she started to manage our finances. Even I had mostly forgotten about it. Then, apparently, Lisa made some wire transfers amounting to over two million dollars from the Haitian Bank to her UBS account," said Cindy.

"Real money transfers, not just wire requests. So where did the account get so much money to begin with?" asked John.

"Well, the money was frequently withdrawn as cash at the Swiss bank's branch in Santo Domingo, generally after the deposits were wired to the bank. That cash was then deposited in Lisa's account at the Haitian bank."

"You mean the same money was basically circulating, causing the total wire transfers to the Swiss bank to appear to be pretty high?"

"Excellent! You're analyzing things like a real banker now, John!" Cindy said with delight. "When the U.S. government went after Americans holding foreign accounts, this one showed up, of course."

"So you really went after her with vengeance," he said with admiration.

"I had more than one reason to."

"You are one devilish woman!" John exclaimed.

"But not the one who wears Prada," she teased back.

"By the way, I am dying to know who came up with the idea of an anonymous Valentine's Day gift to Marcus."

"It was both Caitlin and me," Cindy said with a sly smile.

"That must have caused some tension in their lives!"

"I sure hope so."

"I never thought that you had even a shred of revengefulness in you. This is absolutely unbelievable. I had no idea this is what you were up to, nor did I have any idea how far you would go."

"Well, you told me that you were taking care of ZRK and that I should figure out a way to take care of *them*. So that's all Caitlin and I did."

"You know, if someone didn't know the truth, we would be considered a family of accomplished criminals!"

She demurred at that jest. "How about instead, a close family capable of defending itself by strategic planning and flawless execution?"

"Fine, but that still makes us a family of potentially super smart criminals," he said and laughed.

"No, not really, I truly believe that each act has to be seen in the light of the intent behind it. Our intent was pure and in self-defense. However, you are not exactly a naïf yourself. What about the *Journal of Innovation*? Who added one more edition—the new, very last one with an article by a make-believe Jonathan Demarcolus —to the Journal in its online incarnation?"

"An anonymous benefactor?"

She poked him playfully. "Sure. And I happen to know that benefactor fairly well. And he's not anonymous to me."

"But who came up with the idea of adding the last edition, do I know that person?" said John with a wink in his eye.

"I don't," unconvincingly responded Cindy, and they both laughed.

She asked, "By the way, was Caitlin involved in the blogger incarnation of yours?"

"Yes, but to a limited degree."

"We better watch out for our girl, she is dangerous. We shouldn't be teaching her these things."

"Why not?" John asked.

"I don't know, it just seems like a path filled with too many risks. I just want her to have a happy, normal life," Cindy said with distant looking eyes. "I do have one question remaining, though. You explained about the reward for ZRK—but how exactly does Jake fit into the rest of this?"

"Jake worked for the digital counterintelligence unit at the FBI. He is a true patriot. Jake stayed honorable to his oath. He and I in fact accidentally but effectively worked together on Newtidbits.com. On the one side, he had the responsibility to protect us and make sure we didn't fall into ZRK's hands involuntarily, and simultaneously to prevent us from voluntarily switching to the dark side. Unfortunately, he was still immaturely obsessed with you and wanted to torture us together to the extent possible. So after Jake deliberately ran into you at the ice cream shop—to send the message that he was on the case—it was he who staged the kidnapping attempt at the gas station in Wanton. And he was the one who sent the threatening e-mail to Caitlin."

"Scum bag," a visibly angry Cindy blurted out. "How long ago did you find this out?"

"A few months ago. But later he realized his mistake and apologized."

"Why didn't you tell me then? I wouldn't have been worried to death for you and the children," she said with mild indignation.

"I forgot?"

"Really? Do I sense some competition, maybe a tiny bit of jealousy?"

"Not really," he said unconvincingly.

"So Jake was really a good guy after all! I told you I have a good eye to pick the right ones!"

"No, just the nutty ones!" John said, and they both laughed.

"You know, this blogger thing was very dangerous," Cindy pointed out.

"It was necessary, in the national interest. That monster had to be stopped," John protested.

"Yes, maybe what you did was in national interest. What Caitlin and I did was in our family's interest. I had to protect you, my dear nutty husband, and my children."

It was getting late. The weather was cool, with a gentle wind. They continued to talk.

Cindy then said, "Wait! One more question I forgot to ask. How did TENXUTS stop?"

"I suspected it was Norm's handiwork. I confirmed it through the back channel."

After a while, John said, "You always said I lived on the edge; you were always worried about me crossing the boundary, going to the dark side, becoming—"

"Darth Vader?" she interjected.

"—Okay, becoming Darth Vader. But then, who actually crossed the boundary here, and by the wide margin?" he asked with a small loving nudge.

She looked pleased. "Yes, but that was different. It was for the right reasons. And Cate deserved what she got. I hate her! Those two made our lives, and our children's lives, miserable."

"Hey, I only adventured in my head! You plunged in like an infantryman, for real!"

"Really, you already forgot the adventure of heart or need I remind you in more detail? You better have no more adventures of heart either or you are in serious trouble going forward."

"Knowing you the way I do now, I wouldn't dare. However, I am still entitled to my dreams," John said.

"Yes, fine. But please, no more nightmares," she said.

He said, "It's funny. You did what you were always afraid of me doing, and I did things more like you. We clearly have been mutually influencing each other after all these years."

"Yeah, entirely your fault, you corrupted me. I was such an innocent pup."

"Oh, really? You were the cool and laid-back one and got transformed into a fiery inferno, whereas I was the mental adventurist who kept tight strings on my head."

She replied, "Well, I am driven by my heart and you by your head. At least mostly, I suppose that's what makes us a perfect couple."

"What about our kids? Caitlin was actively involved too, we wouldn't want her crossing the chasm to the dark side for convenience."

"Her compass works right. We've seen that," Cindy said. "Now we all have to change our hats again and quickly move back to normal."

"*Normal?* What's that?" he yowled, and they laughed.

They had talked through the chilly night.

"I wonder what Cate is up to right now?" asked Cindy.

"Who cares?" John shrugged.

The sun was lightening the sky.

*   *   *

In Cate and Marcus's apartment only a few miles away, all the dots connected, with many curved lines for Cate. She had been beaten at her own game. She stared at Marcus apparently sleeping in the bed, regretting that she gave him such a hard time about receiving a Valentine's Day card and for not trusting him. She kept wondering what had gone wrong, when did it all go off the tracks? *I messed it all up; with just a bit of patience, a bit of time, I would have had Gavin, he would have been mine and I would not have been here today. He actually loved me; he loved me! I missed it completely!* She thought in tortured waves of self-recrimination, sobbing gently into the pillow.

Her girls were fast asleep in the other bedroom in this small place, largely oblivious to, or maybe just forgiving of, the turmoil in their innocent lives. Cate stared at the ceiling, felt it pushing down on her. Marcus was right, they were cornered. The perfect trap. The reality and the nightmares had fused; it all became so foggy. *Who was she, who is she, who would she be?* She was losing her grasp on those concepts as separate entities. The existence and nonexistence disappeared, as did night and day. She sensed circles of darkness, concealed within circles of darkness. A void that replaced her inner emptiness. Perhaps there was the past, perhaps there is a future. Who can say?

In a rage, she threw the book on the floor and screamed.

Marcus was startled and jumped out of the bed. He saw her. It was as if she had gone insane, wild eyes staring and a finger stabbing at the book as if it was something alive and poisonous. Knowing reality ahead of real life is the worst possibility of all.

"Were you having bad dreams?" Marcus asked tenderly, his heart breaking at the misery that now tortured his wife, his high school sweetheart.

Rushing floodwaters cascaded toward a future unknown, with no sign there might be a rock to cling to in the torrent. Their lives had made a full circle just as John's and Cindy's. These lives also intersected at more than one point in time. Real life was living in fiction, and the fiction was narrating true life, all connecting in a complete circle, the distinction now having disappeared.

A few miles away, John and Cindy came in from the chill. It was six thirty in the morning, and the girls wouldn't stir for at least another ninety minutes. They climbed into bed for a brief sleep till the new day began.

"Pleasant dreams," he said as they burrowed snugly into the warmth under the comforter.

"And no more nightmares," she said.

— The End —

CPSIA information can be obtained at www.ICGtesting.com
Printed in the USA
BVOW031513071212

307312BV00001B/3/P